First Men

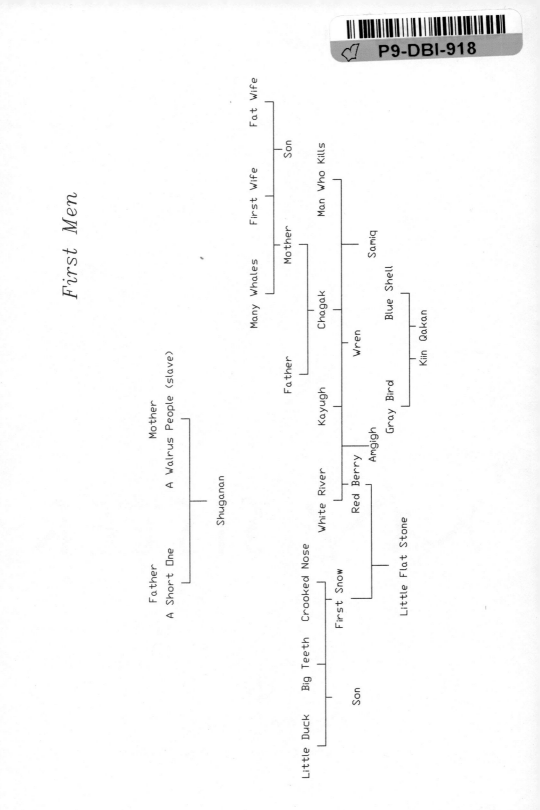

MY SISTER

DOUBLEDAY

New York London Toronto Sydney Auckland

THE MOON

Sue Harrison

PUBLISHED BY DOUBLEDAY
a division of
Bantam Doubleday Dell Publishing Group, Inc.
666 Fifth Avenue, New York, New York 10103

DOUBLEDAY and the portrayal of an anchor
with a dolphin are trademarks of Doubleday,
a division of Bantam Doubleday Dell Publishing Group, Inc.

Book design by Chris Welch

All of the characters in this book are fictitious,
and any resemblance to actual persons, living
or dead, is purely coincidental.

Library of Congress Cataloging-in-Publication Data
Harrison, Sue.
My sister the moon / Sue Harrison. — 1st ed.
p.   cm.
1. Man, Prehistoric—Fiction.   I. Title.
PS3558.A67194M9   1992
813'.54—dc20   91-29102
                                            CIP

ISBN 0-385-42086-2

Copyright © 1992 by Sue Harrison

All Rights Reserved
Printed in the United States of America
March 1992

1   3   5   7   9   10   8   6   4   2

FIRST EDITION

For my parents
Patricia Ann Sawyer McHaney
and
Charles Robert McHaney, Jr.

For my grandfather
Charles Robert McHaney, Sr.

And for Neil's parents
Shirley Louise Batho Harrison
and
Clifford Joseph Harrison

With Love, Gratitude and Respect

Author's Notes

The basic story line of *My Sister the Moon* is borrowed from an Aleut sea otter legend—an incest story. Other legends used in the book include the moon myths of the Pueblo and the Osage; the Aleut raven's marriage story; the Inuit oral histories of a mother hiding the son of an enemy; blue ice men legends; Ojibway twin sons stories; tiger legends from the Orient (which have counterparts in Aleut whale-hunting traditions); Aleut Shuganan and "Outside Men" stories; and the raven-trickster legends, which have parallels throughout most Native American cultures and are so ancient that their roots can be found in the monkey-trickster stories of the Orient.

At the time of *My Sister the Moon*, basketry in the far north was in its infancy; therefore, I hypothesize that the coil and sew technique was used to make baskets, and the simple over-and-under weave used for most matting. These techniques were gradually joined by or replaced by (depending on the culture) the more complex twining weave, which is used today by those few artisans who still make the exquisite Aleut ryegrass baskets and mats.

In an effort to imitate the oral traditions of Native American storytellers, I have begun *My Sister the Moon* with a story already told (Chapter 36 of *Mother Earth Father Sky*). In the storytellers' tradition, this narrative of Kiin's birth is related in a slightly different way and with a slightly different emphasis so it can serve as a foundation for *My Sister the Moon*.

In many Native American cultures, names are seen as having special powers. Throughout a lifetime, a warrior or hunter may possess several names: a "real" name, given by an honored relative or a person respected in regard to spiritual powers; a nickname, which is used instead of a "real" name to protect the holder of the real name against an onslaught of curses or spells by those intending harm; a "pet" name used by family members and close friends; names chosen by the nameholder himself to commemorate an occasion in his life; and a spirit name, often kept secret, which was earned in spiritual quest or fasting. In *My Sister the Moon*, as in *Mother Earth Father Sky*, characters whose thoughts are open to the reader are given names which are presented in a Native American language. These names represent the character's spiritual nature or destiny. Very occasionally a character will also be given a spirit name, as in the case of Kiin (Tugidaq).

At the time of *My Sister the Moon*, stone-knappers on the Eastern Aleutian islands were producing only unifacial blades, although in other parts of North America knappers had developed the beautiful and technically superior bifacial Plano points.

Glossary of
Native Words

AKA: (Aleut) Up; straight out there.

ALANANASIKA: (Aleut) Chief whale hunter.

AMGIGH: (Aleut—pronounced with undefined vowel syllable between "m" and "g" and unvoiced ending) Blood.

ATAL: (Aleut) Burn, flame.

BABICHE: Lacing made from rawhide. Probably from the Cree word "assababish," a diminutive of "assabab," thread.

CHAGAK: (Aleut—also chagagh) Obsidian. (In the Aleut Atkan dialect, red cedar.)

CHIGADAX: (Aleut—ending unvoiced) A waterproof parka made of sea lion or bear intestines, esophagus of seal or sea lion, or the tongue skin of a whale. The hood had a drawstring and the sleeves were tied at the wrist for sea travel. These knee-length garments were often decorated with feathers and pieces of colored esophagus.

IK: (Aleut) Open-top skin boat.

IKYAK, pl. IKYAN: (Aleut—also, iqyax, pl. iqyas) A canoe-shaped boat made of skins stretched around a wooden frame with an opening in the top for the occupant; a kayak.

KAYUGH: (Aleut—also, kayux) Strength of muscle; power.

KIIN: (Aleut—pronounced "kēēn") Who?

QAKAN: (Aleut) The one out there.

SAMIQ: (Ancient Aleut) Stone dagger or knife.

SHUGANAN: (Origin and exact meaning obscure) Relating to an ancient people.

SHUKU: (Ancient Tlingit—pronounced "shoe-KOO") First.

SUK: (Aleut—also, sugh; ending unvoiced) A calf-length, hoodless parka with a standing collar. These garments were often made of birdskins and could be worn inside out (with the feathers on the inside) for warmth.

TAKHA: (Ancient Tlingit—pronounced "tawk-HAW") Second.

TUGIDAQ: (Aleut) Moon.

TUGIX: (Aleut) Aorta, large blood vessel.

UGYUUN: (Aleut) Cow parsnip or wild celery (Poochki, Russian). A plant useful for food, dyes or medicine. The peeled stalks when cooked taste somewhat like rutabaga. The stalk's outer layer contains a chemical that can cause skin irritation.

ULAKIDAQ: (Aleut) A multitude of ulas; a group of houses.

ULAQ, pl. ULAS: (Aleut—also, ULAX) A dwelling dug into the side of a hill, raftered with driftwood and/or whale jawbones and thatched with sod and grass.

WAXTAL: (Aleut) Desire; pity.

The native words listed here are defined according to their use in *My Sister the Moon*. As with many native languages that were recorded by Europeans, there are multiple spellings of almost every word as well as dialectal differences.

PROLOGUE
SUMMER,
7055 B.C.

Chuginadak Island, Aleutian Chain

Prologue

C hagak sat at the roof hole entrance of the ulaq, on the thick sod that was the ulaq roof. She was scraping the last bits of flesh from the inside of a fur seal skin. Samiq and Amgigh nursed beneath her birdskin suk, each baby cradled in a sling that hung from Chagak's shoulders.

Kayugh's daughter Red Berry played with colored stones at the grassy edge of the beach. Now and again, the girl called to Chagak, but the waves hissing into the dark gravel of the shore drowned out her tiny voice.

Chagak wished the noise of the sea would also cover Blue Shell's sobbing, but she could still hear the woman weep.

She thought of Blue Shell's new baby daughter, and for a moment she stopped her work to fold her arms over Samiq and Amgigh. Two fine, strong boys, she thought. And though Amgigh was Kayugh's son, not hers, it seemed that Amgigh belonged to her as much as Samiq did. It was her milk that gave him life. But why did the spirits bless her and not Blue Shell? Why was one woman chosen to receive sons, another given only daughters?

"A son!" Gray Bird had shouted at Blue Shell when the first pains of Blue Shell's labor had begun, and Chagak had resented his words. Did any man know the pain a woman endured to give birth? If Gray Bird had suffered in the birthing as Blue Shell had, would he now be so anxious to kill the child?

"I have had enough sorrow," Chagak said, boldly directing her words toward the sacred mountain Aka. But then she heard voices raised in anger, and Kayugh and Gray Bird came from Big Teeth's ulaq.

Kayugh scanned the beach, and in long, quick strides he overtook his daughter. He pulled her into his arms and held her against his chest. Red Berry clung to him, her small face white against his parka. Then Kayugh turned to face Gray Bird.

For a moment the two men stood without speaking. Kayugh was two hand-lengths taller than Gray Bird, and the wind ruffling the feathers of his parka made Kayugh look even larger than he was.

His jaw tightened and he said, "Have you forgotten that we are the First Men? Have you forgotten that we have begun a new village? Do you think you can have a village without women?" His voice started out low and soft, but as he spoke, anger began to edge his words.

Chagak did not look at Gray Bird. Instead, she kept her eyes on Kayugh's face, ready to grab Red Berry from his arms if Gray Bird attacked.

"Who will bear your grandchildren?" Kayugh shouted. "That?" He pointed to a rock. "That?" He pointed to a tangle of crowberry heather growing near the ulas.

Kayugh clasped Red Berry at her waist and held her out toward Gray Bird.

Do not cry, Chagak pleaded silently with the child. Please, do not cry. But Red Berry held herself stiff and still, her eyes shifting between Gray Bird and her father.

"She brings me joy," Kayugh said. Then in a voice so low that Chagak strained to catch the words, he added, "Her mother was a good wife to me. Her spirit is with this child. I would kill any man who tried to harm my daughter."

Slowly he set Red Berry down. The child stood for a moment

looking at her father. Chagak held out her arms. Red Berry ran to her and climbed into her lap.

Then Gray Bird spoke. "If Blue Shell's daughter lives, I will have to wait three, perhaps four more years for a son. The seas are rough; the hunts are hard. Perhaps I will die before then."

Chagak looked at Kayugh. Would Gray Bird's words soften Kayugh's resolve? But Kayugh did not speak and Gray Bird continued, his voice like ice in the thin, cold air. "Each man rules his own family."

Kayugh took one step forward, and Chagak began to slide slowly back, holding Red Berry against her with one arm.

"Chagak!"

Chagak jumped then rose slowly, searching Kayugh's face.

"Give me my son."

She did not want to obey. Amgigh was too small to be caught in a fight between two men. She hesitated and Kayugh called again. Chagak pulled the baby from beneath her suk and quickly wrapped him in the furred skin she had been scraping.

She took the child to Kayugh. Red Berry followed her, one hand clinging to the back of Chagak's suk.

Chagak handed the baby to Kayugh and he held the child toward Gray Bird, opened the fur wrapping so Gray Bird could see the baby's well-formed legs and arms.

"I claim Blue Shell's girl child as wife for my son," Kayugh said, then he turned and held the baby toward the island's mountain Tugix. "I claim Blue Shell's daughter for my son."

Gray Bird spun and strode to his wife's birth shelter.

Chagak thought that Kayugh would go after him, but he stood where he was, Amgigh now wailing in the chill of the wind. But soon, Gray Bird returned. He held Blue Shell's baby wrapped in a coarse grass mat. He opened the mat and turned the child so Kayugh could see her tiny body. In the coldness of the wind, the baby's skin quickly mottled and turned blue.

"Wrap her," Kayugh said. "She will be wife for Amgigh."

Gray Bird wrapped the child, moving her too quickly to his shoulder. The small head jerked against his chest.

"If you kill her, you kill my grandsons," Kayugh said, and he stood with his eyes fixed on Gray Bird until the man returned to the birth shelter. Then Kayugh thrust Amgigh into Chagak's arms, hoisted Red Berry to his shoulders and walked to the beach.

The summer was nearly over when Blue Shell came to Kayugh. Chagak, now Kayugh's wife, watched from the corner of the ulaq as the woman lifted her suk and showed Kayugh the daughter suckling at her breast. But Chagak also saw the bruises on Blue Shell's face, a long cut that ran across her belly.

"She is alive," Blue Shell said, her voice low. "But Gray Bird has told me I must stop nursing her."

Kayugh sighed. "Big Teeth says I was wrong. I should not have promised Amgigh, forced Gray Bird."

Blue Shell shrugged. "I will do my best to keep her alive." She pulled down her suk, tucked it around the baby. "Gray Bird will not let me name her."

Chagak drew in her breath. The child would have no protection without a name. She would not even have a soul. She would be nothing.

And Gray Bird's promise to give the girl as wife for Amgigh, what of that?

Blue Shell turned to leave, but then looked back at Kayugh. "Gray Bird says that he has given his promise, and so he will not kill the child, but he says that you do not have to keep your promise. He says you should find another wife for Amgigh."

When she left, Kayugh paced the ulaq.

"You cannot change him, husband," Chagak said. "Gray Bird is Gray Bird."

"Big Teeth was right. I should have let the girl die. Now I cannot keep my promise. I cannot give my son a wife who has no soul. Who can say what spirits may come to her, to live in the emptiness she will carry?"

For a long time, Chagak said nothing. When Kayugh finally sat down, she went to the food cache and brought him a piece of dried fish. "There is a chance that Gray Bird will decide to give the girl a name," she said to Kayugh. "Perhaps he will see that a child without a name is a curse to his ulaq, or perhaps he will name her if he thinks he can get a good bride price for her."

Kayugh smiled, a half-smile that told Chagak of his frustration. "So Gray Bird will let her live. And he knows that each time I see the girl, I will remember that he is keeping his promise and I cannot keep mine."

SPRING, 7039 B.C.

Chuginadak Island, Aleutian Chain

1

L ight from the seal oil lamps caught the shine of the trader's eyes. Blue Shell's daughter shuddered.

"A good way to use the night," her father said, and he reached over to cup his daughter's left breast. "One seal belly of oil."

Blue Shell's daughter held her breath, but she made herself look at the man, made herself meet his eyes. Sometimes that worked. Sometimes they saw the emptiness in her eyes, saw what her father would not tell them: that she had no soul. And a woman without a soul—who could say what she might do? Perhaps pull away bits of a man's spirit when he was lost in the joy of her thighs.

But this trader's eyes were dull, greedy for the touch of her. And the girl was afraid he would see only the shine of oil on her arms and legs, the length of her black hair. Nothing more.

"She is beautiful," Gray Bird said. "See, good dark eyes, good round face. Her cheekbones are tall under her skin. Her hands are small; her feet are small." He said nothing about her mouth, how words came from it broken and stuttering.

The trader licked his lips. "One seal belly?"

He is young, Blue Shell's daughter thought. Her father liked to trade with younger men. They thought more of their loins than their bellies.

"What is her name?" the trader asked.

Blue Shell's daughter caught and held her breath, but her father ignored the question.

"One seal belly," he said. "Usually I ask two."

The trader's eyes narrowed. "She has no name?" he asked and laughed. "One handful of oil for the girl."

Gray Bird's smile faded.

The trader laughed again. "Someone told me about your daughter," he said. "She is worth nothing. She has no soul. How do I know she will not steal mine?"

Gray Bird turned toward the girl. She ducked but was not quick enough to avoid the hard slap of his hand against the side of her face.

"You are worthless," he said.

Gray Bird smiled at the trader and gestured toward a pile of sealskins. "Sit," he said, his voice soft, but Blue Shell's daughter saw the tightness of his lips and knew that he would soon be biting the insides of his cheeks, shredding the soft skin of his mouth. She had seen him spit out clots of blood after a bad trading session.

The girl stepped back against the thick earthen wall of the ulaq and worked her way toward her sleeping place. She waited until the two men were engrossed in their bartering, then she slipped through the woven grass dividing curtains that separated the space where she slept from the ulaq's large main room. She could still hear her father's voice, now low and whining, as he offered her mother's baskets and the skins from the lemmings her brother Qakan had trapped.

She knew Qakan would still be sitting in the corner, that he would still be eating, grease dribbling from his chin to the bulge of his fat belly, his small dark eyes blinking too often, his fingers stuffing his mouth with food. But he would be watching. The one time Qakan seemed to take interest in anything besides food was when their father bargained with traders.

She heard her father's giggle, almost a woman's laugh, and knew that he would now work on the trader's sympathy: Here he was, a man trying to provide for his family. See what had happened to him because of his generosity, because of the softness of his heart.

"It is my daughter; she is the one," Gray Bird began as he always began, the same story the girl had heard many times.

"What could I do? I have a good wife. She did not want to give up this daughter. She begged me. I knew I might be killed in a hunt. I knew I might not survive to have a son, but I let this daughter live."

And so he continued. Yes, he had refused to name this daughter, had denied her a name and thus a soul. But who could blame him? Had she not pushed ahead of brothers that might have been born, this greedy daughter, born feet first, thrusting her way into the world?

And each time Gray Bird told the story, Blue Shell's daughter felt the hollowness within her grow. It would have been better if her mother had given her to the wind. Then perhaps her father would have named her, and she would have found her way to the Dancing Lights, been there now, with other spirits.

Yes, that would be better than growing old in her father's ulaq. No hunter would trade for her; no man would pay a bride price for a woman without a soul. Men wanted sons. Without a soul to mingle with a man's seed how could she bring forth a child?

Besides, she thought, I have fifteen, perhaps sixteen summers, but still have had no time of bleeding. I am woman, but not woman, without soul, without woman's blood.

And she remembered one rare time when her mother had stood up to Gray Bird. Blue Shell, angry, had screamed: "How should I know why the girl has no blood flow! *You* would not give her a name. How can a father expect a girl without a name to bleed? What will bleed? The girl has no soul."

"It is Kayugh's fault," Gray Bird had said, and Blue Shell's daughter heard a whining in his words that reminded her of Qakan.

"He promised his son. He will give you a bride price . . ." The sharp sound of a slap had cut off Blue Shell's words.

"He has no honor," Gray Bird said. "He does not keep his promises."

Then Gray Bird had begun to yell, calling Blue Shell the foul names he usually reserved for his daughter.

Blue Shell's daughter had huddled, ashamed, in her sleeping place, and even the grass mat she pulled over her head did not block out her parents' angry words.

But later that night when the argument had ended, she remembered what her mother had said. Kayugh would offer a bride price. Kayugh had promised a son. . . .

A son! Which son? Amgigh or Samiq? And though she realized she had no right to ask, she had sent a plea to their mountain, to Tugix: Please let it be Samiq. And deep within, in that empty place saved for her soul, she felt a small flickering, and by morning the flickering had grown into a flame so strong she could not bear to look into its brightness: wife to Samiq. Wife to Samiq. Wife to Samiq.

Suddenly, the curtain to her sleeping place was thrust aside. Blue Shell's daughter backed against the wall. In the past three years her father had succeeded in trading her five, perhaps six times. Each time she had fought, and the next morning her father had added his beatings to the bruises the traders had given her. But now the girl saw that it was Qakan who peered at her.

Qakan belched and rubbed his belly. "You are lucky this time," he said, but there was no sympathy in his eyes. "Tonight you sleep alone. Our father is a poor trader. . . ." The curtain dropped back into place and Blue Shell's daughter sighed her relief. A night alone, a night to sleep. And she would not let herself think of the summer stretching ahead of her, the traders who would visit. Tonight she was alone.

Amgigh fingered the nodule of andesite. He planned to shear it in two with a blow from his largest hammerstone. He would get seven, eight good flakes from each half, and maybe five of those would make harpoon points.

He held the andesite in his hand, felt the weight of it pushing against his fingers. How many sea lions in that rock? he wondered. It was a question he asked himself each time he found a nodule of stone, each time he made a blade. Five sea lions for each blade? No, at best two. Two sea lions for each of five blades. Perhaps ten sea lions in the rock. If the winds and spirits were favorable. If the hunters were skilled.

Perhaps one of those sea lions would be Amgigh's first. He should have taken a sea lion before now. Samiq had taken his first three years before.

Each time Amgigh returned from a hunt without a sea lion he saw the disappointment in his father's eyes. But did his father realize that when Big Teeth or Samiq, First Snow or even Gray Bird took a sea lion, it was Amgigh's point that killed the animal? His careful work. The precision of his otter bone punch, the strength of his hammerstone.

So who in this whole village had taken the most sea lions?

Blue Shell's daughter stood on the beach and watched the sea. The wind pulled dark strands of her long hair from the collar of her suk and snarled them across her face.

She watched the sea for no reason. The trader had left; there were no hunters out in their ikyan, no women fishing.

But it was good to see the waves push up as though to reach the sky. What had Samiq told her? That the sea spirits were always trying to capture a sky spirit.

Samiq was only a young hunter, sixteen summers, perhaps seventeen, but he was wise. He asked questions and pondered many things, and Blue Shell's daughter was always glad when he came to her father's ulaq. She found herself watching for him when she went out to gather sea urchins or when she walked the hills picking crowberries.

A song started, began its humming in the girl's throat, and brought words—whole and unbroken—into her mouth. It was a song about the sea, about animals that live in the sea, and its words rose and fell like the waves.

Still singing, Blue Shell's daughter squatted at the edge of the sea and pushed a basket out to scoop up water and gravel. The basket, lined with seal gut, was one her mother had made of ryegrass; the grass was coiled and sewn so tightly that water took many days to work its way from inside to outside. The girl stood, swirled the mixture in the basket, then dumped it out. She had taken the baskets to the refuse heap and emptied them of night wastes then came to rinse them in the sea. She had meant to hurry. Her father would be angry if she stayed on the beach too long. But again, the sea had caught her eyes, had caught and held her like the eagle catches the ptarmigan.

Two days before, her father had beaten her for her slowness. Even yet the welts stiffened her back, and she walked like an old woman, slowly, carefully. Her heart, too, had felt bruised, sore with the silence of the rest of that day, her mother avoiding her eyes, her brother Qakan jeering with each smile of his too-fat lips.

At least she had been wearing her suk. Usually when she was in the ulaq, she wore only her grass apron and was bare from the waist up. The suk had blunted the blows, kept the stick from slicing her skin.

But who was she to expect better? She was less than the rocks, less even than the shells that littered the beach.

She stopped singing and held up two baskets, open sides to the wind, so they would dry. But then her eyes fell on a whiteness buried in the beach grasses. A bone, she thought. But it was too large to belong to a bird, even an eagle. She pulled it from the sand.

It was a whale's tooth.

A whale's tooth, Blue Shell's daughter thought. Here? This close to the ulas?

It was as big around as four of her fingers, as long as her hand. It had to be a gift from some spirit. But, of course, not for her. Perhaps she was supposed to take it to her father so he could carve it into something and trade it for meat or skins.

She had seen other carvings—the people and animals that the old grandfather, Shuganan, had made. And though Shuganan was now in the spirit world, his carvings still held great power.

And to Blue Shell's daughter, it seemed that it did not matter how many days Gray Bird spent carving, nor how many times he forced his family into silence as he worked, his carvings could not match Shuganan's.

Often, when Blue Shell's daughter was not guarding her thoughts, a part of her, something inside her head, laughed at the small animals and misshapen people her father made. Once when she was not even tall enough to touch the low sloped roof of her father's ulaq, she had told her mother that Gray Bird's carvings were ugly. And Blue Shell, horror in her dark eyes, had clamped a hand over her daughter's mouth, dragged her up the climbing log and out of the ulaq to the river. There she scooped water into the girl's mouth until the words were washed away, swallowed whole in large painful gulps down the girl's throat.

And afterwards in the ulaq, the ache in the girl's throat moved down into the empty center of her chest, and Blue Shell's daughter realized the extent of the difference between herself and all other people in the world, even her mother. The pain of that knowledge was worse than the ache in her throat, worse than any beating her father had ever given her, and since then words had not come easily, but seemed to wrap themselves around her tongue, shred themselves through her teeth and come out broken. So each time Blue Shell's daughter looked at Gray Bird's work, she reminded herself that the carvings looked ugly only to her, that things of the spirit were as nothing to her.

She was seeing through empty eyes. Even later when she was older, and questions rolled hard and bursting in her head, she would not let herself wonder why she had always been able to see the beauty in Shuganan's work.

Blue Shell's daughter clasped the whale tooth and climbed to the top of her father's ulaq. Tossing the baskets through the roof hole, she made her way down the notches of the climbing log, but before she could turn, before she could hold the tooth out to show her father what the spirits had sent him, she felt the burn of his walking stick as it sliced across the top of her shoulders.

Instinctively, she crouched. She dropped the whale tooth to the grass-covered floor and shielded her head with both arms. Fear pushed at her, wanted her to pick up the whale's tooth and give it to her father. It would earn her three, even four days without punishment. But before she could speak, before she could cry out, her father swung his stick, first against her ribs, then across the fragile bones of her hands.

The girl held her pain in the hollow at the base of her ribs, in that space where most people hold their spirits. The pain lodged there, round and glowing like the heat of the sun. She closed her eyes, shut out her father's anger, but even in the darkness of closed eyes she saw the white of the whale's tooth, and it gave her courage not to cry out.

The blows stopped.

"You are too slow!" Gray Bird shouted. "I have been waiting for you."

Blue Shell's daughter lifted her hands from her head and stood. Glancing back over her shoulder, she saw the sweat on her father's narrow face, saw his knucklebones strain against the skin as he gripped his walking stick. She imagined his hands on the whale tooth, his lips pursed as he planned what small sad animal that tooth would become. Then Blue Shell's daughter no longer felt pain, only anger, anger that gathered until it was as heavy as a stone inside her chest.

She had never owned anything. Her suk was one her mother

had worn until the birdskins were as brittle as dead leaves. Even Samiq's small gifts of shells or colored stones were taken from her, her father or brother prying them from her hands.

She had found the whale tooth. It was hers.

She turned slowly to face her father, and as she turned she carefully placed one foot over the tooth. She listened as her father screamed at her, and she made herself stay still when he raised his stick. She kept her eyes wide and open, and would not let herself wince.

No, she would not give him the tooth. What more could the spirits do to her than had already been done? She was nothing. How could the spirits hurt nothing?

She stood there until her father was through yelling, until with one final swing at her head, he set his walking stick in its niche dug into the earth of the ulaq walls. He brushed past her and went into his sleeping place. Then she picked up the tooth and slipped it under her suk, into the waistband of her woven grass apron, and left it there, smooth and warm against her side.

2

It was night and Blue Shell's daughter was tired. Her mother, brother and father were in their sleeping places, but she enjoyed having the main room of the ulaq to herself, and so had decided to work a little longer on the basket she was weaving.

Her ribs hurt each time she took a deep breath, and all day she had felt as though she could not get enough air. She dipped her hand into the water basket and closed her eyes as she moistened a strand of grass with her fingertips.

Each time she wove baskets, smoke from the oil lamps seemed to settle close over her, prickling against her eyes until they were dry and itching.

She felt her father's presence before she saw him, a sudden heaviness in the air, the oil and fish smell of him. She opened her eyes and saw that he was standing before her, his walking stick held across his body as if he were preparing for an attack. He looked down at the basket she was weaving.

"I need that basket," he said. "Do not sleep until you finish it."

Blue Shell's daughter looked up at him but tried to keep the fear from her eyes. It was a storage basket. Good for dried fish, for berries and roots. Her father did not need it.

She wanted to tell him that it was only a woman's basket, that her mother's baskets were much better than hers. And though she opened her mouth to speak, the words caught at the back of her throat and would not come out. She pushed with all the air in her lungs. Nothing came except the sound of her own breath and a bleating, "A-a-a-a-a. . . ." It was the sound of the emptiness she held within herself. Others had spirits; others had words.

"If you have to," Gray Bird said, "you will work all night."

Blue Shell's daughter took another long breath, would not let herself think of the emptiness she held within her body. She opened her mouth, began slowly, "N-n-no," she said and saw the surprise in her father's eyes. When had she ever told him no? Her father stared at her for a moment but said nothing. He snorted and kicked at the grass on the floor then turned and went into his sleeping place.

Blue Shell's daughter waited until she heard him settle into his sleeping robes, then again she formed the word in her mouth, felt it round and strong against her tongue. "No," she whispered. "No." She felt the power of the word as it traveled back into her throat and down to the center of her body.

She stood, and when she bent to pick up her partially woven basket, she felt something trickle down the inside of her thigh.

Even in the dim light of the ulaq, she knew. Blood.

She was having her first bleeding. She was a woman. A woman! Even without a spirit, without a soul, she had received the gift of bleeding. How was it possible?

Perhaps it was that one word, spoken to her father. But what had given her the courage to stand up to him? She smoothed her hands over her suk, over the small mounds that were her breasts. She felt the bulge of the whale's tooth against her side. Yes, of course, it was the tooth.

Samiq bent over the bone hook he was shaping. His mother was nursing his baby sister, Wren, and at the same time smoothing seal oil into her husband's hair.

Samiq glanced at his brother Amgigh and Amgigh scowled at

him. Samiq turned his head and pretended he did not see. I am a hunter, he reminded himself as he felt the familiar anger rise. This spring he had already taken three seals. He did not have to make any reply to his brother's foolishness.

Samiq had always been able to best Amgigh at any game, whether it required quickness of the mind or strength of the body. Though Amgigh was taller than Samiq, he was very thin and tired quickly. But there was a fierceness in him, a determination that Samiq admired. Even when Samiq beat Amgigh in a race, finishing far ahead, Amgigh did not stop running until he, too, had reached the final line. It was a good thing, that determination, their father said. Important for a boy, even more important for a man. And though Samiq was more skilled with the spear, Amgigh's clever hands knapped the spearhead, and so their father always said that Amgigh's family would never be hungry.

But there was a part of Amgigh that Samiq did not like, the contrary spirit that made Amgigh take a favorite toy from their sister and hold it high above her head until she cried; the part of him that laughed when Gray Bird derided his lovely daughter in front of other men.

And looking into his brother's eyes, Samiq knew that it was this contrary spirit that now spoke, as Amgigh, still holding his scowl, said, "Blue Shell's daughter—they say she has finally become woman. Her mother makes a hut for her now back in the hills."

Their mother looked over at them. "How do you know this?" she asked.

"I saw it. Do you think because I have no sea lion teeth on a string at my neck that I cannot see?"

Samiq flushed, looked down at the necklace his mother had strung for him. She had promised one for Amgigh when he brought in his first sea lion. What more could she do than promise? Amgigh had to take the sea lion.

"Amgigh," their father said, "if you have something good to say to your mother, say it. Otherwise, say nothing."

Amgigh smiled, holding his lips out wide and clenching his teeth. Wren reached out and yanked her mother's hair and Chagak slapped absently at her hand. The child began to cry.

"I will oil my ikyak," Samiq said, suddenly ready to be away from his parents and brother, away from the crying of his sister. "Perhaps First Snow needs someone to talk to. He is alone in that new ulaq with our ugly sister."

His father grinned at him. "And if Red Berry hears you, do you think she will be sharing any food or saving you meat from First Snow's seals?"

Samiq pulled his parka on over his head and climbed out of the ulaq. A sharp wind cut in from the north to sweep across their wide beach. It was night, but not quite dark, the moon full.

So Blue Shell was making a bleeding hut for her daughter, Samiq thought. Did that mean Gray Bird had finally named the girl, had allowed her a soul?

Samiq walked down the beach. He stopped now and again to pick up small stones and throw them into the water. He would give the girl a present, something to let her know he was happy for her. She deserved some happiness.

"You are a hunter," his inside voice said. "Perhaps you could give more than a gift. Perhaps by the end of the summer, you could pay a bride price." His mother wanted him to take a wife from the Whale Hunters, but he did not think she would object to Blue Shell's daughter. Who worked harder, who smiled more, even though her back carried the scars of her father's beatings? He would start saving sealskins. He was ready to be a husband. Did his dreams not tell him he was a man?

3

*B*lue Shell's daughter lay back on the grass that softened the floor of her shelter. The hut had no walls, only a peaked roof of driftwood and grass mats that slanted down to the ground and was staked to the earth with bone pegs and kelp twine. Her mother had taken all night and part of the morning to build the shelter. She had woven the roof tightly to keep out the wind, and had given her daughter an oil lamp for heat and light.

The girl had not been allowed to help, only to watch, to wait in the darkness while her mother gathered grasses and driftwood and brought mats from their ulaq. Her mother had said little as she worked, but twice she turned to smile at her daughter and the girl had been surprised. She had seldom seen her mother smile, could never remember hearing her laugh. So, her mother was pleased then, glad that her unnamed daughter had become a woman.

The girl wondered about her father. She had heard Gray Bird's bellowing when Blue Shell, wakened from her sleep, had shooed her daughter from the ulaq. Gray Bird, Qakan, too, had been wailing about curses. Was there woman's blood on their weapons? Had she been in their sleeping places that day?

But now perhaps her father would get a bride price for her.

Perhaps she would take her place as wife to one of Kayugh's sons. Perhaps Samiq.

When Blue Shell finished the hut, she told her daughter that she would return with food and water. She would also bring strips of sealskin so the girl could weave hunting belts for the men.

The first days of being a woman were a time of power. Blue Shell's daughter had heard stories of girls in first bleeding who had cast whales up on the First Men's beaches, but she carried no hope that she could do such a thing. How could a woman without a name have that much power? But if the men sent sealskin to weave into hunting belts, she would make belts, strong and beautiful, to bring them luck in their hunting.

She took the whale tooth from under her suk and stroked it, studying the dents and scars in its surface. The top of the tooth where it had been broken from its roots was worn almost smooth. The tooth must have lain in the rain and sun for a time, and before that been in the sea. Perhaps it carried the same power as an amulet.

She had never been allowed an amulet. Once as a child, she had fashioned a small pouch from a scrap of sea lion hide and filled it with pebbles and shells she found on the beach. She hung the pouch from a rawhide thong around her neck, but when her father saw what she had done, he jerked the pouch from her throat, pulling so hard that the thong left a gash at the back of her neck. "No amulet," he had said. "A girl without a soul is nothing to the spirits. They will not protect her. They do not even see her."

But now she had the tooth. And perhaps the tooth itself had chosen her. Why else would she have found it, she, not her father, not Kayugh or Crooked Nose, not even Samiq? Perhaps it wanted to give her power, as much power as any amulet could give.

She had worn it only a day and already it had made her a woman. Blue Shell's daughter moved her head so she could see out through the door opening of her hut.

She listened to the wind, watched as it pushed clouds into the gray curve of the sky. For these days, nine days alone in her bleeding hut, she could forget about her father. She could forget that she had no spirit. She could forget about words, words that flowed smoothly from the mouths of those around her, but that came to her only with effort: each word a new and difficult task, pried from her mouth one at a time like a woman pries chitons from a rock.

Yes, she could forget. But one thing, one thing she would remember—the reason she was here. She was a woman. Even without a name, without a soul, without the gift of words. Even so, she was a woman. She hummed under her breath, a small tune, a song without words to the whale's tooth.

O n *the second day* of her bleeding, Blue Shell's daughter
wove hunting belts for Samiq and Amgigh.

She cut sealskin into narrow strips and wove it slowly and
carefully. She strung in shells she had drilled for beads, and
always kept her mind on seals and sea lions as she worked. She
laid a sealskin over her grass sleeping mats, so the belts would
not touch the grass, and her mother bound the girl's hair into a
tight braid at the back of her head. If even a tiny piece of grass
or a strand of her hair were woven into the belt, the sea animals
would know and would not come near the hunter, or worse,
would bite a hole in the bottom of his ikyak so the hunter
would drown.

On the third day, she made belts for Big Teeth and First
Snow, and on the fourth day for her father. On the fifth day,
Qakan sent his sealskin. With each man's sealskin, Blue Shell's
daughter had only had to close her eyes to see a belt, finished
and beautifully decorated, but for Qakan she saw nothing.

It is because he hates me, she thought, and could not help
remembering the times he had stolen her food or had lied to
their father, accusing her of breaking cooking stones or touching
a hunter's weapon.

Qakan had fourteen summers, but had never taken a seal. He
did not even paddle his ikyak well, and their father blamed her

for Qakan's poor skills. She was the curse in their family, he often said. She was the reason her mother had been barren since Qakan's birth. She was the one who kept Qakan from slaying seals.

It was her father's way to blame others for his own shortcomings. But then, Blue Shell's daughter thought, I am also like that, blaming Qakan because I do not want to weave his belt. She warmed her hands over the flame of her oil lamp and thought for a moment, then pulled the whale tooth from her suk. She ran her fingers over the smooth curve of its sides, stroked a furrow that had been eroded into the base of the tooth. Yes, she would make Qakan a belt and use all her good thoughts of seals and sea lions to give it power.

On the eighth day of Blue Shell's daughter's confinement, Samiq sat at the top of his father's ulaq and watched the sea. He watched for the ruffling of water that would tell of herring, watched for the shimmering darkness that comes before a storm, but sometimes he also turned and stood, stretching to his full height to see the small peak that was the top of Blue Shell's daughter's hut. Tomorrow she would come out, would be given the woman's ceremony. Perhaps, Samiq's mother had said, Gray Bird would allow his daughter, now woman, to have a name.

The girl had been strong even as a child, taking beatings and scoldings without tears, without pleading. Chagak said that even though Blue Shell's daughter was a woman without a soul, the belts she made would have power.

Already this spring three hunts had brought Samiq honor. And with the belt, who could say? He might take two and three seals in one hunt as his father sometimes did.

He turned back toward the sea, watched the high rising of the swells. He flared his nostrils; there was nothing. No smell of seal or whale, not even the lesser scent of cod.

A good day to oil my chigadax, he thought and stepped down through the roof hole to the top notch of the climbing log. His father sat in a corner of the ulaq's central room. Wren was on his lap; she sucked two of her tiny fingers and her other hand was wrapped in the soft tangle of her hair.

"Anything?" Kayugh asked.

"Nothing," Samiq answered. His mother was sitting, her back to them, weaving a grass mat that was suspended on pegs pounded into one wall. Above the weaving was a shelf crowded with the small ivory animals carved years before by her grandfather Shuganan.

Chagak looked over her shoulder at Kayugh, and he cleared his throat.

Samiq squatted beside his father. He reached out and smoothed the dark strands of his sister's hair.

"The last time your grandfather Many Whales came to visit," Kayugh began, "he asked that you be allowed to live with him in the Whale Hunters' village this summer." He paused, glanced first at his wife and then at Samiq.

Samiq's heart quickened, thumped hard into the veins of his neck. "And you will let me go?" he asked.

"Long ago I promised such a thing to Many Whales, part of a bride price for your mother."

"You promised that one of your sons would go live with him, learn to hunt the whale?"

Kayugh looked at his wife and again back at Samiq. "Yes."

"And you choose me over Amgigh?"

Chagak started to speak, but Kayugh interrupted her. "I do not choose either of you above the other, but Amgigh will soon be a husband. He must stay here in this village with his wife."

The rushing joy that Samiq had felt dropped cold and hard into his belly. "Blue Shell's daughter?" he asked in a whisper.

"Gray Bird has decided to give her a name, so your father will keep the promise he made when Amgigh was a baby," Chagak said.

"Amgigh knows?"

"We will tell him when he and Big Teeth return from their hunt."

"He has not even taken a sea lion yet," Samiq said and realized that he spoke in a high and squeaking voice like a boy.

"He will," said Kayugh. "Perhaps today."

"Yes," murmured Samiq, seeing the sternness in his father's eyes.

"Your father will help Amgigh pay the bride price," Chagak said, then added, "We have decided they will live here, in this ulaq."

Samiq nodded and tried to keep the surprise from showing in his eyes. Among the First Men, it was customary for a man to live with his wife's family, at least until the first child was born. But, Samiq reminded himself, it was not the custom among the Whale Hunters, and his mother was half Whale Hunter.

"She will be our daughter, will have our grandchildren," said Chagak, lifting her head so Samiq saw the tight set of her jaw. "She needs to be away from Gray Bird. He beats her."

Samiq rubbed a hand across his forehead. Yes, who did not know that? But a girl belonged to her father, and he could beat her, kill her, if he wanted.

"I think she will be safer now, if Gray Bird knows he can get something for her, sealskins or oil," said Kayugh. "I will tell Gray Bird that Amgigh will not take a woman with broken bones."

"Amgigh will be a good husband," Samiq said, and his voice sounded again like the voice of a man. It would be better for the girl if she were in this lodge, and even though Samiq wanted her for himself, he would rather see her with his brother than given to some hunter who came to their beach with skins and meat to trade.

Samiq stood. "I will go outside and watch for Amgigh."

His father nodded but Samiq saw him lift his eyebrows in question to Chagak. Samiq climbed from the ulaq. He squatted in the grass that grew in the sod of the roof.

To hunt the whale, the greatest of all sea animals. What hunter would not feel his spirit grow large and boasting at the thought of taking such an animal? Yes, he had the better share. After all, any man could take a wife, become a husband. Very few could learn to hunt the whale.

Samiq fixed his eyes on the sea and watched for Amgigh's ikyak. He thought of whales, huge and dark, thought of their breath spouts flowing high, and would not let himself think of Blue Shell's daughter, would not let himself feel the ache in his heart.

5

By *the ninth day,* Blue Shell's daughter had finished all the belts and had woven a gathering basket as well. That evening she would return to her father's lodge. Chagak had once told her about the woman's ceremony Chagak's parents had held for her after Chagak completed her first bleeding. In those days, a girl had to live alone for forty days after her first bleeding. Then there were feasts and gifts.

But when Chagak's daughter Red Berry had come to her first bleeding, the men decided that this new village on Tugix's island was too small for one of their women to sit idle, weaving only belts and baskets for forty days. They borrowed a custom of the Walrus People: only nine days alone, only nine days to weave belts and baskets. As Big Teeth said, "Were not Kayugh's own parents once Walrus People?"

Blue Shell's daughter had heard Chagak's protests: Why take the chance that spirits would be angry? Why take the chance that hunting would be cursed?

But Kayugh had said, "Who does not know that the number four is sacred to men; that the number five is sacred to women? Nine is a good number, a strong number. Nine days is the right choice. Besides, who can doubt that the Walrus People understand the ways of spirits?"

It seemed that Kayugh was right. Red Berry, now First Snow's wife, already had a healthy son. And the hunting was good, had been good many years.

Blue Shell's daughter remembered the feast Kayugh had given when Red Berry's nine days were ended. She remembered the many gifts Red Berry received.

Blue Shell's daughter knew that no celebration would mark the end of her own confinement, but it was enough that she had escaped her father's beatings for nine days, enough to be allowed to work without fear of a stick across her back. She sighed and pushed open the mat that covered her door opening.

Her mother would soon come to get her and take her back to her father's lodge. She shuddered, wondering whether her long absence had irritated the man or if he would treat her with more respect now she was a woman.

Perhaps he would be carving his small crooked animals and would pretend she was not there. Idly, she let her fingers caress the whale's tooth that hung at her side. But even if he did beat her, perhaps the tooth would give her added strength, make it easier for her to endure the pain.

Of course, if her father saw the tooth, he would claim it as his own, would cover it with his carvings of men and seals and little circles that were supposed to be ulas.

Her hand closed over the tooth and she pulled it from her waistband. She would not be able to carry it with her or he would see it, but how could she keep its power for herself if she did not carry it?

Blue Shell's daughter stared at the smoke hole in the peak of her roof and wished that the special powers she had during her first bleeding were great enough to make the tooth invisible, like the wind. She crossed her arms over her upraised knees and closed her eyes. No, she thought, it is enough that I am allowed to be a woman. How often had Qakan taunted her saying that she would always be a child, always stay in their father's ulaq to work and to be beaten?

Yes, she might always be in her father's ulaq, but if she could keep the tooth, perhaps she would have some protection. Blue

Shell's daughter laid the tooth against her cheek, and in the moment that it touched her skin, warmth against warmth, she saw it not as tooth, but carved into the whorls of a whelk shell. Her father would not care about a shell. He would think she carried it to hold oil to grease the cooking stone or soften skins.

She had watched her father carve, knew from his conversations with Qakan how difficult it was to carve ivory. "A whale's tooth has a hollow center," her father had told Qakan, "a narrow passage that tapers up into a point deep within the tooth. A carving has to follow the hollow, make allowances for it. But a whale's tooth is not as difficult to carve as walrus tusk." Her father had reached into the basket where he kept ivory, wood and bone for carving. He handed Qakan a walrus tusk. "See," he had said and pointed to the inside of the tusk. "It is different here. It does not obey the knife."

Qakan had yawned and looked bored, but Blue Shell's daughter had listened, and she remembered what her father had said. A walrus tusk is centered with a hard and brittle ivory that chips erratically under the pressure of a blade, and when the ivory chipped, her father became angry, sometimes angry enough to lash out at her with his carving knife.

And, Blue Shell's daughter thought, if it is difficult for my father to carve a whale's tooth, it will be even more difficult for me.

But then it seemed as though the tooth caught her thoughts, as though its voice called to her, and she saw the tooth marked by her father's knife, made into something it should not be.

She picked up the short-bladed woman's knife that lay next to the pile of hunters' belts and pressed the knife against the tooth, felt the blade bite into the smooth surface. A narrow strip of ivory curled and fell, and the girl's heart lurched within her chest. She dropped both knife and tooth.

What had made her do such a thing? What had made her think she could carve something as sacred as a whale's tooth? She was a woman. Only a woman, and worse, a woman without a soul.

Blue Shell's daughter rubbed her hands down over her face. Perhaps even now, with one small chip, she had destroyed the tooth's power. She thought of Shuganan's beautiful carvings. Each glowed with an inner spirit; each was beautiful to see, and when she looked at those carvings, she felt joy.

Then she thought of her father's carvings, flat and mis-shapen. Ugly. No, she told herself. It is me. I do not see what is there. But then she remembered Chagak's stories of Shuganan, of his gentle spirit, and she thought, Perhaps the difference between Gray Bird's and Shuganan's carvings is the difference between the two men's souls. But at least her father had a soul. And compared to her father, what was she? Why did she think her knife would be strong enough? Did her hands have the skill to make a tooth into a shell?

Again she held the tooth against her face. It was still warm, so perhaps she had not destroyed it, had not forced the spirit out of the tooth into the thin, cold air of her shelter.

But again she saw the tooth as shell, saw it so clearly that it was as though the tooth were already carved. And her hand moved to pick up the knife, as though the tooth itself were directing it. So blocking the fear from her mind, she began to carve. She carved carefully, slowly, pushing the image of the shell from her mind down into her hands, down into her fingers as they gripped the knife.

Samiq squatted in the lee of the hunter's beached ikyan and oiled his chigadax. That morning, Amgigh had brought in his first sea lion. Their mother sat now with the hide staked out on the beach. She scraped away flesh left on the underside of the skin and the wind carried off the smaller bits of debris.

But in the midst of the joy over Amgigh's first sea lion, Kayugh had asked both Samiq and Chagak to leave the lodge so he could talk to Amgigh. Samiq knew their father would speak to him of Blue Shell's daughter. Yes, and how would Amgigh feel, a young man filled with the pride of his first sea lion kill, to learn that his brother would be going to hunt the whale while he, Amgigh, would stay in the village and take Blue Shell's daughter as wife?

Samiq scooped yellow oil from the basket he cradled between his knees and rubbed it into a seam. Amgigh had never been afraid to show his anger. Who could say what he would do this time? Perhaps refuse to take the girl, perhaps go to another village, live there, hunt there. And who could blame him?

Samiq looked back toward the ulaq and saw Amgigh striding toward him.

"So," Amgigh called out, his voice high and hard, "you have been chosen to be the hunter and I am to be a husband."

"It was not my choice," Samiq said, and he looked up at his brother, met his eyes so Amgigh would see he spoke the truth.

Amgigh laughed, a hard laugh, edged in bitterness. "You would choose Blue Shell's daughter then?"

Samiq looked down. How could he answer his brother? What man would choose a woman over the chance to learn to hunt the whale? But then why, he asked himself, did the pain in his brother's eyes find an answering ache in his own chest?

"It is for our father to choose."

"You are the better hunter."

"How can anyone know that I am the better hunter?" Samiq asked. "In my last hunt, I took no sea lions. This morning you did. In the hunt three days ago I was the one to kill a seal. And the hunt before that neither of us took a seal and Gray Bird did. Is Gray Bird better than we are?"

Amgigh smiled, a true smile that crinkled his eyes and broke out over a laugh. He squatted beside Samiq. For a moment he did not speak, then he laid his hand on his brother's arm.

"I have pieces of obsidian left," Amgigh said. "Large enough for two good knives."

Samiq nodded. Yes, their father had taken Amgigh with him to the mountain Okmok. They had brought back obsidian to trade with the Walrus Hunters and some for Amgigh to knap.

"The knives will be brothers as we are," Amgigh said. "You

take one with you to the Whale Hunters and I will keep one with me. They will remind us of our bond. Then, when you return, you will share the Whale Hunters' hunting secrets with me."

There was hurt, but also hope in Amgigh's eyes, and some of the weight that had settled into Samiq's chest lifted. "I will tell you everything I know. We will hunt together. Men from other tribes will tell stories of the hunts we make."

Amgigh nodded. A smile pulled at one corner of his mouth, but he looked down, traced a pattern in the beach gravel. "Until you get a wife," he said, "I will share Blue Shell's daughter with you."

And Samiq bent low over his chigadax, afraid of what his brother might see in his eyes.

"Daughter?"

The girl jumped and tucked her partially carved tooth under a mat. She leaned forward to pull open the door flap. At first, she thought her mother had come, but then she realized that the voice belonged to Chagak.

"A gift from Kayugh's ulaq," Chagak said and laid a bundle outside the door. She reached in to touch the girl's hand and then quickly turned and left.

Blue Shell's daughter pulled the bundle into her hut and tied the door flap open to let in light. The bundle was wrapped in grass mats, and when she saw what was inside, her surprise made the breath catch in her throat. A suk. The finest she had ever seen. The skins were fur seal, tanned to such suppleness that she knew Chagak had worked a long time stretching and scraping them.

She unrolled the garment and laid it across her lap. The back of the suk had been made with the darkest fur, and was banded at the bottom with a ruff of white cormorant rump feathers hung with shell beads. The sleeves were cuffed with tufts of brown eider feathers and on the outside of the collar rim

Chagak had sewn a strip of pale ribbon-seal fur, trimmed into a pattern of ripples, a blessing asked from the sea.

Blue Shell's daughter hugged the suk close to her, and she felt comfort in the cool softness of the fur. She slipped the old suk off over her head. Her mother had worn it a whole year before Gray Bird had allowed his daughter to have it, and so the cormorant skins were very frail. It seemed that she spent as much time repairing it as wearing it, and during the past winter it had not been warm enough, even with bundles of grass stuffed inside as a lining.

Blue Shell's daughter moved to the center of her shelter where the middle pole lifted the roof high enough for her to stand. There she pulled on the new suk, feeling the softness of the inside skins against her breasts. It fitted her perfectly. The sleeves ended just above her fingertips and the bottom edge fell below her knees. She looked down at herself and wished that she dared run from her shelter to the edge of the stream to see her reflection in the water.

She crouched, drawing her knees up into the suk. It was long enough to touch the ground when she squatted and so would keep her bare feet warm.

It is true then, she thought. I am to be a wife to one of Chagak's sons. Why else would she make me a suk? Amgigh did not want her; sometimes he even joined Qakan's taunting. It would be Samiq. But then she pulled her thoughts from such a hope. Perhaps she would never be a wife. But for now, for the rest of this day, she had this beautiful suk. She would not allow herself to think beyond that.

6

*B*y *the time the* sun was sinking for the night, Blue Shell's daughter had finished the tooth. She had carved carefully, scraping and cutting until the surface of the tooth was whorled like a whelk shell. She held the tooth near her oil lamp and looked at it with critical eyes. It was not perfect—a hard ridge of ivory, something her knife could not shape, ran the length of one side, and there was a chip on one edge—but it looked like a shell.

Besides, she reminded herself, she would be careful to conceal the tooth under the edge of her apron. And perhaps the tooth carried its own power to deceive, to fool her father's eye and protect itself from his knife.

She raised her suk and tied the tooth to the belt of her apron. She was smoothing her hands over the fur of the suk when her mother came to the shelter.

"You must come out," she called, and the girl saw the surprise in her mother's face when she stepped outside wearing her new suk.

"It is from Cha-Cha-Chagak," Blue Shell's daughter said.

Her mother made an uncertain smile and nodded.

The tightness that had seemed to bind Blue Shell's daughter during her time in the tiny shelter suddenly left, and she spread her arms out, catching the wind with her fingertips. She began to laugh, and she turned so she could see Tugix, the great mountain that guarded their village.

"Be still," her mother said. "You are a woman now, not a child."

And the daughter answered, "I have n-n-never been a ch-ch-child."

Her mother looked away and the girl closed her eyes, for a moment regretting the words. But then anger pushed up from the hollow in her chest, pushed up and brought with it the remembrance of the many times she had been beaten, times when her mother had been silent or had left the ulaq.

Blue Shell pulled at strands of hair the wind had whipped into her eyes and said, "I have something for you."

She led the way to a knoll nearer the beach and squatted down out of the wind. She reached into her suk and pulled out a packet wrapped in sealskin and tied with strips of hide.

"This is for you," she said untying the bindings. She unfolded the sealskin and the girl saw that the packet contained a small basket. It was woven from the ryegrass that grew near their beach, and the fitted lid was linked to the basket with a plait of sinew.

She lifted the lid. Inside were a sealskin thimble, birdbone needles and an ivory awl.

"You will need these," her mother said.

"Yes."

"It is not as great a gift as Chagak gave you," Blue Shell said. She looked out over the beach, away from her daughter's eyes.

"Y-y-you m-m-made the . . . b-b-basket," her daughter said, the words coming slowly.

Blue Shell nodded.

"It is . . . it is . . ." Blue Shell's daughter wanted to say beautiful, wanted to thank her mother, but the words caught and stopped, and there was nothing more she could say. She waited, hoping her mother would see the gratitude in her eyes, but her mother did not look at her, and Blue Shell's daughter tried to remember if her mother ever looked at her, ever allowed the meeting of eyes. No, no, but perhaps that was so she did not have to see the emptiness in her daughter's heart, so she was not reminded that her daughter had no soul.

For a time Blue Shell said nothing, but then she stood, her back to the sea, and the wind parted her hair in a pale line down the back of her head. "You will be given two ceremonies this night," she said. "The ceremony of becoming a woman and the ceremony of naming. Your father has chosen a name for you."

The daughter heard the words, made a small choking sound, a laugh with tears caught in it. A name. A name! This time she sought her mother's eyes boldly, waited, unblinking until her mother looked at her.

"I am glad you have become a woman," her mother said. The words were quiet, almost lost in the cries of guillemot and gull.

The wind suddenly swirled down around them and spun their hair into tangled black clouds around their heads. They both reached up to brush the strands from their faces, and for a moment their hands, in reaching, touched, then quickly pulled away to smooth hair back into place.

The girl stood beside her father's ulaq. She could see the beach. Someone had made a heather and seal bone fire, and the wind carried the smell of burning seal fat and crowberry heath. All the people of her village were gathered there: her father, shortest of the men; her mother, tiny and, according to Crooked Nose, once beautiful; her brother, Qakan, taller now than their father; Big Teeth and his two wives, Crooked Nose and Little Duck and Little Duck's son. How many summers did the boy have, seven, eight? And of course, Kayugh, a hunter whose family was never hungry. Chagak, holding their daughter Wren, stood beside him; their oldest daughter, Red Berry, and Red Berry's husband, First Snow, were next in the circle, then Samiq and Amgigh.

How Blue Shell's daughter had hated that beach. The flat expanse of dark gray shale and gravel with only a few standing boulders gave no place to hide from her father or Qakan.

But tonight, it was a place of joy.

Her mother had told her to watch for Kayugh's signal—his hand lifted, pointing to the path of the sun. She waited anxiously. Her nervousness, once only a knot in her belly, now spread to numb her fingertips and toes.

She ran her hand back through her hair. She had combed it with a notched stick and rubbed seal oil into the length of it. It fell, long and smooth, to her waist.

"You are beautiful," her mother had whispered to her. The words had surprised Blue Shell's daughter so much that she had not answered her mother, only watched as Blue Shell joined the others on the beach. And she wondered if the others, too, would see the difference in her, if they would see that she had changed from an ugly girl into a beautiful woman.

Kayugh raised his arm and Blue Shell's daughter lifted her head. She walked slowly to the beach. As she neared the circle of people, she saw there was a space for her between her father and Kayugh.

She felt the muscles of her shoulders tense as they always did when she was close to her father. But then it was as if someone spoke to her, as if someone said, "You are a woman," and in that moment she looked up to see Samiq watching her. He was not as tall as his father, but his shoulders were wide and strong. His cheekbones were high, his eyes as dark as cormorant feathers. He smiled and Blue Shell's daughter's eyes widened. The ceremony was a solemn thing. No one, her mother had told her, was supposed to smile, but the girl's happiness began to flow up from her chest and she had to look away to keep from smiling back.

"You have gifts?" she heard Kayugh ask, and she realized that the ceremony had begun.

Blue Shell came forward and laid the belts that her daughter had made on the sand in the center of the circle.

As her mother laid each belt out full length, the women made small sounds of appreciation. It was probably something the women did at every new woman ceremony, Blue Shell's daughter reminded herself, but their admiration for her work still gave her joy.

Her mother stepped back into her place in the circle and Kayugh spoke again.

"We have come to make the woman's ceremony," he said, "but your father has also asked that you be given a naming ceremony."

Blue Shell's daughter looked at her father. He stood facing straight ahead, as if she were not at his side.

Kayugh turned toward her and placed his hands on her head. "Your father says . . ." he began, then stopped, cleared his throat. Kayugh closed his eyes, and for a moment Blue Shell's daughter thought she saw him clench his teeth, but then he looked up at the sky and said, "Your father says that your name is Kiin."

Blue Shell's daughter felt the heat of sudden embarrassment push up into her face. Her father had chosen to name her *Kiin*. Kiin, a name that was a question—Who? So she was still to be someone unrecognized, a daughter, a woman, but a stranger.

There was the dampness of another hand on her head, her father's hand.

"You are Kiin," Kayugh said, bending to whisper the name in her ear. And hearing the name again, Blue Shell's daughter was suddenly angry, and wished that somehow her father was as much a man as Kayugh, that he had been able, in spite of his hatred for her, to choose a name that was a true name.

But then the joy of the moment came to her. She was soon to take her place as a woman of the First Men, and more importantly, she had been given a name. No matter what that name was, no matter how insulting, it allowed her to claim a soul.

They had no shaman in their village, so Kayugh as chief hunter made the ceremonies, and now he began a chant, something said in words she did not understand. She stood with her head bowed under the weight of the two men's hands.

Then she felt Kayugh slip something over her head, and looking down, she saw a sealskin pouch hanging from a thong. It was an amulet. She knew it would contain the First Men's sacred stone, obsidian.

Again the thought came, I have a spirit now. I have a soul. She felt something moving within her chest, a fluttering like the wind. It pressed out to fill her, pushed against her fingers and her toes. Kayugh ended his chant and Gray Bird lifted his hand from her head.

Kiin raised her eyes to the people in the circle and saw herself as one of them. Joy seemed to lift her from the ground, and when her mother stepped forward to the center of the circle, Kiin nearly forgot to join her.

Kayugh lightly touched her arm and Kiin suddenly remembered her place in the ceremony. She walked to her mother's side, waited as her mother picked up one of the belts. It was for Kayugh. Kiin took it to him, laid it over his outstretched arms, and she, in turn, took the gift he offered her, two sealskins.

The next belt was for Big Teeth, a man of jokes and laughter. On his belt, Kiin had made pictures in the sealskin, men in ikyan hunting seals. Kiin knew the pictures would give him extra power in his hunting, and she saw a flash of gladness in his eyes when he took the belt from her and gave her a harbor seal skin.

Her father was next. He took his belt and gave her two stone lamps in return. First Snow gave firestones and a seal belly of oil. Then it was Samiq's turn. Would he see that of all the belts, his was the most beautiful?

As Kiin laid the belt over Samiq's outstretched arms, she looked up at him, dared to meet his eyes.

"It is beautiful, Kiin," Samiq said, and his voice seemed to make her name beautiful. Then from beneath his parka, he pulled a long strand of shell beads. He reached forward and slipped it over Kiin's head. The necklace hung against her suk, white and shining even in the dim firelight, and she looked down at it in wonder.

Perhaps she could dare to hope, could begin to see Samiq as one who would be husband. But then he said, "This I give as a gift from me and from my brother Amgigh."

And in surprise she looked at Amgigh who stood with a smile crooked on his face, but his eyes hard. Kiin gave him his belt and waited to see if he would speak to her, but he said nothing.

The last belt went to Qakan. It had few decorations but was intricately woven, the strips of sealskin moving in and out like sea waves. She had cut seal shapes out of a darker piece of hide and sewn them into the woven waves. Her brother snorted when she gave him the belt, and she looked at him in surprise. It was not as bright and flashing as the older men's belts, but it was beautiful and should give him great power over seals. He handed her his gift, two woven grass berry bags, bags Kiin herself had made, and Kiin was suddenly angry. What right did Qakan have to despise her gift when his was so poor?

She lifted her head and looked into Qakan's face. "I-I-I w-w-wish you power in your . . . hunting," she said, something that was true, for each man's hunting helped the entire village. Then her anger rose, flooded her throat. It brought, as anger almost always did, flowing words, nearly smooth, and Kiin added, "I-I thank you for the berry bags. It must have taken you many hours to weave them." Her words were quiet. She knew no one but Qakan could hear her, but she also knew any accusation of woman's work would humiliate him.

Qakan's face darkened and Kiin fought the impulse to look away. I have a soul, she told herself. He cannot hurt me. But then she felt a voice within, the moving of her spirit, and in her mind, her spirit said, "His ignorance does not excuse yours." Kiin blushed and stepped back to the center of the circle.

As she knelt to place the berry bags with her other gifts, she looked up at the faces of the people around her. They can see the value of Qakan's gift, she thought. Let them make the judgment.

Quietly then, Kiin stood. Her mother had returned to her place beside Crooked Nose, and Kiin was alone. The people were silent, and Kiin felt the weight of their stares. She lifted her head and waited for the words that would come next.

Finally Kayugh spoke. "You are a woman," he said. "You are a woman," said Big Teeth. "You are a woman," her father repeated. First Snow, Samiq, Amgigh, and finally Qakan each said the words.

"You are a woman," Kiin's spirit said.

7

"You have many beautiful gifts," Red Berry said to Kiin, and Kiin, afraid the words would stick in her throat, made no reply but merely smiled and nodded.

Red Berry, Samiq's sister, was the youngest of the wives. She carried a baby son in a sling under her suk, and as Red Berry bent to help Kiin gather her gifts, the baby began to whimper.

Kiin laughed. "G-g-go. F-f-feed him."

Red Berry glanced down the beach. "Samiq is coming. He will help you. This little one needs his bed."

She hurried away and Kiin looked up. The men were squatting around the fire, eating food their wives brought them. Samiq was striding toward her, holding a dark piece of dried seal meat.

"Are you hungry?" he asked. He tore the meat in two and gave a piece to Kiin. Then before Kiin could thank him, he added, "You have a new suk."

"Y-your m-m-mother," Kiin said.

She lifted the string of shell beads that lay against her breast. They glittered in bands of soft colors. She wanted to thank him for the necklace, but though she tried, the words were gone, pulled from her throat as though some spirit had stolen them.

Samiq leaned close to her and slipped his hand under the necklace. "These three," he said and his fingers stroked three of the beads, "are from shells I found during our long hunt when my father killed the walrus." He moved his hand to the next bead. "This one is from a necklace that once belonged to a grandmother, someone who died before I was born. This bead is from a bone of my first seal. Most of the beads are cut from shells I found on our beach or places nearby. I have been making this necklace for you for many years."

"Th-thank you," Kiin said.

Samiq smiled. "It is better than berry bags," he said.

Kiin laughed.

Samiq's eyes darkened and he studied her face. "At least these last few days you have been safe," he finally said. "Away from your father and brother."

"It w-w-was l-l-lonely," Kiin said. She saw the surprise in Samiq's eyes. "I m-m-m-missed my mother," Kiin explained, then said softly, the words for once coming easily, "I missed you." But then she blushed and she wished she had not spoken. A woman did not say such things to anyone except husband or children.

Samiq looked away, toward the sea, and for a long time did not speak. When he finally turned toward her, he said, "Soon you will belong to a husband and your father will leave you alone." He spoke softly so the sound of his words washed in and out with the rush of the waves. Then he turned and walked away from Kiin.

Kiin watched him, watched the sway of his straight shoulders as he walked, the gleam of his black hair as the wind swept it back from his face, and she remembered his fingers pressed lightly at her throat, the shell beads white and pink against the brown of his skin.

Samiq went back to the fire, squatted beside Big Teeth. Kiin smiled. Of all the older men in the village, Big Teeth was her favorite. When he was on the beach working over ikyak or weapons, Kiin had seen him throw back his head and laugh, as if he told jokes to himself. But why not? Other men made songs as they worked. Why not make jokes?

Big Teeth and his wife, Crooked Nose, had always been kind to her. There had been many times that Kiin would have lain outside all night after one of her father's beatings, times when she would rather be in the cold of the night winds than return to her father's ulaq. But Crooked Nose would come for her and take her to Big Teeth's ulaq. They would give her something to eat, perhaps several of the puffin eggs Crooked Nose had gathered and stored in the oil and sand in the food cache at the front of their ulaq. It was a delicacy Gray Bird never allowed Kiin even though she was the one in their family who climbed the cliffs to find eggs.

Kiin would go back to her father's ulaq in the morning. She would pretend she had no bruises, would pretend she had not spent a night in another ulaq. It was the best way, and if Qakan mentioned the beating and asked where she had been, Kiin would shrug and say nothing.

Kiin glanced toward the ulas. All of the women except Chagak had left the beach. She was still bringing food to the men. A gathering bag of eggs hung from one arm, and she carried a sea lion stomach container that Kiin knew was stuffed with dried halibut.

Kiin hurried to help her.

"Thank you," Chagak said. "My husband told me they will be a long time yet."

"I w-w-will st-st-stay to help," Kiin offered.

They carried the sea lion stomach between them. It was a large one, as big around as Kiin's waist, and its length reached from her shoulders to her knees. She and Chagak laid it near the men where Chagak had covered the beach gravel with long grass mats.

Kiin began to pull the fish from the sea lion stomach. She noticed that the men stopped talking when she and Chagak approached, but Kiin had not missed her father's words, "She will make a good wife. Her mother has trained her well. You see the parka I am wearing. My daughter made it. I will not give her easily."

Kiin's heart began to beat so fast that her hands trembled as she laid out the fish. Samiq must have asked for her.

If she knew she would belong to Samiq, if she knew she would soon be his wife, her father could beat her every day, and still she would not die.

But the hope was too wonderful, and so Kiin tried to turn her thoughts to other things. That way, if her father said no, perhaps the pain would not be as great.

She and Chagak finished setting out the dried halibut and the eggs, then Chagak whispered, "I will help you carry your gifts to your father's ulaq."

They slipped away from the group of men. Soon the edge of the sun would push into the sky to end the short night. Already, it was light enough to see their way to the piles of gifts that lay above the tide flats on the beach.

Kiin folded her gifts into the sealskins Kayugh had given her. Then each woman picked up a sealskin and carried it up the slope of the beach toward the ulas.

Their small village had four ulas: Kayugh's, Big Teeth's, Gray Bird's, and the new ulaq that belonged to First Snow.

Chagak had told Kiin stories of the large village that she had lived in as a child. There had been eight, ten ulas, and Chagak had explained that these were much larger than even Kayugh's ulaq and often several families lived in each. And Kiin had heard the men's stories about the warrior tribe called the Short Ones, terrible men who killed other men for the joy of killing. They had attacked Chagak's village and only Chagak had survived. She had left the village then, had left her sacred mountain Aka, and went to her grandfather, Shuganan, the old man now dead.

And the men told stories of the great battle fought on the Whale Hunters' beach. All the Short Ones were killed, and Kayugh and the men came back to this beach, the beach that belonged to the sacred mountain Tugix. And here they lived, safe and well since that terrible battle.

And now, we, their children will make families, Kiin thought.

Then someday, perhaps when I am a grandmother, our village will be large and we will be a strong people again.

She smiled at Chagak, though Kiin knew that in the darkness, the woman could not see her smile. They climbed the slope of Gray Bird's ulaq. Chagak pulled up the door flap that covered the opening in the center of the roof and Kiin climbed down, then lifted her arms so Chagak could hand her the gifts.

Kiin glanced around the ulaq. Her mother was not in the large main room, but a seal oil lamp still burned, giving a dim light.

My mother must be asleep, Kiin thought.

Gray Bird's ulaq had a large center room with small areas curtained off at sides and back. Gray Bird's sleeping place was at the back of the ulaq, the place of honor, and Qakan's was beside his. Kiin and her mother had sleeping places on each side of the ulaq, and at the front was a food cache.

Kiin climbed back up the notched log and closed the door flap. Chagak had already begun to walk to her own ulaq.

"Sl-sleep well," Kiin called softly.

Chagak turned and waved, her words light with laughter as she called back, "I do not think you will sleep, so I will only wish you a good night."

Kiin smiled and sat down at the top of the ulaq so she could see the beach. The men were still gathered at the fire, even though the flames were gone and glowing coals were all that were left of the crowberry heather and seal bones that had been stacked as high as her waist. Kiin pulled her knees up inside her suk and covered her bare feet with her hands. The wind coming from the sea was cold, and Kiin shivered.

She rested her arms on her upraised knees and dared to let thoughts of Samiq as husband come to her mind. This day had been the most beautiful in her life. Finally the spirits of Tugix rejoiced over her. Finally she had all things a new woman would want—a beautiful suk, a necklace, perhaps even the promise of a husband.

And though Kiin had hated the nights she was forced to

spend with traders, it would be different with Samiq, with his arms around her, with his hands touching her.

Samiq had always been a friend. He often fought with Qakan to protect her from Qakan's sudden anger. And when her father beat her, it was usually Samiq who took her to Chagak or Crooked Nose to have her cuts washed, her bruises layered with wet willow leaves.

But to have Samiq as husband—to have him hold her during the night . . .

At first Kiin did not realize that her father was shouting. But when Qakan raised his voice, Kiin heard him, and she saw that her father and Qakan were striding away from the other men.

They are angry with me, Kiin thought. I did not bring enough food.

She slid down the side of the ulaq and hid in the heather and long grasses that grew at the back of the sod mound. Kiin held her breath as her father and brother climbed the ulaq and went inside. The other men were also leaving, and they walked by without seeing her. When Samiq passed she almost reached out to him. But no, Amgigh and Kayugh were with him, the three walking together to Kayugh's ulaq. Kayugh looked angry, and Kiin saw that even Amgigh's lips were pressed tightly together, his hands clenched into fists.

In a sudden panic, she wondered if in some way her father had been able to take away her name, if perhaps she was again without her soul, but she felt the fullness of her spirit moving within her, and its quiet inside voice said, "Wait. Stay where you are; I am here."

She reached for the amulet that hung at her neck. Since Kiin now had name and soul, she knew she could lift her thoughts to the spirits of grandmothers who lived in the place of Dancing Lights.

Please, let me keep my spirit, she begged. Please don't let my father take it from me.

She moved back to lean against the ulaq, her head pressed against the grass. The sky was streaked with the beginning of morning. I will wait until my father goes to his sleeping place, she thought, and carefully crept to the top of the ulaq, where she crouched, listening, trying to tell whether Gray Bird and Qakan were in the main part of the ulaq.

She heard her father's voice, still sharp in his anger, and was surprised to realize that his anger was directed at Qakan. "If you were a hunter, you could pay for your own woman. Kayugh is a fool and has offered a good price for the girl. What else can I do? Tell him no? I will not refuse his offer."

"Then give me the sealskins he trades for her," Qakan said. "I will take them to the Whale Hunters and get a woman for myself."

"You do not want a Whale Hunter woman. They are more like men than women. They think they own their husband's ulaq. Go to the Walrus People. Get a good wife. A woman who knows how to please a man."

"You will give me the skins to trade?"

"I need the skins."

Kiin heard her brother snarl, heard his words grating at the back of his throat. "I will take Kiin, then," he said. "I will trade her."

Kiin heard her father laugh, and the long low sound caught in her teeth, making them ache. It was the same laugh he made when he was beating her.

"You can meet her bride price?" he asked.

"She is worth nothing, so I give nothing," Qakan answered.

"Kayugh will give me fifteen skins."

Fifteen skins! Kiin thought. Fifteen skins, enough for two brides, even three. Her heart slowed, and again she felt the soft movement of her spirit. She was safe. Kayugh had offered enough to ensure her safety. She would be wife to Samiq. Wife. Qakan could do nothing.

8

E ach day, Kiin tried to stay near her father's ulaq. Perhaps it would take Samiq into the next summer to save enough sealskins for her bride price, she told herself. You are foolish to wait so near the ulaq, risking your father's anger, risking a beating, just because you hope to see Kayugh and Samiq coming to the ulaq, coming to bargain for a wife.

But still, each time she went to the cliffs to search for eggs, or into the smaller hills behind the village to dig roseroot, she found herself stopping to look back toward the village. And on the third day, when the men went hunting, she could not keep her eyes from scanning the sea.

During those three days, she also noticed that her father did not speak to her, but that Qakan followed her with his eyes, a scowl on his face, his thick lips drawn into a pout. Qakan went with the men on the hunt, but Gray Bird stayed in the ulaq. He must carve, he told Blue Shell. The spirits demanded it. The ground had trembled the night before. Had she not felt the spirits moving deep in the earth?

But when Gray Bird sat down to carve, Blue Shell took her basket pole outside and Kiin was left inside to weave mats.

"Mat weaving is a quiet thing," Blue Shell whispered to Kiin. "It will not disturb your father. And if he needs something to drink or eat, you will be here to get it for him."

Kiin did not answer. Blue Shell usually went outside when Gray Bird began to carve; Kiin was left to face his anger if the carving did not come easily.

Kiin sighed and began splitting grass stems with her thumbnail then sorted them according to length.

For most of the afternoon, she worked, splitting and sorting grasses then weaving them into coarse mats, using her fingers and a forked fish bone to push each weft strand tightly against the strand of grass above it.

Her father sat close to an oil lamp, his head bent over his work. Soot from the lamp gathered in the damp creases of his forehead. Kiin seldom looked at him, though occasionally, he broke the silence with muttering, once making derogatory statements about Kiin's mother, another time hissing words against the wood he was carving. Kiin had turned, thinking he was speaking to her and saw that he was carving something shaped like a man, one leg crooked and shorter than the other, the wood rough where his knife had worked, the rough areas, already marked with soot from his fingertips.

Kiin sighed and returned to the straight, clean rows of her mat, and for some reason, her fingers sought the smooth surface of the whale tooth shell that hung at her waist.

She had nearly completed the mat when her father spoke to her, and the suddenness of his words made Kiin jump. "Kayugh will pay a good price for you," he said.

Kiin looked at him and raised her eyebrows, pretending surprise.

"Bride price," her father said and set down his small carving knife.

"I-I-I-I," Kiin began, angry with herself as the words caught. Her father uttered a short, harsh laugh. But his laughter seemed to give Kiin her voice, and she said, "I am to be a w-w-wife then?"

"Kayugh has promised me fifteen sealskins," Gray Bird said. Slowly, he stood, grimacing as he straightened to his full height. Unlike Kayugh, he did not have to stoop under the lower edges of the sloping ulaq roof. He flexed his hands. They were smooth-skinned, like a child's hands.

"You will live in Kayugh's ulaq and eat Kayugh's food, but do not forget that you are my daughter. I was the one who let you live, though most girls would have been left to the wind spirits."

A few days before, if her father would have spoken to her for such a long time, Kiin would have kept her eyes lowered, her head bowed, but now she saw the uncertainty in the man, and felt the strength of her own spirit, pressing against the walls of her heart, pulsing with the beat of her blood. And so she did not look away, but kept her eyes open, locked with his eyes, so his spirit knew she was growing strong.

"Yes," she said. "I will stay in Kayugh's ulaq." And she said the words without stammering, as though the decision was her decision and nothing to do with what her father wanted.

Gray Bird raised his chin and thrust out his chest. "You will bring food to us," he said. "When Kayugh or your husband or your husband's brother takes a seal, you will ask for a share for your father," he said.

Kiin stood and moved a step closer to her father. She straightened to her full height and realized that she was nearly as tall as he was. Anger smoothed her throat, pulled her words into long lines that flowed easily from her mouth. "If you need food," she said, "I will ask Kayugh."

Her father smiled, and the smile tightened his thin lips and made the string of hair that hung from his chin tremble. He nodded.

But then Kiin added: "I will not have my mother starve."

Gray Bird blinked, and for a moment, the muscles of his arms tensed and he raised one hand, but Kiin did not move. Let him hit her. She would show Samiq the bruises, tell him to lower the price he had offered for her. Perhaps then she could become a wife more quickly, without waiting through one summer and maybe another for the skins to be gathered.

But then she heard the call from the beach, the high trilling of women's voices, and her father turned away and climbed from the ulaq.

"They have seals," he called down to her, and Kiin was surprised he would tell her.

She waited until she was sure he had time to walk to the beach, then she slipped into her suk and climbed from the ulaq, pausing at the top to count the ikyan. Yes, all the men were back. Samiq's and Amgigh's ikyan were towing seals.

The hunters had taken four fur seals. Big Teeth and First Snow had killed one together, both men's harpoon heads in the seal's flesh. Samiq had one, as did Kayugh and Amgigh. Qakan had taken nothing.

Chagak, Crooked Nose and Red Berry began butchering, but Blue Shell and Kiin waited. They held their women's knives in their hands, ready but unable to help until asked. Otherwise, it would appear that they claimed a kill for their ulaq. But soon Chagak turned toward them and gestured toward the seals Amgigh and Samiq had dragged up the beach.

Kiin smiled, and for a moment let her eyes meet Samiq's eyes, but to her surprise, he looked away and said gruffly, "You should take Amgigh's seal."

She turned from Samiq and she let herself smile into Amgigh's eyes. What did it matter which seal she took? she asked herself. They were brothers, and a wife to one brother was often considered second wife to the other, cooking for both, sewing for both.

She began cutting, working quickly to separate the hide from the carcass until she was ready to call the other women to help her turn the seal and continue the skinning.

When she looked up she realized that Amgigh had stayed beside her. "Give the flipper meat and fat to your father," he said, then left to join the men as they inspected their ikyan for tears or gaps in the seams.

The flipper meat and fat—the best part—to her father? Kiin watched Amgigh walk across the beach, and her stomach suddenly twisted as though she had eaten the most sour of lovage stems. Why had Samiq told her to skin Amgigh's seal? Why did Amgigh give a gift of meat to her father? Surely she was not to be bride to Amgigh. Samiq was the older of the two brothers. Besides, Samiq had made her the necklace.

She clasped the beads at her neck and heard the quiet voice of her spirit repeat Samiq's words, " 'This I give as a gift from me and from my brother Amgigh.' "

9

They came three days later, Kayugh's arms piled high with sealskins, Amgigh following with four new fur seal skins, rolled skin side in. Kiin was sitting with her back to the climbing log as she pounded dried seal meat into a powder to mix with dried berries.

When she heard Kayugh's voice, she scooted to the dark side of the ulaq near the food cache and watched as first Kayugh then Amgigh tossed furs down to her father and then slid down the climbing log.

She waited, hoping Samiq had come with them, but there were only Kayugh and Amgigh, and when Gray Bird gestured for Kayugh to sit down, leaving Amgigh standing beside the climbing log, she knew. Amgigh was to be her husband.

Her lungs suddenly seemed too heavy for her chest and her heart seemed to stop beneath their weight. Slowly, she squatted on her heels. Slowly, she crossed her arms over her upraised knees. Not Samiq, she thought. Not Samiq.

But then her spirit spoke, moving within her chest, fighting the heaviness of her lungs, until Kiin could breathe again. "You will have a husband," her spirit said. "A man to care for you. And you will live in Kayugh's ulaq, with Chagak. With Samiq. You will have warm clothes, enough to eat, and Amgigh will give you babies, sons to be hunters, daughters to be mothers. Remember, remember, last summer, even a few days ago, you thought you would never be wife, never belong to any man but your father."

Kiin watched Amgigh, watched as he shifted his weight from one foot to the other, saw that he turned his head away from the men when his father told Gray Bird of Amgigh's strength, of his good eyes, of his skill with harpoon and knife. "What boy, what man, climbs more easily to the bird holes in the cliffs?" Kiin's spirit whispered. "What man takes better care of his ikyak? And does any man try harder than Amgigh, in throwing the spear, in running? He will be a good husband. A good husband."

Yes, Kiin thought. He would be a good husband. And he was a handsome man. Much like Kayugh, with long arms and legs, leaner than Samiq, but with shining eyes and white teeth; clear, smooth skin.

Gray Bird and Kayugh were speaking of hunting, of the sea, of the weather. Kiin heard them, but did not listen; she had heard this politeness before; any time men met to discuss more important things, the politeness came first. But suddenly her father stood, strode to the pile of sealskins. She watched as he inspected each skin, and she was thankful that Chagak was not here to see the casual disdain with which he regarded her careful work.

He would not know, Kiin thought, that Chagak's sealskins were the finest Kiin had ever seen, better even than Blue Shell's, and Blue Shell's brought high trades with the Whale Hunters.

"I asked fifteen hides," Gray Bird said. "There are twelve here."

"We have these," Kayugh said and gestured toward the four rolled skins, only partially scraped.

"You bring work for my wife?"

"Chagak will finish them. I wanted you to see that they are waiting for you. We will give them to you when they are finished."

"So you would take my daughter for twelve skins?"

"Sixteen," Kayugh answered, his voice firm.

Amgigh's hands clenched and unclenched. Did he want her so much that his wanting made him nervous? Or was he insulted by her father's words?

"Sixteen," Gray Bird said, "but only twelve now. Four on your promise."

"Three on my promise and an extra skin because you waited for the three," Kayugh answered.

Gray Bird made a rude noise with his lips. "On your promise?" he said.

"Have you known me to break a promise?" Kayugh asked.

For a moment Gray Bird said nothing, then he looked up at Amgigh. "He hunts?" Gray Bird asked.

"Yes," Kayugh answered.

"He will be able to feed my daughter, bring in seals for oil and skins?"

"Yes."

"You see my daughter," Gray Bird said, and he strode to Kiin's side and pulled her suddenly to her feet. "She is not too thin." He pinched Kiin's legs, her arms, cupped a breast with one hand. His fingers were cold against Kiin's skin. "You will keep her fat?"

"Yes," Kayugh said.

"Yes," Amgigh answered, and Kiin blushed for she knew Amgigh was not supposed to speak. In trading for a first bride, the father traded; the son watched.

Gray Bird pulled Kiin's new suk from a pile of furs where she had carefully laid it. "You see she does fine work," Gray Bird said.

Kiin felt blood rise to her cheeks, and the heat from her skin rose to burn in her eyes. Blue Shell must not have told Gray Bird who gave Kiin the suk. And Kiin must remember now to tell her mother what Gray Bird had done. If Blue Shell ever told Gray Bird that Chagak had made the suk, if Gray Bird realized that he had become a fool in his trading, he would beat Blue Shell until she could not stand.

61

Amgigh took a long breath, and Kiin, looking from the shadows, caught Kayugh's eyes. She shook her head. Don't tell him, she begged silently. Please don't tell him. Think what he would do to my mother. He might, in his embarrassment, refuse Kayugh's offer, allow Qakan to trade her to people from another village.

Kayugh held his hand up toward Amgigh and stared at his son until Amgigh dropped his head.

"Kiin has many talents," Kayugh said. "That is why I want her for my son."

Gray Bird puffed out his chest, strutted to the center of the ulaq and squatted beside Kayugh.

"He thinks he has won," Kiin's spirit said. "He thinks he has bettered Kayugh in his game of trading."

Kayugh looked over Gray Bird's head to Amgigh and nodded. Gray Bird turned and watched as Amgigh unlashed a knife from his left wrist. He laid the knife across his palm and held it out to Gray Bird, handle first.

"My son makes knives," Kayugh said.

Kiin saw Gray Bird's back suddenly straighten. Amgigh's knives were treasured by all the men. Big Teeth said he had known no finer. This particular knife was short bladed, the right size to fit inside the sleeve of a man's parka. The blade was black, nearly translucent at the edges, knapped from Okmok's obsidian. The knife was hafted with seal gut to a smooth piece of ivory, marbled yellow and white. The end of the handle was plugged with a stopper of walrus ivory. Amgigh pulled the ivory plug from the handle and shook out three birdbone gorges. Amgigh slipped the gorges into the knife handle and pushed the ivory plug back in place.

Gray Bird smiled and reached for the knife. He tested the edge with his finger, held it up to the light from an oil lamp. He pulled out the plug and examined the gorges.

"You will have the four skins back to me in"—he paused—"twenty days?"

"Yes," Kayugh said.

"Take her," Gray Bird said motioning toward Kiin, then he turned his back to his daughter and the men, and dragged the twelve finished skins into his sleeping place.

Kiin's eyes widened. It was done. So quickly, it was done. She stood, uncertain what was expected of her, but when Kayugh said nothing and Amgigh remained with his back toward her, she pulled a seal bladder container from the storage cache and using the flat of her knife blade, pushed the meat she had ground into the container.

She picked up her sewing basket and suk, then taking one of her mother's largest baskets, filled it with her naming gifts. She hurried into her sleeping place to gather grass mats and sleeping furs. When she came back into the main room of the ulaq, she found that Amgigh was waiting for her. He took the bundle of mats and sleeping furs from her arms and watched as Kiin put on her suk and picked up the basket. Then still without speaking, Amgigh led the way up the climbing log. Kayugh was already at the top of the log, the rolled green skins in his arms.

The wind was strong and it pulled at the basket Kiin held, but for a moment she stood on the top of the ulaq, watching as Kayugh and Amgigh walked to the high mound of Kayugh's ulaq. Kiin looked toward the beach, listened to the rumble of the waves. The sky was gray, darker near the center and light where its edges met the far limit of the sea. Even the beach was gray, and the tide pools reflected the sky.

Then she saw Samiq standing alone beside the blackness that marked the place of her woman's ceremony fire. His back was toward her, but he turned. He turned and slowly raised one arm, one hand toward her, fingers splayed. And without thinking, Kiin stretched one hand toward him.

10

S*amiq watched as Kiin* followed Amgigh to Kayugh's ulaq. Anger pressed hard into Samiq's chest, but he was not sure whether he was angry with Amgigh for taking Kiin as wife, with his father for making the trade, or with Kiin for walking so easily in Amgigh's wake, as if she had always been wife, as if she wanted Amgigh as much as Samiq wanted her.

You are foolish, he told himself. She is safe now, away from Gray Bird, safe in our father's ulaq. You cannot be her husband; you are going to live with the Whale Hunters. You will be away for the summer, perhaps longer. Would you rather she was unprotected, beaten and abused in Gray Bird's ulaq?

But he stayed on the beach. The wind turned toward night, cold and bitter, numbing his hands, stiffening his knees, so that he walked slowly, like an old man.

Kiin stroked the whale tooth shell that hung at her side, then folded her hands in her lap. Chagak had given Kiin a corner in the large room for her sewing basket and weaving supplies, and Kayugh had pointed to the sleeping place that would be hers, one near the front of the ulaq. There Kiin spread out her sleeping skins and stacked the grass mats that protected the furs from the packed dirt and rock of the ulaq floor. But now she had nothing to do.

During other visits to Kayugh's ulaq, she had felt no awkwardness, had helped Chagak prepare food or care for Samiq's baby sister, but today Wren was sleeping, tucked away in Chagak's sleeping place, and when Kiin had offered to help Chagak with the food, Chagak motioned her to sit down, to be still. Tomorrow, Kiin would help, tomorrow she would cook and sew, but today was a day to sit, to talk and to do nothing.

Kiin could never remember having a day to do nothing. Her hands could not stay still; her fingers clasped and unclasped until Kiin, embarrassed that her actions were more like those of a child than a wife, tucked her hands up inside the sleeves of her suk and began playing a game in her mind, a game of naming berries—salmonberry, red currant, crowberry—then naming fish—greenling, herring, halibut. . . .

After bringing Kiin to the ulaq, Amgigh and his father went into one of the sleeping places, one to the left of the honored back room, Kayugh's sleeping place. Kiin heard the murmurings of their voices, but could not tell what either man said. Finally when Kiin had named all fish in the world, all berries on the island, all people in their village and the names of any Whale Hunter people she could remember, Kayugh came back into the main room of the ulaq. He stood for a moment in front of Kiin, smiled at her, then said, "My son will be a good husband to you. What food we have is yours. The furs we have are yours. You belong to this family now. I am your father and you are my daughter."

For a moment Kiin sat very still. She wished she had asked her mother questions about the giving of brides. Crooked Nose had told her of men's ways and how to please a man, but nothing of ceremonies. Perhaps Kayugh's words were only a politeness, but perhaps they were a ceremony and there was something Kiin was expected to say in reply.

Finally she said in a very soft voice, "Is-is th-th-this a ceremony?" She could not raise her eyes to Kayugh's face, but then he reached down and cupped her chin in his hand, lifted her head so she could see that he was smiling.

"It is a welcome," he said. "Only that."

"Th-thank you," Kiin said. "I w-w-w-will be a g-g-good w-wife to Amgigh. I will be a g-g-good daughter to you and Ch-Chagak."

"A sister to Wren and Samiq?" Kayugh asked still smiling.

"Yes," Kiin answered and would not let herself feel the small ache that had lodged beneath her breastbone since she had seen Samiq from the top of her father's ulaq.

"Then you may help your new mother with the food. We plan a feast," Kayugh said.

Kiin hurried to Chagak's side, but Chagak said, "Sit. Rest. Enjoy the day."

"Please," said Kiin, her voice a whisper, and Chagak looked at her with widened eyes, then said, "Yes, you are right. Sometimes it is better to have something to do."

She handed Kiin a basket of eggs that had been boiled in their shells and cooled. Kiin took the basket to the center of the ulaq where the roof hole let in light, and she began to peel the eggs. Chagak was the only woman in the village who made these eggs, and they were one of Kiin's favorite foods. After peeling, each egg was sliced into quarters and each quarter dipped in seal oil. Chagak usually arranged the slices in a pattern on a grass mat, the egg quarters spreading from the center in a large circle like the petals of a white and yellow flower.

Kiin's flower did not turn out to be as lovely as the ones Chagak made, but Chagak clicked her tongue in approval when Kiin had finished, and Kiin's skin warmed with pleasure at the praise. Chagak set out dried halibut, fresh herring fried in seal oil and thin slices of seal meat that she had cooked on sticks over an outside fire. There was a basket of peeled ugyuun stems to be eaten with the fish, and goose fat mixed with dried berries.

Finally Chagak sat back on her haunches and smiled at Kiin. "A feast," Chagak said and brushed her hair back from her forehead. With her large slanting eyes, full mouth and tiny nose, she was a beautiful woman. The most beautiful in their village, Kiin thought. She was small, but not as small as Kiin's mother, Blue Shell. And Blue Shell herself had once been beautiful, Crooked Nose had said, though now the woman's hair was heavily streaked with gray, her nose crooked from one of Gray Bird's blows.

Chagak looked up at Kayugh. "Bring your sons," she said, then she and Kiin stood up and took their places behind the climbing log. At this feast, as at most feasts, the men would eat first, the women bringing water, slicing meat. Kayugh called Amgigh from his sleeping place then left the ulaq saying, "I will find Samiq."

Amgigh squatted beside the food. He did not speak, but sat with his arms resting easily atop his knees. He was wearing a grass apron, the panel edged in a darker grass and woven with a checkered pattern as were all of Chagak's weavings. Perhaps now that Kiin was daughter, Chagak would teach her to weave like that.

Amgigh's shoulders and back shone with oil and his hair was combed out straight and smooth, and hung like a fall of black water to his shoulders. He did not look at Kiin but Kiin noticed that his hands were not still, and she heard the snapping sounds from his finger joints as he cracked each knuckle.

Finally, Kayugh returned with Samiq, the two sliding quickly down the climbing log, Samiq shedding his parka and taking his place across from Amgigh, his back to Kiin. His hair was tangled and his skin was not oiled, but Kiin's eyes wanted to watch him rather than Amgigh, so that finally she did not allow herself to look at either man.

And when the men had finished, leaving the food to Chagak and Kiin, Kiin sat so she could not see the men, but though she did not look at them, she found herself listening for Samiq's voice, admiring the wisdom of his comments, hearing his stories with more interest than she had in either Amgigh's or Kayugh's tales. So she began to talk to Chagak, saying things about weather and the sea, about sewing and cooking. She asked questions even though the words were broken by her stuttering, anything to pull her mind from Samiq, anything to help her be a true wife to Amgigh, in her thoughts as well as with the work of her hands.

After the food was eaten, after Chagak had brought Wren from her sleeping place and nursed the child, then Kiin knew it must be time. The sky at the top of the roof hole had darkened for the night. By now she was usually asleep. But everyone seemed to be busy, so Kiin pulled a skin from her sewing basket and used her awl to poke holes in one side. She would make Amgigh a pair of sealskin socks, something to keep his feet warm in the ulaq.

But now Kayugh suddenly stood before her, and Kiin quickly put away her sewing. He clasped her hands and pulled her to her feet. Kiin's heart beat hard, so hard that she was sure Kayugh could see it thrusting against the walls of her chest. Kayugh said nothing but brought her to stand before Amgigh. Amgigh sat very straight, and when he looked up at Kiin, his eyes reflected the yellow flames that danced at the circle of wicks in the nearest oil lamp. Samiq was sitting beside his brother, and Kiin, her head lowered, could not keep from glancing at Samiq's face.

His eyes, too, reflected the circle of lights but beneath the light, she saw pain, and so she quickly looked back at Amgigh. Her husband, Amgigh. "Not Samiq," her spirit said to her. "Not Samiq. Amgigh." And Kiin fixed her eyes on Amgigh's face and did not let herself look away.

Amgigh stood and Kayugh took his hand, laid it on top of Kiin's hand, then he raised the two hands, laced their fingers together both arms upraised.

"She is your wife," Kayugh said to Amgigh, then led them to Amgigh's sleeping place and pulled aside the curtain while Amgigh led Kiin inside.

11

Kiin *heard the curtain* brush closed behind them. She knew that most nights Amgigh would come to her in her sleeping place, but this night, their first night together, they were in Amgigh's sleeping place. Soft fur seal pelts were spread from the ulaq wall to the entrance, and when Kiin stepped onto the furs, she could feel the padding of heather and grass mats beneath.

"Sit," Amgigh whispered. He squatted down, his back to the door.

Kiin heard Chagak's voice coming from the other room and Kayugh answering her. They laughed and Samiq laughed with them. A part of her wanted to go to them. To leave this little room and her new husband, to be in the light of the seal oil lamps, to sew and to hear whatever they were talking about.

Kiin sat down facing Amgigh. Light pricked through the weaving of the grass door flap and settled, shining, in Amgigh's hair.

Slowly Amgigh reached out to her; slowly he touched her hair, then her face. Kiin felt the gentleness of his fingers, and her spirit whispered, "He will not beat you. He will be a good husband; be a good wife."

So Kiin lifted her arms and pulled off her suk. She had not had time to prepare as she would have wished: to smooth oil over her back and shoulders, to crush dried fireweed blossoms into her hair and comb them out, leaving their delicate smell, or to smooth the calluses of her hands with lava rock, but she knew her hair was shining and her body graceful, breasts round and soft. Perhaps that would be enough.

"You are happy to be my wife?" Amgigh asked, moving close to whisper the words. He pressed his thumbs gently down her cheeks to her lips.

If he had asked whether she wanted him above all other hunters, Kiin could not have answered. Even now she had to pull her thoughts from Samiq sitting in the next room. But since Amgigh had asked whether she was happy, she could give a true reply. Reaching out to lay her hands on the tops of his shoulders, she leaned forward so her breath carried the words to his ears, so that in whispering she would not stammer. "Yes, I am happy, Amgigh. Thank you for taking me as wife."

Then his hands moved slowly down to the band of her apron, untied hers and then his own. Carefully, Kiin laid the whale tooth shell aside. Then Amgigh leaned her back against the furs of his sleeping place.

Other times, with other men, Kiin had fought. It had seemed the only way to keep her honor, even though it meant bruises— bruises from the trader who had purchased her for the night, and later, when the trader complained, when he showed the marks of Kiin's teeth on his skin, another beating from her father. Even the few times when a trader had been gentle, she still fought. She fought the trader and she fought against the betrayal of her body, against that part of her that would give in, that would become like the Whale Hunter women, laughed at for their eager ways.

But now Amgigh was her husband. She did not have to fight. He must have been with other women, in other villages. She would show Amgigh that she could please him as much as any woman.

She began moving her fingers slowly in circles down his belly, slowly, slowly. Chagak laughed again; again Kayugh replied. Kiin heard Samiq's voice, and for a moment her hands stopped. "No," her spirit said. "Amgigh, not Samiq."

I am wife, Kiin thought, and again she stroked Amgigh's smooth oiled skin. Wife to Amgigh, Kiin thought, and made her hands move with the rhythm of her thoughts. Wife to Amgigh. Wife to Amgigh.

Amgigh held Kiin even after her slowed breathing told him she was asleep. He had taken her quickly. Perhaps in a little while, he would be ready again. Then he would wake her, but for now it was good just to hold her, to feel her softness against his skin.

Having a wife is better than hunting whale, he told himself. He knew Kiin had had other men. Gray Bird sold her as hospitality. How many evenings had Amgigh watched from the ulaq roof as Samiq paced the beach? How many times had he seen the anger on Samiq's face as Kiin emerged the next morning and hobbled to the edge of the sea to wash blood from her face, from her legs, her arms? And when Samiq had seen Amgigh and Kayugh laden with furs and walking to Gray Bird's ulaq, he had stopped Amgigh, stared deep into Amgigh's eyes. "Be careful with her tonight," he had said. "Be gentle." And Samiq would not let him pass until Amgigh had nodded his agreement.

Amgigh had had a woman before—an old Whale Hunter woman who had sneaked into his sleeping place once when he went with his father on a trading trip. She had taken him quickly, had ridden him as though she were the man. And the next day Amgigh had felt fumbling and stupid.

But with Kiin . . . Her hands had been strong, moving over his stomach, then to his shoulders and down his back to buttocks and thighs, teasing him until the throbbing in his loins told him he could wait no longer. But he had remembered Samiq's request. He had been gentle.

In the darkness Amgigh smiled.

Samiq would marry a Whale Hunter woman, loud and used

to ruling her man. Yes, Samiq would learn to hunt the whale. But he had promised to teach Amgigh. Then Amgigh, too, would know. Amgigh would know and have Kiin as well. Amgigh sighed and pulled Kiin closer so he could smell the sweetness of her hair.

Perhaps by next spring, Amgigh thought, I will have a son.

12

Q *akan woke early, even* before his mother had trimmed lamps and emptied night baskets. He climbed to the top of his father's ulaq and in the dark of early morning looked out over the ulakidaq, looked out over the beach.

He was hungry. He should have pulled something from the food cache, but now he was sitting on the ulaq. It would be too much trouble to go back inside. Besides, his mother would soon be up. She would bring him something.

He yawned. Everything was still. Even the wind had died leaving the sea to roll almost calmly into shore. A movement from one of the other ulas caught Qakan's eye. Probably Chagak. There was no laziness in the woman. But no, it was Kiin. Kiin out to empty the night wastes.

Qakan smiled, almost laughed. Kayugh had paid sixteen skins and a knife for her.

So Kiin was wife now to Amgigh. And though Kiin's marriage brought laughter into Qakan's mouth whenever he thought of the price Kayugh had paid, it also brought anger. Because of his father's greed, Qakan must forget the plans he had made so carefully, plans that had taken him more than three years to devise.

Why was Kayugh willing to pay so much? He knew Kiin was nothing. For years she had had no name, no soul. Gray Bird said

she would never be wife, and when Gray Bird grew old, too old
to hunt, what would happen to her? She would come to live
with Qakan, to take his food, food that Qakan would need for
his own wives, for his children. For himself.

How many times had his father told him, told hunters from
other tribes and traders who came to their village, that Kiin had
taken Qakan's right as firstborn, as first to suckle his mother's
breasts, as first to claim a place in his father's ulaq? And who
could say what other powers she had taken from him? Yes, their
mother weaned Kiin early so she could bear another child—a
son—for her husband. And though most infants weaned that
early would have died, his sister—full of greed for life—had
lived, had lived.

She had walked early, her little legs strong as she learned to
help their mother, the girl carrying loads too heavy for a small
child to carry, and she also talked early, saying words too hard
for a small child to say, and all the while, he, Qakan, had lain
and watched her, content to watch, because she had taken his
power, the power to walk and talk. But finally Qakan knew he
must fight back, and he, too, walked and talked. And the spirits
saw his efforts, and they took some of his sister's many words
and gave them to Qakan, leaving the girl to stammer and stut-
ter. The years passed and finally Qakan had thought of his wonderful plan. While still a boy, Qakan had thought of it. And
now he was ready to become a man.

Qakan blinked his eyes, yawned again, looked out toward the
gray expanse of the sea. He hated the sea, the water forever
around his ikyak, even above him, hanging gray in the clouds.
He hated the weight of the harpoon in his hands, the lines that
twisted and knotted, the ikyak moving with each small jerk of
legs or arms. He hated the stink of the chigadax. No, he was not
a hunter. But who could say, perhaps Kiin had grabbed that
power, also, and held it like a seed in her womb, hoping her sons
would be hunters.

But even if he could not hunt, Qakan had more power than
his sister. It did not matter what she had done to him; he would

still become a man, and he would do this by learning to trade. Who were more honored than traders? Not hunters, no. Their hunting provided only the skins and pelts for the traders. The traders were the ones who brought goods from one tribe to another. They were given the choice women of any tribe to warm their beds at night; they slept in the chief hunter's honored sleeping place. And traders with their brightly marked iks were the ones who had the best furs, the finest parkas, the most beautiful weapons.

So Qakan had planned, and had waited. And then one day his father had come back successful from a hunt, had come back with a sea lion when Kayugh and Big Teeth and First Snow took nothing. Qakan had watched, waited during the dividing of meat, during the praise songs sung by the women, waited until after his father had eaten well. And then, as though some spirit were aiding Qakan's plan, his sister had spilled hot broth on their father's feet.

It had been an accident, an accident, she had pleaded. She had tripped on Qakan's leg just as she passed their father.

Qakan had watched the beating, watched though his mother hid her eyes. He had seen Kiin shudder with the force of each blow. But silence was broken only by the sound of his father's stick against Kiin's flesh, of his father's harsh breathing. And Qakan knew that it was only because Kiin had no soul that she did not cry out. How could a person without a soul feel pain?

Then, after the beating, after Kiin had pulled herself up the climbing log and left the ulaq, perhaps to stay outside for the night, or to lose her pride and beg for a place in another ulaq, then Qakan had settled himself beside his father, had said a few words about Kiin's stupidity, and waited in silence until Qakan's mother also left the ulaq.

Then Qakan leaned close to his father, smiled and praised his father's hunting success.

Yes, Qakan had said, who would deny that Gray Bird was a good hunter, taking a sea lion when others brought back nothing. But how sad, Qakan went on to say, that Gray Bird's good heart had allowed Qakan's sister to live, had allowed that greedy one to take the strength that should have come to Qakan. So now Qakan would never be the hunter his father was. No, not ever. He would never know the pride of having village women sing to him. No, not ever. But there was one thing the greedy sister did not take; she did not take the cunning mind. That had come complete to Qakan: the cunning, cunning mind.

And Qakan watched as the scowl that was on Gray Bird's face changed slowly, slowly to something more nearly a smile. Yes, Qakan was smart, Gray Bird had said. Not a hunter, not strong with muscle, but strong in his mind.

"Perhaps there will be something for me in that," Qakan had said. "Perhaps there will be some honor for me, something. . . ." And he had let the word trail off into the flickering oil lamps of the ulaq. And he said no more. That night.

13

Kiin woke and gently pulled herself from Amgigh's arms. She had been wife for three days and four nights, and each night before she fell asleep, she told herself to wake early, to start the lamps and prepare meat so Chagak could stay in her sleeping place, nursing Wren.

Kiin fastened her apron around her waist and gently covered Amgigh's shoulders with a fur seal pelt. She slipped into the large central room of the ulaq and using a braided reed took fire from the few burning wicks in the oil lamp nearest the smoke hole and lit the other lamps. She pulled eggs and meat from the storage cache and began to arrange them on Chagak's woven mats.

The ulaq was quiet. Once she heard a murmur from Samiq's sleeping place and once Wren gave a short, quick cry. There was nothing more. When Kiin had arranged the food, she straightened the floor mats carefully so they did not overlap. Wren was learning to walk and tripped easily over mat edges.

It is a good place, this ulaq, Kiin thought. There was no hatred, no sudden anger; Kayugh never beat Chagak, seldom raised his voice in anger. And though there were times when Samiq and Amgigh disagreed, there were more times when they worked together, building ikyan, repairing their mother's ik or as partners while hunting seals.

Kiin stretched her arms over her head and yawned. It had been days since her father had beaten her. The bruises of his last beating had faded. It was good to walk without pain, to face others without embarrassment over eyes swollen and black, teeth loosened by her father's fists.

It was good to wake in the morning with her husband's arms around her, to wake and know there would be no beatings, no taunts from her brother. Even the one time Kiin had visited her father's ulaq, Gray Bird had treated her well, telling his wife to bring food and asking Kiin if her husband planned a hunting trip soon. And though Qakan scowled each time he saw her, Kiin kept her eyes straight ahead, as though she did not see him, as though he were nothing more than a bit of fireweed fluff caught in the wind.

Kiin took a seal stomach container of oil from the storage cache and, lifting it, carefully poured oil into a small wooden bowl. Then setting the seal stomach back into the storage cache, she poured the oil into the oil lamps, allowing it to seep in slowly from the edge so it would not cover the burning wicks and douse their flames.

When she had finished, she smoothed the oil left in the bowl onto her fingers and combed them through her hair. Her hair was long, hanging to her waist, and her father had often threatened to cut it so he could sell the long strands to the Walrus People whose women made patterns on chigadax and seal gut boots with designs sewn in hair.

And now there was no danger, no threat. Amgigh had told her her hair was beautiful, and once when they were alone in her sleeping place, he laid her back, spread her hair out over the sleeping mats and stroked it like a man strokes the sides of his ikyak the morning after he has slept with his woman.

Kiin heard a rustling from Chagak's sleeping place. Wren crawled out, and when Kiin reached her hands toward her, the little girl pushed herself up and tottered across the ulaq floor. Kiin held her breath as the fat baby feet padded over the mats and grass, and she held in her laughter when several paces from

Kiin's outstretched hands, Wren flung herself forward. Kiin caught the child and lifted her in a joyful hug, shushing Wren when she began to laugh. But then Kiin heard another laugh and looked up to see Samiq watching her. Kiin's eyes met his, and in that glance, she felt a sudden lurching of her heart, a twisting of her spirit, so that she looked down quickly, and hid her face in Wren's hair.

Then Chagak was also in the room, and Amgigh, but Amgigh's smile faded when he saw Samiq.

"Tomorrow, brother?" he asked.

Samiq's answer was a grunt, then he walked to the climbing log, laying his hand quickly on Wren's head as he passed. Amgigh watched until his brother had left the ulaq, then came to stand behind Kiin.

"There is f-f-food," Kiin said. She set Wren down and looked up at Amgigh.

"So you think we need nothing more than food," Amgigh said, and his words frightened Kiin. The anger in his voice was too much like her father's anger.

For a moment Amgigh's fingers gripped her shoulders, too hard. For a moment, Kiin felt pain. But then his hands were gentle, stroking her hair, lingering against her cheek. "I will eat later," he said and also left the ulaq.

Kiin watched him go, then glanced down at the food she had laid out. There was a heaviness in her chest, almost a dread. What had she done? Was there grass in the food? Was the meat spoiled, the oil rancid?

But no, everything looked as it always did. The meat was clean, not white with mold, and the oil smelled sweet.

Then Chagak was beside her, whispering, "He is upset because tomorrow Samiq leaves to go to the Whale Hunters. Samiq's grandfather, Many Whales, will teach him to hunt whales."

The words came to Kiin like a blow, knocking out her breath. "It will be better," her spirit said, but a part of Kiin wanted to scream out in protest. And she realized that much of her joy in being Amgigh's wife was to see Samiq each day, to prepare food for him, to help Chagak make his clothing.

"You belong to Amgigh," her spirit said. "To Amgigh. Samiq is a brother. You belong to Amgigh."

Kiin turned to Chagak, saw the sadness in Chagak's eyes. "H-h-how l-l-long will he be-be gone?" Kiin asked.

"For this summer, perhaps the winter and next summer also."

"And-and Am-Am-Amgigh?"

"He and Kayugh will go with Samiq, stay a few days and then return to our ulaq," Chagak answered. "Each of our sons was given a gift. Samiq will learn to hunt the whale. Amgigh was given a wife."

Quickly Kiin turned away; quickly she arranged more meat on the mats. What man would choose a wife above learning to hunt the whale? What man would want her above the honor of being a whale hunter? And when Samiq came back next summer or the next, it would be worse. Any man could find a wife, even a poor hunter like her father. But few men ever learned to hunt the whale. Amgigh will hate me, Kiin thought, must hate me already.

That day seemed long. Kiin stayed inside the ulaq except to empty night baskets and bring water from the spring. The ache that had begun in her heart spread to her arms and legs, so she felt stiff as though she still lived with her father, her muscles sore from his blows.

She did not see Samiq or Amgigh again until the day was over, the twilight of the summer night nearly upon them. They came in together, the two laughing, talking, and when Kiin offered food, first to Amgigh, then to Samiq, she drew her spirit up within herself, as strong as she had been when meeting her father's upraised walking stick, and made herself look into Amgigh's eyes. If Amgigh hated her, she would see it, for who does not know that hatred always lodges itself in the spirit and shows itself in the eyes?

So Kiin looked but saw no hatred, a glimmer of something, perhaps anger, perhaps sadness, but no hatred.

In her relief, she turned to Samiq, handed him a bowl of fish Chagak had baked outside on her cooking stone, and in that moment, their eyes met. Samiq's spirit reached out so quickly to Kiin that she could not look away. And though Samiq's eyes were crinkled, nearly closed with his smile, Kiin could not miss the sadness there, a greater sadness than any that might have been in Amgigh's eyes.

Then Amgigh clasped Kiin's arm. "Wife," he said, "my brother leaves tomorrow to go to the Whale Hunters. I have promised him something to remember, something to draw him back to this village when he has learned what there is to learn." He clasped her hand and laid it against Samiq's shoulder. "Go to Samiq tonight. Let him know what he is missing in choosing whales over having a wife."

14

Samiq held his breath and waited for Kiin's reaction. Amgigh should have talked to Kiin privately, asked her if she would spend the night with Samiq, that way she could have refused him if she wished, without embarrassment, without appearing to defy her husband.

Then Samiq thought, Perhaps Amgigh enjoys having the power of husband over Kiin, enjoys demanding her obedience.

But no, that was Gray Bird, not Amgigh. Amgigh was young, a new husband. Had First Snow not made similar mistakes in dealing with Red Berry? Even now after the two had been husband and wife nearly two years, Samiq still noticed that occasionally First Snow's thoughtlessness made Red Berry grind her teeth in anger, or more often laugh in frustration. And Red Berry was sometimes foolish also, rushing down to the water to bid him luck on hunting trips, when every hunter knows a wife should watch from ulaq roof not beach, that a hunter must not touch his wife before entering his ikyak. Otherwise the sea animals, smelling the earth smell of women, would be offended and never give themselves to the hunter's harpoon.

Samiq saw Kiin's eyes widen, and for a moment, she looked at him, but then she looked away, lowered her head and murmured something to Amgigh.

"Good," Amgigh said, and laughing, slapped Samiq's back. "Go now. Have a long night," he said.

But Kiin answered, her face reddening, "I-I have w-w-work first." Then she turned away from them and busied herself at the storage cache.

They began to eat, but Samiq suddenly found that nothing tasted right. His stomach burned as though he had eaten uncooked bitter root bulbs.

The evening passed slowly. Samiq's mother seemed to hover over Kiin, talking in a low and soothing voice, and his father withdrew to a corner, turned his back to the main room and worked on his harpoon.

So, Samiq thought, do I refuse Kiin, insult her and my brother, give him nothing to trade for the Whale Hunters' secrets? Do I make him feel that I am the one who has been given the better life? Or do I take Kiin?

There was a pulling within, that need of his body, and the desire for Kiin. Then anger came, turning Samiq's thoughts away from Amgigh and in toward his own wants.

She should have been my wife, not Amgigh's, Samiq told himself. Let Amgigh go to the Whale Hunters; let him learn. Let him live with their noisy women. I am Kiin's true husband. I care for her more than Amgigh does.

So, without looking at his father or his mother, without looking at Amgigh, Samiq stood and walked to where Kiin worked. He clasped her wrist and gently pulled her to her feet.

"Come," he said and took her into his sleeping place.

Amgigh watched them, watched the curtain close behind Kiin. In his mind he saw Kiin, naked, wrapped in Samiq's arms, and pain stabbed into his chest, made him catch his breath. He sat very still, his head down, until he could breathe again. Then he stood, stretched. He pulled his parka from a peg on the wall and slipped it on, then climbed from the ulaq.

Clouds were gray in the black night sky, and between the

clouds he saw stars. Amgigh sat down on the ulaq roof and tried to hold his thoughts away from Kiin and Samiq. What was a wife compared to hunting whales? he asked himself. What was sharing a wife compared to the power a man gained when he killed a whale?

Amgigh pulled a stem of grass from the ulaq roof and shredded it between his fingers.

One night. He shared Kiin for only one night. But Samiq would remember that sharing, would remember that sharing and the promise he had made Amgigh to teach Amgigh to hunt the whale. Then there were the obsidian knives. Two knives: knapped from the same stone, brothers as Amgigh and Samiq were brothers.

Amgigh had knapped the blades as all First Men did, knapping the stone on only one side. But from the time Amgigh was a boy, he seemed to have the lighter touch, to know where the stone would yield to the pressure of his bone punch, how to make the flakes come cleanly, softly. Even knapping only one side of the blade, he had managed to thin the edges almost to translucency.

His father said that stone spoke to Amgigh, and Amgigh thought perhaps, in some way, that was true. Especially with these two obsidian blades, the stone seemed to speak. From the first blow of his hammerstone, the blades had spoken to him of their beauty, of their balance.

But there seemed to be spirits around him as he worked. Their voices spoke of fear, of anger, of pain. Twice Amgigh stopped his work, stopped and listened, but his desire to finish the blades spoke louder than the spirit voices. And who could say whether those spirit voices were good or evil, whether they spoke truth or lies?

He had told Samiq he would make him a knife, an obsidian knife, and if he did not, what would Samiq think? That Amgigh was angry? That Amgigh did not want Samiq to come back to the First Men, to teach them to hunt the whale? The knives were a part of Samiq's promise to return.

But as Amgigh continued to work on the blades, he realized that one knife was somehow wrong, too heavy in his hand. When he had finished knapping them, he had set the blades side by side and had not been able to tell any great difference between them. But one was not right.

"Too heavy, too heavy," Amgigh's spirit seemed to whisper to him. And Amgigh knew that inside that blade some other stone was caught in the darkness of the obsidian, perhaps a nodule of quartz, something that would weaken the knife.

Amgigh climbed back down into the ulaq, nodded at his parents. He went into his sleeping place, leaving the curtain open to let in light. He began to pack his belongings into a sealskin bag. He should be ready if his father wanted to leave early in the morning. He pulled a basket from the weapons corner of his sleeping place. Inside were his finished blades—andesite lance heads, small obsidian blades for crooked knives, a few rounded blades for women's knives. He sorted through them, picked out several of the best to take with him to the Whale Hunters. Perhaps they would have something to trade.

When Gray Bird had told Amgigh that Qakan would soon leave on a trading trip, Amgigh had given a number of blades to Qakan. He had told Qakan, "Blade for blade, nothing less." Amgigh needed to see the work of other blade-makers. He had already surpassed the skills of his father and Gray Bird, of the blade-makers among the Whale Hunters. He hoped Qakan would make a good trade. But who could tell what Qakan would do? Who could trust him? But as Kayugh had said, better to give Qakan a chance than to have him live in his father's ulaq forever, Qakan eating but never hunting, too lazy even to gather sea urchins, to dig clams.

Amgigh picked up the two obsidian blades he had made for himself and Samiq. They were beautiful, as fine as anything he had ever made. He had hafted each blade to handles he had cut from pieces of whale jawbone, and wrapped the handles with the black baleen of the humpback whale.

He held one blade in each hand. One blade, the one he had

knapped first, lay in his left hand. The other blade lay in his right. Amgigh sighed. The stone itself spoke to Amgigh's soul, told of its own imperfection. He would leave the flawed blade here, in his sleeping place, take the other blade to the Whale Hunters, give it to Samiq to remind Samiq of his promise to teach Amgigh to hunt whales.

But then Amgigh heard laughter, a woman's laugh, and knew it was Kiin. Kiin with Samiq. Again, he saw her in his mind, naked, Samiq's hands on her breasts, Samiq's hands between her thighs.

Amgigh closed his eyes, clenched his teeth. He wrapped the good blade and put it back in the weapons corner of his sleeping place. He wrapped the flawed blade, put it in the pack he would take to the Whale Hunters.

Kiin's heart beat so hard that she felt the pulse of it along the insides of her arms. She was glad Samiq's sleeping place was dark so Samiq could not see her eyes. What would he think if he saw her fear? What would he think if he saw her joy?

"Your husband asked you to do this," her spirit murmured. "You are doing only what he asked." But she felt uneasy. Perhaps there was a part of her that wanted this too much. Perhaps this wanting had seeped out during her sleep and entered Amgigh's dreams. Perhaps it was only her selfishness, her own desires that prompted Amgigh to give her to Samiq. Then what good would come of it, of her own selfish wanting? Samiq was brother. Amgigh husband.

But Samiq drew her down beside him, spoke to her in whispers while he held her hands. "I am sorry. I am sorry to take you so soon from your husband. But, you see, it gives Amgigh something to trade, something that is worthwhile. He was the one who wanted to go to the Whale Hunters. I wanted to stay here, to be your husband. I do not need to hunt the whale, but Amgigh . . ." Samiq reached up, stroked Kiin's cheek then dropped his fingers to the bead necklace he had given her.

"When I made this, I thought I made it for my wife," he said.

Kiin felt his fingers tremble. She clasped his hand. "When y-y-you g-g-gave it to me, did y-y-you know?"

"Yes, my father had told me."

"And y-y-you were angry?"

"Yes, but mostly glad that you would be here, living in this ulaq, away from . . ."

"Yes."

Then for a long time, Samiq did nothing, did not move, did not speak, until finally Kiin began to straighten mats and furs, making a comfortable bed for him. But then he clasped her hands again.

"Lie down," he said.

His breath was warm against her neck and she lay down. "Amgigh wants this," her spirit said. So Kiin pushed away the uneasiness she held within herself and began to untie the knot that held her apron.

But then Samiq said, "No. We can't." He turned her and put his arms around her, lying with his chest pressed against her back.

"Amgigh-Amgigh wants it," Kiin said.

"No," Samiq answered. "Amgigh wants to learn to hunt the whale. Only that."

Kiin made herself lie still, tried to think of other things besides Samiq warm and close beside her. She thought of birds: red-legged kittiwakes, fulmars and gulls, imagined herself drawn up by their wings, hovering over Tugix's island, looking down at the ulakidaq. She thought of whales, the giant long-flippered humpback and the smaller minke, imagined herself swimming with them to their own villages under the sea.

And finally the warmth of Samiq's skin against hers, the weight of his arms over her and the rhythm of his breathing pulled her into dreams.

———

Her father was screaming at her. Something she had done or not done. He raised his walking stick, brought it down hard against her face, over her shoulders. Others were watching as her father beat her, as he raised his stick again and again. She would never be a woman, he was screaming, never be a wife, never a mother. She was nothing. She had no soul, was worth nothing.

Kiin curled herself into a ball, protected her eyes and ears from his stick. "You are Kiin," her spirit told her. "Kiin. You have a soul. He cannot take it away from you. Even with his stick. Even with his beatings. You are Kiin. Kiin. Kiin."

But the beating continued, then hands were reaching for her, pulling her away from her father, pulling her from the pain, whispering her name: "Kiin, you are safe. You are here with me. I won't let anyone hurt you. Kiin, Kiin."

It was Samiq. Kiin reached up to him, pulled him close to her. "Samiq, my husband," she whispered. "Samiq."

She stroked the smooth skin of his chest, the soft darkness of his hair, and she felt his hands against her back, reaching down to clasp her close as she wound her legs around him. She felt his man part grow and stiffen against her, and she could not keep herself from touching him. . . .

"Please," she whispered, "please, I want to be your wife."

Kiin woke early. Samiq lay with one leg thrown over her legs, his hand over hers. Slowly she pulled away from him, sat up and straightened her apron. For a moment, she allowed herself to look at Samiq, at the smooth brown of his skin, the darkness of his hair.

"It was a dream," her spirit told her.

Yes, it was a dream, Kiin thought. She looked at the smooth unmarked skin of her arms and legs. Her father had not beaten her. It had been a dream.

She went out into the main room of the ulaq, set out food

and packed several storage containers with dried fish for Samiq, Amgigh and Kayugh to take with them.

When the food was out, Kiin took Amgigh's parka and settled herself on a mat near her sewing basket. The parka was torn under one arm and she wanted to repair it before he left. She wanted the Whale Hunter women to know she was a good wife.

"A good wife . . . after Samiq?" some spirit seemed to whisper.

"It was a dream," Kiin's own spirit answered, and the words slid through Kiin's mind as she punched awl holes on either side of the tear and selected a piece of sealskin for a patch. She was tying a strand of twisted sinew to the end of her needle when she saw the door flap of Samiq's sleeping place open.

She glanced up. Samiq stood watching her. She smiled, and as she smiled, his eyes caught her eyes, held them. And suddenly she felt as though she were again in his arms, and she remembered his body strong and moving against her body and the warmth of him within her, and she knew it had not been a dream.

"Wife," Samiq said, the word so soft, Kiin heard it only by seeing the sound of it on Samiq's lips. "Wife."

15

Kiin did not follow the others to the beach. Perhaps it would have been all right for her to do so. It was not a hunting trip. Amgigh would not curse himself if he touched her or allowed his eyes to linger too long, his thoughts to stray to nights spent with his wife. And Samiq . . . No, he was not her husband. He could not be cursed by her presence. But Kiin thought it would be better for her to stay in the ulaq. She would cut sea lion esophagus for boot tops, and in that way show the spirits that she expected the quick return of her husband and her husband's father. But as she worked, she felt her own spirit pressing out against her skin, pushing on her legs and feet until she could no longer sit still.

She rolled up her work and began striding from one side of the ulaq to the other, pacing until finally her feet brought her to the climbing log.

No, she thought, I do not need to go outside. I do not need to see Samiq one more time. But then her feet were on the climbing log and then she was at the top of the ulaq, as though her body moved without the consent of her spirit. She looked toward the beach. The three ikyan were gone, Samiq's, Amgigh's and Kayugh's. Big Teeth's, too, was gone, but Kiin knew he would travel with them only that day.

Kiin turned to go back into the ulaq, but then thought of

Samiq's sleeping place. It should be cleaned out with new heather laid over the floor, the skins shaken and aired. Perhaps it would be best if she did this now. But first she would have to go up into the hills to find heather. Yes, she decided, and returned to the ulaq only to pick up her woman's knife and slip into her suk.

She left the ulaq, then climbed quickly through a shallow ravine that was sheltered from the wind, and from there to the top of the cliffs that stood at the back of the beach. The ikyan would go south and west around Tugix's island and to the close island where men hunt sea otters, then across the stretch of water that separates that island from the Whale Hunters' island. Kiin shaded her eyes and looked out toward the sea. Finally she saw them, not as far away as she had thought. Samiq's ikyak was first then Kayugh's and Big Teeth's, last, Amgigh's. Kiin watched Samiq's sure, quick strokes, the straightness of his back as he sat in the ikyak. Amgigh looked like a boy beside him, his paddling more tentative.

Yes, Kiin thought, Kayugh made the right choice. Samiq is the one who should go to the Whale Hunters. He should be the one to hunt the whale. He is the man.

Qakan had watched the four men leave the beach. Amgigh laughed and made jokes, but Samiq was serious, saying little. Samiq had stooped, picked up a few pebbles from the beach—a promise that he would return to this village. Then he had scanned the ulakidaq. Qakan knew he was looking for Kiin. Why he wanted her, Qakan had never been able to understand, but he knew that Samiq did want her, had always wanted her. Even as a boy, Samiq would suddenly begin to boast and laugh whenever Kiin was near. And during this past year, each time Samiq came to their ulaq, he watched her, his eyes stopping on Kiin's small pink-tipped breasts, on her lengthening legs.

Ah, Qakan understood that part of Samiq's wanting. Did he not feel the same when he saw women from other tribes? On rare occasions Whale Hunters brought their wives with them on trading visits. Then one of those wives might come for a night into their ulaq, to his father's bed, and Qakan listened to the groaning and laughter, and he hated his father for keeping the woman to himself.

Once, Qakan crept from his own sleeping place to the edge of his father's sleeping curtains. There, as he watched his father undress the woman, Qakan's own man part grew long and hard. And Qakan had wondered if Kiin had learned her greed from Gray Bird. Surely other men shared their women with their sons.

So Qakan understood Samiq's desire, and though Qakan thought Kiin was too thin and too quiet, for some reason Samiq wanted her as wife. But in this one thing, Samiq would not have his way. Qakan smiled. Samiq, the boy who always threw farther and better than the other boys, who could outrun them, who was stronger, a better hunter, who even, for no reason anyone could understand, caught more fish on his carved clamshell hooks, Samiq could not have, would never have Kiin.

But then, neither would Qakan.

All his careful plans. All the years that Qakan had lain in his sleeping place at night and thought of quick retorts, replies that would show his intelligence, his wit. All the nights he had planned while others slept.

It had taken months for anyone to notice, to comment on his jokes, on the strength that came out through his words.

Then the day came, two moons before Kayugh and Amgigh brought Kiin's bride price to Gray Bird's ulaq. Gray Bird was on the ulaq roof, the two of them together, alone, the women on the beach digging clams at low tide. Qakan was direct, telling his father rather than asking. His father was weak—Qakan did not doubt that—and Qakan knew that a request was often met with refusal only because refusing gave Gray Bird some feeling of power.

"I am not a hunter," Qakan had said. "I want to be a trader. I will bring honor to you and bring you furs and shells and harpoons from other villages."

But instead of commenting on Qakan's desire to become a trader, Gray Bird had said, "No, you are not a hunter. If spirits hid the roots and berries from the women, the seals from the hunters, still you would not even be able to bring in a puffin."

And Qakan, angered by his father's words, gritted his teeth and said what he always said, what he had first heard from his father: "It is not my fault. I want to be a hunter, but the girl, your daughter, she took my strength."

Gray Bird spat a blade of grass from his mouth and looked away from his son, looked toward the sea.

For a moment Qakan waited, then when his father did not speak, Qakan said, "Traders bring as much honor as hunters do and sometimes more skins."

Slowly Gray Bird turned his head, slowly he looked at Qakan. "You want to be a trader."

"Yes."

"You think you can bargain, can make a man take less for his goods, for his furs or shells than he thinks they are worth?"

And this was the question Qakan had hoped his father would ask. It was a question he had heard discussed among traders, those who came to his father's ulaq, who came to use Qakan's mother for the night, to cast hopeful eyes on Kiin but to look away when Gray Bird told the story of Kiin's shame.

"No," Qakan answered and held his smile inside his mouth when he saw his father's eyebrows raise. "I would not make a man take less than what he thinks his furs are worth. That makes enemies. I would make him think he is getting more, but he would not be. I would trade fine seal furs for shells rare on this beach, but common on another or for whale meat which the Whale Hunters have in abundance."

His father had nodded and nodded again, then he said, "But you must have something to trade. What do you have?"

Qakan lowered his eyes. His father should not see the mocking there. What did Qakan have to trade? Many things, many, many things. Woman's knives carelessly left on the beach, chunks of ivory from his father's carving basket—things Kiin or Blue Shell were beaten for losing. And each time traders came, each time they visited Gray Bird's or Big Teeth's or Kayugh's ulaq, later that day or the next, things were missed—women's sewing needles, awls, crooked knives, small things that could be easily hidden in the sleeve of a parka. Ah yes, everyone said, traders. Some could not be trusted.

So Qakan kept his eyes hidden and said, "Perhaps you and Samiq and Kayugh have extra furs, something I could take with me to trade, and in return, I will bring you walrus tusks or bear hides, something you might like to have."

Again his father nodded. "What would you get in exchange, for bringing us walrus tusks or bear hides?" he asked.

"Good food, honor among other tribes." Qakan laughed, "Women for my bed."

Gray Bird smiled, a crooked smile, and his chin hair quivered.

"Perhaps," Qakan said, gathering his courage, "perhaps you could let me have one thing."

"What?"

"My sister."

His father had turned sharply, his eyes widening. "Who would give anything for her?" he asked. "She has no soul. She has never even had a bleeding time."

"Who beyond this village knows that?"

"A few traders," his father said. Then with his eyes on the sea, he said, "She is not ugly. How many furs do you think you could get for her?"

"Ten," Qakan had said. Ten, though he thought perhaps even twenty.

"Ten," Gray Bird said. "If you got ten, I would expect you to give me eight."

"Eight," Qakan said. Only eight, better than he had hoped.

But then Amgigh had come with his offer of sixteen skins and one of his obsidian knives.

So Qakan had watched as Amgigh and Samiq and Kayugh and Big Teeth left. Yes, he had still prepared for his trading, had managed to get Big Teeth to give him fishhooks and skins, and his mother to make a birdskin suk, even Kiin had given him a number of her finely woven baskets and Chagak allowed him to take five grass mats, the ones she wove with dark checkered borders. Before he left, he would take the bundle of sealskins Kayugh had given as Kiin's bride price. But how much better to have Kiin, too.

16

The last time he turned, Samiq saw her. She stood high on the edge of a cliff, her hair fanning out behind her in the wind, her slight body only a thin line against the gray of the sky.

Keep her safe for Amgigh, he prayed to Tugix. Keep her away from Gray Bird and Qakan. He repeated that prayer during the first long day of paddling and even in the evening after Big Teeth had left them, and Samiq, Amgigh and Kayugh made camp for the night on the sea otter island.

They hauled their ikyan up from the beach to a place where four boulders formed a circle, then set the ikyan as windbreaks between the boulders. Kayugh had filled and lit oil lamps— hunters' lamps, small and light, chipped from stone and easily carried inside an ikyak.

They ate dried seal meat and goose fat, a good thing to soothe the throat after a day of salt water. Later, Kayugh laid out mats for sleeping, but Samiq could not sleep; his mind was full of thoughts of Kiin, of their night together. She was wife to Amgigh, but had she not called him husband in her dreams?

Before they left, Samiq had confided his fears for Kiin's safety to Big Teeth, but Big Teeth had merely smiled. "Gray Bird is afraid of your father and of you and even Amgigh. He will not hurt Kiin. And Qakan . . ." Big Teeth had thrown back his head and laughed. "Qakan has decided to be a trader. I gave him ten fishhooks and some skins to trade for me. I think he plans to leave in the next few days. When he returns, if he returns, Amgigh and your father will be back in the village."

Samiq had nodded. Big Teeth was always right. Kiin was safe, but still fear hung over him like some spirit, battering against his mind, whispering of the many ways Kiin could be hurt, ways that left no mark on the body, things that could be done to destroy the soul.

Samiq slid over to his ikyak and untied a sealskin packet from its side. The packet was filled with rendered seal fat. He smoothed the fat over his hands and his cheeks, then he reached for his chigadax.

He smoothed seal fat into the garment's many horizontal seams, then oiled the strips of seal gut to keep them supple and prevent tears. He had needle and sinew thread, and like all hunters, he knew how to repair his clothing, but he could not make it watertight.

He had often watched his mother sew, and once had watched Kiin work on Gray Bird's chigadax. Each watertight seam was a double seam, sewn one way, then turned and sewn back another.

He had watched as Kiin pushed the needle into the skin she was working and deftly brought it up without letting it pierce through to the opposite side of the seam. It did not look difficult, but when he had to repair his own chigadax, the needle seemed to go its own way, so that Samiq had to be satisfied with smearing fat over his stitches to keep out the water.

When Samiq finished oiling his chigadax he began to work on his father's. It was something he could do to keep his mind from thoughts of the next day when he and his father would be with the Whale Hunters.

What would it be like to hunt the greatest of all animals? Would his skill in hunting sea lions give him an advantage among the Whale Hunters? Perhaps he would not be skilled enough to take a whale, and his grandfather would make him return to the First Men, a boy again, no better than Qakan.

———

The next morning, they ate as they repacked their ikyan, but the food upset Samiq's stomach, and when they were again on the sea, it seemed that Amgigh paddled too quickly. Why rush? They had all day to get to the Whale Hunters' beach.

The water was choppy, and they saw no sign of seal or whale, but gulls followed above them, circling and calling as though directing their path through the sea.

They sighted the Whale Hunters' island that afternoon. "There!" Kayugh said suddenly, and Samiq straightened in his ikyak, holding his paddle vertically in the water to steady himself. Yes, Samiq could see the island. It was large, with a long flat beach that rose toward a jumble of hills and the jagged peaks of a mountain. The day was misty. The sun was only a light place in the clouds, and so Samiq could not see the entire island, but it seemed large, and the beach was three, four times as long as Tugix's beach.

Kayugh pointed toward a ridge of rock that stretched into the water. "Stay away from the south side of the beach," he called. "Too many rocks."

As they neared the island, Samiq could see long mounds set near the hills, six perhaps seven, that he thought must be ulas. A stream cut along the north side of the beach and Samiq paddled his ikyak away from the current he knew would come from the flow of water entering the sea.

He slowed his ikyak and followed his father. Kayugh had come to the village before and so would remember where boulders lay hidden under water, but even so, Samiq kept his eyes to the sea, searching for any rocks that could tear holes in the bottom of his ikyak.

"They see us," Kayugh called back to Samiq.

There were six, eight men on the beach, three with spears in their hands. Kayugh made a sign, a hand raised, waving, then lowered and raised again. The men on the beach looked at one another, then shouted. As Samiq neared the men, he saw that they were directing them toward a section of smooth rock that extended into the beach.

Kayugh paddled his ikyak over the rock, and as a wave brought him into the shore, he loosened the shoulder strap and drawstring that bound him into the ikyak and stepped out. Several of the Whale Hunter men picked up the ikyak and carried it to a high place on the beach. One of the men slapped Kayugh on the back in greeting and both laughed.

Samiq watched as Amgigh directed his ikyak over the rock. A wave suddenly pushed Amgigh's ikyak sideways, and two Whale Hunter men pulled Amgigh up while two others lifted the ikyak, Amgigh dangling in their grip until Kayugh could untie the drawstring that bound Amgigh to the craft.

Samiq clenched his paddle and waited for a wave to send him over the rock. A good wave brought him well up onto the beach. Samiq steadied himself with the paddle and pulled at the bindings that would let him slip easily from the sea lion gut hatch skirt.

Samiq usually tightened his hatch skirt with three knots, each made to loosen easily. The first knot untied with one jerk, but the second did not, and Samiq sat in the ikyak, struggling with one hand and his teeth to untie it.

"The next wave will take you into rocks," someone said and handed him a knife.

Samiq cut the knot and jumped from the ikyak, lifting it from the water before the wave hit.

"You are quick, Samiq," the man said and Samiq looked up to see the hunter called Dying Seal, a man who occasionally came to their village on trading trips.

Samiq was surprised that Dying Seal remembered his name, but he smiled and answered, "Only with knots."

Dying Seal laughed. He was wide-shouldered and short-legged like all the Whale Hunters, but unlike the others, Dying Seal was not given to boasting. When the Whale Hunters came to the First Men's village to trade, there was always a feast, always a time of telling stories, but Dying Seal's stories were of other hunters' kills, not his own. Even so, his abilities in the ikyak and with the harpoon were well-known.

"You come to trade?" Dying Seal asked.

"No," Samiq said, but then answered, "Yes. A different kind of trading."

Samiq carried his ikyak up the beach and laid it beside his father's ikyak. Kayugh and Amgigh were speaking to a hunter who sometimes came to the First Men's village to trade. His name was Hard Rock. Dying Seal joined them, but Samiq knelt to inspect the bottom and sides of his ikyak for tears. Let the Whale Hunters see that he valued his ikyak above talk of weather and the sea. He had many days to talk to Whale Hunters. Why listen now?

But as Samiq ran his hands over his ikyak, the wind brought Hard Rock's words to Samiq's ears: "Many Whales is old. He is probably asleep."

"He is still your chief?" Kayugh asked.

Hard Rock snorted.

"Yes. He is our chief," Dying Seal answered.

"I need to speak to him. I have brought his grandson. Many Whales wants him to learn to hunt the whale."

Again Hard Rock snorted, then using his chin to point at Amgigh and back toward Samiq he asked, "Which boy belongs to Many Whales?"

Samiq stood. "We are hunters. We belong to ourselves," he said, and looking at his father noticed that the man's lips had thinned, the muscles of his jaws tightened.

"Samiq has come to learn your ways," Kayugh said. "We need Amgigh to stay with us. We cannot give up two of our hunters."

Hard Rock stared at Samiq. The man's eyes were heavy, dark, like small black stones.

"Come," Dying Seal said to Kayugh and motioned also to Samiq and Amgigh.

Dying Seal led them to the first long ulaq. He climbed to the opening at the top of the mound and, looking back at Kayugh, said, "Wait."

Samiq turned to see that Hard Rock had stayed with the ikyan, the man now squatting beside the boats, a scowl on his face. Samiq looked back at his father, but Kayugh's eyes were on the line of ulas that made up the Whale Hunters' village. There were eight in all, Kayugh had told Samiq, but Samiq could see only seven, these making a line between the hills and the beach like the footprints of a giant man.

"Where is the eighth ulaq?" Samiq asked, and Kayugh pointed to a place between two hills, some distance from the other ulas. "That is Hard Rock's ulaq."

"Why did he build it there?"

"He says that he will someday be chief and the chief should live in a place apart from others."

Samiq shook his head. "What do the other men say about that?"

"The other men say he is lazy. With his ulaq set between two hills, he did not have to build walls, only a roof."

Samiq laughed, but an uneasiness crept into his mind. He would be living with these people. He would have to hunt with them, even with Hard Rock. Again his belly began to ache, and he felt a shameful longing to be a child once more, to return to his own village, to sit beside his mother as she sewed or wove mats, to have nothing required of him except that he gather a few eggs, collect berries or sea urchins.

As if his father knew his thoughts, Kayugh laid his hand on Samiq's shoulder. "You do not have to stay," he said.

Amgigh suddenly leaned forward. "You have a promise to keep," he said.

Kayugh raised his eyebrows and looked at Samiq. "I told Amgigh I would teach him to hunt the whale," Samiq said. "I will stay unless Many Whales says I cannot."

He saw the pride in his father's eyes, and Kayugh said quietly, "If you learn to hunt the whale, you can teach all of us."

"Yes," Samiq began but stopped speaking when he saw Amgigh's eyes suddenly narrow.

"Not Qakan," Amgigh said.

"Qakan must first learn to hunt the seal," Kayugh answered. He looked up as Dying Seal emerged from Many Whales' ulaq.

"Many Whales will see you," Dying Seal called.

Samiq followed his father up the side of the ulaq, but Dying Seal jumped to the ground. "You will not go with us?" Kayugh asked.

"He wants to see you and Samiq alone." He laid his hand against Amgigh's arm. "Not Amgigh," he said.

Samiq saw anger flush red into Amgigh's face.

Kayugh and Samiq climbed down into the darkness of Many Whales' ulaq. When Samiq's eyes had adjusted, he saw that Many Whales' ulaq was large, higher and longer than the ulas of the First Men. The main room was lined with tall boulders, each nearly as high as Samiq's waist, each with a hollow at the top that held oil and a mound of moss that acted as a wick.

"It is good you are here," Many Whales said. "Sit down."

The old man sat on a mat in the center of the ulaq. He wore an otter skin parka decorated with fur and feathers at each seam. On his head was a cone-shaped wooden hat. Whale Hunters wore such hats when they came to the First Men's village to trade, and Samiq had wanted one since he was a small child. His mother had told him that the Whale Hunter men made the hats from a slice of wood so thin that it could be steamed and bent into shape, the edges laced together like a seam up the back of the hat. The wood of Many Whales' hat was smooth and shiny as though it had been rubbed with oil. Long sea lion whiskers were sewn into the hat's seam, and feathers and shells dangled from one side.

Kayugh sat down on one of the grass mats that was opposite the old man and motioned for Samiq to sit beside him. On Many Whales' left was his wife, a short fat woman, her black hair pulled tightly back from her round face and bound with a strip of furred otter skin into a tail at the nape of her neck. They both sat cross-legged rather than on their heels as Samiq and Kayugh did.

The woman motioned toward two mats, one layered with thin, dark slices of meat, the other holding four shell bowls filled with melted fat. Many Whales selected a slice of meat and handed it to Kayugh then motioned for Samiq to take a piece as well. Samiq watched Many Whales dip his meat into the melted fat then fold it and put it into his mouth. Samiq did the same.

It was a rich, sweet meat, something Samiq first thought was walrus then knew was whale. And again, the realization of why he was here came to him and his heart began to beat too quickly.

"Long ago you promised me you would bring my grandson back to me. I knew you would come," Many Whales said.

His voice was low and strong, like the voice of a young man. The Whale Hunters were once First Men, the stories said. And it was true that the Whale Hunters spoke the same language as the First Men, though some words were pronounced differently, and every word was quick and clipped as if in hunting the whale, the people had learned to move with more speed, even in their speech.

"Once long ago our people saved your village," Kayugh said, and Samiq was surprised by his father's abruptness. Usually conversations began slowly with many comments on hunting and the sea, on wives and children.

"Yes," Many Whales said. "For that reason, I gave you my granddaughter and my grandson."

Samiq was suddenly still, sitting very straight. He noticed that Fat Wife was leaning so far forward that her large breasts pressed against her knees.

Samiq drew his thoughts back to his father's words. What had Many Whales meant when he said he had given Kayugh his granddaughter and grandson?

"And in return, I said I would bring your grandson back when he was a man so he could learn to hunt the whale."

Many Whales said nothing, but his wife answered, "Only the men of this village can hunt the whale. Besides, this boy does not look like a hunter. He is heavy-boned. His shoulders are too wide."

Samiq was surprised that she would say anything at a men's meeting, and he waited for Many Whales to reprimand her, but the old man only nodded.

"I remember that Chagak suckled two boy children," she continued. "One was her son, our grandson, the other your son. How do I know this one is ours?"

The words were like stones set over Samiq's heart and he struggled to understand what Fat Wife was saying. He was not Kayugh's son? Who then was his father? He looked at Kayugh, willed the man to look at him, but Kayugh kept his eyes fixed on Many Whales.

Finally Kayugh started to speak, at first quietly, as if to himself, as if Many Whales and his wife and even Samiq were not in the ulaq. "Samiq is already honored in our village for the number of seals he has taken. He is skilled in the use of the ikyak. He is your grandson. I would not lie to you."

Kayugh stood up and Samiq also stood beside him. "Your traders are welcome always," Kayugh said, a traditional farewell between all trading villages.

Again, the abruptness of Kayugh's words surprised Samiq, and he struggled to hold his questions within his mouth, to keep silent and act as if he knew what Kayugh was doing. Kayugh started up the climbing log that led to the roof hole of the ulaq.

"It would be good to have a son in our ulaq," Fat Wife said. "A life for the son we lost fighting the Short Ones."

"You are willing to give him to us as son?" Many Whales asked.

"Grandson," Kayugh answered. "He is my son."

"Take him outside," Many Whales said. "Make your decision and come back to us."

Samiq followed Kayugh from the ulaq and slid down to the

leeward side of the mound where he and his father could talk without fear that the wind would carry their words to others on the beach.

"Do you want to stay?" Kayugh asked.

But instead of answering, Samiq said, "You are not my father. Who is my father?"

For a long time Kayugh did not speak. Finally he said, "Your father, husband to your mother, Chagak, was son of Shuganan, the carver."

Samiq nodded. He had heard the stories of Shuganan. Of his power in the spirit world. His mother had also told him of her village that was destroyed by the Short Ones, and of her mother who was one of Many Whales' daughters.

"Is Amgigh your true son?" Samiq asked. His heart had moved from its place in his chest, moved like a spirit moves, and he felt it first in his temples, then at his wrists, now pounding at the backs of his knees.

"Yes, he is my son and the son of another wife, not your mother."

Again, Samiq's heart moved, now to beat in a quick rhythm at the base of his throat. "We are not brothers, then?"

"When I took your mother as wife, you became brothers and I became your father."

"You should have told us the truth. From the time we were small children, you should have told us."

Kayugh cleared his throat, did not look at Samiq. "We thought it would be better to raise you without knowing. What good is gained by speaking of the dead? Who can say what curse, what anger might have come to our ulaq if your mother spoke of your true father, if I spoke of Amgigh's true mother?"

Samiq closed his eyes, rubbed his fingers across his eyelids. "So Amgigh was not chosen to learn to hunt the whale because he is not grandson to Many Whales," he said.

"Yes."

"But if you were the one who could choose, you would have chosen Amgigh. . . ."

For a moment, Kayugh looked up into the sky, and when he looked back at Samiq again, Samiq saw the concern in the man's eyes. "You would have been my choice because you are the better hunter," Kayugh said. "You will stay?"

"Yes," Samiq answered, but in his mind he was already seeing the many times Kayugh had seemed to favor Amgigh over him, the times Samiq had won in races or had brought back the largest fish, but Amgigh had received the praise.

Kayugh nodded. "Then learn to hunt," he said. "Learn to hunt the whale, and come back to teach Amgigh."

17

When his father and Samiq went into Many Whales'
ulaq, Amgigh climbed to the top of the ulaq and
waited, watching the sea. Many Whales—grandfather to
Amgigh's mother and chief hunter of the Whale Hunters—why
had he chosen Samiq over Amgigh? Or had Kayugh been the
one to choose? Even so, why leave Amgigh outside? What
secrets were being told to Samiq that Amgigh could not hear?

Many Whales had visited the First Men's village before, but
he had never seemed like a grandfather. He showed no interest
in either Samiq or Amgigh, only giving each boy a nod, perhaps
asking if they had taken their first sea lion yet. Let the old man
ask now. Amgigh had taken both sea lion and wife.

Three young women walked slowly around Many Whales'
ulaq. Two were almost beautiful, not as beautiful as Kiin, but,
Amgigh thought, it would not be terrible to spend a night with
one of them. The third woman was as large as a man, her face
dirty, her front teeth broken to jagged stumps. She, of the three,
spoke the loudest, and when she caught Amgigh's eyes on her,
she took off her otter fur suk, flipped the front of her apron and
giggled.

Amgigh waited until the three were behind Many Whales'
ulaq, and then he slipped down the curve of the roof and
walked to the beach. Whale Hunter men were repairing ikyan,

Sue Harrison

and women were digging roots at the edge of the beach. Amgigh went to his ikyak, ran his fingers over seams and the sea lion skin patch that his mother had sewn over a thin spot near the keelson. He oiled seams and skins, and when he had finished, he pulled the bundle of knives from inside the ikyak. He found a flat place on the beach and spread out a sealskin, then arranged the knife blades and lance points in a circle, points out, on the skin. He sat down, spread a thick piece of sealskin over his left thigh and wrapped his left hand with a strip of sea lion skin, then took his punch from the basket and began to retouch a dull knife.

He did not look up as the Whale Hunters began to gather; he did not look up to acknowledge their comments or their offers for his blades. Yes, they would give whale oil, furs, nights with their daughters. Let them regret Many Whales' choice; let them wish the old man had chosen his other grandson, the grandson who could make the most beautiful blades they had ever seen.

But then he heard his father's voice and Samiq's. Samiq broke through the Whale Hunter men to stand beside Amgigh, Samiq's hand possessively on Amgigh's shoulder. Amgigh looked up at Samiq. He paused to toss the wrapped obsidian knife into Samiq's hands, and he smiled as Samiq unwrapped the knife, as Samiq held it up for the Whale Hunter men to see.

Then Samiq squatted down beside him, laid his hand on Amgigh's arm. "It is too beautiful. It should belong to you, not me," Samiq said.

"I have one like it," Amgigh replied, but he could not meet his brother's eyes. Then Amgigh turned to the Whale Hunters. "Otter furs and necklaces," he said. "I will trade my blades for otter furs and necklaces." And looking at Samiq from the corners of his eyes, Amgigh said, "I need gifts to take back to my beautiful wife."

18

K iin woke early and went out to the kelp rocks to fish for pogy. She caught three, each as long as her forearm, wrist to elbow. She cleaned and split them then took them to Chagak's cooking stone. She had started a fire under the stone before she went fishing, and now the stone was hot. She laid the fish, skin side down and watched as the heat turned the fishes' green inner flesh flaky and white.

Still squatting beside the cooking stone, Kiin ate one fish then took the other two back for Chagak and Wren, then she left the ulaq to watch the sea. Who could say when Amgigh and Kayugh would return? Perhaps today.

Kiin sighed and looked out toward the water. It was still early, but she saw that Crooked Nose had already been out in her ik and was now coming in, her small open-topped skin boat filled with cod. Kiin smiled and hurried down to the beach to help Crooked Nose pull the boat ashore.

"Have you b-been fishing all n-night?" Kiin asked when she saw the many white-bellied fish in the bow of the boat.

Crooked Nose laughed. "No. But the spirits favored me."

Under a rock at the edge of the ikyan racks, Kiin saw Crooked Nose's carrying net. She ran over and got it, then brought it back to Crooked Nose.

The net was a circle. When it was spread flat on the ground, it was as wide as the length of a tall man. Crooked Nose loosened the gathering cord and she and Kiin held opposite sides, flipping fish from the boat into the net. Then together, they carried the full net to the place where the women cleaned fish. There, during low tide, the waves would not reach them, but at high tide, the sea would reclaim the fish innards.

They set down the net and Kiin reached under her suk to the pocket in her apron where she kept her woman's knife. The flint blade was slightly curved, the straight back edge blunted to fit easily into Kiin's hand. She grabbed a fish from the pile and slit it from gills to tail, then reached in and with two quick slices detached the innards at top and bottom and pulled them out with her hand. Crooked Nose had brought drying sticks—short ones, the width of Kiin's hand, to place inside the fish and hold them open for quicker drying, and long ones to string ten, fifteen fish through mouth and gills and hang them over drying racks.

Kiin inserted a short stick, embedding the ends in the flesh, then laid the fish on a piece of old ikyak cover that Crooked Nose had laid out.

"Your suk is beautiful," Crooked Nose said, slicing into another fish.

Kiin grimaced at the slime that was clinging to one of her sleeves. "I sh-should be-be wearing m-my old one," Kiin said.

"Go and get it. The fish will wait."

Kiin lowered her head and pretended to test the sharpness of her knife blade against her thumb. "I-I left it in m-my father's ulaq."

Crooked Nose snorted. "I will get it for you," she said and left before Kiin could stop her.

"Do n-not s-s-say that I wanted it," Kiin called after her, but was not sure that Crooked Nose heard her.

Kiin knew that Crooked Nose was not afraid of her father. Gray Bird was a small man, and Crooked Nose was taller, perhaps even stronger.

Kiin pulled several fish from the net and gutted them, then

she looked toward the ulas. Crooked Nose was coming toward her, Kiin's old cormorant suk in her hands. "Your father sends his greetings," she called to Kiin.

Kiin's eyes widened and then she began to laugh. She could never remember her father sending his greetings to anyone, especially her.

"Oh, s-so n-now I am wife, he-he has decided I am w-worth greeting?" Kiin said, trying to make her words light.

Crooked Nose smiled and said, "Go and wash your hands before you change your suk."

Kiin went to the edge of the stream and squatted to scour her hands with gravel. She used wet sand to remove the slime and fish blood from the sleeve of her suk, then pulled the garment off over her head. The wind was cold against her breasts and she shielded herself with the suk as she walked back to Crooked Nose.

The woman pointed with her chin to the place she had laid Kiin's old feather suk and Kiin slipped it on over her head and smoothed it down over her apron.

The women worked in silence for a time and then Crooked Nose asked, "Do you feel different, now you are a wife?"

Kiin pursed her lips and finally said, "It is m-more be-because I have a soul than because I am a w-wife." She held a fist against her breast. "It is g-good to feel a sp-spirit m-moving in here."

"Your father should have named you long ago," Crooked Nose said. "But at least your mother did what she could for you."

Kiin was surprised by Crooked Nose's words. What had her mother done for her? Even Kiin's new suk had been made by Chagak. Blue Shell would not defy her husband to honor the daughter he hated. How many times had Blue Shell only watched, crying but doing nothing to stop him, while Gray Bird beat Kiin?

"I w-would never allow my husband to b-beat one of my children," Kiin answered. "He could b-b-beat m-me instead."

"I am not saying that all your mother did was right," Crooked Nose answered. "But you must realize that your father's anger at you is because you are not a son. There is no other reason. You are a beautiful woman. He often boasts of your beauty. Big Teeth has told me."

Kiin's surprise kept her words in her throat. Her father considered her beautiful? "But m-my mother . . ." she finally said.

"Should have stopped him?" Crooked Nose said. "Yes, at least she should have tried. But you must remember what she did for you."

Kiin frowned and Crooked Nose said, "Your father wanted to kill you after you were born."

Kiin nodded. "Qakan has t-told me that many t-times."

"Kayugh forced your father to let you live by promising Amgigh as husband for you. Your father took his revenge in not giving you a name. That way Kayugh could not keep his promise, could not give you to Amgigh. How could he ask Amgigh to give up all hope of having sons? Or to chance that you would steal Amgigh's soul?"

"I would never steal a man's soul."

Crooked Nose shrugged. "But your mother, she could have given you to the wind. She could have let you die. Then there would be no arguments, no anger in our village."

"But Kayugh might have been angry. . . ." Kiin began.

But again Crooked Nose shrugged. "There are many ways for a new baby to die. It is easy for someone to smother a child and say it died sleeping.

"Your mother had to watch you all the time. She never left you alone. Even when she went out to fish, she bound you to her back. And think how simple it would have been for her to obey your father, to smother you some night and tell no one what had truly happened and so bring peace back to your father's ulaq."

Crooked Nose stopped speaking, but Kiin did not say anything. It had been so easy to resent everyone in her family, to hold her loneliness and fear around her so closely that the joys of life could not get through.

"Do you understand what I am telling you?" Crooked Nose asked.

Kiin looked up and met the woman's eyes. "Yes," she said.

Crooked Nose smiled and stood up. She grabbed a stringing pole, and she and Kiin began to thread the gutted fish on the stick. When the first stick was full, they carried it up the beach to a flat rocky place in the lee of the cliffs. There the men had set up drying racks. With the rise of the cliffs at the back, the racks were more protected from the birds, and one woman watching could keep gulls and ravens away.

Each driftwood rack had wide, forked supports, and each support was braced in an upright position by piles of rock and beach gravel. Each support held three poles, one in the fork at the top, two in niches carved in the sides. Kiin and Crooked Nose laid the pole of fish in the forked niche of the nearest supports.

"You guard," Crooked Nose said and handed her a long stick to keep birds away. "I will go back and string another pole."

Kiin crouched beside the rack. Gulls were wheeling, calling to each other, skirmishing for position in the sky above the racks. Kiin stood, swung the long stick in a circle over her head. The gulls retreated, swooped away toward the pile of fish innards that she and Crooked Nose had left for the tide. Kiin crouched again beside the racks.

"Do you need help?" a voice asked.

Kiin, startled, looked up. It was Qakan.

"Crooked Nose is d-down on the b-beach. Help her c-carry poles."

"I would rather help you," Qakan said.

Kiin's thoughts went back to the night before she became wife to Amgigh. She and Qakan had been alone in their father's ulaq, Kiin weaving mats, Qakan leaning against a heap of sealskins stuffed with goose feathers.

"Do you think I will be a good husband?" Qakan had asked, then he had pulled back the flap of his apron to show her the man part of him.

"N-n-no," Kiin had said in disgust. "You-you w-w-would not have the strength to make s-s-sons."

She had run then, up the climbing log and outside, and Qakan had been too lazy to follow her. She had waited outside the ulaq until her mother returned from gathering sea urchins, but since then, until this day, Qakan had not spoken to her.

A sudden burst of joy filled Kiin's chest. It is good, she thought, to be away from my father's ulaq, to be safe from Qakan.

"Kiin!" Crooked Nose called, and Kiin looked down the beach to see that Crooked Nose had two more poles of fish. She rose to help, but Qakan hurried to Crooked Nose's side and took one of the poles.

They carried the poles to the rack and set them on supports at the same time so the rack would not tip one way or the other.

"You can stay with the rack," Crooked Nose said to Kiin. "I told Chagak to come to my husband's ulaq. Little Duck and I plan to work on baskets."

After Crooked Nose returned to Big Teeth's ulaq, Kiin squatted on her heels and pulled her suk down over her knees. Qakan crouched beside her.

"I will be leaving soon," Qakan said.

Kiin looked at him, raised her eyebrows.

"To trade," he said. "I am a trader," he added, the words belligerent as if he expected Kiin to disagree with him.

Kiin stood up, swung the bird stick over the rack.

"I need more things to trade," Qakan said. "Have you finished any more mats or baskets? If you give them to me, I will bring you something good for them."

Kiin looked at Qakan, smiled a slow smile. "I have t-two berry bags," she said. "S-someone gave them to me." She saw the red creep into Qakan's face. "They are in Kayugh's ulaq. B-but I c-cannot leave the racks now."

"I will go," Qakan said.

Kiin shrugged. Qakan pushed himself to his feet. "I will bring you something good," he said again.

Kiin turned her back to Qakan, swung her stick again toward the gulls. Qakan will be gone, she thought, perhaps for the whole summer. What could be better?

Then she remembered what Crooked Nose had told her. Blue Shell had wanted Kiin, had, in her own way, protected Kiin. A hardness that had long been in her heart seemed to lift itself out of her chest.

And Kayugh had promised his son Amgigh as husband to save her life. She could never allow herself to wish for Samiq as husband. She was alive because of Amgigh.

But how could she forget the times Amgigh turned his head in embarrassment at her bruises? Samiq, not Amgigh, had sat beside her, comforting her with gentle words until her thoughts were pulled away from the ache of her muscles, the pulsing wounds on her back and arms.

Once, when her father had beaten her so hard that Kiin could not remember how she had made her way from his ulaq to Kayugh's, Chagak had made a bed for her in the large central ulaq room, near the warmth of several oil lamps. Then Samiq had taken her hand, had said he wanted her to be his wife, said that he would pay the bride price, whatever her father demanded.

"I want you as wife," he had said.

Kiin had studied Samiq's face, the wide, strong forehead, the high, slanting cheekbones. Then her eyes seemed to be caught and held by the power of Samiq's eyes.

"I promise you," Samiq had said, running a finger down the curve of her cheek, "someday you will be my wife, and I will keep you safe."

But the promise had been the promise of a boy, something Samiq could not keep. So Amgigh was her husband and he was a good husband. Perhaps already she carried his child. Kiin reached up to adjust one of the fish racks and in reaching she heard her spirit whisper, as though it spoke softly to something inside Kiin, as though Kiin were not supposed to hear, "Or perhaps you carry Samiq's child."

Kiin stroked the whale tooth shell at her side. No, she thought, Samiq was with the Whale Hunters, would take a Whale Hunter wife.

She remembered the whale that had washed up on the First Men's beach several years before: meat, bones for ulaq rafters, and oil, smokeless and clean, for lamps. It was good that Samiq would learn to hunt the whale. Good for Samiq and for the First Men.

The Whale Hunters came to trade, once, twice in a year. Kiin knew some of the hunters who came, at least by name and face —Dying Seal and another man, sullen and always arguing, called Hard Rock. They were Samiq's people now. He would take a Whale Hunter wife. Kiin belonged to Amgigh.

Qakan called out. No one answered. He smiled and climbed down the log into Kayugh's ulaq. Kiin's corner would be the farthest from Kayugh's sleeping place. Yes, there were Kiin's baskets, not good enough to be Chagak's work. Qakan squatted on his haunches and looked through the pile of mats and furs Kiin was working on. The berry bags were rolled together at the bottom of the pile. He took them. A woman's knife was under them. Qakan picked it up. The blade was something Amgigh had made. No one else could knap rock to such thinness. Qakan slipped the knife up his sleeve. He walked around the ulaq, stopped before Kayugh's sleeping place, put his hand on the curtain then drew back.

Why take the chance that Kayugh's anger would call spirits to curse Qakan's trading trip? He went on to Amgigh's sleeping place. Kayugh had the power of killing men. Who had not heard of his battle with the Short Men? But Amgigh was really only a boy. His curse would be small, certainly not strong enough to harm a trader.

Besides Amgigh's blades always brought good trades. He pushed aside the curtain and went in, saw where Amgigh kept his weapons. Short spear, seal harpoon, bola, a container of fishhooks. Blades, a basketful.

Laughter filled the spaces in Qakan's lungs as he spilled the blades out over Amgigh's sleeping furs. Blades, beautiful, beautiful blades. Who made better? A man could take Amgigh's blades alone and become a successful trader.

Qakan picked up the basket and as he did, he saw the sea lion skin wrapping. He set down the basket, sat cross-legged on Amgigh's sleeping furs and picked up the bundle. When he felt the weight of it, the balance of it in his hands, he knew. But even so, when he unwrapped it, his breath hissed out in a long whistle: obsidian, knapped to a narrow-edged blade. The facets of the knapping caught the light, illuminated the blackness of the knife. The handle was wrapped with black baleen, shredded fine as hair.

He rewrapped the knife, pushed up the front of his parka and slipped the bundle into his apron's waistband. "I am Amgigh's brother," Qakan said out loud, said to whatever spirits lived in Amgigh's sleeping place. "I am Amgigh's brother. Remember, his wife is Kiin, my sister. Amgigh can make himself another knife. I will trade this one and the knives in the basket. I will bring him back something that even Samiq will envy."

19

Gray Bird threw his head back and laughed, long and hard. At first the laughter embarrassed Qakan, but then his embarrassment gave way to anger. His father was a fool. Was he blind to what Qakan offered him?

Gray Bird, his small eyes as dark and hard as mossberries, said, "She belongs to Amgigh. I cannot give her to you."

"Amgigh is gone."

"For three, perhaps four, days."

Qakan leaned toward his father. "That is enough."

Gray Bird narrowed his eyes. "What do you mean?"

"What if Kiin should die, an accident in her ik? Would you have to give back the bride price Amgigh paid?"

Gray Bird shrugged his shoulders. "No. She was wife. I gave no promise of how long she would live. But the four skins Chagak has yet to finish scraping, perhaps I would not get those." Gray Bird looked down at his hands, picked at the dirt under a fingernail. "Tell me," he said, "why do you want to kill your sister?"

Qakan sneered. "I would not kill her. It would just seem that she was dead. But listen to what I have to say. I need your help."

Gray Bird straightened and looked around them. They were

in the lee of his ulaq, the wind coming only in gusts broken by the roof grass.

"There is no one near," Qakan said. "All the women are in the ulas and so is Big Teeth. Kiin is watching the fish racks."

But Gray Bird shook his head. He picked up his walking stick and prodded at the grass near his feet. "I cannot help you," he said. "Do what you must do, but tell no one. There are spirits that will hear, and you do not know if they favor you or your sister."

"They favor me," Qakan said. Again the anger rose within him, pushing blood up into his face until his head felt too large for his body. "She is only a woman with no power."

"She has found favor with someone for she has a good husband."

"You were the one who gave her a name. You were the one who gave her whatever power she has."

Gray Bird stood and pushed past Qakan. Looking back over his shoulder he said, "She has brought me more sealskins than you have. If you were a hunter I would have more regard for your plans."

Words rushed into Qakan's mouth so quickly that he knew some spirit must have put them there. "You speak to me of hunting? You?"

Gray Bird whirled, raised his walking stick, his hand trembling. His lips curled back until Qakan could see his teeth, but Qakan did not wait to hear what his father would say.

Enough. He would take Kiin himself, without his father's help. And any furs he got for her would be his own, none owed to his father. He strode to the beach without looking back. His ik was packed; he would leave now. At least they would think he was leaving now.

The first day the men were gone, Kiin and Chagak had talked much, laughed much. They kept Wren out of her cradle most of

the day, allowing her to walk all over the ulaq without worry
that she would bother the men. For part of the afternoon, Kiin's
mother, Blue Shell came over and the three women worked on
baskets, each weaving, while Chagak told a story, or while Kiin
sang, first a song of weaving then one of the sea.

Even the second day was not terrible, and Chagak had
praised Kiin for the cod Crooked Nose had given them, as
though Kiin herself had caught the fish and not just helped
Crooked Nose with the cleaning. But today, the third day, the
ulaq seemed too quiet, too empty. When Kiin had lived in her
father's ulaq, she and her mother were glad each time Gray Bird
went away hunting. But with Amgigh and Kayugh gone, it
seemed the ulaq was dark, even with all lamps burning, and
there was no joy of laughter in the long evenings. And Samiq
. . . he would not be returning. Not this year, perhaps not the
next. But Kiin could not allow herself to feel the hollowness his
absence left. She was Amgigh's wife. Perhaps when Samiq returned to the First Men, she would have given Amgigh a son,
and perhaps Samiq would bring a wife from the Whale Hunters.

A sudden ache filled Kiin's chest, and she heard her spirit
whisper, "Yes, and it will be best if he does. She will be a sister
to you and to Amgigh. A daughter to Chagak and Kayugh. A
second mother to Amgigh's sons."

Kiin's fingers sought the smooth surface of the whale tooth
that hung at her side, and she stroked the ivory until some of
her pain left. She had been too long in this ulaq. It would be
good to take her mother's ik out to the kelp rocks and fish. That
evening she and Chagak could have a small feast, something to
ease their waiting.

Chagak was in her sleeping place, feeding Wren, and Kiin
called to the woman telling her she would soon be back, that
she planned to go only a short way from shore.

"Wait," Chagak called to her. "I have something I want to
give you."

Kiin, puzzled, waited until Chagak came out of the sleeping

place, Wren in her arms, the child suckling, her mouth pressed tight against Chagak's right breast.

"This," Chagak said and handed Kiin the carving that she wore around her neck, something, Kiin knew, that the grandfather Shuganan had made for her. The carving was of woman, husband and child, the faces of the man and woman most surely Chagak and Kayugh. The whale's tooth ivory was yellowed with age, dark with the oil Chagak rubbed into it to keep the ivory from drying and splitting.

"I-I-I c-c-cannot," Kiin stammered. "It-it is yours. Your-your g-g-grand . . ."

But Chagak held up her hand to silence Kiin and slipped the thong around Kiin's neck, adjusted the carving so it hung between Kiin's breasts.

"It is yours now," Chagak said. "It will give you babies, and your babies will be a joy to me as well as to you."

Kiin tried to speak, but again some spirit pushed itself into her throat, held back the words. So Kiin leaned forward, pressed her cheek against Chagak's cheek, let Chagak see that tears had come into her eyes.

Chagak smiled and said, "Someday you must give it to one of your sons' wives. That way it is always a gift."

Kiin clasped the carving in both hands, studied the faces, the woman's suk, the feathers and seams etched into the ivory. For a moment her thoughts went to her father's poor carvings, but she closed her mind against the man. Why let thoughts of Gray Bird spoil her joy?

"So, you go to fish?" Chagak asked.

"P-p-perhaps for pogies," Kiin answered.

"Ask your mother if she wants to go with you," Chagak said. "The wind is strong. Do not go alone."

Kiin smiled. Chagak, always the worrier. Kiin grabbed her suk and pulled it on over her head. She climbed from the ulaq, one hand still clutching the ivory carving.

She walked to her father's ulaq, and her chest tightened even as she climbed inside, but to her relief, her father was not there. She called, but the ulaq was empty. Perhaps her mother was digging roots or gathering heather in the hills. Kiin did not mind. Yes, the wind was strong, pushing down from the north, sweeping out toward the south sea, but she would stay to the south side of their cove so the waves would not pull her ik away from the kelp rocks. Sometimes it was better to be alone, to go slowly in the ik, watching for sea otters or seals.

The ik was on the beach beside Chagak's, but Qakan's ik, the one he and Kiin's father had made when Qakan decided he would become a trader, was gone.

Yes, Kiin thought, that morning Crooked Nose mentioned that Qakan had left the night before on his first trading trip. She said that he had taken most of the fish from their drying racks. Who would expect anything different from Qakan?

But he was braver than Kiin had thought. There were many problems a man alone would face, even a trader who skirted the beaches and inlets. It would not be an easy trip, even if he went only to the Whale Hunters. Besides the berry bags, Kiin had given him a number of baskets. He promised he would bring her something in return, something from another tribe. But Kiin expected nothing. She was used to Qakan's smooth words of praise when he needed something, his quick scorn when he had whatever it was he wanted.

It did not matter to Kiin. She was a wife now, and perhaps soon she would be a mother. Let Qakan do what he wanted.

She lifted the ik, pushed it out into the water until the waves were lapping at the bottom of her suk. Then she climbed into the ik and began to paddle. When the current caught the ik, Kiin used her paddle to direct the craft until she reached the kelp rocks. She was tying a line to a fishing gorge when she noticed a large number of chitons glistening on the rocks just under the water. She leaned out and, pulling her woman's knife from its pouch at her waist, she used the flat of the blade to pry the chitons loose.

She worked until she had a pile of chitons, each as long as her hand, their dark, jointed shells curled like tiny ulaq mounds. Then using her paddle, she pushed the ik away from the rocks. Why bother to fish? The chitons would be feast enough.

She would have to paddle hard to get back to the beach. The current was forcing her away from the cove, but she was used to paddling; her arms and back were strong. She had taken several hard strokes when she heard someone call to her, and looking up, saw an ik.

She stroked again, maintaining her ik's place in the current, then waved. It was Qakan. Yes, who could doubt when he had painted his ik so hideously with bright trader colors.

She allowed the current to take her back toward the rocks, then let her ik drift into a still place between two boulders. Only one day, one day alone on the sea had been enough for Qakan. Kiin was not surprised. He would never be a man. He, not Kiin, would be the one who lived forever in their father's ulaq.

When he was close enough, she called to him. "I thought you were going to be a trader."

Qakan shrugged and brought his ik close to hers. "It was a bad night," he said, his voice pitched high into the whine Kiin was used to hearing. "There were spirits on the beach where I stayed."

Kiin nodded. She had little doubt that he had spent the night in the cove on the west side of Tugix's island. The First Men had a camp there and even a small ulaq. The beach was a place where fur seals stopped when swimming from the south sea to the north.

It was not a terrible place to stay. Kiin once went there herself when she was just a young girl. She had stolen Crooked Nose's ik and paddled to the cove, determined to live there away from her father. Kayugh had found her the next day and brought her home, but the night had not been terrible. There had been no spirits.

Qakan looked down, would not meet her eyes, and for a moment Kiin felt an ache in sympathy with his shame. How terrible to be lazy and afraid like Qakan. "I have gathered many chitons," she said. "Do you have a basket I can fill so you can take some back to our mother?"

He nodded and handed her one of her own baskets, one that she had decorated with yellow curls from puffin tuft feathers. She wanted to hand it back to him, to ask for one less beautiful, but then her spirit whispered, "Why add to his pain?" So she took the basket and began to scoop shells into it.

Kiin was looking down, did not see Qakan raise his paddle above her head, did not raise her eyes until she heard the swoop of the paddle blade as it sped through the air.

It caught her at the left temple, gashing through her skin and knocking Kiin to the bottom of her ik. For a moment she looked up at Qakan, saw there was no shame in his eyes, no fear. Slowly she forced her lips into one word, "Why?" But Qakan only laughed and then the sky turned red and the ocean was black and Kiin saw nothing at all.

20

K*iin woke to pain.* Her head ached and her back felt as though someone had beaten her, had flailed her until her skin was broken and raw. Her stomach was heavy with the pain, as though she needed to vomit, and when she tried to open her eyes, she could not.

I am in the ik, she thought, as she felt the pull of water against the sides. Then came fear, as sudden and cutting as her pain. If she were in the ik, then the currents would have taken her far out into the sea. She must find the paddle. She grabbed the sides of the ik and sat up. The pain settled below her stomach, and she felt a rush of warmth between her legs. She opened her eyes. She saw two of everything, her body divided at her chest, four legs, two overlapping at the center, and blood covering all. She closed her eyes.

No, she thought. It is not the time for my bleeding. It is still new moon.

Then a voice came from above her, a voice and laughter.

"Amgigh will not want you now. Not even Samiq. I have taken your soul again, Kiin."

Kiin did not act as if she had even heard, but she felt her spirit moving within her body, pushing, pushing against her skin, flitting from head to heart to feet, and suddenly Kiin knew that Qakan had taken her as a man takes a woman. Had taken her in anger and with great force, and had torn her in the taking.

Slowly she lay down again. She crossed her arms over her chest. Let the blood flow. Let it stain Qakan's trading ik, let it bring him the curse of woman's blood. What did she care.

"I am going to use you as trade," Qakan said. "You will bring a good price. You think Amgigh will come after you?" He laughed. "No one will. They all think you are dead. Even if Amgigh did find you, he would not want you. You are spoiled, like rotten meat."

Kiin opened her eyes, moved her head so she could see Qakan, his fat round face only a blur. Blood still oozed from her wounds, and she shuddered at the thought of Qakan upon her, thrusting into her, leaving his flow, the thick white milk burning like juice from an ugyuun plant. But he was wrong. He had not taken her spirit. It was strong within her and moving in anger. Kiin closed her eyes and mouth, lifted her hands to her ears to hold her spirit in. She would not let it escape. She would keep her spirit, and though she was not strong enough to fight Qakan now, soon her head would clear, then she would fight. She would never let Qakan trade her. She would kill him first.

Qakan looked at his sister and laughed. She was lying in the bottom of the ik, legs drawn up, hands over her ears. Qakan dipped his paddle into the water and pushed the boat ahead in hard, smooth strokes. He laughed again, and the laughter floated out in front of them. He was a man now, had proven himself a man. In his pride, he felt his man part thicken again. Yes, he was now a man, as much as Amgigh, more than Samiq. Had Samiq ever taken a woman? Perhaps by now among the Whale Hunters he had been in a woman's bed, who could say? But Whale Hunter women were ugly, more like men than women.

Qakan pulled his paddle into the boat and held it over Kiin's head. Water from the dripping edge poured over Kiin's face and down her neck. She flinched but did not move her hands from her ears. Qakan pushed the paddle under her arm and lifted, trying to pry the hand from her ear, but Kiin was strong, stronger than Qakan thought she would be. Qakan lifted the paddle. He should hit her again. He wanted her to be afraid of him, but then he stopped. No, he needed her to paddle tomorrow, and besides, why leave another gash? The wound on the side of her forehead would already make one scar and there were scars on her back from their father's beatings. Qakan must begin to think like a trader. Kiin was more valuable to him without scars.

And besides, she was already afraid of him. She had covered her ears just to hide herself from his voice.

"You are nothing, Kiin," he said to her, repeated it until it bounded back to them from the cliffs they were passing, from the thick ice rivers that flowed from the mountains into the north sea. "Nothing, nothing, nothing . . ."

21

Amgigh expected Kiin to be watching from the ulaq, to be waiting as a wife should wait, hoping for the return of her husband. It was evening, and he would not have to sit for long in the ulaq before he could go to his sleeping place, invite Kiin to follow him. Then he would ask her to rub his aching shoulders.

He could almost feel her hands upon him, the tiredness of his muscles passing from his body into her small, strong fingers. Then he would pull her to him, stroke her until he was ready to take her. . . .

It was good to be a man. To have a wife.

He pushed his paddle hard into the water and thought of the Whale Hunters. He and his father had spent two days with them, trading for whale oil and the otter skins for Kiin, but it had been a difficult two days. The younger Whale Hunter women were bold, always beside him, laughing, flashing their eyes, but the grandfather Many Whales and his woman, Fat Wife, had treated him like a boy, not a man. They had not even offered him the comfort of a woman at night; he and Samiq had been given one sleeping place to share, as though they were children.

The cliffs gradually pulled back from the shore, opening into the wide shallow cove that was the First Men's beach. Amgigh glanced back at his father. He was only the length of an ikyak behind him.

Someone was on the beach, Big Teeth, yes, and two women. Kiin? No, it was Amgigh's mother. Crooked Nose was beside her. Where was Kiin?

He scanned the beach, then the ulaq roofs. She had known he would be back this day or the next. Would she have gone into the hills to collect roots, to the cliffs to snare birds? Was she no better wife than that?

Angrily, Amgigh pushed his ikyak ashore, loosened the hatch skirting and stepped out onto the beach. He picked up his ikyak, then felt a hand on his shoulder. It was Gray Bird. The man had blackened his face with charcoal, sign of mourning, and Amgigh felt the sudden tremble of his heart as it jumped from its place in his chest to settle high in his throat.

"Kiin?" he asked, his voice choked by the nearness of his heart.

Then Kayugh was beside him, his hand for a moment on Amgigh's shoulder. "She is dead?" Kayugh asked.

Gray Bird nodded. "We found her ik in the kelp. There was a hole in the bottom."

"You did not find her body?" Kayugh asked.

"No," Gray Bird said and lifted his head to look out at the sea. "She is there with the sea spirits." He looked at Amgigh. "Perhaps she will guide seals to your harpoon."

Amgigh could not answer, could feel nothing but a sick emptiness in his belly, a full rushing in his head. He looked at his mother, felt a sudden and foolish hope that she would tell him Gray Bird was wrong. Kiin was alive. But then Amgigh noticed that she, too, had darkened her face with ashes and that she had cut a section of her hair short so that it hung in a fringe over her forehead.

He pulled his knife from its wrist sheath, and looking toward the sea, slashed it across his face, laying a cut open from cheek to jawbone. He wiped the knife in the beach gravel and then walked into the sea, scooped up a handful of water and splashed it against his face. The salt of the water burned in the wound.

"She was a good wife," Amgigh said, speaking to no one, speaking to everyone, speaking to the spirits. "She takes a part of my soul with her into the sea."

Gray Bird waited two days. He watched Amgigh, watched as the young man went from sorrow to anger and to sorrow again.

In early morning the third day, Gray Bird pulled himself from his sleeping place, startled his wife with his early rising. Blue Shell, her matted hair cut short, her arms and legs marked with slashes she had made in mourning her daughter, had not yet set out food.

"Feed me, woman," Gray Bird growled.

He ate quickly, then said to her, "I have taken a new name. You will call me Waxtal."

Blue Shell looked up at him, her eyes wide, and waited as though for an explanation, but why tell her his reasons? Did she need to know? Women were whisperers, telling secrets to small, bothersome spirits. Perhaps when traders came to his ulaq, he would tell the story of his daughter, of her greed and how he let her live. Then he would tell how the water spirits took her. And the traders would need no explanation. They would know why he was called Waxtal. Did he not have pity upon his daughter, in spite of her greed?

Gray Bird stood, pulled on his parka and climbed from the ulaq. Amgigh was on the beach, as he had been each morning since his return from the Whale Hunters. He sat beside his ikyak, a sea lion bladder of seal oil in his lap, but his hands were still. Only his eyes moved, scanning the surface of the sea.

Gray Bird sat down on the other side of Amgigh's ikyak. Finally Amgigh looked up at Gray Bird, shook his head as though to clear it and asked, "Qakan—he went to trade with the Walrus People?"

Gray Bird shrugged. "Perhaps. Perhaps only to other First Men villages."

"My knife is gone," Amgigh said. "All my knives."

Gray Bird waited, said nothing.

"I think Qakan took them."

Again Gray Bird shrugged. "He had a pack of your knives, three short-bladed, two long," Gray Bird said.

"Yes, I asked him to trade them for me, but now all my knives are gone and a special knife, obsidian, long-bladed. I made two, one for Samiq, one for myself."

"If you did not give it to him," Gray Bird said, "Qakan would not take it. Perhaps your mother put it in a special place; perhaps before she died, Kiin did." Gray Bird cleared his throat. "You will hunt today?" he asked.

"Perhaps. If my father wants to hunt."

"I will hunt with you if he does not."

"Perhaps, Gray Bird, I am not sure. . . ."

Gray Bird coughed, again cleared his throat. "I have taken a new name."

Amgigh looked at him, for the first time pulling his eyes from their study of the sea.

"To honor my daughter."

"You did not honor her during her life," Amgigh said, and Gray Bird heard the bitterness in his words.

"I let her live. I let her take the power she needed for her life from her brother. Now he is a trader, not a hunter as both he and I had wanted."

Amgigh hunched his shoulders as though pulling himself away from Gray Bird's words. "What is your new name?" he asked.

"Waxtal."

Amgigh grunted.

"You are the first to know," Gray Bird said.

For a time they sat without speaking, then Gray Bird said, "And Samiq, will he change his name?"

"I do not know," Amgigh said. "Perhaps the Whale Hunters will have a new name for him. If he takes a whale."

"He is a good hunter, a strong man," said Gray Bird. "You think he will return to us or stay with the Whale Hunters?"

"I think he will return. He has promised he will teach me to hunt the whale in return for nights with my wife."

"But you have no wife."

Amgigh shrugged. "He will not know that until he returns. Besides, he promised to teach our father to hunt the whale. A man always keeps the promises he makes to his father."

"And you think he does not know?"

"Does not know what?"

"That Kayugh is not his true father."

Amgigh turned, his eyes suddenly narrowed to dark slits, his mouth tightened into a fine line.

"You did not know?" Gray Bird asked and felt a billowing of gladness begin in his chest.

"No," Amgigh said slowly.

"And did you know that Chagak is not your mother?"

Amgigh's eyes widened.

"If you do not believe me, ask her. Ask your father."

"Kayugh is my father."

"Yes and Chagak is Samiq's mother."

"And Red Berry?"

"She is Kayugh's daughter and daughter to your true mother, a woman who died shortly after your birth."

"They should have told us. It would have been easier then to understand why Many Whales wanted Samiq and not me."

"They should have told you," Gray Bird said, "but perhaps they were afraid Samiq's true father or your true mother would come back from the Dancing Lights, settle into Kayugh's ulaq, use their spirit powers to harm the children that were not their own."

"Yes."

"Now you understand why your father chose a wife for you before choosing one for Samiq."

"Yes."

"And Kiin was a good wife to you."

Amgigh bit at his bottom lip, then he picked up a thin piece of driftwood and began making long deep lines in the beach gravel. "Who is Samiq's father?" he finally asked.

Again Gray Bird shrugged. "Shuganan's son, Chagak says. But I have often wondered. Shuganan was tall and thin, and Chagak, she is not tall, but she is fine-boned, thin. Samiq is heavy-boned, wide with muscle. He does not look like one of the First Men."

"But Shuganan's wife was a Whale Hunter and so was my— Chagak's—mother. Whale Hunters are a big people with wide strong muscles."

"Yes," said Gray Bird. "But also tall."

"Who else could Samiq belong to? Not Big Teeth."

"No," Gray Bird said. He stood, adjusted his parka. "Perhaps you should ask Chagak." He picked up the bladder of oil from Amgigh's lap, began coating the seams of Amgigh's ikyak.

22

For two days Kiin lay in the bottom of her brother's ik. The rocking of the boat made her head ache, and whenever Qakan forced her to drink a bit of water, to eat a mouthful of food, she vomited.

She did not try to help him make camp, to cook food or arrange sleeping mats. She stayed in the ik, and much of the time she slept, but when she was awake, she planned. Each day, her head hurt less. Soon she would be strong again, stronger than Qakan. And who could say? Perhaps some grandmother spirit had seen what Qakan did to her. Perhaps some grandmother spirit would help Kiin escape.

On the third day, as Qakan awkwardly pushed the boat from the beach where they had spent the night, he said, "So you are going to die."

Kiin said nothing, and she kept her eyes closed against the light of the new day. But though Kiin said nothing, she heard her spirit speak—the words clear in Kiin's mind: "No, Kiin will not die. You will die, Qakan."

Kiin felt the ik lurch as Qakan settled himself on his padded seat of sealskin. "It is sad you will die without a soul," Qakan said.

Kiin opened her eyes only a little, a slit that she hoped Qakan would not notice. Her brother looked down at her. His face was smudged with dirt, his birdskin parka torn on one shoulder, his hair dull and matted. He looked like a boy, not a trader; he looked like someone who would know little, who would be easily overpowered. She felt her spirit swell within her chest, felt strength once more in her arms and legs, and she realized that her eyes now saw what was true, not spirit images, doubling and tripling each rock, each blade of grass.

"So you will die without a soul and go nowhere," Qakan continued. "You will not go to the Dancing Lights and you will never see Samiq again."

Kiin's heart jumped in her chest. Why mention Samiq when Amgigh was her husband? Did her feelings for Samiq show themselves so clearly that even Qakan knew?

"M-m-my husband is Am-Amgigh," she said, her voice cracking from days of silence.

Qakan looked at her, and through the fringes of her eyelashes, Kiin saw that he smiled, the smile he used when he was preparing to hit her, when he was ready to tell lies about her to their father.

"So you are alive again," Qakan said.

Kiin moved her head slowly and opened her eyes wide to stare at the gray sky above them. Yes, she was stronger, and her head hurt only where Qakan had hit her, and that pain was the tenderness of a bruise, not the deep ache that pulled her into terrible dreams and made Qakan's voice seem like some high whining of the wind.

"I brought you to help me paddle and to catch fish and prepare food," Qakan said. "I did not think I would have to take care of you like you were a baby."

"Amgigh w-w-will come for m-me," Kiin said. She raised herself slowly and gritted her teeth as both sky and ik seemed to spin. "T-t-today or t-tomorrow he will find us and he w-will kill you for t-taking me."

Qakan laughed. It was a laugh that their father used, a laugh that seemed to start in the throat and arch up into a high, thin note like the call of a guillemot. The fat under Qakan's chin trembled and his belly quivered beneath his parka.

Qakan, a trader, Kiin thought. Why would anyone deal with him? But then Kiin's spirit whispered, "Many men will want to trade with him. Qakan is a boy, easy to trick. He will take seal-skins and come home with lemming skins."

"Amgigh will not follow us," Qakan said. "He thinks you are dead."

Kiin pulled herself to sit erect in the ik. She faced Qakan, saw the truth of what he said in his eyes.

"I put a hole in the bottom of our mother's ik and wedged it between some rocks near the south cliffs. The whole village will think the water spirits have taken you."

Kiin raised her chin, stared at Qakan until he looked away. "I w-w-will send my s-s-spirit to Amgigh during his dreams s-s-so he will know the truth," she said.

"You have no spirit," Qakan spat out. "Everyone in the vil-lage thinks you are dead. Your spirit was afraid to stay in a dead body. It left you while you were asleep. It went to the Dancing Lights without you."

Kiin smiled, nearly laughed, but did not reply to Qakan's foolishness.

Qakan cocked his head, watched her for a moment. "You think I brought you with me only to sew my parka and prepare my food? No. I will sell you when we come to a Walrus People village."

Kiin kept the smile on her face, but a small portion of the anger that had been growing in her chest suddenly changed to fear. Yes, she would bring a good price, if not as wife, then as slave, and traders said some of the Walrus People kept slaves.

"Th-they will not w-w-want a woman without a s-s-soul," she said and allowed the mocking of her spirit to show in her eyes.

"I will not tell them." He looked at her as though she were a child, as though he were scolding her. "You should not tell them either. It will be better for you if you are wife rather than slave."

"S-s-so I become w-w-wife," Kiin said. "And s-s-someday I

ask to visit my people, t-t-to return to my village. I w-w-will t-tell our father and my husband what you did. Perhaps he or Am-Amgigh will kill you. P-p-perhaps Kayugh will."

Qakan shrugged. He dipped the paddle into the water and said, "Our father already knows. And Amgigh will get another wife. A better wife than you, and he will not want you back."

Kiin heard the words, gritted her teeth in anger. Of course, her father knew. How else would Qakan have accumulated the furs and skins, the oil to take on a trading trip? But then she thought, He knows Qakan will trade me to the Walrus People, but does he know that Qakan forced himself on me, used me like a wife?

"And he-he knows you cursed yourself and your t-t-trading trip by using your own s-sister as a w-w-wife?" she asked and snorted when she saw Qakan's face redden.

"I will get more for you if you carry a child," Qakan said, his voice low.

Kiin leaned toward him. Anger forced her words out, flowing and clear, as though her spirit spoke and not Kiin herself. "And you think you will give me that child. You think Amgigh has not already put a child in my belly? You will get nothing," she said. "You have cursed yourself and this ik. You see the blood in the bottom of this ik. It is my blood. Woman's blood. If you take this ik too far out on the sea, the sea animals themselves will bite a hole in this ik and we will both drown."

Qakan hunched his shoulders as though to protect himself from her words. "If I am cursed," he said, "then you are doubly cursed. If you return to our people and tell them what has happened, do you think Amgigh will want you? Do you think a hunter of the Walrus People will want you? Do not speak to me of curses. I am a trader. I have too much power to be cursed by what happens with a woman. It is the woman who carries the curse. Already it has taken your soul."

"You are wrong, Qakan," Kiin said. "I still have my soul. I feel it, strong, here." She pressed her fist against her chest.

Qakan smiled. "Perhaps you are right," he said. "Perhaps your soul is still there. It takes a long time for a soul to leave some-one who still lives, but perhaps it is smaller already. Perhaps each time you speak, a small part of your soul comes out in your words, comes out and is taken by the wind up to the Dancing Lights."

At his last word, a large wave slammed against the ik, pushing it toward an outcropping of rock. Qakan sucked in his breath and paddled, yelled for Kiin to help. She grabbed a paddle from the bottom of the ik and thrust it against the rock. The rock ground into the wooden blade. Kiin's arms felt weak, but she held the paddle steady, pushing with all her strength while Qakan pulled the boat with long, deep strokes.

Finally the wave was beyond them, and Kiin watched as it foamed against the beach, its power draining into the dark gravel, the wave hissing as it pulled itself back into the sea.

"Keep the paddle," Qakan said. "We will go faster if you help."

Kiin tightened her hands on the paddle's smooth shaft. Her eyes followed the shaft to the blade. "Take him now," Kiin's spirit whispered. "Take him now. He is tired and you have your strength back."

"I-I-I will paddle only if you t-t-turn the ik bac-back toward our island," Kiin said.

Qakan pulled his paddle from the water and raised the blade toward her.

He lifted his chin, gesturing toward the partially healed gash that marked the side of Kiin's forehead.

"You have forgotten what I can do with this paddle?" he asked.

Kiin, the wood of her own paddle cool against her hands, looked at her brother's smooth, plump fingers and felt no fear, but she drew back and pulled her paddle from the water to hold like a protection between herself and Qakan.

Qakan threw back his head and laughed.

For a moment Kiin waited, waited until Qakan's laughter spread itself up into his cheeks, until his cheeks curved up to force Qakan's eyes closed. Then Kiin clasped her paddle like a hunter clasps a lance, and she plunged the blade into the soft bulk of Qakan's belly. Kiin's thrust knocked Qakan backward in the ik, and as he fell he dropped his paddle. Kiin lunged forward, grabbed her own paddle and thrust it again toward Qakan, but this time, Qakan caught the blade before it hit him, caught and held, his hands so firm that Kiin was amazed by his strength.

He must have the help of some spirit, Kiin thought, but what spirit would help Qakan?

She tried to twist the paddle from his grip, but the twisting made the ik turn so the bow no longer faced out into the sea. Waves slapped against the ik, and water spilled in over one side.

"Kiin, stop!" Qakan yelled. "We will drown. The ik . . . look. . . ."

"What does it matter?" Kiin's spirit whispered. "Even a child could make it back to shore from here." Kiin jerked the paddle toward her, then released it so quickly that the blade smashed into Qakan's mouth. She jumped forward, landed with one knee in Qakan's stomach, the other in his groin. Qakan moaned. He lost his grip on the paddle, but then he reached out for Kiin, caught her hair with one hand, and before Kiin could wrench away, his arms were around her, forcing her face into his chest, squeezing her ribcage until she could not breathe, until her heart felt as though it did not have room to beat. He moved his hands to her throat, pressing his fingers into her windpipe. Kiin's lungs ached with the need to breathe, and as she struggled, her eyes dimmed, seeing all things gray, all things shimmering with spirit images.

Then Qakan was pushing her away, one of his hands still tight on her neck, the other drawn back in a fist.

Kiin pulled in a long breath.

"H-h-hit me," she said, the words rasping from her throat. "The-the Walrus People w-w-will give you a good price for a w-w-woman with s-s-scars on her face."

Qakan's lips drew back into a grimace. Blood bubbled from between his teeth.

"You are stupid, Kiin," he hissed, and the words forced a spray of blood and spittle from his mouth.

Kiin tried to turn away, but Qakan twisted his hands into her hair and raised her head, slammed it against one of the ik's wooden ribs. Pain burst from the back of Kiin's skull into her eyes, and once again all things doubled, once again all things blurred.

"Why fight me?" Qakan asked, the question broken with long shuddering breaths. "Amgigh will not want you now. Even Samiq will not want you. Besides, would you curse Amgigh by being his wife after you have lain with your own brother?"

His words pushed into Kiin's head, and she felt the weight of them slip down her throat into her chest, settle heavily beside her heart.

Qakan was right. She carried a curse. Could she live with Amgigh or Samiq and take the chance that the curse might spread to them?

The weight of the curse spread in her chest, spread and pushed her soul into a thin layer at the inside of her skin, until finally she was hollow, her soul brittle, like the shell of an egg, and holding nothing but her breath and broken words.

23

They were *watching him* again. Their giggling took his thoughts from his work, and his knife slipped, gouging another piece of wood. Samiq closed his eyes and arched his back to ease the strain in his shoulders. His grandfather had given him an old ikyak frame from which to make an ikyak of his own, one, his grandfather said, made the right way, in the manner of the Whale Hunters, an ikyak the sea animals would respect.

Samiq tried to keep his thoughts from the man who had first owned the ikyak frame, the hunter who had shaped the jointed keel, the gunwales and deck beams. He had been skilled, that ikyak maker. The frame was solid, the joints well-fitted. But Samiq could not help wonder whether the man had been a good hunter, one who had brought meat for the village, or if he had cursed this ikyak frame with his laziness, with disrespect.

Most of the framework was still good, even the joints where the deck beams met the gunwales. The Whale Hunters used baleen lashings to hold joint to joint, and where wood rubbed against wood, they inset small plates of whale tooth ivory into the framework.

"See," his grandfather had told him, pushing at a piece of wood with a fingernail, "water softens the wood, peels it away until the waves can pound it into nothing. Ivory keeps the wood from wearing."

Yesterday Samiq had painted the frame pieces with ochre, blood red, mixed into a paste and spread on with a piece of hard-bristled hair seal skin. The ochre protected the wood from the rot of wetness, from the scalding salt of the sea.

The wood frame of a Whale Hunter's ikyak was, Many Whales told Samiq, like the bones of a whale, jointed so it could move in the sea, so it would shape itself to the waves, bend with the swells. The First Men's ikyan were poorly made, he told Samiq; the First Men's ikyan were stiff and awkward.

Many Whales' words settled into Samiq's chest like splinters and seemed to rub against Samiq's heart each time he breathed. So Samiq told himself that if a Whale Hunter boy went to the First Men to learn to hunt sea lions, perhaps he would have to learn to use the First Men's ikyan. He would without doubt have to give up his large awkward lance, and instead learn to use the finely balanced barbed seal harpoons of the First Men.

Samiq slipped one end of the curved deck beam into its socket in the gunwale. A good fit, Samiq thought. Snug, but not so tight that the joint would snap if a wave bent the ikyak.

Fat Wife had agreed to sew the sea lion skins Samiq had cut for the covering. At least when the ikyak was done, Samiq would be able to get away from the young girls for a time, even if Many Whales would not allow him to go beyond sight of the beach.

He looked with longing at the ikyak he had brought from his own village. It lay above the high tide line, the craft made in the manner of the First Men, without the top ridge or the pieced keelson of the Whale Hunters' ikyan. He could take it, now, go back to his own village, to his own people. To Kiin and to his mother, to his baby sister Wren. But then he would disappoint Kayugh and Amgigh. To help his people, he must become one of the Whale Hunters. And for this year at least he must please Many Whales and even Fat Wife.

It would be easier if Fat Wife were more like his own mother. Then he would be able to talk to her about the First Men, about his family and his village. Then he would not feel so alone. But Fat Wife seemed to want Samiq to forget the First Men. She did not want him to sit as First Men sat; she did not want him to talk as First Men talked. She had even insisted on making Samiq a new parka, though when she finished he could see little difference between it and the one his mother had made him.

Many Whales had laughed at Samiq's seal harpoons, at their fine slender points, their light bone foreshafts. But when he inspected Samiq's throwing board, the old man had merely grunted, and Samiq held a smile within his cheek, knowing that the throwing board was as fine as a man could make. It had belonged to his grandfather, Shuganan, and was given to Samiq because it was the exact length of Samiq's forearm, from the tip of his longest finger to his elbow.

The throwing board was an extension of Samiq's arm and allowed him to throw a spear or harpoon much farther than he could without it. Nearly the width of Samiq's hand, it had a hook at one end that socketed into the shaft of Samiq's spear. The spear lay in a groove the length of the throwing board. Samiq held one end of the board, allowing it to extend, horizontal to the water, back over his shoulder. When he threw, a hard, sidearm throw, the board followed the arc of his arm, but the spear stayed horizontal, finally connected to the throwing board only by the hook at the end of the board.

Samiq's throwing board always aimed his spear true and the hook in the end never slipped. Many hunters more gifted than Samiq had poorer throwing boards. "Perhaps it is the power of the many kills your grandfather made with it," Kayugh had explained to Samiq. And that was the explanation Samiq gave to Many Whales.

But each day, Samiq was left standing on the beach, watching as the young men of the village went to hunt sea lions or seals. And during those days, he remembered what Kayugh had told him:

"Do as the old man says. Show interest in his words and

stories, and after he has taught you to hunt whales, come back and tell us. We will become as the Whale Hunters, only greater, for we are better sea lion hunters."

Yes, Samiq told himself whenever his spirit ached to see his own island, to return to his own ulaq, Kayugh has treated you like a true son. Now honor Kayugh as true father. Learn to hunt the whale so you can teach him, so you can teach him and his son Amgigh.

Samiq laid his knife on the ground and inspected the ikyak. He had tied each joint with stiff ribbons of baleen, had set the ivory rub plates into their sockets and glued them with a mixture of powdered kelp and his own blood. Many Whales would have difficulty finding reason to reject this framework. Perhaps today, Fat Wife could start sewing the covering.

The whispers of the girls stopped as Samiq picked up his knife and walked toward Many Whales' ulaq. But soon he heard someone hurrying behind him. Samiq turned and saw the girl called Three Fish following him. Her two friends hid their smiles behind their hands and huddled together, watching from the beach.

Three Fish was tall and wide like all the Whale Hunters, and her smile showed a mouthful of broken teeth. How could she be a good wife if even in her youth her teeth were chipped and broken? How many seal flipper boots would she make, crimping the soles with her teeth, before she had no teeth at all?

"Where are your friends?" Samiq asked the girl.

Three Fish giggled and flung her arm back toward the two girls. "They think you are a giant and will eat them," Three Fish said and giggled again.

Samiq did not answer her. He felt a wariness in talking with any girl of the village. Though he had little experience in the things of the sleeping place, he knew the three girls behind him had been taken soon after their first bleeding. Among the Whale Hunters, any man but father, grandfather, or brother had the right to ask favors, although a married woman could be given only by her husband. These three were eager to share his bed, and they spent much time following him, flipping their aprons as they walked. And although Three Fish brought little desire to Samiq's heart, the other two, Small Flower and Speckled Basket, were not ugly.

But during the first day Samiq spent with the Whale Hunters, Many Whales had said, "No night walking. Night walking will make grass grow between your toes, and you will curse yourself forever with the sea animals."

Samiq had been puzzled by the strange warning, and asked Crooked Bird, a young man of the village, what Many Whales had meant.

"No visiting," Crooked Bird had said and then laughed, his laugh opening Samiq's mind to the possibility that Crooked Bird did not like him. "No sleeping with women. You are not yet a man."

Then Samiq knew that if in Many Whales' eyes he was a boy, to all the Whale Hunters, he was a boy. A man hunted whales, and Samiq did not even have a proper ikyak.

So there was one strange comfort in Three Fish's giggling, and the thought came to Samiq each time he heard her laugh: someone sees me as a man.

Fat Wife was sitting in the large central room of the ulaq, the room lit by whale oil lamps, these lamps burning more cleanly than the seal oil lamps of the First Men.

Samiq waited respectfully for Fat Wife's acknowledgment, and when she looked at him, he squatted down to speak.

"I am ready for the cover now, Grandmother," he said.

"You have completed the frame?" Fat Wife asked.

"Yes."

"Sit then, and I will speak of something Many Whales has told me. Perhaps he will tell you himself, but perhaps not. It is something you should know."

Samiq settled himself on the floor mats, cross-legged as was the custom of the Whale Hunters. Fat Wife laid down the basket she was finishing, and Samiq noticed how crude her work was compared to his mother's. The image of his mother sitting with a basket inverted on a basket pole, made a heaviness in his chest, and Samiq brought his thoughts back to Fat Wife, her greased hair drawn back tightly from her round face, her small eyes glittering in the light of the oil lamps.

"We are a great people," she began in the Whale Hunters' now-familiar litany, the beginning of any plan or story. "You are more than a boy, but not yet a man. In the village of the People, to be a man, you must hunt the whale. But since you already hunt the seal, you will not go with the boys, learning slowly over the years." She leaned forward, looked into Samiq's eyes and said, "Many Whales will instruct you." She settled back and adjusted the mat that was folded up over her knees. "It is a great honor."

Samiq, unsure of what to say, finally replied, "Yes, Grandmother, it is a great honor."

Fat Wife smiled and reached out to pat his knee, and Samiq forced himself not to recoil. Among his own people, touching was limited to a man's wives and children. But then, Samiq told himself, Fat Wife did not see him as a man. He felt his face color, and he hoped Fat Wife did not see.

But she leaned forward again, now patting his cheek, and said, "You look much like your grandfather, but wider, stronger. Perhaps someday I will find out what Seal Hunter mothers feed their sons to make them grow so strong. Do you know?"

Samiq tried to think of some plant or animal eaten by his people that the Whale Hunters did not use, but he could not. In eating, all seemed the same. "I do not," he finally answered, wishing he could tell her, wanting to please her. "But when I return to my people, I will ask," he added.

But Fat Wife quickly pulled away from him, frowned and narrowed her eyes. She lifted her head and said, "You are no longer a Seal Hunter. You are one of us. Many Whales has decided to give you a new name—Whale Killer."

Samiq's eyes widened and he could not keep the dismay from

his voice, but he spoke softly as though he reasoned with a child, "My name is Samiq. It is a name honored among the First Men."

"Kayugh has given you to us!" Fat Wife said. Her eyes were intense as she studied Samiq's face, and Samiq was suddenly very tired. He remembered his mother's words, often spoken when the clamoring of many people filled the ulaq: "I need to speak to the sea." And now he said the same words to Fat Wife, but did not miss the smile on her face as he left the ulaq.

24

Kiin *pulled another strand* of ryegrass from the pile at her side. Each day, after she and Qakan beached the ik for the night, Kiin worked on baskets. It gave her something to do, some reason to keep her eyes from Qakan's mocking face, to pretend she did not hear his complaining.

Qakan had brought the grass from their father's ulaq—stolen, probably, Kiin thought, from the dried grass their mother kept in flat layers in a corner of her sleeping place. Each time Kiin touched the grass, felt it smooth against her fingertips, her spirit seemed to see her mother weaving baskets. But Kiin pushed the ache of memories away. She was here now with Qakan; she was not a child who could climb on her mother's lap and hide from the fears of each day's living.

Sometimes she paused in her work and stroked the whale tooth shell, sometimes she touched the necklace that Samiq had given her or the carving from Chagak, but then her fingers went again to the grasses as she twisted and held the strands with one hand and bound them in tight stitches with her weaving needle. She smiled when she remembered Qakan's fear of the carving she wore, his mumblings about the trades he could make for it. But who was fool enough to touch one of Shuganan's carvings without permission of the one chosen to be the carving's owner? Not even Qakan would take that chance.

Kiin had just finished the circular bottom of another basket when Qakan came from the beach. It was a good beach with cliffs that blocked the wind on one side and talus slopes that led to the mountains on the other. Kiin turned away from Qakan, hoping he would ignore her, but he ran to her and grasped her arms. His eyes were bright with a look that Kiin had come to dread, and she tried to pull away from him, tried to turn so that if he hit her he would not strike face or stomach.

"I saw a whale. It is a good sign for us," Qakan said, and he let go of her arms and bent over, hands on knees to catch his breath.

He is too fat to run so hard, Kiin thought. But then something in Kiin's spirit whispered that the whale might be some message from Samiq, and she bent down to ask Qakan, "Is it s-s-still there?"

Qakan nodded and Kiin took several running steps toward the beach, but he called after her, "Wait for me, Kiin." His voice held the whine that was a sign of anger to come, and so Kiin stopped and looked back at him. "You will see it better from the cliffs," he said.

Kiin turned from the beach and began to climb the layered rocks that led up to the cliffs. She did not look back. She knew Qakan could not keep up with her, doubted that he would even try to follow her; he was too lazy to run so far.

At the top of the cliff, Kiin shielded her eyes, straining to see the whale in the waves.

"You did not wait," came Qakan's accusing voice, his words broken with hard breathing, but when she did not turn he asked, "Do you see it?"

"N-n-no," Kiin answered, but there was an uneasiness in her spirit, something within whispering a warning. Qakan had come too quickly. He had run, and Qakan did not like to run.

"I did not lie. I saw a whale," Qakan said, and the strange tone of his voice made Kiin look back at him. He was crouched low, squatting on his heels. In his eyes, Kiin saw the truth.

There was no whale. He wanted her here, on the cliffs, but not to see a whale.

Kiin had run out on a narrow extension of the cliff top, and now that Qakan was behind her, she could not get around him.

She tried to keep her eyes on the sea, but something seemed to pull her head back toward Qakan, to see what Qakan was doing.

Qakan smiled at her, his crooked smile, so much like their father's smile. "I could push you off the cliff and you would be dead," he said and laughed.

His laughter made Kiin shudder and she moved away from the edge of the cliff. "I-I w-w-will bring you much in t-trade," she said and fixed her eyes on Qakan's hands, ready to move if he moved.

"So will Kayugh's furs."

"I-I-I wi-will bring more," Kiin said, trying to move without seeming to move.

Qakan shrugged. "Perhaps," he said. "But remember what I told you about the Walrus People." His face was still red from running, but he spoke easily now, without pauses for breathing. He broke off a stem of grass and began to chew the end of it. "The Walrus People place a high value on a woman who has had a child. So, you see, you will not be worth much."

But Kiin ignored Qakan's words. She knew he spoke only to distract her.

He moves slowly, she thought. I could jump over him. . . .

Kiin looked out toward the sea and said, "W-wait, I think I s-see something." When Qakan looked, Kiin turned and began to run, but Qakan lunged toward her, and as Kiin jumped, she caught her foot on a fold of his parka.

She stumbled and Qakan grasped one of her ankles, pulling her down beside him. The fall knocked the breath from Kiin's chest, and she could not speak.

"You are afraid of me, Kiin," Qakan said and began to laugh. "Do you think I will kill you?" He crawled to her side, then straddled her and sat on her chest, pinning her arms with his knees.

A gust of wind rose from the drop of the cliffs and blew Kiin's hair across her eyes. Qakan reached into his parka and pulled out a long-bladed obsidian knife. Kiin gasped. Amgigh's knife, the one he kept carefully wrapped in the weapons corner of his sleeping place. It was one of a pair, Kiin knew, and Amgigh had taken the other with him to the Whale Hunters to give to Samiq.

"Your hair is in your eyes," Qakan said. "Let me fix it for you." He grabbed a handful and cut it close to her scalp.

Kiin's breath had returned to her body and she began to try to wiggle free, lifting her legs to hit Qakan in the back with her knees. "The s-s-spirits s-see you. They know you t-took Amgigh's knife. They-they s-see what you do-do to me. They will k-kill you."

Qakan laughed, his smile bringing up one corner of his mouth. "Not for a woman without a soul." Again, he laughed and his whole body shook with the laughter.

Qakan grabbed another handful of her hair, his knife poised to cut.

"C-cut m-m-my hair," Kiin said. "It w-will grow back. But n-n-not before we r-reach the Walrus People."

Qakan frowned and loosened his grip. Kiin took a long breath.

"You are right," Qakan said. "The Walrus People like long hair on their women." He moved his knife close to her neck. "Do you remember something else I told you about the Walrus People? Do you remember?" He pressed Amgigh's knife to her skin, and Kiin felt the sharpness of the blade. She held herself very still, but suddenly Qakan rose up and dropped down hard on her chest. Again, she could not draw a breath, could not speak, even when Qakan leaned back and pushed one hand between her legs, his cold fingers thrusting into the warmth of her woman parts.

She bucked against him, nearly throwing him from her chest,

but he caught himself and taking both hands, grabbed Kiin's hair and jerked her head up, then slammed it against the rocky ground.

The pain made Kiin cry out and Qakan laughed.

"You w-w-will be c-c-cursed, Qakan. I am w-with child," Kiin said, her teeth clenched.

"You lie," Qakan said and slid one hand into the neck of her suk.

Kiin writhed against his touch, but Qakan raised the knife and hit her hard across her face with the tang. The blow opened a cut on her cheek and blood began to flow into Kiin's left eye.

Qakan leaned back, slowly moved one hand up the inside of her thigh, and the shift of his weight released one of Kiin's arms. She put all her strength into a punch aimed at Qakan's belly, but Qakan turned as she moved, and Kiin saw that he had a rock in one hand. At the same moment as the punch landed, she felt the impact of the rock above her left temple.

Then darkness.

Qakan laughed. Again he raised himself and dropped hard on Kiin's belly. But Kiin only groaned; her eyes rolled back in her head, showing the whites beneath the partially closed lids.

He looked at the rock in his hand. There was blood smeared on the edge of the stone. Kiin's blood. Woman's blood.

He threw the stone over the cliff, waited to hear if it would hit the water. *It will mean good luck if it hits the water,* Qakan told himself. But he heard only the clatter of stone against stone.

Kiin's fault. Kiin could even curse stone.

He lifted the shell necklace she wore. It was a gift from Amgigh and Samiq, something, Qakan knew, that Kiin treasured.

He gripped the necklace until the shell beads pressed dents into his hands, then with a hard twist he broke the strands of sinew and dropped the necklace to the ground.

Again Qakan lifted himself from her body and again slammed himself down on her. A groan, only that. She was weak. She would never defeat him. He stood, looked down at her. What was she compared to him? He squatted beside her and reached out, pushed his hand up under her suk. But then he remembered her words. She was with child. A lie. When did Kiin ever tell the truth? But perhaps . . .

It would be his child, of course. His child. He stood, kicked at Kiin to see if she would open her eyes, but she only moved her head, side to side, muttered something, her words garbled as they always were.

Yes, Qakan thought, let his father laugh at him. Let Amgigh and Samiq scorn his hunting skills. Still he was a man, more a man than either of them. And in Kiin's belly perhaps there was proof of that.

He lifted his foot and pressed it down against Kiin's breasts. He could not remember that she had had a bleeding time during their journey. Perhaps she was telling the truth. Why not tell the truth if it would spare her a beating? What a joke on the Walrus People. Yes, a child, but his child. Child of a brother. Cursed, yes, they would be cursed and would be giving him gifts for that cursing!

Qakan laughed, a laugh that came up hard from his throat, clattering like the rock he had thrown from the cliff. He looked out toward the sea. His stomach growled. He looked at Kiin. Her eyes were still closed, her breathing shallow. He could carry her down, but it would not be easy. Besides he was too hungry to wait for her to wake up. And the wind was rising, bringing spray in from the sea. The cliffs were always too windy.

He shrugged. Tonight he would have to get his own food. But that would be good. He would eat. Eat! Kiin hoarded all the fish she caught, giving him a few this day, a few the next, as though he were a child. Tonight she would not stop him. Tonight he would eat.

He left Kiin on the cliff.

When Kiin awoke it was night. She tried to sit up, but a sharp pain in her back forced her to roll over first, then push herself up.

She pulled her suk close around her. Her face and head hurt, but there was no pain between her legs. Then Qakan had not taken her, had believed her when she said she was with child. Perhaps he even thought the child was his own. Perhaps that was why he did not take her. No man would wish to curse his own son.

She was relieved, but with the relief she felt fear. Qakan had easily overpowered her. Did that mean that her soul was weak? Perhaps Qakan was right in saying that her spirit was slowly slipping from her, perhaps with each word she spoke.

She stood but her head began to throb, and dropping to her hands and knees, she vomited. She vomited until there was nothing left in her stomach, then she lay back on the ground and closed her eyes.

I will stay here until morning, she thought. But then I will go some place to hide so Qakan will not find me.

For a long time, she did not move, but finally she began to notice rocks pressing against her back and legs, and she sat up, slowly, so her head would not spin. She cleared a place on the cliff then pulled up handfuls of grass to make a padding for her bed.

She sat down on the mound of grass and watched the sky. Clouds shifted and moved like sand ripples over the sliver of moon. She rubbed her eyes, pressed her hand carefully to the cut on her cheek, but then something beside her bed caught the moon's light. Kiin reached out. It was the shell necklace Samiq had given her. Qakan must have ripped it from her neck, but since it was knotted between every shell bead, only several of the smallest beads were missing.

She grabbed her amulet and felt for the carving Chagak had given her. It was still there.

Then a voice came to her. Perhaps her spirit spoke, or perhaps it was the voice of the cliffs or the sea, "You must fight Qakan. Qakan will harm too many people if you do not. You are the only one who truly knows how evil he is."

"No," Kiin answered, speaking the word aloud. "No, no, no." She would hide, would find places in the cliffs, in the hills. He would never find her.

But again, the voice came, "You must go back. You must go back."

Again Kiin told the spirit no. Her voice, clear and loud, did not break on the word. "Why should I care about Walrus People?" she asked, flinging the question out to the cliff, to the sea, to the moon. "Why should I care what evil Qakan brings to them?"

For a time there was nothing, but then the answer came, soft like a grandmother's voice, rising from around her, from the shell necklace warm in her hands, from Chagak's suk, fur smooth against her skin, from Shuganan's carving that hung at her neck: "Because they are people."

"They are not my people," Kiin said, but then bowed her head, suddenly knowing whatever spirit spoke, whether spirit of moon or wind or sea, that spirit was right.

"Tomorrow," Kiin whispered, singing the words so they would not catch in her throat, "tomorrow, I will fight Qakan again, and if I win, I will go back to my own people, and if I do not, I will tell the Walrus People the truth, no matter what Qakan does to me."

She curled her legs up into her suk and lay back on the grass. The wind caught in her hair, buffeting like a ptarmigan trapped in her mother's bird nets.

25

"**P**ush," *Qakan said to Kiin.* Kiin leaned against the stern of the ik and pushed as Qakan plunged his paddle into the water and thrust the boat out through the waves. The water was cold against Kiin's legs; rocks cut into her bare feet. Again she pushed.

Early that morning Qakan had climbed the cliffs and shook Kiin out of her sleep. "I did not touch you last night," he said when Kiin opened her eyes to look at him. "You carry my son." He said the words with belligerence, his lower lip thrust out like a child's. "It is not Amgigh's son."

Wearily, Kiin rolled away from him and pushed herself up.

"If you lied to me . . ." Qakan began.

"I did not lie," Kiin said, though she was not sure. She had missed her bleeding at the full moon, but her mother had told her that at first, until the moon was used to seeing her as woman, her bleeding times would not follow the regular ways of women.

"Push!"

Kiin pushed again and jumped to catch the thwarts as the ik slid into deep water. Once in the boat, she pulled on her suk, using the bottom edges to dry her feet and ankles.

Yes, I lied, Kiin thought. I lied, Qakan, and today, we will begin our journey back to our people. If Kayugh says I am cursed, then I am cursed. Perhaps he will let me live in the village in my own ulaq. Perhaps I can help each family with sewing and weaving. It would be better there than here or traded as slave to the Walrus People. But if I cannot find a way to go back or if you are stronger than I think you are, then I will go on, to warn the Walrus People.

So she waited as the morning passed, watched as Qakan grew tired from his paddling.

Finally, she began to fish. She had not been surprised to see that all the dried fish were gone. Qakan must have spent the whole night eating. But she would need food during the long return to her people. The dried seal meat and roots Qakan had brought for the journey were not enough, even for a normal man, and Qakan ate as much as two or three.

She uncoiled a kelp fiber fishline, tied a gorge to the end and lowered it into the water. The line jerked and Kiin brought it up, coiling it around her left hand. A small herring flipped and turned, fighting the gorge hook in its mouth. Kiin pulled the fish into the ik, slit and gutted it, then pulled the gorge out of its throat and tied the fish inside the bow of the ik, belly open so the flesh would dry in the wind.

"I am hungry," Qakan said, his voice a whine.

Kiin cut off the fish's head and handed it to him without speaking.

Qakan pulled his paddle from the sea, but before laying the paddle in the bottom of the ik, he swung it up over Kiin's head and laughed as water dripped down her neck. Kiin had learned that Qakan soon tired of the game if she pretended the water did not bother her, so she sat still, trying not to move.

Finally, Qakan laid his paddle down and began to eat the fishhead.

Kiin squeezed some of the water from her hair, then fastened a bit of fish gut to the gorge and again lowered her line.

Qakan would seldom take the ik into deeper water where Kiin

could catch halibut. Qakan stayed close to the land, skirting beaches. To avoid hunters of other tribes, he told her, but Kiin knew that the true reason was his fear of the water. It was not difficult to see the terror that whitened the corners of his eyes when the waves were too high, or the wind was too strong.

After the first two, three days they had lost sight of Tugix, then Aka, Chagak's mountain, but they passed many mountains, and it seemed that most of them had angry spirits, for clouds of smoke and sometimes the haze of ash swathed the peaks.

As they went on toward the Walrus People's villages, the valleys between mountains were often filled with ice, the ice like blue rivers which flowed from the mountains into the sea. Sometimes the ice extended so far that Qakan had to guide their boat around it, and as they passed, Kiin could feel the rush of cold wind pulling itself from the surface of the ice to settle in the bottom of the ik.

"Spirits," Qakan would whisper, his face pale and sweating, but Kiin felt no fear. If they were helping spirits, they might carry away her curse, if harmful spirits, perhaps they would sink the ik. She would drown but so would Qakan.

Kiin remembered her father's stories of the blue men who live in the ice rivers. Sometimes they would pull a man from his ikyak and take him with them into the ice. Gray Bird said he had once seen the dark form of a man frozen within a river of ice.

Sometimes the ice was like a cliff, white under the water, then blue as it rose into the sky, as though the light gave it color. At first Kiin had been afraid to look into the blue depths. How would she feel if she, like her father, saw a man frozen there? And what if the spirits decided to lock her within the ice? But then she thought, Would that be worse than to be sold as wife, carrying a curse to any man who chose her? Would it be so terrible to live within the still blue, seeing only sky and sea, gulls and otter, to hear only the sounds of the water, the groaning and cracking of the ice?

And if she did carry Qakan's child, it would be frozen within her, unable to do harm.

Kiin caught another fish, hung it beside the first. "I brought enough food for our journey," Qakan said. "But you have slowed us down. I thought you would help me paddle. If you would paddle, we would get there quicker."

"I will p-paddle," Kiin replied, meeting Qakan's eyes. He spat a mouthful of fish at her.

"Back to Tugix's island," Qakan said.

Kiin lowered her head and sighed. "N-n-no," she said, making her voice weak and trembling. "We have c-c-come too far. I d-do not know the way b-back." She raised her eyes, saw the doubt in Qakan's face. "I w-would rather help you p-paddle to the Walrus People than s-s-starve here."

Qakan scowled at her, but handed her the paddle from the bottom of the ik and crawled to the bow of the boat, then he lay back, his own paddle balanced on his belly.

Kiin paddled swiftly and willingly the rest of that morning and through the afternoon. But while she paddled, Kiin made plans, prepared herself to fight by remembering Qakan's lies and the times he had beaten her; she remembered the curse he had given her, a curse that threatened both the First Men and the Walrus People. And so she allowed her anger to grow until it filled her chest so full she could barely breathe.

Then, finally, late in that afternoon, Qakan's eyes began to close. His breathing deepened until Kiin knew he slept. Kiin pulled her paddle from the water and raised it over Qakan's head, holding her breath and waiting until the anger that filled her chest could flow into her arms and give her strength. Too late, she saw the rivulet of water drip from the paddle blade onto Qakan's head. He awoke with a jerk as Kiin swung, and his movement made her paddle glance off his head.

The ik shuddered, and Kiin braced herself against the gunwale. Qakan turned, swung his own paddle and hit Kiin in the ribs. The pain made Kiin bend double, and before she could straighten, Qakan was on her, his hands closing over her neck, stopping her breath until Kiin knew she was dying. But then he let her go. He reached into one of his packs of trade goods and pulled out a coil of babiche. He tied her ankles together and then tied her wrists behind her back, Qakan pulling the rawhide cords so tight that Kiin's fingers soon grew numb.

Again she had failed. Perhaps she was not supposed to return to the First Men; perhaps the spirits of those First Men already at the Dancing Lights saw her curse as too great. Perhaps they protected her people's village.

Yes, she could fight against Qakan, but why fight against the spirits? They would want what was best for the people. Did Kiin think her wisdom was greater than theirs?

She leaned against the side of the ik and looked toward the shore. No, she decided. She would not fight. She would go with Qakan.

They stopped early for the night, but with Qakan, Kiin had grown used to late starts and early ends to each day. Kiin pointed with her chin toward the abundance of sea animal bones at the high tide line and said, "They will make a g-good fire and s-save our oil." Qakan hesitated, but then untied her ankles and wrists.

"First help me with the ik," he said.

Kiin flexed her swollen fingers against the pain of returning feeling. Then she gripped the side of the ik and helped Qakan pull it into the grass above the beach.

They unloaded the ik and turned it over to make a shelter for themselves and the trade goods. Kiin began to pick up bones, pulling them from the sand and dumping them into a heap a short distance from the ik.

Few north sea beaches had reefs, but from the way the waves broke, Kiin knew this one did. "There m-might be octopi here," she called to Qakan. One large octopus would make a good meal, with meat left over.

Qakan looked out at the cold water and Kiin knew he was considering the trouble of launching the ik again.

"I will dry the ink sack and make it into powder for black paint. You know hunters will trade for black paint powder," she said.

"No," Qakan finally answered. "Find sea urchins. That will be enough. I have sulphur, I will start the fire."

Kiin shrugged and returned to the ik to get a gathering bag. She walked the length of the beach, and filled the bag with large, green-spined sea urchins from the edges of tide pools and niches between rocks on the tide flats. When the bag was full, she returned to the fire where Qakan was sitting eating the last of the fish she had caught that morning.

"Qakan, what will we eat t-t-tomorrow?" Kiin asked, but Qakan acted as though he did not hear her.

Kiin set the bag of sea urchins down and began cracking them with a stone. Qakan finished eating the fish and reached for the opened sea urchins. He unsheathed his sleeve knife and used the blade to scoop out the urchins' ovaries. He ate so fast that Kiin could not keep up with him. Finally he paused, his mouth full of sea urchin, and said, "I have been thinking about trading for a wife for Samiq."

When Kiin did not answer, he grabbed an opened shell from her and said, "Kayugh asked me to bring back a woman for him. Did you know that?"

Kiin kept her head lowered and broke open another sea urchin. Was Qakan telling the truth, or taunting her with a lie?

"You do not believe me?" he said. "Look for yourself. Whose sealskins are in the bow of the ik? Kayugh's and Samiq's."

Kiin remembered the bundle of hides, smooth and fine, well-tanned. Yes, they must be Kayugh's sealskins. No woman in the village prepared skins as well as Chagak. But perhaps they were the hides Amgigh had given her father for Kiin's bride price. Or perhaps Qakan had stolen them from Kayugh's ulaq.

"At first, I thought I would trade Kayugh's sealskins for an old woman," Qakan said and laughed, his laughter spraying meat from his mouth. "Some old woman who had no more sons to give, someone with rotted teeth and aching hands."

Kiin paused and laid down the stone she was using to open the sea urchins.

"More," Qakan bellowed.

Kiin set her teeth and locked her eyes to Qakan's. "The rest are mine," she said.

Qakan pushed himself to his feet, and belching, grabbed the bag of urchins from her hand. He dumped them out, flipped two of the smallest back to Kiin and holding his knife, blade up, said, "I will eat these. You should have found more."

Kiin did not answer.

Qakan sat down, broke wind with a satisfied grunt and lifted an urchin ovary to his mouth on the blade of his knife. Finally he said, "Yes, I was going to bring Samiq an old woman, but now I am thinking of a young woman, someone who likes men." He laughed. "Someone who will not want to save herself for her husband. It is a long trip back to Tugix."

Kiin looked away, toward the sea, toward the dark eastern sky. Qakan was still talking, telling her how he would bed Samiq's woman, how he would be a trader, having many women, earning his power as a trader not a hunter, not in the cold waters as a hunter. Someday he would have his own tribe, he said, a tribe of sons stretching from the Whale Hunters of the west to the Caribou People of the east.

"It is only a boast," Kiin's spirit whispered, but Kiin knew that Qakan had a strong spirit. How else could he already be a trader, his trade goods enough to make others see him as a powerful man?

Kiin's hand crept up to the amulet that hung at her neck. That afternoon when Qakan tied her wrists and ankles, he had threatened to take her amulet, but she had reminded him that any threat to her spirit was a threat to his child, and so he had allowed her to keep the amulet, and now she clung to it, clung to it and prayed that Qakan's boasts would never come true, that Samiq and her people, even the Walrus hunter who would take her as wife, would be protected.

26

$\int$ amiq fingered the spearhead that Many Whales had given him. It was an obsidian blade, narrow and as long as a man's hand.

"It will be many summers before you are skilled enough to use it well," Many Whales told him, "but you will learn, and tonight in the ceremony you will become a Whale Hunter. It is right that you take this weapon."

The old man slowly climbed out of the ulaq and once again Samiq was alone. It had been a long day of thinking, the ulaq left dark except for one small oil lamp placed on the floor, not a woman's lamp, but a hunter's lamp that could be taken in an ikyak.

Many Whales had painted Samiq's face with red ochre, and then Samiq prepared himself, singing the song that Many Whales had taught him, trying to make up a song of his own as all hunters were expected to do. But none of his thoughts would fit together to make a song; and finally his words seemed to drift away and hide themselves in the shadows of the ulaq, and his mind was filled with images of hunters taking whales with harpoons and floats made for sea lions.

Then his thoughts had strayed to Kiin, and he remembered her ability to make songs, her voice pure and clear in the singing, the words something beautiful to please the spirits. But some spirit seemed to whisper to him: You will curse your hunting by thinking of women.

So Samiq took the spearhead to his sleeping place and laid it in the baleen basket his mother had made him. He would keep it there with the blades and harpoon heads he had brought from his own people, the bundle of feathers from his first bird and a piece of hide from his first seal. He would save the spearhead until he had special need for its power. He placed the lid on the basket and held it for a moment, his fingers stroking the fine weaving wrought by his mother's hands. And he thought of the person he had become, a man of two peoples.

Living with the Whale Hunters, he had begun to think of himself as a boy, not a man. Fat Wife was always ready to correct him—his speech, his habits—and Samiq often felt that if she could, she would reach into his head and change his thoughts.

Samiq set the basket in the folds of his sleeping robe and walked back into the ulaq's main room. He stretched his arms over his head, jumped to touch the rafters of whale jawbone. He wished he could be outside, could run, could feel the wind.

Without the sun and the tides, Samiq did not know how long he had been in the ulaq, how long until the feasting and ceremony would begin. He knew it would still be light outside when the ceremony started. The end of summer was near, but the sun was still strong enough to give long days. Fewer whales were sighted now than had been in the spring, but the village's caches were already full, and when there was a sighting, one of the younger men was given the opportunity to spear the whale.

Samiq thought back over the days he had spent with Many Whales. The old man was like the sea lion, stiff and slow on land, skilled and graceful in water. His ikyak seemed to be a part of him, the paddle an extension of his arms.

Samiq had considered himself skilled with the ikyak until he saw Many Whales. Even Kayugh could not compare with the old man, and Samiq, watching, soon found that he improved greatly with his grandfather's instruction.

Many Whales took him into the roughest seas, and Samiq learned to value the flexibility of the Whale Hunters' three-piece keelson, the ikyak bending with the swells.

The Whale Hunters used a double-bladed paddle, and though at first the paddle seemed awkward in Samiq's hands, soon it was as though he had always used it, had always paddled with such ease and speed. He learned to be silent in the fog, when sound carried easily, to blend the lapping of his paddle with the rhythm of the sea. He learned to throw his spear in the highest waves, his throwing board firm and sure in his hand.

Samiq sat down, his thoughts on the whales. "Watch them in the water," the old man had said. "Watch them. Think how the whale feels to be so big, to swim far down into the sea. If you can become like a whale in your mind, you will always know how to aim your spear."

For a time then, sitting in the ulaq, Samiq tried to become the whale, swimming beneath the water, moving with the push of the sea, but then a shaft of light came from the top of the ulaq and Fat Wife's face was a round moon floating in the darkness, calling him to come.

Samiq climbed from the ulaq. He was nervous, but he held his shoulders straight as he followed Fat Wife to the beach. He could tell from the sky that the sun would soon set. Clouds west and north of Atal, the Whale Hunters' small mountain, were edged in pink.

"Sit here," Fat Wife commanded. "You will receive your marks."

Samiq looked around, wondering which woman would make the black lines that would mark his chin and proclaim him a Whale Hunter, a man.

"Stay still," Fat Wife said, and her smile reminded Samiq that she gained some pleasure in ordering his movements.

Then Many Babies was bending over him. Yes, she would be the one, Samiq thought. Her husband was Hard Rock the alananasika, chief among the whalers.

She washed Samiq's face with sea water, wiping the red of

the ochre away. With a piece of charcoal, she drew three lines down his chin.

Samiq averted his eyes as she dangled the needle before him. A fine piece of sinew was tied to the end of the needle, the sinew black with charcoal. When Many Babies drew the thread through his skin, it would leave a dark line that would mark him forever as a Whale Hunter.

Many Babies grasped his face in her left hand and pinched the skin where the needle would enter. The prick of the needle was quick as she thrust it through the fold of skin, but Samiq shuddered at the sound of the thread as it was pulled through.

Fat Wife bent close to Samiq's face, the woman watching as Many Babies pushed the needle again into the skin, and after each puncture, Fat Wife dabbed away the blood with a ragged bit of sealskin.

When she had finished the first line of marks down the center of Samiq's chin, Many Babies pushed her thumb into his mouth, held the flesh away from his teeth, and thrust the needle into the skin to the left of the first line. She made three lines in all, the lines side by side, down the center of Samiq's chin.

The pain made Samiq clench his teeth, and soon the muscles in his neck and shoulders began to ache, but finally the marking was complete. Many Babies blackened Samiq's chin with charcoal and said to him, "Leave this two days." Then Fat Wife was smoothing seal oil reddened with ochre over the rest of his face.

Samiq stood, wanting to join the other men who had begun to gather around the cooking pits. "No," Fat Wife said, pressing him down. "Wait for Many Whales."

The women left, and Samiq sat alone. His chin stung, and beads of blood that still seeped from each needle hole dried and made his skin itch. Samiq clasped his hands together to keep from scratching. "You have suffered worse things," his inner voice said, and Samiq forced himself to watch the men as they practiced dance steps on the beach.

Each man wore his chigadax and most also wore a long otter

skin apron that hung nearly to the ankles. Every hunter had a wooden hat, the whaler's hat, decorated with feathers and seal whiskers. Samiq studied the men carefully, and seeing the manner in which they carried themselves, decided how he would dance and walk when he was allowed to join them.

The women fed the hunters, but still Many Whales did not come. Samiq waited as the hunters ate. He had not eaten since the night before, and his empty belly was like a stone pressing against his spine.

After the men had eaten, the children were fed. Watching the small ones dance around the cooking pits, Samiq thought of his sister, Wren. She would grow up happy, loved. But then his thoughts went once more to Kiin, to the times he had found her bruised, bleeding from her father's beatings.

But now even Kiin was happy. Samiq knew his mother would treat Kiin as a daughter, nor was Chagak one to be angry or cross as were so many of the Whale Hunter women who seemed driven by some spirit to destroy the calm of the ulaq with their loudness and arguing.

"Samiq!"

The voice startled him, and he looked up to see a huge misshapen face, something that looked like it was carved from a giant curl of wood. The face was as tall as a man, head to knees, and was colored in reds and blues. The eyes were painted on, but in the wide slits at the bottom of the nose Samiq thought he saw the glow of someone watching. Man or spirit? Samiq wondered. But then he noticed that the face had ordinary man's feet beneath the curve of its giant chin. And when the face said, "Come!", the voice was much like Hard Rock's voice.

Samiq followed until they came to Many Whales who sat on a feather robe that had been spread over the top of a boulder. The masked one pushed Samiq to his knees, but Samiq's eyes were drawn to Many Whales. The old man seemed to have gained strength and size as he sat atop the boulder, his feather-trimmed chigadax and tall seal gut boots glowing pink and gold in the light of the long sunset.

He held a carved staff in one hand and made a chant in words that Samiq did not understand.

Many Whales handed Samiq a bundle, an otter skin ceremonial apron on top, a whale-tongue-skin chigadax at the bottom. "Stand!"

The other hunters who stood near Many Whales pulled the apron from Samiq's bundle and slipped it around his waist, stripping his grass apron from him. Then someone pulled the chigadax on over Samiq's head.

"There are boots, also," Many Whales said, leaning forward, his shining eyes visible even under the shadow of his wooden hat.

Two of the men helped Many Whales from the rock, and the masked one handed him something wrapped in a sea lion skin. The shape was evident and Samiq held his breath as Many Whales unfolded the skin to reveal a gleaming wooden hat. It had been painted with red and black stripes. No sea lion whiskers bent from the ivory overlaid seam at the back. Those, his grandfather had told him, were given each time the hunter took a whale. Many Whales' hat had more whiskers than any other hunters' hat, even more than Hard Rocks'.

Many Whales held the new hat over Samiq's head, again chanted strange words. Then bending closer to Samiq he said, "Black is for the whale. Red is for blood." He paused, looked at the hunters gathered around them. He placed the hat on Samiq's head, lightly touched the tattoos on Samiq's chin. "You are Whale Killer, a man of the Whale Hunter people," Many Whales said.

Samiq reached up to touch the hat. The wood was cool and smooth under his fingers. Samiq, Whale Killer, he thought, a man of two people. Samiq. Whale Killer. And in the midst of his joy, he felt a sudden sadness, and he reminded himself that what he did was done for the First Men, that he obeyed Kayugh. Then he looked again at Many Whales, the old man truly grandfather, and Samiq held himself straight, squaring his shoulders.

No one spoke, and in the stillness Samiq could hear the strong beat of his own heart. Then suddenly, louder than his heartbeat, Samiq heard the pounding of the watcher's signal. The men around him turned, and Samiq saw a young boy running toward them.

"Whale! Whale!"

The masked one suddenly threw the mask from his body and Samiq saw that it was Hard Rock, the alananasika. He wore only his apron under the mask and as he ran toward his ikyak, his wife Many Babies hurried from their ulaq bringing Hard Rock's chigadax. As he dressed, the boy came to him, his thin voice carrying to Samiq's ears.

"It is there, close to the shore."

Samiq looked toward the sea. Even in the gray of the early night, he could see the whale; the mist of its blowing was white against the sea. Hard Rock climbed into his ikyak and sent the small craft into the waves with quick thrusts of his paddle. Samiq could no longer see the whale, but he watched Hard Rock until the ikyak was only a small darkness in the water.

Samiq thought he saw an arm raise, a lance fly, but he could not be sure, and finally he turned back to Many Whales.

Crooked Bird, a young man having the same number of summers as Samiq, one who had laughed as Samiq learned the first lessons of whale hunting, looked at Samiq and Samiq noticed the fast beating of the veins in the man's neck, the tightness of his fists, and Samiq realized that Hard Rock had chosen to go for the whale, had not allowed one of the new hunters to gain experience and perhaps the honor of taking a whale. But Hard Rock was alananasika; who could argue with his choices?

Then Many Whales called to Samiq, the old man laying his hand on Samiq's shoulder.

"Whale Killer," Many Whales said, "you have been given a great honor. The whale has recognized your manhood. You will be a great hunter."

And then, as though some spirit drew his eyes, Samiq again

looked at Crooked Bird. Crooked Bird's lips were curled, his teeth clenched, and something in Samiq knew that Crooked Bird's anger was not directed at Hard Rock, but at him, the newest hunter, the hunter whose manhood ceremony had been honored by a whale.

27

ven before the ceremony fire had burned down to coals, Hard
Rock returned. "The whale gave itself to my spear," he said,
a smile lifting one corner of his mouth.

It was time now for the retrievers to go out, to follow the
whale until the poison in Hard Rock's spear had time to work.

But Many Whales looked beyond the man to Samiq, and
Samiq met his grandfather's eyes. "Hard Rock's spear is in the
whale," the old man said, "but your magic brought him to us.
You must also become one with the whale."

Samiq saw the anger in Hard Rock's eyes, and he waited for
him to protest, but the man said nothing, only turned his back
and walked to the small whaler's hut, the place where the
alananasika used his powers to draw the whale to the Whale
Hunters' retrievers, to keep the whale from swimming to another village.

That night, the men built a small hut for Samiq. It was close
to Hard Rock's hut, and when it was completed, Samiq went
inside, as Many Whales told him, secluding himself to become
the whale, to sicken as the whale must sicken.

It was not an easy thing to become something he was not, an
animal he knew little about. Sometimes, Samiq dreamed of
being an otter, of sleeping in the sea, wound in kelp, the waves
his bed, and once he had dreamed he was in his ikyak and the

ikyak had grown legs and tail. In that dream Samiq had truly been otter, but now, his belly ached with hunger and his mouth was parched for water, and in his discomfort he could be nothing but a man.

How long would he be in the hut, one day, two days? How long since he had eaten? Since the day before his ceremony. He should sleep, though sleep seemed elusive, pushed away by his need to become whale.

But perhaps the only way to become whale was in the same way he had become otter—through his dreams.

Samiq, Whale Killer, closed his eyes, let his thoughts go to the cold gray of the sea. He saw the waves, dark as shale, solid, shining like wet rock. But then that image was swallowed by the pain of his hunger until the pain grew into something that stretched beyond himself, and it pulled him down, into the darkness, through the waves, away from the wind. The quietness pressed into his ears, the darkness into his eyes, and he was at peace. But then he heard the deep, hard roaring of other whales, the low voices of blues, the higher calls of the minke, the killer whales, their song the song of a pack, each voice a different pitch so even a few sounded like many.

Something forced him from the depths up to the warmth of the sun, and he suddenly knew the place that held Hard Rock's spear, felt the pain of poison traveling through his body. With each movement, each twist, the poison slowed his heart, and the pain spread: to his belly, to the joints of his flukes, even to the great muscles that moved his tail.

Safety lay in the deep parts of the sea. He would surface for air, then dive, but with each dive he had less strength until he could not dive at all. The waves moved against him, hurt him as they pressed into his skin, but he had to stay at the top, near the wind, near the wind. . . .

Something cut his lip. A small pain among many pains, but he could not move.

"Whale Killer."

The rocks gouged into his belly, tore through his skin. There was no water and the weight of his body crushed in on itself. He could not breathe, could not breathe, could not breathe. . . .

"Whale Killer."

He opened his eyes and looked into Fat Wife's face.

"Whale Killer, the whale is here. Come. You must eat a hunter's portion."

Samiq shook his head trying to understand Fat Wife's words.

"The whale," she said. "It is on the beach."

Samiq stood, and leaning on Fat Wife's arm, he walked into the brightness of the day. The huge carcass lay on the beach, the whaler's line still through the upper lip. Already the men had begun to lay the whale open, exposing the thick white layer of blubber under the dark skin.

And for a moment Samiq looked away, unable to bear the sight of the flaying, the cutting of that which he had been.

In the next few days, there were five sightings. Three whales were taken. The beach was slippery with blood, and new storage pits were filled with meat, more new ones dug.

"Never have so many whales been taken," Many Whales said as he and Samiq watched the women working over the cooking pits. "I have spoken to Hard Rock," Many Whales continued. "He has agreed that you should be the hunter if another whale is sighted."

Samiq turned in amazement. "Hard Rock has said this?"

The old man smiled. "Yes. He has also said that there will be no more sightings this summer. He saw that in his last fasting."

Samiq laughed. During the last fasting, Samiq had requested to go with the retrievers, the men who went after the whale once it had been speared. Many Whales did not want him to go, but Hard Rock had intervened saying that his own power had always brought the whale before; this time would be no

different. There was no need for Samiq to fast. Samiq had been
allowed to go.

The three retrievers had followed the whale for two days.
Samiq's place was in the second ikyak, and he stayed back as
Many Whales had taught him, waiting until the man in the first
ikyak, Dying Seal, saw the whale.

"It will make circles," Many Whales had told Samiq. "And it
will cry like a small child cries, a noise like 'oogh . . . oogh.'
You must learn to listen for this sound or you will think it is only
the sea talking to the mountains."

Suddenly, Samiq had seen the black hump of the whale's
back, and he watched Dying Seal, the man maneuvering with
his paddle in one hand, his other hand on his throwing board,
fingers wrapped tightly over the board, his arm partially cocked.
The spear was attached to the ikyak with a long coil of braided
kelp, and Samiq saw that Dying Seal had not bound the stone
tip to the shaft, thus leaving the weapon blunted, to be used as
a tester to see if the whale still lived.

After watching the whale for some time, Dying Seal raised his
arm over his head, and pulling his arm back nearly to the stern
of the ikyak he had hurled the spear. On impact, the blunted
weapon hit the whale and fell into the sea, then Dying Seal
pulled the spear back through the water, coiling the line as he
pulled.

The whale did not move.

Dying Seal fitted the spear shaft into his throwing board and
threw once more. Again the whale did not move.

"He is dead!" Dying Seal shouted, and Samiq moved his
ikyak closer, watching as Dying Seal slit the animal's lip and
strung a braided kelp cord through it, the cord as thick as
Samiq's wrist. Dying Seal held the line in his hand and threw it
to Samiq. Samiq turned his ikyak back toward shore and attached the line to his stern, then threw the excess line to the
third retriever, Crooked Bird.

Crooked Bird missed the first toss, and the line slipped down the side of the ikyak into the sea. Bending to grab it, Crooked Bird upset his ikyak, floated upside down in the water. Samiq suppressed a smile and pulled the line back in, coiling it to throw again, waiting until Crooked Bird righted himself, his chigadax wet, his lashes dripping water to his cheeks. Dying Seal did not laugh, but Samiq had seen a smile on the man's face when Crooked Bird was still in the water.

Again Samiq threw the line and Crooked Bird caught it with one hand, steadying his ikyak with the blade of his paddle. They pulled together, hauling the whale through the water, singing as they paddled, honor to the whale, honor to the hunter, honor to the Whale Hunters. Who could match them in skill? Who could match them in bravery?

When they reached the shore, Many Babies brought Hard Rock from his hut. The days without food and water had drawn his face, making him look like an old man, and Samiq wondered if he, too, had appeared feeble and old after the days he spent in the hut, if perhaps to become a whale, a man gave not only a few days of dreams, but also years of his life.

The people stood and watched as Hard Rock cut the harpoon from the side of the whale. He cut out a large portion of meat also, the swelling caused by the wound. Hard Rock cut deeply, then he took the chunk of flesh up the beach to bury it. The poison that killed whales was also able to kill men.

28

"No," *Many Whales said to* Samiq.
Samiq paced from one side of Many Whales' ulaq
to the other then stopped to squat in front of his grandfather.
"Only a trading trip," Samiq said. "Only that. To trade oil and
meat. We have more than we need." He did not say what he
truly wanted, to return to Kayugh and his mother, to Amgigh
and perhaps be given another night with Kiin. He was now a
man, felt the strength of that manhood, wanted Kayugh to see
what he had become, wanted Kiin . . . wanted Kiin . . .
wanted Kiin. . . .

"You are one of us, now," Many Whales said. "Perhaps next
summer we will make a trading trip. Next summer or the summer after that. Perhaps then we will go to trade. Or perhaps
Kayugh and your brother will come here."

"You promised that I would be here among you for a year,"
Samiq said and felt his heart beating hard, pushing heat into his
ears, throbbing against his eardrums. "Then I would go back to
teach my people."

Anger snapped from Many Whales' eyes, and he replied,
"They are not your people! You belong to us. You will stay with
us. Perhaps at times you will visit to trade. That is all. And then,
in many years, when you have become a skilled hunter, then

you will be told the secrets of our poisons, the manner in which we call the whales to our shores.

"Already you have sat in the alananasika's hut. How many other young hunters have done so? Only you."

Many Whales leaned forward and rudely pointed at Samiq with two long and bony fingers. "What is the first thing a hunter learns?" he asked. "What is the thing even boys know? A hunter must wait, must be patient."

Samiq's anger made his words thick and hard in his throat and he said, "I ask only to fulfill the promise given to my father. Among the First Men words spoken are promises to be kept." Samiq waited, watching his grandfather's face for the telling signs of anger: the rapid pulse at neck or temple, the subtle coloring of jaw and cheek. But the anger had faded from the old man's eyes and now he looked small, shrunken, as if the argument had taken a portion of his life.

And Samiq wondered if this man, a man who could not be trusted, was truly his grandfather. How had his mother, Chagak, conceived a child from the spirit of these people? And Samiq closed his eyes against the uncleanness he suddenly felt within himself.

"Words are only words," the old man said softly. "What is in the heart is what is true. All men know that promises may be of the heart, or not. The one who hears is the one who must decide. The words I spoke were the best way for me to bring my grandson home to his true people. The truth was in my heart. Perhaps Kayugh knew that. Perhaps I saw the truth in his heart also. Perhaps he is willing to wait many years to learn to hunt the whale. Perhaps, he would give you to me for only the hope of learning. Perhaps that is Kayugh's truth.

"You know that Kayugh is not your true father, that he came to the Seal Hunters after your father's death. Amgigh is his son, not you. Does it seem so strange that he is willing to trade one who is not true son for the hope of learning to hunt the whale?

"What is the truth in your own heart? Where do you belong? Will you go back to Kayugh unable to teach him? Will you return to the Seal Hunters to weave baskets? Or will you stay here and become alananasika, learn the poisons and the chants?"

The old man's words pounded against Samiq like the waves pound the cliffs of the First Men's beach. The ache was so deep that he could give no answer and he finally stood and walked to his sleeping place, but as he reached his curtains, he heard Fat Wife's words, nearly gentle: "There is too much meat for us. We have enough for two, three winters. Ask the hunters to trade with the First Men. Tell them to trade generously."

"Perhaps a trading trip," the old man mumbled. "I will speak to the other hunters. But Whale Killer stays here. I do not want him to go back. It is too soon."

Anger burned, clogged Samiq's throat with its heat. So, in spite of the ceremony, in spite of the whales his spirit had brought in, he was man, but not man, his opinions amounting to nothing.

How many seals did it take to give enough oil for one man for a year? Twenty-five, thirty? Without Samiq's hunting, and with Qakan useless, his people would have trouble bringing in enough seals. If the Whale Hunters would be willing to trade whale oil for knives, for caribou sinew. . . .

Samiq saw Fat Wife glance toward him, but Samiq looked away and quickly entered his sleeping place. He picked up the basket in which he kept his spearheads. Running his hands against the basket's smoothly woven sides, he thought of his mother's hands also touching the basket, and he thought of what Many Whales had said about Kayugh. Kayugh was not his father. But was not a man who raised a boy, fed him, taught him to hunt, a true father?

Samiq pulled on his parka, not the new one Fat Wife had made him, but the one his mother had sewn him from puffin skins. He walked from his sleeping place to the climbing log without looking at Fat Wife or Many Whales, left the ulaq without speaking to them.

He cut up the side of the hill that rose above Hard Rock's

ulaq and through the long ryegrass that grew chest high from the edge of the beach until the grass gave way to crowberry heather and the first mosses that crowded the rocky hillsides.

He heard the whisper before he saw the hand, heard the hiss of words, "Be quiet," before the hand grasped his wrist and pulled him down into the grass. Then he was looking into Speckled Basket's dark eyes.

She was naked, her apron folded and laying on the grass beside her, her suk under her like a sleeping mat. Her mouth was curled into a smile.

"Usually I wait for Crooked Bird," she said, "but he did not come today."

Samiq jerked his hand away from her grasp, stood, but Speckled Basket looked up at him through her eyelashes, pursed her lips into a pout.

"You are a man now," she said and brushed her fingertips against her chin. "You have hunted whales. Are you afraid of women?"

Yes, he was a man, Samiq thought. No matter what Many Whales thought. He was a man. Samiq squatted beside Speckled Basket, reached out to cup one of her small breasts in his hand. She reached up under his parka, began to stroke the insides of his thighs. He almost stood, almost pushed away. His inside voice whispered, "What will you do if Many Whales finds out?"

But then he let his eyes follow his hands, and he smelled the warm woman smell of Speckled Basket as she spread her knees. Why should he care what Many Whales thought? Did the old man care about him?

29

hen they had argued, Samiq had known the hardness of the man who was his grandfather. And now, before the hunters of the village, he again felt the man's stubbornness, a hardness covered by persuasive words.

"We trade then?" Many Whales asked.

No one answered, and Samiq thought that everyone agreed. Some of the men had already gotten to their feet, eyes scanning the horizon, watching the sea, testing the sky. But then, Hard Rock stood, several men standing close to him, and Samiq, watching Many Whales, saw the old man stiffen, a sadness in his eyes.

"You are wrong," Hard Rock said. His words were low and soft, but forceful, and Samiq felt the thrust of them even where he stood at the back of the circle of men.

"The women must work harder, drying the meat and storing oil so we will eat for many months. Perhaps next year there will be no more whales."

But Many Whales answered quietly, "We will trade meat for meat. Seal for whale."

"There is no argument in that," Hard Rock continued, "but what of the oil? Seal oil is nothing. Or will you trade bird grease for our whale oil?"

Samiq felt the beginning of defeat in the argument and

waited, his breath tight in his chest. His people needed the meat. The oil even more.

"Will you take baskets?" came the insult.

Many Whales did not answer.

"Whale Killer," Hard Rock called, and Samiq raised his eyes to meet Hard Rock's stare. "What can your people trade for oil?"

Samiq looked at Many Whales, but there was no answer in the old man's eyes, and Samiq knew he must give his own answer. "The First Men have always been traders," he began slowly. "You have traded with them. I do not need to remind you about the things stored in their ulas. I do not need to tell you about the sealskins packed with fish. Sinew of caribou, strong and fine as woman's hair. Seal oil and meat. Baskets. Healing roots." He shrugged. "Ivory, obsidian as well. My brother makes fine knives." He drew the knife Amgigh had given him from the scabbard at his waist and held it up so the men could see the long black obsidian blade.

An intake of breath, silence, then the sudden babble of many voices.

But once again Hard Rock spoke. His words were harsh, and Samiq suddenly realized that the argument was not over the trading. The Whale Hunters did not need so much whale meat, and to trade with the First Men was a time for celebration and feasting. The argument was over whose voice would rule the people. Many Whales was once a great hunter, but now he could no longer take whales. His value was in teaching his skills, sharing his wisdom. But Hard Rock was a hunter, now bringing more whales than any other hunter ever had. He was the rightful chief.

Samiq studied his grandfather's face. The old man's eyes were closed, his hands clasped loosely in his lap.

Hard Rock still stood, and now he looked at the men gathered around him. Some of the men stared out toward the sea; others sifted the beach gravel between their fingers.

They do not want the choice, Samiq thought. It is too difficult.

"I will not trade," Hard Rock finally said. "My portions will stay in the village. But each man must choose for himself. I will not decide for anyone but myself."

This is the fair thing, Samiq thought. Each man must decide what he will do. And he felt a greater respect for Hard Rock, and he understood why Many Whales had closed his eyes, understood that Hard Rock was worthy to be leader.

The men left, some walking to the stream, others gathering at the edge of the sea. Samiq watched his grandfather, waited as Many Whales sat with eyes still closed.

Images of Speckled Basket as she lay beside him in the grass suddenly crowded in to fill Samiq's mind, to cloud his thinking.

When Samiq had returned to the ulaq, Fat Wife had squinted her eyes at him and told him Many Whales had gone to speak to the men, that Samiq should join them, but before Samiq was able to leave, Fat Wife circled him, chortling as she brushed bits of grass from the feathers of Samiq's parka.

She said nothing, but Samiq felt his cheeks begin to burn, and as Samiq climbed from the ulaq, Fat Wife called after him, "Next time have Speckled Basket pick the grass from your parka, then Many Whales will never know."

And remembering her words, Samiq's face again burned. How did she know it was Speckled Basket? Did the woman speak to spirits?

Many Whales cleared his throat and opened his eyes, and Samiq's thoughts were drawn back to his grandfather. What would Many Whales think when he found that Samiq had disobeyed him? How could Samiq defend himself? What man did not need a woman? But what hunter did not deny himself that pleasure to strengthen his power for hunting? No wonder Many Whales did not consider Samiq a man. A man did not let his anger dictate his actions. A man practiced control in all things.

"They have left?" Many Whales asked Samiq.

"Yes, Grandfather," Samiq said and found he could not meet his grandfather's eyes. He had not only disobeyed, but also cost his grandfather the leadership of the Whale Hunter people. He had never considered himself to be selfish, but suddenly all his anger seemed foolish, and the remembrance of his time with Speckled Basket was like a rock lodged in the center of his chest.

But then Samiq's inside voice said, "What you did with Speckled Basket was the action of a boy, not a man, but your concern for your own people is not a selfish concern. Each man must consider the needs of his people. Why else hunt? Is your life worth nothing more than seal meat and oil? No, you hunt for your people, so they might live. There is no selfishness in that."

"You understand?" Many Whales asked, and it seemed to Samiq as though Many Whales had also heard Samiq's inside voice.

"Yes," Samiq answered.

"He will be a good leader," Many Whales continued, and Samiq realized that his grandfather spoke of Hard Rock.

"Hard Rock makes his own way, leaving others to follow or not," Many Whales said.

"They would have done what you asked," Samiq answered.

"Yes," the old man replied. "But it was time. This is the best way. No one was dishonored."

Samiq stood and waited as the old man pushed himself to his feet.

"You understand that there will be little whale oil or meat to trade with your people, that the alananasika's portion is the largest and if others trade their meat, they cannot be assured that Hard Rock will share with their families during the winter?"

Samiq nodded.

"You understand why Hard Rock questioned you?"

Samiq smiled. "I am of the Seal Hunters."

"No," Many Whales answered. "That is not the reason." He cleared his throat and adjusted the collar of his parka. "As a man grows old, he becomes wise in the ways of others. He learns to watch the eyes, the set of the jaw, the working of the fingers. I have watched Hard Rock. He is afraid the whales have come because of you. That is why he says you will be the hunter if another whale comes. He wants to see if you have the power to call in another whale, and if a whale does come, Hard Rock wants to see if you have skill enough to take it.

"Most years many of the whales speared do not die or are washed to another beach. Many times the hunter cannot get close enough to set his spear, or if he does, the whale overturns his ikyak. This year, every whale speared has been taken. Someone has great power. Hard Rock is afraid it is you."

30

*S*amiq was the first in the village to see the sighting fires, and
the young boys who watched for the fires had only begun to
call when Samiq joined them, crying, "Whale! Whale!"

He met his grandfather at the top of the ulaq, the old man
squinting at the lookout's fire, and when Samiq was close
enough to hear, Many Whales said, "You are the whale hunter.
The whale hunter does not call out. Come inside. Fat Wife has
your chigadax."

Samiq took his spears from the weapons corner of the ulaq,
and Many Whales handed him the carved ivory box that held
the poison Samiq would put beneath the spearheads. Samiq
tied the heads on with strands of sinew. The sinew would break
once the harpoon entered the body of the whale, leaving the
poisoned tip to fester deep in the whale's flesh.

He pulled on his chigadax and for a brief moment clasped
the amulet that hung from his neck.

Many Whales placed his hand on Samiq's wrist. "I saw the
spouting," the old man said. "It is the low wide spout of a
humpback. You could not ask for a better whale to take first
time out. But watch for his flukes. They are long and he will use
them like a man uses his arms." He released Samiq's wrist. "Be
strong," he said.

Then Samiq climbed from the ulaq. The people waited for

him, staying back a small distance as he walked to his ikyak. Samiq noticed that Hard Rock was not among the people, but Samiq lifted his head and walked as a hunter should walk, eyes on the sea, spears heavy in his right hand. He was a whale hunter, and for the first time since coming to his grandfather's ulaq, he felt he had a place in the Whale Hunters' village.

Samiq carried his ikyak into the water and climbed in, stretching his legs out before him. He pulled the hatch skirting close around his chest, fastening it over his shoulder with the braided cord Fat Wife had made. He lashed his spears to the top of the ikyak and pushed himself out into the ocean with his paddle.

Once free of the turbulence of the shore, he skimmed easily in the sea, scanning the water from the top of each swell. For a long time he saw nothing, and he wondered if he had taken too long in dressing, in launching his ikyak. But then he saw the widening circle of bubbles, the foaming just beneath the surface, and he steadied his ikyak, the paddle nearly vertical in the water, Samiq ready to turn or dart forward. Suddenly the water darkened, and Samiq knew the whale was breaking the surface.

As Many Whales had said, it was a humpback, its long, white-edged flippers pale against the water. The whale came slowly, turning as it rose, showing the ridge of its back. The water roared, and the sound was immense, hammering against Samiq's ears. Samiq moved his ikyak forward and arched his arm back, ready to fling the first spear.

But then the largeness of the animal, the churning of the water, made Samiq unsure of his skills. The whale was a mountain, and Samiq was suddenly only a boy, and he realized how small his ikyak was against the sea, how weak against the whale. He tightened his hand over his throwing board, but could not make his arm move, could not throw the spear.

Then the whale was again deep in the water.

Samiq shook with disappointment. You are a child, he told himself. Only a boy, afraid to be a hunter. Perhaps your grandfather is right. You should return to the Seal Hunters and weave baskets. But then he remembered something else his grandfather had told him: that many men fail the first time they go out to hunt the whale. That even Hard Rock had turned his ikyak and fled from his first whale.

So Samiq pushed away the fear that had settled into his stomach like a rock, and again he held his harpoon ready. He spoke to himself, not in anger, but as if he were speaking to another hunter, with kindness, with encouragement.

"The whale might come again. You are strong. Be ready. Be ready."

He paddled his ikyak toward the northern horizon, taking his bearing from the yellow haze of the sun and the gray line of the shore, and again he saw the darkening of the water. Again he saw the sea turn green as the whale neared the surface, but this time Samiq drew close, taking the chance that the whale would flip his ikyak.

Samiq raised the spear, holding his ikyak steady with the paddle, stiffening his fingers on the throwing board as the animal broke the surface. For a moment, Samiq's eyes were on his ikyak, on the water that rushed up with the whale and flooded over the bow. The water was like the surf in a storm, and it forced the ikyak down like a sea lion diving. The sea covered the bow, covered the bindings that held Samiq's other spears. Samiq swung his paddle back, forcing it into the white foam, churning the water until the bow of his ikyak pulled itself up.

Then the whale turned, exposing a white side, and Samiq forgot about his ikyak, forgot all things except the whale. He tightened his hand on his spear thrower, leaned back against the stern of his ikyak and hurled, aiming, as Many Whales had told him, so his spear would hit beneath the flipper.

It was not a beautiful throw. The spear spun then wobbled, caught in the foam, but some spirit seemed to carry it to the whale, and Samiq thought he heard the animal moan as the spearhead entered its body. The heavy layer of blubber under the whale's dark skin closed around the spear shaft, and a thick gush of red pumped from the wound as the whale dove, leaving a slick of oil and blood on the surface of the water.

Samiq fought to keep his ikyak from turning over in the froth from the whale's dive. He pulled a sealskin float from its ties on the top of his ikyak, made sure a ballast rock was firmly attached to the float and hurled it into the water where he last saw the whale. Then he turned as quickly as he could, pushing his ikyak toward the shore with long, hard strokes, the waves giving him speed. Hunters were standing on the beach, and as he approached them, Samiq lifted his paddle over his head, the signal that the whale had been hit. Several men climbed into their ikyan, pushing them into the sea, paddling out toward the whale. But Samiq went to the alananasika's hut, to give himself to the whale as he wanted the whale to give itself to the Whale Hunters. Gift for gift. And in his becoming, Samiq gave thanks to the whale, to the animal that would lend its flesh so the Whale Hunters could live.

It was the third day. Samiq marked the time by the noises of the village. He had become whale again, felt himself sicken, knew he was near death. But now, suddenly, he was only himself. What had happened?

He waited, listening. Yes, there were voices coming from the beach. He heard Hard Rock and Dying Seal. They had returned. Was the whale now on the beach, or had it been lost?

Suddenly the door flap of the hut was drawn back and Many Whales stood in the opening. The light that shone around the old man blotted out his face, and Samiq could see only the outline of his grandfather's thin arms and legs, the hunch of his shoulders.

He stood without speaking, and finally Samiq asked, "The whale is beached?"

"Yes," Many Whales said quietly, still standing in the doorway, the old man making no move to help Samiq stand.

"It is time for me to remove the poison?"

"Yes."

Samiq stood, suddenly uneasy. There was a harshness in his grandfather's manner that Samiq did not understand.

Many Whales turned and Samiq followed him from the hut, but Samiq stopped at his first sight of the beach, for there was no whale.

"There," Many Whales said, gesturing toward Samiq's ikyak, "go to your whale."

Samiq turned toward the old man, seeking the meaning of his grandfather's words. Several other hunters had gathered, Hard Rock with a broad smile on his face.

"Your grandfather tells you to go to your whale," Hard Rock said. "But I say, 'Stay here.' The Seal Hunters will recognize your spear will they not? You have banded it to match your seal harpoons. Surely, they know not to eat your poison."

But Dying Seal laid a hand on Samiq's shoulder and said, "The choice you made is a choice every hunter makes, to feed his people. You have power. We have never seen such power."

But Hard Rock pushed past Dying Seal, spat on the ground near Dying Seal's feet and looked into Samiq's eyes. He spoke low so Samiq heard the growl of anger under his words. "You will never be alananasika. Your power is nothing. Do not think you can rule people like you rule whales!"

Hard Rock turned and the others followed, leaving Samiq and Many Whales alone on the beach. And Samiq felt as though he were still in the dream of his becoming, as though the world that his eyes saw was not real. He had not called the whale to the First Men's beach. What man had power to do such a thing?

"I did not . . ." Samiq began, but Many Whales cut off his words.

"Will you stay or go?" Many Whales asked.

"I still have that choice?"

"Yes."

For a moment Samiq let himself think of Kiin, of his mother, of the First Men's village, but then he remembered his promise to Kayugh, to Amgigh. There was still much he needed to learn about hunting whales.

"I will stay," Samiq said.

Many Whales nodded.

"I did not send the whale . . ." Samiq said, but Many Whales again cut off Samiq's words.

"You are hungry?"

Samiq drew in a long breath. "Yes," he said.

"I will have Fat Wife bring you something."

Many Whales walked toward the ulas, but then he turned, his eyes now softer. "Samiq," he said, "a man's power is not only what he knows it to be, but also what others think it to be." And then in a quiet voice that spun out in the wispy fog that was settling over the beach, he said, "If the Seal Hunters were my people, I would have done the same."

31

Amgigh *was in his ikyak* near the kelp beds when he saw the whale. It was a humpback, large, swimming in circles, and the froth of its wake was dark, as though the blackness of the animal's skin colored the water.

Amgigh's breath caught in his throat and the pulse of his heart quickened to pound hard along the veins of his arms. A whale! Food for days. Food and oil. He turned his ikyak and paddled quickly back to the beach, shouting as he neared the shore, shouting until Gray Bird, Kayugh, First Snow and Big Teeth were all on the beach.

"Whale, whale, whale, whale!" Amgigh shouted. "A humpback. Bring floats, bring harpoons."

When he saw that the men had understood, he turned his ikyak back toward the kelp beds. He did not realize he was holding his breath until he again saw the whale, still circling, then he drew in air, holding it in his lungs until his heart slowed and his arms no longer trembled.

He kept his ikyak beside the whale, far enough away to avoid the animal's foaming wake, but circling as the whale circled until Amgigh saw his father's ikyak coming toward him on the water.

"The others follow," Kayugh called and pulled his ikyak next to Amgigh's.

Amgigh looked at his father, saw the older man shake his head, saw the joy shining in his eyes. Amgigh's chest was suddenly filled with pride. For some reason the spirits had sent this whale to him. Perhaps to show that he was as good a hunter as Samiq, that he of the two brothers was the one who should have been sent to the Whale Hunters. Or perhaps to make up for the loss of his wife. Who could say? The whale was a gift. Why question a gift?

"They bring floats?" Amgigh asked. The whale, being humpback, would sink once it died, and unless a storm brought sudden strong waves, the carcass would stay in the sea, tangled and lost beneath the kelp.

"Yes," Kayugh answered.

A call came and both men turned, seeing Gray Bird, Big Teeth and First Snow behind them, seal bladder floats lashed front and back to each ikyak.

"What do we do first?" Amgigh asked.

"It is your whale, you decide," Kayugh answered.

Amgigh felt a prickling of fear at his father's reply, but kept his eyes on the whale, watching as the whale's circles grew smaller, his path in the sea less sure.

"He is dying," Amgigh said. "Perhaps his meat will be no good."

"Perhaps," said Kayugh. "But we will use the oil in our lamps."

"Yes," Amgigh said, his voice low.

"So . . ." Kayugh said.

"So," Amgigh answered, taking a long breath, then waiting until the other men had drawn their ikyan close. "First, each man should throw two harpoons and each harpoon should have two floats." He paused and looked at his father then at Big Teeth. Big Teeth was smiling but seemed to have no objection. His father's face was serious, as though he were concentrating on what Amgigh said. The fear that hovered close in Amgigh's chest suddenly seemed more like excitement, like the feeling a man has when he first sights the dark head of a seal above the waves. Amgigh raised his voice and turned his ikyak slightly so he was talking to all the men, not just his father. "Keep one harpoon tied to your ikyak with a long coil of line."

"The whale will pull us down with him into the sea," Gray Bird said.

Gray Bird's protest made Amgigh angry, and once again the fear returned, tightened Amgigh's throat until his voice was high and squeaking like a boy's voice. "The whale is too weak to dive against the floats," Amgigh said.

"What do you know about whales?" Gray Bird asked. "What do you know about strength and weakness?"

"You have a knife?" Big Teeth suddenly asked Gray Bird.

Gray Bird slipped a knife from its sheath at his wrist and held it aloft.

"It is sharp?" Big Teeth asked.

"Ask him," Gray Bird said and pointed at Amgigh with the tip of the blade. "He made it."

"It is sharp," Amgigh answered, his teeth gritted at the insult.

"Then perhaps you are strong enough to use it to cut the line to your harpoon if the whale dives," Big Teeth said, and as he talked, he was tying a coil to his harpoon and checking the floats, loosening them from the ikyak.

Gray Bird's face darkened, but Amgigh, his courage strong again because of Big Teeth's words, suddenly pushed his ikyak toward the whale and when he was close enough, threw his harpoon. The harpoon landed hard and strong into the side of the whale.

The whale shuddered, and Amgigh whooped. Then Big Teeth, Kayugh and First Snow hurled their harpoons. Last of all, Gray Bird threw his.

The whale heaved, wrapping the lines around his body, and pushed itself down into the water. The force of the animal's dive suddenly jerked Amgigh's ikyak into the foam of the animal's wake. The water bubbled and hissed over the bow of the ikyak, and Amgigh saw that the other hunters had longer lines, their ikyan still safely away from the roiling water.

Again, the whale jerked. Amgigh's ikyak sped through the water, twisting until the line had wrapped itself twice around the bow of the craft. The line tightened, pulled taut. Amgigh heard the wood skeleton of his ikyak groan. His father called to him, "Cut the line. Cut the line."

Amgigh pulled his sleeve knife from its sheath, but then the whale turned again, and this time the tip of the ikyak went into the water. Suddenly, the craft stood poised on end. Amgigh, leaning back to keep his balance, clasped his paddle with both hands and the knife slipped from his fingers.

The whale dove, taking Amgigh down with it into the sea. The salt water burned as it rushed up Amgigh's nose. He released his paddle and fumbled with the ties of the hatch skirting, but his fingers were slow and awkward in the cold water.

Then his lungs were burning, and he fought the desire to breathe in. What chance would he have if he took a breath of water?

Below him the whale was huge and black, blotting out the sea, filling Amgigh's head with its immensity. His spear and the spears of the others bristled in a dark cluster from the whale's side.

The whale turned, wrapping the ikyak more tightly into the lines. But in the turning, Amgigh saw another spear, a spear banded with dark markings and rings of white.

Samiq's spear.

Then Amgigh knew. The whale did not belong to him. It was Samiq's whale. Samiq had sent it, not some spirit. Samiq. Yes, of course, how could he have thought otherwise? All things belonged to Samiq. Samiq had taken the first seal; Samiq threw his spear the farthest; Samiq caught the most fish. Kiin, though she was Amgigh's wife, had belonged to Samiq. Who could not see it in her eyes each time she looked at Samiq? And now this whale. Even the whale.

All things were Samiq's.

32

K*ayugh watched in horror as* Amgigh's ikyak disappeared with the whale. Kayugh had cut his own harpoon lines, and his knife was still in his hand. Then suddenly, before his mind could give reason not to, Kayugh was slashing at the hatch skirting that bound him to the coaming of his ikyak.

Dimly, he heard Big Teeth's voice, his call: "No-o-o-o . . ." as Kayugh dove into the sea.

Kayugh pulled himself down into the water, pulled in desperate strokes as his mind spun with questions: How deep? Six, ten, twelve men deep? The water pressed into him; the cold slowed his arms, numbed him until even his heart seemed slow, and he felt the pumping of it press into his ears and throb against the pressure of the sea water. Each stroke brought him further into darkness, and in the darkness there were voices:

Is man an otter that he can swim?

You think Amgigh is still alive? He cannot be.

How will you find him? It is too dark. It is too dark.

And he saw Chagak's face drawn in sorrow, scarred in mourning. For Amgigh? For her husband?

Almost he turned back, but then in the half-light, he saw the ikyak, buoyant from sealskin floats in stern and bow. It pulled at the whale, the blunt end of the stern up toward Kayugh.

With lungs bursting, Kayugh made his arms move again in wide strokes. He reached toward the ikyak, missed, reached again, caught hold, pulled himself toward Amgigh, toward Amgigh's white face, toward Amgigh's open staring eyes.

Blackness pressed in from the edges of Kayugh's mind, slowed his thoughts, dimmed his vision. The whale no longer dove, but held itself steady in the twilight of the water. Kayugh moved his arm to Amgigh's skirt hatching, tried to cut, tried to cut. He could not feel the knife, watched the slow bumbling of his hands as though he watched someone else. He fought against the impulse to breathe in. Pain, pain, in chest, in ears. The knife cut, finally cut.

Amgigh lifted free of the hatch, began to rise as if the sea itself pulled him out. Then Kayugh dropped the knife, wrapped his arms around his son, kicked against the water, kicked as he had seen otters kick. He no longer knew which way was up toward the sky, which was down, but he moved away from the whale, away from the ikyak.

In the blackness, the cold was no longer cold, but he could not move his arms and legs, and his body felt thick and stiff. He drew in a breath; water flooded his mouth, nose, flooded into his lungs. He choked, drew in more water; fought against the pain of it in his lungs.

But then there were hands, grabbing the hood of his chigadax, pulling him from the sea; Gray Bird's voice: "Hold on to Amgigh. Hold on to Amgigh. . . ."

And it was as if he were a spirit watching.

Choking, coughing, water poured from his mouth and nose, arms guided his legs back into his ikyak, Big Teeth bound their ikyan together, Gray Bird slung Amgigh over the front of his ikyak.

Then Kayugh was ashore; carried to his ulaq. He struggled to open his eyes, but could not.

He drifted in and out of sleep, listened, even in his dreams, for mourning songs. There were none. Only lullabies, lullabies.

To which child, what baby? Red Berry? Amgigh? Samiq? Wren?

And in the midst of the songs, First Snow's voice: "Tell Kayugh that the whale washed ashore."

Chagak's voice: "Do not speak to me of whales."

33

*C*hagak stroked her son's hair back from his forehead. For two days he had lain in the ulaq, his eyes closed, his chest barely moving.

Kayugh had come back to the village nearly dead himself, his ikyak lashed to Big Teeth's, Big Teeth paddling for them both. Amgigh had been lying across the bow of Gray Bird's ikyak. Chagak had been on the beach with the other women, all of them waiting to see if their hunters could bring in the whale.

When Gray Bird untied Amgigh from the ikyak and set him gently on the beach, Crooked Nose had begun the mourning song, but Chagak had knelt beside Amgigh and had heard what Gray Bird did not hear, the rattle of Amgigh's breathing.

She leaped to her feet and screamed that her son lived, was alive, then she had watched as Big Teeth used his strong arms to force the water from the boy's lungs.

Even Gray Bird—Waxtal—had helped suck the mucus from Amgigh's throat, and instead of boasting afterwards, only shrugged at Chagak's thanks and said that Amgigh had been a good husband to his daughter.

And some of Chagak's mistrust of Gray Bird lifted, so that during the nights when Gray Bird offered to sit with Amgigh so Chagak could sleep, she gratefully accepted his offer.

For two days Kayugh slept, his body racked with shaking, but finally he awoke, finally he sat up, ate, talked, and then fought against Chagak's wish to keep him with her in the ulaq, until finally she said no more, but let him go outside, let him sit on the ulaq and watch as the women flensed the whale. The whale lay, huge and bloody, on the beach, and Chagak hated the sight of it.

Whales had taken Samiq from her, had taken him to her grandfather's people; a whale had nearly taken Kayugh, and now she fought a whale for Amgigh's life.

She picked up a whale carving that Amgigh kept in his sleeping place. It was one of Shuganan's carvings, and for many years, each time Chagak looked at it, she had seen Shuganan's hands holding his crooked knife, Shuganan's eyes studying, studying, seeing in the ivory what no one else saw until his carving was complete. But now looking at the carving Chagak did not see Shuganan. She saw Samiq leaving in his ikyak; she saw Amgigh white and still. Both sons taken from her.

She had once won their spirits by taking two eider ducks with her bola. But what was the power of an eider duck compared to that of a whale?

Yes, she thought, her anger making her thoughts loud and pounding in her mind. Yes, she thought as the other women rejoiced over whale meat and oil, flense it, break its bones. It has taken my sons, has taken my beautiful sons.

And in her sorrow, she remembered the other losses in her life: her family, her village, her brother Pup, Shuganan. Now she had lost two more: Samiq to the Whale Hunters, Kiin to the sea. Would she lose Amgigh, too?

She remembered the whale that had washed up on Shuganan's beach the morning of Samiq's naming ceremony. After presenting Samiq to the four winds, Shuganan had placed the baby's hand against the side of the whale. Chagak remembered her uneasiness. Perhaps even then she had known that the whale would take her sons. Perhaps even then.

Chagak sighed and pressed her hands against Amgigh's face. The first day, she had used the serrated back edge of a yoldia shell to comb seal oil through Amgigh's hair, but the combing had seemed too much like something done for one who had just died, and this day Chagak had left Amgigh's hair without combing, had even mussed it a little so he looked like a man sleeping, not one laid out for a burial ceremony.

"Wake up, wake up, wake up," she called to him. But Amgigh did not seem to hear her.

Then the voice of the sea otter came to Chagak, and Chagak did not want to listen, but she reminded herself that the otter had been a gentleness in her soul since she and Shuganan had killed Samiq's true father long ago. "The whale is good," the otter said. "The whale is food. It is oil for your lamps, skin for your husband's chigadax, bone for building ulas. It is good. Samiq sent it. It is good."

"Samiq sent it," Chagak said aloud. "It is good." But still within her spirit, she felt the grating pain of anger.

Then Amgigh groaned and Chagak, heavy with fear, leaned toward him. He moved his head and Chagak caught her breath.

"Amgigh," she whispered.

Amgigh blinked, and for a moment his eyes were open.

"Amgigh, Amgigh," Chagak called. "Open your eyes. Look at me. Do you know who I am?"

Again Amgigh groaned, again moved his head, blinked open his eyes. He smiled, only a small trembling at the corners of his mouth, but it was a true smile, and Chagak, her tears mingling with her laughter, heard him say, "Mother."

Then someone was coming down the climbing log. Kayugh, Chagak hoped, and she opened the curtain of Amgigh's sleeping place and peered out. It was Gray Bird—no, Waxtal, Chagak reminded herself. His face was grim, but Chagak pointed with her chin toward Amgigh, and suddenly Waxtal was smiling.

"Go, get Kayugh," he said to Chagak. "I will stay with your son."

Chagak leaned forward, clasped Amgigh's hand. "Waxtal was the one who saved you," she said. "Your father and Waxtal." Then she stood and hurried from the ulaq.

———

Waxtal watched until Chagak had ascended the climbing log, then he closed the curtains of Amgigh's sleeping place and leaned toward Amgigh. He had waited and waited; five nights and five days he had waited. He had sat and watched Amgigh, and at first he had been patient, willing to wait, but then he had become angry. The young man slept too long. Some spirit must know what Waxtal planned, and so kept Amgigh sleeping, kept Waxtal waiting, laughed at Waxtal's growing anger.

Perhaps it was Shuganan's spirit. Shuganan would know what Waxtal knew—that any man's spirit was easier to direct when he had just awakened from a sleep, when dreams still held a portion of his thoughts. And perhaps, since he was now spirit, Shuganan would know what Waxtal planned.

But Shuganan's spirit must not be as strong as Waxtal had feared, because now Amgigh was awake, and Waxtal was alone with him.

"I am glad you are alive," Waxtal said to Amgigh, and he forced himself to say the words slowly, to hold back what he wanted to say until he knew Amgigh understood him. "You can hear me?" he asked, leaning closer to Amgigh.

"Yes," Amgigh said, the word hoarse and whispered.

Waxtal smiled. Yes, Amgigh heard him. Yes.

Waxtal cleared his throat. "They say that Samiq sent the whale as a gift," Waxtal said. "But I told them Samiq has had enough praise. I told them that it was my son Amgigh, once husband to my daughter Kiin, who brought in the whale. He should have the honor."

Waxtal watched as Amgigh's face flushed. Amgigh's eyes closed for a moment then opened again.

Again, Waxtal leaned forward and whispered into Amgigh's ear. "There is something I must tell you so you can protect yourself."

He paused, waited until Amgigh nodded.

"I told you Samiq is not true son to Kayugh and you are not true son to Chagak. But Chagak has been a good mother to you and Kayugh has been a good father to Samiq. That is the way it should be. But think of this: What power does a mother give her sons? Nothing . . . only the food she prepares and the clothes she makes. But a father, he gives the spirit. And Samiq's true father was an evil man. Most people do not know this. Only Chagak and I. Not even Kayugh knows the truth about Samiq's father. If Kayugh had known, he would not have let Samiq live."

Waxtal watched as Amgigh's eyes narrowed, as his forehead creased. Then Amgigh's eyes closed, but Waxtal could not take the chance of losing him, of letting him drift into sleep. He clasped Amgigh's shoulder, shook him.

"Amgigh . . ."

Amgigh's eyes jerked open, focused on Waxtal's face. "How do you know?" Amgigh finally asked, his voice stronger. "How do you know when my father does not?"

"Because Chagak has kept it a secret so Samiq would be allowed to live," Waxtal answered. "Because I was with Shuganan, the grandfather, when he was dying, and during his death, his spirit fought with the spirit of Samiq's true father.

"You saw the spirits?"

"I heard the voices."

"Who was Samiq's father?" Amgigh asked, and raised himself on one elbow.

The movement made Amgigh cough and soon he was spitting up phlegm, gagging in his struggle to speak.

Then Waxtal heard Chagak and Kayugh, their voices clear from the top of the ulaq.

"Lie down," Waxtal told Amgigh. "I will tell you later. But it is something that must be kept secret. I promised Chagak long ago that I would tell no one. But you, you must know. Samiq may be changing. Perhaps that is why he sent the whale. Perhaps now that he lives with the Whale Hunters, Shuganan can no longer protect him. Perhaps his father's spirit has had a chance to come to him, to push some of its evil into Samiq's soul."

Amgigh lay back against his sleeping mats, and though he closed his eyes, he raised his hand to clasp Waxtal's hand.

Amgigh's fingers were cold, and Waxtal shuddered. He remembered the whiteness of Amgigh's face when Kayugh had brought him up out of the sea, water dripping from both men, seaweed tangled in Amgigh's hair. Amgigh had been dead, Waxtal was sure. Had he not held Amgigh's body as Big Teeth helped Kayugh climb back inside his ikyak? Had Waxtal not lashed Amgigh, dead, to the bow of his own ikyak? What power did Chagak have, so that when the boy was finally on the beach she merely leaned over him and he was again alive, again breathing?

She is a woman, only a woman, Waxtal reminded himself. Her powers are nothing compared to the powers of a hunter. And I, like Shuganan, carve. The power in that is the power of a shaman. Why else could a man call a spirit from a piece of ivory, a chunk of wood?

Waxtal loosed Amgigh's hand and tucked it under the seal-skins that covered him. Once more he whispered into Amgigh's ear, "It is better if your mother does not know that I have told you."

He waited, hoping that Amgigh would in some way acknowledge his words, but then Kayugh and Chagak were in the sleeping place, Kayugh's face wet with tears. Waxtal stood and for a time he watched them, but then he left them alone, and slipped silently up the climbing log to stand for a long time atop Kayugh's ulaq, to stand looking east toward Aka's island, toward the trader's route.

34

They paddled, for days and days, through two full moons and on toward another. The sea water softened the ik's hide covering, and they were forced to stop more and more often to repair the seams, patch the hides. Qakan had not thought to bring the slices of seal blubber Kiin needed to stuff the seams of the ik so water would not seep in, so Kiin filled the leaking seams with bits of fish fat, and each night she patched and repatched until her fingers bled.

The sea spray made the skin peel from their faces, and Kiin's hands cracked and split from the salt water, but still they went on. Twice, they found ulakidaq, both First Men villages. At each place they traded for food, and Qakan was given a woman for the nights they stayed.

Kiin was surprised that though Qakan seemed incompetent in the trading—his words slow, and his face often showing his perplexity in making a decision—he always came away with more than he had given, and so now the ik was weighted down with extra furs, chunks of ivory, unusual shells, even two seal stomachs filled with dried meat.

They had left the last village four days before, though Kiin had urged Qakan to stay. Winter would soon be upon them and with winter would come the storms—times when even the best hunters, most skilled with their ikyan, would not want to be out on the sea. But Qakan would not listen to Kiin, would not listen to the hunters of the village, but instead went on. They would go until they found the Walrus People, he told Kiin. The Walrus People's village would make the two villages they had visited seem small and unimportant.

So Kiin, seeing the stubbornness in Qakan's eyes, took up her paddle. What else could she do? At night Qakan still kept her wrists tied, her ankles hobbled, and at each village, Qakan had told the people that she was a slave. And they, seeing her as slave, had given her the hardest chores, the most hated work; and their men would not ask for her other than to inquire if Qakan would sell her for the night. But to Kiin's surprise, Qakan would not.

"The Walrus People will pay more," he told her. "I save you for them. I have heard stories about what men have done to women slaves bought for the night. Besides," he would say and lean over to pat her stomach, "I do not want to curse my son."

In the days since they had left the last village, Kiin's spirit seemed to grow smaller and smaller until it settled as small as a pebble, hard and sharp against her heart. And sometimes in the night, huddled in their shelter of grass mats and sealskins, she awoke with her blood pounding, echoing in her chest, the emptiness within as great as it had been when she had no spirit, no soul of her own.

Kiin flexed her fingers on the paddle. Her knuckles were swollen, her hands and arms cramped with stiffness. This morning the rocking of the ik nauseated her, and for a moment she stopped paddling to curl one hand over the lower part of her belly. Three moons had passed without her woman's bleeding. She sighed. Yes, she carried a child. Amgigh's, she told herself. Amgigh's.

But when her wrists, rubbed raw from the cord that bound them, bled and burned, or when her back ached from paddling most of the day, some voice of doubt would come, would whisper, "It is Qakan's child. Of course, the child belongs to Qakan." And at other times when the cry of some bird or the sight of an otter slipping into the water would give her a bit of hope, another voice would say, "It is Samiq's."

The day after they had left the first village, Qakan had found her vomiting. She had been digging clams in the tide flats of the beach where they would spend the night. Suddenly the nausea had come to her, twisting her stomach until she could do nothing but retch.

Qakan had laughed, had laughed and done a strange jumping dance, his feet clumsy against the ground, his belly jiggling with each of his steps. Then he had bent over Kiin, had shouted into her ear as she crouched holding her stomach, "My son! My son! My son!"

Kiin had closed her eyes, pretended Qakan was not beside her. Then the nausea was gone as quickly as it had come. She had walked away from Qakan, up the slope of the beach to the fringe of ryegrass that grew at the edge of a long, sloping hill. She broke off some of the grass and chewed a few stems to soothe her stomach. Then she turned and called back to Qakan.

"Your s-son?" she said, her voice raised to sound strong against the wind. "You d-d-did not g-g-give me a ch-child. It is Amgigh's son. The child was in my b-b-belly before you t-took me and he is strong enough to st-stand against the seeds of your s-spirit. He has Amgigh's b-b-blood and Kayugh's b-blood, Ch-Chagak's and Shuganan's. How c-could you even hope it is your son?" And the wind passing through Kiin's hair blew away Qakan's taunts.

For days after that, Qakan had acted more the part of a man, complaining less, once even helping her set up their crude skin and grass mat shelter. But this morning, Qakan was once more a child, peevish and pouting, slapping Kiin when she was loading the ik, screaming at her that she was too slow. And shortly after they had begun paddling, he began to shout his anger at the fog, directing Kiin to keep the ik so close to shore that twice they ran aground on gravel spits, and Kiin had to climb from the ik and push them free.

At least the sea is calm, Kiin told herself, but then she noticed the blackness of huge boulders just under the surface of the water.

"Rocks, r-r-rocks," she called to Qakan. When he did not answer, Kiin looked back at him and saw that he was not watching the water. Instead he kept his head turned toward the shore.

"Rocks!" she said again, and sinking her paddle into the water, pushed the ik away from one of the boulders.

"Qakan!" she called out. "Listen to me. . . ."

"Kiin, shut your mouth," Qakan said, then, "There! Turn." And he began paddling on the left side of the ik, forcing the ik to the right until Kiin thought they would run up on the beach. But then she saw an opening in the hills, a rocky place that forced the sea into something more like a river. The water was choppy and pushed through the narrows quickly as if anxious to get through, then the sea widened again, into a bay, and Qakan pointed toward a hill where Kiin could see ten, twelve ulas.

"Walrus People?" she asked.

"No," Qakan said. "First Men. Twice I came here with my father. They are First Men, but they are not like us. They speak differently, too quickly. And their women are ugly. I could get much for you here, but they do not treat their women well. It is better for you to go to the Walrus People."

Kiin scowled. More likely he was afraid Amgigh or Samiq would someday come here, would find her and know what Qakan had done.

It was low tide and the water was shallow. Qakan pulled out a length of twine, hobbled Kiin's ankles and bound her wrists a hand-length apart in front of her. Then he motioned for Kiin to jump out, to push the ik ashore. With wrists and ankles bound she was awkward, but she managed to jump without falling, and then she pushed the ik up on the gray sand beach.

Children came first, then the women. The women were dirty,

unkempt, each woman's hair a mass of tangles. Their children were filthy, their faces splotchy with the rash that comes from eating raw unpeeled ugyuun stems.

Even though they were traveling, Kiin tried to keep herself clean, kept her suk in good repair, even pulled her fingers through her hair each evening to untangle it.

One woman stepped out from the group and greeted Qakan. The woman was tall, and her long, sharp-nosed face reminded Kiin of the curved cutting edge of a woman's knife.

"You have come to trade," she said, and gripping her digging stick, stood on tiptoe, trying to see over Qakan's shoulder into the ik.

"I will speak to your men," Qakan said.

The woman shook her head. "They hunt today. Later, they will return." She turned to look at Kiin, and Kiin lowered her head. The woman glanced at Kiin's bound wrists and said, "She is not your wife."

"A slave," Qakan said.

Perhaps Kiin would have said nothing. Perhaps she would have acted as she did at the other villages, doing the chores the woman gave her to do. But then the woman said, "The men will be happy tonight. You will be able to sell her many times."

And Kiin was suddenly angry. Would she lower her eyes to these women who were too lazy to keep their children clean?

"N-no," she said. "I am n-not a s-slave. I am his s-sister. He stole me from my husband's ulaq, though I carry my husband's ch-child."

Qakan turned, his mouth open wide, as though he would swallow the words Kiin had said. He raised his hand, and Kiin ducked so his blow hit her head, not her face. Qakan clasped his hand and screeched. "She lies," he said, then knotted his fist and drew it back to hit Kiin. But the tall woman blocked Qakan's hand with her digging stick.

"We do not want you here if you beat women," she said. "I have no great powers to tell whether or not you lie, but if she tells the truth, we do not want you here. Besides, we have little to trade. The hunting has been poor. Our mountain has been angry and its ashes drive the seals away."

She turned, walked back up the beach, but Qakan followed her. "I have fur seal skins," he said.

She ignored him, as though he had said nothing.

"A most beautiful suk," he said and ran back toward the ik, rummaged through the packs until he pulled out the suk his mother had made. He unrolled it, held it up. "Look!" he said, running his hands down the sleeves.

Some of the younger women's eyes grew round, and Kiin saw the wanting in their faces. But the tall woman stopped and, without turning, raised her digging stick until its pointed end was high over her head. "I told you to leave!" she said and continued walking toward the ulas.

The other women turned and followed, and only the children stayed to stare at Qakan as he called, "I could curse your village, but I will not. Tell your hunters that you chased away a trader. Tell them I have obsidian knives. The finest they have ever seen. I do not have to curse you. Your hunters themselves will curse you when they hear what you have done."

35

There on the shore, with the children watching, he beat her. First with his fists. And Kiin, used to being beaten, tucked herself into a ball, protecting her head and stomach. Her helplessness brought anger, and her anger, tears. What could she do against him, her wrists and ankles tied? But then he stopped, and Kiin, afraid to look up, heard the scrape of a paddle as Qakan pulled it from the ik. Fear pushed her to her feet, and she suddenly realized that she was not as much afraid for herself as for her baby. Amgigh's son. Perhaps Samiq's.

"You will kill your son," she said softly.

Qakan stared at her. Finally he dropped the paddle into the boat. "Push us out," he said. "Three, four days will bring us to the Walrus People's village."

Kiin held out her bound wrists, but Qakan pushed her hands away.

"Perhaps you need to know what it is like to truly be slave," he said.

They traveled for the rest of that morning. Kiin tied a long twisted line of kelp fiber to a thwart of their ik. She weighted the line with several stones, so it would sink to the bottom of the sea, and baited the hook. They were far enough out so that

211

she might catch a halibut. Not a large one—she and Qakan were not strong enough to bring a large one into the boat, but perhaps one the size of Samiq's sister Wren. Kiin rested her paddle across the ik and jerked the line. Nothing.

Kiin smelled the smoke before she saw it. The thin wisps were lost in the fog that hugged the shores and hid the mountains that rose from the sea like a huge spine of rock and ice. She turned back toward Qakan. "Smoke," she said and pointed with a turn of her head.

Qakan, his paddle lying across his knees, was suddenly alert, eyes squinted to see the shore. "Look, there," he said and gestured with his paddle. "We can beach the ik there."

Kiin raised her paddle from the water and let Qakan make the long strokes that would turn the ik toward land, then she, too, paddled, skimming the ik toward the beach.

Gravel grated against the bottom of the ik. "Stay here," Qakan said to Kiin and he jumped out, pulling the boat ashore.

The wind came in sudden gusts, and several large waves crashed into the beach, pushing the ik sideways. The boat tipped, but not far enough to let water seep in over the edge. Qakan jerked the ik one more time, then watched the waves for a moment. When the sea calmed, he shrugged and said, "If waves come, move it farther up on the beach."

Kiin held out her wrists. "With my hands bound?" she asked, but Qakan was already walking away from her. Kiin stood, ready to call after him, but when she stood, she saw a small fire that had been hidden by the fog. Standing near the fire she thought she saw two, perhaps three, men. Kiin groped for the sharp-edged stone that Qakan allowed her to keep to clean fish, but she knew it would be little protection against three men.

As Qakan approached the fire, the fog lifted, as though Qakan's feet, in walking, pushed back the mist, and Kiin could see the men, their faces painted red and black. They stared at Qakan without moving or extending hands in greeting. Qakan had his hands out, palms up, and she heard him say, "I am a friend. I have no knife." He said something else, words that Kiin could not understand, the Walrus People's language.

Qakan had taken two, three trips with their father to the Walrus summer camp and had told her he could speak the Walrus tongue, though Kiin, thinking the boast was another of Qakan's lies, had not believed him. But for the past month, he had spent time each day practicing the Walrus words he knew, mumbling them aloud as he paddled the ik, but he had refused to teach any to Kiin.

When they had left the second First Men village, Qakan had hung a red-dyed otter skin over the bow of the ik, sign of a trader, but when they had seen the smoke of the three men's fire, Kiin could tell that in spite of his boasting, Qakan was afraid.

This was not a village, only a stopping place for hunters. Who could say what village the three men were from, and whether or not they were friendly? Kiin flattened herself in the bottom of the boat and reached slowly toward a paddle. What if the men killed Qakan? Could she push the ik out to sea before they got to her? She did not think so. But she could defend herself better with a paddle than with a small cutting stone.

She was pulling the paddle toward herself when one of the three men began to speak. His words startled Kiin, and she stopped, as though she were a child caught doing some forbidden thing, and peeked over the edge of the ik.

The tallest man of the three had extended his hands to Qakan, and Qakan began to laugh, a high, girl-like giggle that let Kiin know how frightened he had been. The man motioned toward the fire and Qakan squatted on his heels beside it and accepted the dried meat they gave him.

One of the men pointed toward the ik and said something. Kiin's heart quickened. Qakan spoke. Some of his words were in the First Men tongue, most in the Walrus language.

Then he stood and, motioning at Kiin, called out, "Come here."

When she did not move, he strode toward her, a look of irritation on his face. He grabbed her arm and jerked her to her feet. "They want to see you," he said. He pulled her from the ik, but Kiin tripped over the edge and fell, the beach gravel skinning her knees and the palms of her hands.

"Stupid!" Qakan hissed.

Kiin stood up slowly. She brushed off her hands and legs and straightened her suk.

"How much do you think they will give me for a woman who cannot walk?" Qakan said, but Kiin, used to his complaints, did not answer.

He was the one who had put hobbles on her ankles and wrists, tied her feet so she could take only small steps. What did he expect? She walked to the fire, then squatted down and pulled her suk over her knees.

The men stared at her, and Kiin fought the impulse to look away. Instead, she stared back at them, something a woman of the First Men did not do, something she knew would anger Qakan.

The three men looked much alike. They are brothers, Kiin thought as she studied the three faces. The tallest seemed to be the oldest. Lines ran from the corners of his eyes to his jawbone. His cheeks were painted red, his nose black. He had a fine growth of chin hair that wisped down to his chest, and his eyes were thin half-moons. He, of the three, talked the most and the loudest.

The man who looked the youngest had painted the backs of his hands in a design that looked like sea waves. His face was round, his hair greased and cut evenly to shoulder length. The other man, long-faced and thin, had a scar curving from the corner of one eye to the center of his chin. When he spoke the skin over the scar pulled taut.

Each man wore a hooded fur parka and each hood was trimmed with thick silver fur, a kind of fur Kiin had not seen before. The parkas were short, not even reaching the knees, but the men wore fur leggings and sealskin boots.

They continued to speak to Qakan. Qakan said little but laughed often and sometimes pointed to Kiin and laughed again.

After a while, Qakan came over to her and untied the ropes that bound Kiin's ankles and wrists; he cupped her chin in his hand and laughed into her face. But Kiin looked away, rubbing her wrists where the skin was raw from the burn of the ropes.

Then the tallest man pointed to Kiin and the tone of his voice changed. He circled the fire and stood behind her. Kiin sat very still, clenched her fists to keep her arms from trembling.

The man squatted beside her and took one of her hands in his. His face was very close, and Kiin could see that he was older than she had first thought, the paint that covered his cheeks and forehead hiding age lines. She saw, too, that his dark hair was marked with gray, and suddenly she realized that he was father of the other two.

The man pulled up the sleeve of Kiin's suk and pointed to her scarred wrist. He asked Qakan something, and Qakan cleared his throat, finally answering in jerky, broken phrases. The man turned and spat on the ground, then asked another question. Qakan shrugged his shoulders.

The man left the fire and went to a crude lean-to that was propped beside an inverted ik, the boat longer and wider than Qakan's ik and covered with a thick hide that had few seams. The man returned with a small packet and handed it to Kiin.

He said something to Kiin and Qakan translated: "Goose fat for your wrists." Qakan's face was pinched and red. She looked up at the Walrus hunter and thanked him, then spread the grease over her wrists.

The fat smelled strong, nearly rancid, but it was soothing, and when Kiin had finished her wrists, she leaned over and greased her ankles. This brought another murmur from the three men, and the tallest one said something to Qakan, something that made Qakan grin foolishly and jump to his feet, hauling Kiin up beside him.

"Go to the ik," he said to her. "They have agreed to take us to their village."

Kiin bound up the packet of grease and handed it back to the man, but he smiled at her and shook his head. He said something to Qakan and Qakan said to Kiin, "Keep it," and when Kiin still held the packet out toward the man, Qakan pushed it back, making a sound of disgust in his throat. "He said it is yours. You are to keep it."

Kiin smiled at the man, at all three men, and nodded, then walked to the ik, standing beside it as Qakan helped the three men bury their fire and dismantle their lean-to.

They are a good people, Kiin thought as she watched. Too good for the curse Qakan was bringing them. She wondered what Qakan had told them about her wrists, how he had explained. Whatever he had said seemed to satisfy them. They were no longer angry with him. The youngest man often clapped a hand on Qakan's back, and the one with the scar spoke often, making the others laugh as they worked.

The three men loaded their supplies in their boat and carried it to the water. Qakan helped them push it out, and then he and Kiin dragged their ik into the waves.

"They think you are a slave, captured from the Whale Hunters," Qakan said.

Kiin picked up her paddle. "That is what you told them?" she asked.

"How else could I explain your wrists?"

"But they gave me medicine," Kiin said.

"I told you they were a good people." Qakan leaned forward. His fat cheeks made his eyes look like dark slits. "Do you think I would trade you to an evil people?"

Kiin turned around and sat down in the bow of the ik. Why answer?

36

In *the middle of the afternoon,* the Walrus hunters paddled their boat back to offer Qakan and Kiin food.

"Take it and like it," Qakan said to Kiin, his voice jolly, but his eyes hard. "If you were with First Men hunters, we would eat only at night."

Kiin in turn offered the men some of the fish that were drying on the edge of the ik.

"You insult them with your poor food," Qakan hissed at her, smiling as he spoke. But the men, nodding and laughing, took the fish and ate it, and Kiin defied Qakan by giving them more.

After eating, the men pulled ahead again, and after a time of paddling in silence Qakan said, "They are a father and two sons. They made a trading trip before winter."

Kiin did not turn, did not indicate that she heard him.

"The oldest son, the one with the scar, is looking for a wife. He has many things to trade." When Kiin did not answer, Qakan bellowed, "He would be a good husband for you, and he would make me rich with furs and ivory." Then Kiin felt cold water dripping on her neck. She looked up and saw Qakan's paddle over her head.

"Do you th-think he would b-be happy if you hit me?" she asked.

Qakan lowered the paddle into the water and gave the ik a strong thrust that pushed it close to the three men's boat.

"I am trying to help you," Qakan said to her.

"You are t-trying t-to help yourself, Qakan," Kiin answered. "If you w-w-wanted to help me, you would have left me alone so I could be w-wife to Amgigh."

"Amgigh," Qakan said and spat into the water.

Anger knotted in Kiin's breast, and for the first time since they had met the Walrus men, Kiin felt her spirit move within her. "Wife to Amgigh," its voice echoed, and a pain squeezed Kiin's chest so tightly she could not breathe. No, Kiin told herself, I cannot be Amgigh's wife. Not now. And she sat without paddling until the pain left her.

But then looking ahead at the Walrus men she thought, What if the scarred one asks for me? He, too, is a good man. Is it right that I curse him? No, I will escape. Somehow I will escape. The child and I will live alone and curse no one.

They paddled until it was nearly night, then hauled the iks ashore and made two lean-to shelters, one for the Walrus men and another for Kiin and Qakan. Kiin prepared food for the men from their stores and from Qakan's, then she went into a shelter, huddled under some of Qakan's furs and listened to the strange rhythms of the Walrus tongue as Qakan and the three men talked long into the night.

Kiin fell asleep before Qakan came to their shelter, and in the morning when she awoke, she saw that Qakan's eyes were open, his mouth pursed into a small, tight frown. She knew the look. He was afraid. Not angry, not pouting, but afraid. It was the look he had each time their father took him on a hunt. But Qakan avoided her eyes and so Kiin did not ask him what was wrong.

They ate, then launched their boats, Qakan and Kiin again following the Walrus men. A cold north wind began to blow, and Kiin saw the wisdom of the hooded parkas the Walrus men wore. She tucked her hair into the collar of her suk, but the wind pushed through her hair and into her ears until Kiin's head and neck ached with the cold.

A fog hung over the water and the wind pushed it in toward the beaches, but Kiin could see cliffs, and at one place they passed a great mound of blue ice. During the morning, the Walrus men kept their ik close to the shore as Qakan did, but then they suddenly turned, paddling north into the wind, and Kiin, surprised, looked back at Qakan. Qakan, too, paddled to turn north, but Kiin saw the fear in his eyes.

"It is shorter," he said to her. "Last night they told me it would take only the rest of this day and night and perhaps another day to reach their village if we go this way."

Kiin felt anger beginning in her chest. Qakan should have told her. The ik's seams were weak. At least she could have spent the night sewing, strengthening the weak places with sinew thread and patches of sealskin.

"You should have told me," she said, and her anger made her voice strong so that she did not stammer on the words. "Our ik is weak. If the waves grow . . ."

"Shut your mouth!" Qakan said.

Kiin turned and looked at him, her anger suddenly, even in the north wind, making her cheeks hot. She turned and laid her paddle in the center of the ik and said, "You paddle. At least I can stuff the seams with fat."

Qakan opened his mouth, but said nothing, and finally he looked away from her and paddled, his eyes looking right or left, not at Kiin.

For a moment Kiin watched him, then she said, "If you see a leak, tell me. I will bail." Then she began repairing the ik.

There were no mountains, only the sea. Kiin remembered her sadness when she could no longer see Tugix. But there had been another mountain and another. And as they passed, Kiin had prayed to each mountain's spirit, had asked the mountains to take her prayers for protection back to Tugix, back to her people and to Amgigh and Samiq.

Now there were no mountains to carry her prayers, and so Kiin whispered to the sea, sending her requests on the waves. And she hoped that the sea spirits did not look too closely at their poor ik. The tattered covering, the gaping seams would be an insult to the sea animals, to the ones that had given themselves so the ik could be made. So even as she worked, sealing seams with fish fat, tightening stitches with sinew thread, she waited, expecting some sea animal to come under the ik and bite holes so she and Qakan would drown.

But no sea animals came, and when Kiin had repaired all of the seams she could reach, she began to paddle again. For a short time the fog lifted, but then the sun was setting and darkness came. Kiin heard Qakan's breathing, even over the noise of paddling and the sea, long sighing breaths, then short, quick breaths, sometimes moaning, as though his fear spoke in a voice of its own.

When Kiin could see nothing at all, when she no longer knew which way to direct the ik, one of the Walrus men began a chant. Something to sea spirits, Qakan told Kiin. And then Kiin followed the sound of his voice, the darkness and cold pressing in against her eyes like wet fur.

They came to land at dawn, ate and rested, then started again without sleeping, and it seemed to Kiin that her arms moved only because they had paddled so long that they knew nothing else to do. Muscles in her shoulders and back burned, and cramps knotted in her thighs. She said nothing, but Qakan never stopped his whining, and finally his voice became like the high singing of the wind, something Kiin chose not to hear.

They followed the land again, so Kiin no longer feared sea animals, but she tried to watch for rocks. The land was flat, though in the distance there were mountains. Kiin could see them when the fog lifted—white-capped clouds on the edge of the horizon.

They paddled through that day until the sun was only a red

shadow in the darkening sky, and Kiin watched the Walrus men to see if they would stop to sleep. How could she paddle for another night? How could she keep her arms moving?

Then the man with the scar called to Qakan and pointed to a projection of rock that reached out from the shore. Qakan brought the ik alongside the Walrus men's boat and spoke to them. Again the Walrus men took the lead, their large, heavy ik skimming the water with an agility that surprised Kiin. "They p-paddle it like an ikyak," she said to Qakan.

"They are too stupid to make ikyan," Qakan replied.

"Each t-tribe is d-different," Kiin said.

But Qakan shrugged and said, "They say we must watch for rocks under the water."

Even though it was nearly dark, Kiin could see boulders under the waves, some very close to the surface. There were occasional jagged triangles of floating ice, thin and easily broken with a paddle, but a sign of winter. The seas near the island of the First Men did not freeze, but Qakan had told Kiin that in winter the Walrus People's sea became ice.

"They said their village was at the next cove," Qakan called to her.

Something in Kiin grew tight and cold, and her teeth began to chatter, but she kept her eyes to the sea, watching for rocks, thrusting her paddle against them to protect the ik.

When they rounded the point, the rocks were smaller and flatter. Kiin looked up and realized that they were in the cove. A shiver of nervousness made her fingers tingle. The cove water was frozen, but the ice was thin, divided by a path of open water that led to the beach.

Then Kiin remembered something she had heard long ago, something her father had said after a trading journey. That some tribes call the Walrus People Ice Hunters, because in winter they hunt through the ice. Kiin looked toward the beach and wondered if the Walrus People lived in ulas, but in the growing darkness she could see only the red coals of a fire on the beach.

"The men meet on the beach," Qakan said pointing to the

beach fire. "That is where I will do my bargaining. Most of the men will have painted faces; it is a sign of their manhood. Do not ask a man about his paint, what it stands for. It is something sacred between him and the animals he hunts."

"Where are the women?" Kiin asked.

"They meet together each evening also. In the long house."

"What is a long house?"

"You are stupid, Kiin," Qakan said, "and you ask too many questions. Be quiet. The Walrus People like quiet women."

Qakan's words made Kiin angry, but she said nothing. He taunted her to make her angry. He always had. Qakan seemed to be happy only when others were unhappy.

They guided the ik toward the beach, and Kiin could see that a large number of men stood by the beach fire. The three Walrus men pulled their boat ashore, and Kiin could hear their voices, loud with excitement, the men pointing toward the ik. One voice rose above the others, the father's voice, and at his words Qakan laughed.

"He says a rich trader has come," Qakan said and laughed again. "He says the trader has a beautiful woman to sell."

A shout went up from the men on the beach, and Kiin's stomach twisted.

"You will bring me a good price," Qakan said. "It seems they are anxious for wives."

The ik was near the shore, but Kiin could not bring herself to look at the waiting men. Instead she jumped from the boat and guided it toward shore while Qakan paddled. But three, four of the Walrus men pulled off their fur leggings and waded out, breaking through the ice and into the water. Two grabbed the bow of the ik; the third lifted Kiin out of the water and carried her to the beach.

His arms were thick and hard around her belly, and Kiin's heart beat so fast she could not breathe. He was a huge man, much taller than any of the others. His face was unpainted, but he wore a labret through each cheek. He hoisted her up so she was sitting on his left shoulder. Kiin clung to the hood of his parka and looked down at the men around her. In the darkness all she could see of them was their wide smiles, their square, white teeth.

The man who held her shouted something at the other men and then he began to dance. Kiin bounced with each of his steps, and she wished she was a child so she could scream and cry for the man to put her down.

The Walrus men were all around them now, all dancing. Some had pulled off their parkas and one man, one who had helped pull the ik ashore, danced without parka or leggings, only a short apron covering him.

The man who held Kiin was singing, and she clung more tightly to his parka, leaning down to encircle his neck with her arms, and he shouted something in her ear, whether to her or the others, Kiin did not know, but the noise and the bouncing was beginning to make her sick. She searched for Qakan among the crowd of men, and finally saw him leaning against the ik, a smile on his face.

"Qakan," she called to him. "Qakan I am s-sick. Tell them to-to let me down."

"Laugh," he called to her. "Laugh or they will not want you. The Walrus People like women who laugh."

Kiin clamped her teeth together to keep from vomiting. As the man continued his dance, a slow moaning cry pushed up from Kiin's stomach into her throat. Suddenly he stopped, and as if she were a child, he pulled her from his shoulder and set her down.

The men stopped dancing, but orange shadows from the fire curled over them so it seemed they still moved. The giant asked Kiin a question, and she shook her head. The man called over his shoulder to Qakan.

Qakan stalked to the center of the circle. "Stupid woman," he said to Kiin, but showed a smile to the men, patting Kiin's shoulder and stroking her suk.

As he spoke, Kiin studied the faces of the Walrus hunters. They were handsome men and all seemed to be tall. Most had long hair. One man's hair hung over his hood to the center of his back. A few had paint on their faces, but most did not. One man had black lines on his chin like the tattoos of the Whale Hunters, and suddenly an image of Samiq's face, marked with tattoos, came to Kiin, and with the image, a feeling of hopelessness, a realization of how much Samiq's time with the Whale Hunters would change him and how far away Kiin was from her home.

Qakan was still talking to the Walrus hunters, the men leaning forward, sometimes volunteering a word, Qakan correcting himself with a short laugh edged with irritation. But finally he walked behind Kiin, patted her shoulder, and suddenly he jerked up her suk.

Kiin gasped and tried to pull away from him, but her arms were caught in the sleeves, her head buried in the suk. He pulled the suk off, and Kiin stood shivering, wearing only her apron. She wrapped her arms over her bare breasts as Qakan threw the suk to the nearest man. He told the man something, and the man began to study the seams of the garment.

"I told him you made it," Qakan said to Kiin, one side of his mouth raised in a smile.

"But Ch-Chagak . . ." Kiin began, then stopped, ashamed for what her brother was doing. "You-you are full of lies, Qakan," she said, struggling to control the trembling in her voice.

She knew the men's eyes were on her, appraising her body, but she had expected that. What man would take a woman as wife if he had seen her only bundled in a suk? Perhaps under the suk she was marked by some spirit, shown to be cursed. But Kiin knew her curse was something the men would see as a blessing, and something that she, since she did not know their language, could not explain.

The man with the labrets suddenly pointed to Kiin and said something. He was holding Kiin's suk and he threw it to Qakan.

"He thinks you are cold. He thinks you should have your

suk," Qakan said, but he again moved behind Kiin, and this time he grasped her arms, holding them away from her body. He said something and some of the men laughed. Kiin tried to pull away from him, but he jerked her arms behind her back and held them at the wrist with one hand, then reached forward and squeezed her breasts.

Kiin's breasts were sore from her pregnancy, and she winced at Qakan's touch. "Let m-me go," she hissed, but Qakan laughed and said, "I told them you will make a good mother." Then he patted her stomach and said something else, something that made the men gasp, and some stepped forward, bending to look at Kiin's belly.

Then the men were smiling, their voices louder, higher. Kiin suddenly jabbed Qakan in the stomach with her elbow. He let go of her, and Kiin spun, grabbing the suk from his shoulder. "D-d-did you tell them it was your ch-child?" she said to him. "D-did you tell them you are b-both its father and uncle?"

The Walrus men were laughing. But Kiin saw the anger in Qakan's eyes. "Why are you an-angry?" she asked him. "You will get more for me now. I have shown my strength." She squatted on her heels, and pulled the suk on over her head.

"You stupid woman," Qakan said and lunged forward, catching Kiin by the hair, but suddenly one of the men who had brought them to the village was beside Qakan, catching Qakan by his hair. It was the father. He said something low and hard, and Qakan let Kiin go. He asked Qakan something, and Qakan, rubbing his head, said to Kiin, "Go with him. He will take you to the women."

The man led the way up the beach and Kiin followed.

Beach shale gave way to gravel, the gravel to grass. A path wound around a hill until they came to a valley, and even in the darkness, Kiin could see twelve, fourteen mounds, like long ulas, except the roofs were not sod, but scraped hides, peaked in the center. Light from inside the mounds lit the skins so each looked like a small glowing fire on the valley floor. The mounds were arranged around one very long ulaq, this one only dimly lit, and Kiin wondered if these people had a shaman or a powerful chief who lived there.

The man beside her pointed to a ulaq near them and said something, then grasped her hand and pulled her with him to the place. A sudden fear rose up inside her, and she wished she understood his words.

What if he were taking her to be his wife? How could she give herself to any man when Qakan had cursed her? How could she give herself when she knew the man taking her would be cursed?

As they neared the ulaq, Kiin could see a rectangular opening on one side. A flap of woven grass covered the opening. The man opened the flap and a woman's voice greeted him. Then a second woman's voice.

He pulled Kiin inside, and she saw that two old women sat cross-legged, facing each other, a grass mat draped over both of their laps. Each woman was sewing a pattern at an end of the mat. Their needles were threaded with long strands of colored sinew. Both women had the white hair of the very old; both had round faces; lines spread from the corners of their eyes and mouths. They wore hooded parkas as the men did, but these parkas were decorated with strips of fur at the wrists, and the fronts were colored with bright shell beads in a pattern of triangles.

The man said something and one of the women laughed, her mouth opening to show that she had no teeth. She held up her needle and the other woman leaned forward and bit off the strand of sinew dangling from it. They rolled the mat, and the man helped them stand. Then they scurried around the large room of their ulaq, pulling out furred hides and containers filled with roots and dried meats, all the time looking at Kiin and whispering to one another. The man shook his head and laughed, saying something to Kiin, and the old women looked up and joined the laughter.

The man laid his hand on Kiin's shoulder. "You are safe here," he said in the First Men's language, and Kiin stared after him, her mouth open in surprise as he left the ulaq.

A short time before, Kiin had been afraid he would take her as wife, but now, without him, she suddenly felt alone. She stood, her eyes on the door flap, willing him to come back, but finally she turned and faced the women.

They were spreading out a floor mat. "Sit down, little one," said the woman with teeth, and she, too, spoke in the First Men's tongue.

The women began to giggle, a silliness in the laughter, like the laughter of little girls, then the toothless one said, "Long ago my sister and I were born to the First Men. We, too, once came as brides, and we, also, each carried our firstborn when we came."

Kiin's eyes widened and she placed her hands over her stomach.

"Do not be surprised," said the one without teeth. "My sister has a gift of visions. We knew you would come, though we told no one."

She handed Kiin a wooden bowl filled with dried meat and small white slices of some root. "It is important that you eat," she said.

Kiin took the bowl and held it in her lap. How could she eat when they were not eating? They would think she was rude. But one of the old women leaned forward and scooped up a handful of the mixture and pressed it into Kiin's mouth. The food was good, and Kiin was hungry, and so, without looking at them, she began to eat. The meat was rich, like whale meat, but also with the taste of seal. And the white root was pungent, cutting the tallow of the meat.

The women moved closer to Kiin as she ate, making her feel uneasy, and she wondered whether she was expected to share the food, and so she held the bowl out to them, but they shook their heads. Kiin noticed that they did not take their eyes from her face, and suddenly, she remembered stories she once heard of spirit women, whose food carried curses or even death.

But no, Kiin thought. These women were too full of laughter. They seemed more like children than old women.

She took another bite of the meat. Yes, it was rich and good, and the root . . . Kiin was sure she had not tasted it before, but it was much like bitterroot bulbs. Another bite; she was tired. Perhaps after she ate she would tell them how much she needed to sleep. They would understand when she told them she had not slept for two days.

Kiin scooped her fingers into the meat. Was the meat at the bottom of the bowl different? Thick and sticky? No, Kiin told herself. You are tired. All things seem strange when you are tired. Another bite. But this mouthful . . . this mouthful was almost too thick to swallow.

The two old women sat down and again began to work on their grass mat. They were talking—in the Walrus tongue? Kiin was not sure. Their words stretched out, slow and long, as though each syllable were a thread strung from wall to wall.

Darkness pulled at the corners of Kiin's eyes, and she felt as though she were again in the ik, rocking with the swells of the sea. She shook her head. I have spent too many days in the ik, she thought. The waves still seem to move me.

"I am t-tired," she said to the women, and she tried not to close her eyes. But the women stared at her, as if they could not understand what she said.

Kiin searched within for her spirit's voice. It would tell her what to do. But her spirit no longer answered her, and she felt as though she were a child again, without a name, without a soul.

She was suddenly afraid, and tried to get up, but could not. She opened her mouth to speak, but the only sound she could make was a tiny cry, as though not she but her unborn child controlled her voice. Kiin moved her eyes toward the women, and the effort took all her strength.

They smiled at her as though nothing were wrong, and then smiled at one another. Then Kiin closed her eyes, closed her eyes to see darkness. And dimly, softly, sifting in through the grains of her sleep, she heard the toothed one say, "We know about your curse."

37

"We cannot."

"You want to curse all of us?"

"We will be cursed either way. It is better to have the power of the good one to help us in this. Besides, we can kill the evil child after its birth."

"But how will we know which one is evil? Can anyone tell before a child has ten, twelve summers?"

Kiin fought the clouds that seemed to drift in her mind. Where was she? Who was speaking? It was not Crooked Nose or Little Duck.

"You, not I, see visions," said one of the women. "I will do what you say."

"Then let her sleep. It is nearly morning and the men will want to trade for her today."

Kiin suddenly remembered the women's faces: as yellow as dock root and wrinkled, one with teeth, one without. What had they given her to make her sleep so hard, without dreams, as though she had been dead?

And with sudden panic, she remembered that her spirit had seemed to leave her, that she had been alone. In her fear, she opened her eyes, saw the two old women bent over her. Then in that moment, she heard a quiet voice, something from within, yet also from without, for Kiin's spirit and both women spoke at the same time, saying, "Do not be afraid."

A stillness settled over Kiin, and she again closed her eyes. Again slept.

She awoke to the smell of cooked fish.

"Eat, little one."

Kiin opened her eyes. The old woman with teeth was bending over her, holding out a shell bowl full of fish, flaked into sections.

Kiin sat up and took the bowl. She looked into the woman's eyes.

The woman smiled. "There is nothing in it but fish," she said. "Eat it and then we will talk."

"You and-and your s-sister should eat, too," Kiin said.

The old woman looked over her shoulder at her sister and the sister filled two more bowls. They sat down facing Kiin, and when they began to eat, Kiin did also.

When the bowls were empty, the toothless one asked, "Do you want more?"

"No," said Kiin. "It was enough." She felt stronger, her head clear.

The toothed sister gathered the bowls and wiped them out with her hand. Then she sat down again.

When the two women did not speak, Kiin glanced up at them and saw they were both staring at her. She almost looked away, but then realized that they meant to test her power. Had she not seen the men of her village do the same? Kayugh was always winner, able to keep his eyes under his own control, to stare as long as he wished without blinking, without looking away.

Remembering Kayugh, Kiin kept her eyes fixed between the women, so she could see both, but be dominated by neither. She fought each blink until her eyes began to burn, then she turned her thoughts from herself to things that brought joy in her life: the softness of a well-tanned hide, a finished seam of tiny stitches, the morning call of the auklet, the graceful swimming of the otter. These things kept her mind from the pain of her eyes, even when tears formed and spilled to her cheeks.

"She is strong," said the toothless sister.

"She has to be," answered the other. And both sisters blinked, giving Kiin clear victory. And so when they began to speak to her, Kiin was not afraid.

"You should know our spirit names," said the toothed sister. "Though they are something most people, even the people of this village, do not know."

"A spirit name is a sacred thing," said the other sister. "Something that is tied to the soul."

"Then why t-tell me?" Kiin asked. "You d-do not know me."

"We are linked by the bond of our people, the First Men," said the toothed one. "And by my dreams."

Kiin wetted her lips. Had they not told her they knew about her curse? So why take a chance with the sharing of names?

"Do not t-tell me," Kiin said.

But as if they had not heard her, the toothed woman said, "My true name is Woman of the Sun, but you should call me Aunt as do all the people of this village."

The toothless one said, "I am Woman of the Sky, but in this village I am called Grandmother."

Kiin could not answer them. They had given something too sacred. But then she thought, Perhaps they did not give true names. They knew her curse. Or perhaps they were so powerful, they had no fear of her curse. Perhaps they wanted only to know her name. But why? Her name was not as sacred as the name of an old woman. It had not been with her long enough to gain much power, and she had no spirit name.

"I am c-called Kiin," she said.

The old women nodded. "And you have no other name? No true name of the spirit?"

"It is not the c-custom of our village," Kiin answered.

The women looked at each other, then the toothed one said,

"You must have one. It is too dangerous to face our people without one."

"This you must keep secret," said Woman of the Sky. "Do not even tell the man who takes you as his wife."

The women turned to face each other, and though they gestured with their hands, Kiin heard no words. But finally Woman of the Sky said, "My sister names you for she has the greater power."

Kiin felt a strange stirring within her, not from her spirit, but from within her womb as though her baby were afraid. And for a moment Kiin forgot that there was a chance the child she carried was Qakan's. For a moment she was only a mother, frightened by her child's fear. She placed her hands over her belly and asked, "Why is my b-baby afraid?"

Woman of the Sky opened her mouth as if to speak, but closed it. Then again the two sisters began the strange silent movement of hands, the talk without words, and the uneasiness that pulled at Kiin became stronger.

Finally they both turned back to her. The toothed one spoke. "Little one," she said, taking Kiin's hands, patting them as if Kiin were a child, "there is something you must know about the child you carry." She paused and reached into the top of her suk and pulled out an amulet, the leather old and dark. She squeezed the amulet in a slow rhythm, the rhythm of the pulse, the heart beating. "The spirit of the one you carry is strong, too strong for one body." She held Kiin's eyes with her own, and Kiin realized how powerful the woman was, and again the child in her womb moved as though it were afraid.

"A man, perhaps, could contain it. But a child . . ." She shook her head. "A child would die.

"So the infant you carry chose the path of life. He became two. One half taking the good of the spirit, the other half the evil."

Woman of the Sun paused, and Woman of the Sky leaned forward to say, "When you came, my sister had been warned in a dream of your curse. We decided to kill your baby and so protect our people. That is why we gave you the white root. It would not have harmed you, only the child."

"But the child was too strong," said Woman of the Sun. "And then its spirit spoke to mine, telling of blessings as well as a curse, telling of two children, one evil, one good."

"Two children . . ." Kiin said. And suddenly it seemed she could feel two babies, moving, one lying up against her ribs, the other hard and solid within the cradle of her pelvis. And she wondered whether the good one was Amgigh's, the other, the evil one, Qakan's. "S-s-so you cannot kill the evil w-without killing the good," Kiin said.

"Yes."

"But after the b-birth you will k-kill the evil one."

"Yes."

"But who can s-say whether a new baby is g-good or evil?"

"Perhaps their spirits will speak to your spirit," Woman of the Sky answered.

Kiin shook her head. "The evil one will lie."

"The secret will be revealed to you," Woman of the Sun said. "Some way, you will know. Then you must have the power to do what has to be done."

"So we give you another name," said the toothless one. "Something that holds power." She got up slowly and hobbled to a niche in the wall, then drew out a small bladder pouch. Holding it out toward Kiin she said, "If the name we have chosen is a good name, a name of strength, the liquid in this pouch will taste sweet to you, like the goodness of fresh seal oil. If it tastes bitter, we must choose another name."

She brought the pouch to Kiin and sat down. Kiin held it in her hands as both old women closed their eyes and began to chant. There was a tightness within Kiin's chest, a fear that was more than the movement of her children, as the truth of the old women's words sank into Kiin's soul. She laid the pouch in her lap and placed both hands over her belly. Two children. One evil, one good. One to hate, one to love.

Suddenly the old women began to moan, a chant that was

more like weeping. And finally the toothed one said, "You are Tugidaq—Moon."

The sister repeated the words, then said, "Drink."

Kiin raised the pouch to her lips and drank. The liquid was rich and sweet.

38

Woman of the Sun and Kiin sat together in the ulaq. Woman of the Sun had begun another weaving, and Kiin had offered to help her. Woman of the Sky had left the ulaq while it was still morning, and now it was noon.

"She will not tell the men about your babies," Woman of the Sun said.

The thought had not occurred to Kiin, but she nodded, wondering at the trust she now had in the two women.

"Too many of the men would kill both babies at birth, taking good with bad."

"You must do what is best for your village," Kiin replied, her fingers sorting and rolling lengths of grass for the weft of the mat. Then Kiin realized that her words had come easily, without stammering. A good sign, she thought. A good sign.

"Yes," said Woman of the Sun. "My sister and I have agreed that there are only two men in the village strong enough to be your husband. She went to make sure at least one of them makes an offer for you."

Kiin's hands tightened on the ball of grass she was holding. Qakan had little power. His spirit was weak. Why should he be allowed to claim her for trade? The old women had food and a warm ulaq. Kiin would be safe with them. She cleared her throat and asked, "Could I stay here and take no husband?"

Woman of the Sun laid her hands in her lap and looked at Kiin. "Every woman wants a husband," she said. "And the two we seek for you are the most powerful men in the tribe. Ice Hunter is the one who brought you here last night. He is chief hunter, but his wife died two summers ago and in his grief he has not taken another. The other man is Raven. He hopes to become shaman of our tribe. He has two wives, but he is a man who always wants more." She picked up several strands of grass. "I would choose Ice Hunter," she said. "He even speaks the First Men's language. But perhaps he will not make an offer."

Kiin smiled, remembering Qakan's awkward use of the Walrus language when all the while Ice Hunter understood First Men words.

"Ice Hunter seems to be a good man," Kiin answered. "But I do not want a husband. If I stayed with you, I could help in many ways. I could gather sea urchins and bird eggs. I will help you weave."

"We weave death mats," said the old woman. "With the babies you carry, it is best you do not help us much."

Kiin quickly raised her hands from the grass she was sorting, but Woman of the Sun smiled and said, "This is only a ulaq curtain. Something for us."

Kiin cleared her throat. "I will bring food. I can fish, dig clams."

"We are given food for our mats," the woman said. "And Ice Hunter brings us much meat." She smiled. "He is my sister's son."

The words did not surprise Kiin. There was a strength in Ice Hunter that spoke of Woman of the Sky's care. But then Kiin realized the compliment Woman of the Sky was giving her when she asked Ice Hunter to consider Kiin as wife.

"Why do you not want a husband?" Woman of the Sun asked.

For a long time Kiin did not answer, but finally she looked at the old woman and when their eyes met, she said, "I have a husband among the First Men."

"You have other children?"

"No," Kiin said quietly.

"Ice Hunter told us that the man who brought you here owns you as slave. That he captured you from the Whale Hunter tribe. But you are of the First Men. That is one of the things I learned about you in the vision."

"Yes, I belong to the First Men," Kiin said.

"Then why did the man who brought you lie?"

"It is his nature to lie."

Woman of the Sun stared at her, then closed her eyes and began a gentle rocking. With eyes still closed she said, "He claims to be father to your babies. But he hurt you. He forced you. You did not want him."

The old woman opened her eyes. "That is not enough to bring the curse you carry."

"He is my brother," Kiin said softly.

For a long time, Woman of the Sun said nothing. Kiin felt the babies move within her, and she placed a hand on her stomach.

Then Woman of the Sun asked, "Why did you come with him?"

Kiin pulled back the sleeves of her suk and held up her scarred wrists. "He forced me," she said. "He told our people I had drowned, then brought me here."

Woman of the Sun closed her eyes. "Is your other husband a shaman or a great hunter?"

"No," Kiin said, lowering her head. "He is only a boy. Just this summer he took his first sea lion."

"Then you must know you cannot go back to him. He would not be strong enough to stand against the curse of your children. Do as my sister and I say. You will have protection."

The ulaq door flap opened and Woman of the Sky stepped inside. "They are ready for the trading," she said. "Both Ice Hunter and Raven will offer a bride price."

The large ulaq glowed with light. Eight openings in the roof let in outside light, and niches in the side walls were crowded with burning oil lamps.

Woman of the Sun led Kiin into the ulaq, and the people made a way for them, many of the women bowing their heads as Woman of the Sun passed. The old woman squeezed Kiin's hand, and a surge of strength coursed up Kiin's arm. Then instead of looking down, Kiin raised her head, met the eyes of those staring at her.

The children were round-cheeked and fat, many with beautiful eagle skin parkas. One little girl reached out shyly and touched Kiin. Kiin smiled at her. She reminded Kiin of Amgigh's baby sister, and the pain of the remembering made Kiin's eyes burn, but she forced back her tears. She could not return to her people. Even Woman of the Sun said so.

Woman of the Sun stopped to talk several times, but they finally broke out into the open space at the center of the ulaq. Four men sat there, each with a pile of trade goods. Kiin recognized the tallest man, though his face was no longer painted. Woman of the Sun leaned close, and whispered, "Ice Hunter."

Of the other three, one was an old man, bent and white-haired, another was young, perhaps only two or three summers older than Kiin. The third man was neither young nor old. His face was heavily marked with tattoos—straight black lines on his chin like the tattoos of the Whale Hunters, and chevrons, one following another, over both cheeks until the points met and crossed at his nose. His hair, black as a cormorant's wing, was so long that it touched the floor when he squatted beside his trade goods, and it was greased so that the oil lamps were reflected in its darkness. His eyes were narrow and slanted, but the brown circles of his irises were so large that Kiin could not see the white around them except when he looked to one side or the other.

Woman of the Sun raised her hands. The murmur of voices that had filled the ulaq stopped. The old woman said something, the words in the rhythm of the Walrus tongue.

"I told them you were the one to be given as bride," she said to Kiin in a low voice. "I told your man to come and claim you."

"He is not my man," Kiin said, but the old woman left and Qakan took her place.

He smirked at her and said, "I hope you had a good bed during the night. Look, see her?" He pointed toward a woman in the crowd. She was young and carried her head high, and she was beautiful, her cheekbones tall in her face, her lips small and pouting. She smiled at Qakan and slowly closed her large eyes, then turned to say something to a woman beside her. When she turned her head, Kiin saw that a wide section of her hair was yellow, lighter than the gold of willow twigs in early spring.

"I shared her bed," Qakan said.

Kiin's eyes widened, and for a moment she thought that Qakan was telling another of his lies. But then Qakan smiled at the woman, and the look that passed between them told Kiin that her brother spoke the truth.

"She is wife to the shaman, Raven."

Kiin said nothing, but a fear began to grow in her. If the Raven gave wives in hospitality, would not all Walrus men do the same? She had spent too many nights with traders, but could a woman defy her husband?

Then Kiin's spirit said, "Why are you surprised? You have heard your father's boasts after trading visits to the Walrus People."

"How many women did you have?" he would ask Big Teeth, and then claim that he had taken a different woman each night.

"Remember, you do this to protect the First Men," her spirit voice said, the words a comfort to Kiin, something that slowed her heart and pulled her mind from its own thoughts to the realization of what was happening around her.

Qakan sat down, but when Kiin squatted beside him, he hissed, "You must stand." She stood slowly, moving a short distance from him. She felt awkward, standing in the center of the circle, most of the people watching her, but then an old man stepped from the crowd. With a loud voice, he quieted the people then pointed to the four men offering a bride price and returned to his place.

Each of the four men said a few words. Then they laid out their trade goods.

They offered walrus skins, bundles of lemming hides, pouches of shell beads, grass mats and ulaq curtains. The old man offered a basket filled with crude spearheads, one of shiny black obsidian. But the youngest man had a walrus tusk, its surface completely carved with men hunting. When he held it out, Kiin gasped. The piece was as beautiful as anything she had seen. The young man smiled at her, but Kiin dropped her eyes, suddenly remembering that she must go to Ice Hunter or the Raven, no one else.

Ice Hunter had the largest stack of furs. One of the hides was covered with long yellow-white fur. He unrolled it slowly, and Kiin could see that it was stiff, but the fur was long, and Ice Hunter yanked at it with both hands, showing that the hide was well-tanned, none of the fur pulling out.

The Raven offered fewer furs, but the ones he had were furs that carried some special sign of luck. All the lemming skins were banded with white at the neck, and three pieces of walrus hide carried a strip of black hairs the length of the back. Two fur seal skins were pure black, no marks on them.

Qakan looked up at Kiin, squinted his eyes and licked his lips. He spoke to the Raven and the man pulled something from a pile behind him. It was an amulet. The shaman opened the bag and pulled out its contents: an obsidian spearhead, perfect in shape but as small as the tip of a man's finger; a thin bracelet of braided sea lion whiskers; a whale shape, cunningly cut from baleen; a tiny ivory box with fitted lid, inside a chunk of red ochre; a bear tooth; and an intricate braid of dark, coarse hair. Kiin knew the pouch was a hunter's amulet, each object except the spearhead from some animal of great power.

The Raven cocked his head and looked at Kiin through slitted eyes. A chill prickled her skin. She was a woman to be traded. All men looked at her with wanting in their eyes. But the Raven's look was something more, something that made Kiin's spirit pull itself tight against her backbone.

Qakan looked at the other men, asked a question. The Raven's gifts were best. Kiin knew there was no question of their worth. The youngest man turned and spoke to a woman behind him. She dragged out a pile of white furs, long-haired and soft, the bound stack as high as a man's knees. He cut the babiche that held the pile and pulled out several of the furs, each perfect and perfectly tanned.

"Fox furs," Qakan whispered to Kiin and chuckled.

"Fox?" Kiin said. But then she remembered hearing Big Teeth talking about the small, sharp-toothed animals. Larger than lemmings, smaller than seals.

Then the Raven, too, drew out a bundle of fox furs. Some white, some nearly black.

The furs drew a murmur from the people, but Qakan shrugged one shoulder and shook his head. He looked at the old man, but the old man only smiled and held out empty hands.

Qakan stood and pulled Kiin to him. "Lift your suk," he demanded, but Kiin, curling her lips, answered, "They know I am w-with child. D-do you think you can f-f-force more for a trade by acting as though they are so s-stupid as to have forgotten?"

Qakan scowled and raised his hand as though to strike her, but then Woman of the Sun, speaking in the First Men's tongue, said, "She sings. In my vision, I heard her. She makes songs of great power. Every hunter needs songs of power."

Qakan, anger snapping in his eyes, hissed, "Sing."

Kiin looked at those around her then closed her eyes. Always there was a song close to her, rising from her heart into her throat, the words dancing as men and women dance to celebrate something with joy; but this day, the sorrow and fear in Kiin's chest made something not quite a song, more a cry of mourning, lift itself into her mouth, and she began a high chant of sorrow for the old man and for the young man, for Ice

Hunter and for this people. The words came, a new song, something Kiin had not sung before:

> *For your gifts, for your trading*
> *I give you curses.*
> *For the furs you have taken from earth and sea*
> *I give you sorrow.*
> *There is evil here.*

> *Where are your spirits?*
> *Do they not feel what I bring?*
> *Why do you fight to curse yourselves?*
> *Why do you greet me with joy?*
> *There is evil here.*

This song she sang, once, twice, until Qakan, smiling at all those around, turned his back to Kiin but clasped one of her wrists and, keeping it hidden between them, squeezed until the small bones ached.

"You curse us with your song," he whispered.

"They d-d-do n-not understand the wor . . . words," Kiin replied and jerked her hand away, holding her arm and rubbing her wrist so the men who traded for her could see he had hurt her.

Qakan began to speak again in the Walrus tongue, and then so suddenly that Kiin could not react, he pushed his hands under her suk and brought out the whale tooth shell.

Kiin's eyes widened. She had been careful to keep the shell under her suk, afraid that if Qakan saw it too closely and realized it was whale tooth not shell, he would demand to add it to his trade goods.

"This, too, she does," he said, speaking in the First Men tongue, directing his words to the two old women, then speaking again to the Walrus People in their language. "Did she tell you she carved this from a whale's tooth?"

Kiin noticed the sudden light that came into the Raven's

dark eyes and even Woman of the Sun looked surprised. She whispered for a moment to her sister then walked forward to take the shell from Qakan's hands.

She turned it carefully then looked at Kiin. "You carved this?" she asked.

"It is n-nothing. It does n-n-not even look like a sh-shell," Kiin answered, feeling embarrassed that Woman of the Sun should look carefully at her poor work. In her mind she saw the baskets that held her father's carvings, misshapen seals, puffins, too short or too long, animals that looked as though some child had formed them, and she remembered that when she was younger, she had dreams in which all animals were as her father carved them, limping and deformed. She looked again at her shell, at the uneven whorls, the long ridge that marred one side. "I carved it," she said.

"You have a gift," Woman of the Sun said.

"No," Kiin answered. She shook her head. "I s-see here what it sh-should be," she said and pointed to that place in her head, just behind her eyes, where images and dreams seemed to gather. "But-but I cannot make wh-what I see. It d-does not come out right. But my songs . . . they are . . . what they should be."

But Woman of the Sun held Kiin's shell up for all to see, and for a horrible moment, Kiin thought she would trade the shell, take that small bit of power that Kiin still owned, but then the old woman handed the shell back to Kiin and at the same time, Ice Hunter called to someone in the crowd, and one of his sons, the man with the scar, carried something draped in a caribou hide to the center of the circle. Ice Hunter waited a moment until the people were quiet then slipped off the hide.

Kiin's eyes widened. Under the skin was a large face. Carved from wood, it was nearly as tall as a man and brightly painted in reds and blues. The eyes were drawn down at the outside corners, blue tears dripping from them to the chin. But the mouth was open in a wide grin that showed sharp white seal teeth embedded in the wood.

Ice Hunter spoke, and Qakan turned to Kiin, saying, "He tells us it was won in a raid from the Dancing Tribes that live over the mountains and many days to the south. It carries their tribe's power to bring animals before a hunt."

Then the Raven spoke, and Kiin recognized the challenge in his words even though she did not know what he said. He clapped his hands, and Qakan gasped. The woman with the yellow-streaked hair stepped forward and stood beside the Raven's pile of trade goods.

At a command from the Raven, she took off her suk and dropped her leggings, standing with only aprons, front and back. From behind, the Raven leaned forward and cut the waist string of her aprons, letting them fall to the floor. The men in the ulaq grew loud, laughing and talking, and Qakan giggled, but the woman held her head high. She looked at Qakan and slowly licked her lips, then she raised her arms above her head and turned, swaying her hips. Her skin was greased and it glowed in the lamp light.

The Raven laughed, but he reached for her suk, tossing it to her. She slipped it on and sat down beside the trade goods bare-legged.

"I have chosen your husband," Qakan suddenly said in a loud voice, but as he spoke, Woman of the Sun came forward. She stood before Qakan, and the people were suddenly silent. Even the golden-haired girl lowered her eyes.

"It is not your choice," Woman of the Sun said to Qakan in the First Men's tongue. "Your sister is not a slave, so it is her choice. In our tribe the woman decides. You choose two. Then she takes the one she wants."

Qakan's mouth dropped open, and he looked at Kiin. His eyes darkened, and he said, "You told them about the curse."

Kiin shook her head. "Sh-she knew. I d-did not need to t-tell her. She is a . . . d-dreamer of visions. I told them only that I was your s-sister."

"You are an ignorant woman," he said, his voice rising to a high squeal.

Then Woman of the Sun, her words hard and full of power, said, "Make your choice. Choose two."

Qakan drew back his lips in a smile that showed gritted teeth and pointed to Ice Hunter and the Raven.

The old man shrugged and smiled, but Kiin felt a hurting at the disappointment in the young man's eyes.

"Now you must choose," Woman of the Sun said to Kiin.

Kiin looked at Qakan and he whispered, "If you choose Raven, I will give you one of the fox skins for your baby."

But Kiin did not look at the trade goods. Instead, she looked into the Raven's dark face, into Ice Hunter's clear eyes.

She took a step toward Ice Hunter, but then heard her spirit say, "He is a good man. What if the old women are wrong? What if he cannot withstand your curse? He has offered the wooden face, perhaps it holds his power."

Kiin looked at the man and allowed her sorrow to flow out from her eyes, for she wanted him to know he was her true choice. Then she turned to the Raven. "This man," she said pointing to him, and heard Qakan's choking gasp, the low laugh of the golden-hair.

The Raven smiled, his lips drawn out in a square that showed all his teeth, then he stood and shoved the golden-haired woman into Qakan's lap. Qakan laughed out loud, but pushed the woman from his lap and crawled to the pile of trade goods, now his. He pulled out a fox fur and tossed it to Kiin, saying, "You chose well."

But Woman of the Sky stepped forward and said to him, "Give her two fox furs."

Qakan looked at her, surprise showing in his face, but he giggled and pulled out another pelt and threw it to Kiin.

Kiin draped the furs over her arm. The Raven was staring at her, his head tilted back, thin lips curled in a smile. Kiin stood straight, eyes unblinking.

No one heard her spirit's mourning cries.

39

K iin followed the Raven from the long house at the center
of the Walrus People's village to a ulaq set closer to the
hills. She had noticed the ulaq before. It was large and, unlike
most of the Walrus People ulas, had a sod roof. The Raven,
then, was the one who lived in this place, he and his two wives,
though now perhaps the yellow-haired one was no longer his
wife. How could she be? She belonged to Qakan.

And so if the Raven were powerful enough to have such a fine
dwelling, was he indeed a shaman? Something inside Kiin began
to quiver. There had never been a shaman in their village, but
she had heard stories of their power to control spirits. And it
seemed, at least in the stories, that most shamans eventually
used that power for evil. What had Kayugh said? That a man
cannot hold that much power. It creeps into his spirit, steals his
soul.

The Raven pushed Kiin ahead of him into an entrance at the
side of the ulaq. The entrance was a small tunnel woven of
willow branches and covered with grass mats. It slanted down
into the ulaq and was so low that Kiin had to crawl on hands
and knees to get through it. When she and the Raven emerged
from the tunnel, a man greeted them.

The Raven said something in the Walrus tongue, and Kiin,
unsure how she should greet the man, nodded, and since the

man was old, his face lined, his dark hair full of gray, she low-ered her eyes in respect.

The ulaq smelled rank, as though it were filled with rotten meat, but all things looked neat; the mats on the floor were new, the storage containers that hung from the walls, dry and strong.

Two women were crouched on the far side of the ulaq, one woman combing the other's hair. The Raven grunted at the two and rudely pointed. But the women seemed to find no insult in his pointing, and they greeted Kiin. One offered Kiin a length of dried meat, and the other held up a basket of bitterroot bulbs. But the Raven gestured impatiently at them and pushed Kiin through the walrus hide curtains that partitioned the ulaq.

On the Raven's side of the curtains, a large oil lamp hollowed from the top of a boulder was in the center of the room. The only sleeping place Kiin saw was a raised platform cushioned with skins and furs. The stink was even stronger here; the floor was littered with scraps of rotted meat, bones and molded bits of food.

A woman—young, though not as young as Kiin—came for-ward and offered the Raven food. He slapped her hands away and said something to her in the Walrus tongue.

A sly look of joy came into the woman's eyes, and she picked up a large basket and began to cram it with pelts from the sleeping platform.

The Raven waited until the woman had finished then spoke to Kiin, but Kiin shook her head and shrugged. How could he expect her to understand the Walrus tongue? She had been in his village only two days.

The Raven wrinkled his nose, curled his mouth and said something to the woman. She glanced at Kiin, then left the ulaq. The Raven went to a storage skin and pulled out a handful of meat. He squatted on his haunches and ate but offered noth-ing to Kiin.

Kiin felt a small bubbling movement within her belly and wondered if her babies felt as uncomfortable here as she did.

Finally, she sat down. She was wife and so must be ready to make her husband comfortable, to bring water, prepare food, but she had stood for a long time that morning. She might as well be comfortable herself.

Soon the Raven's other wife returned. Woman of the Sky was with her. Kiin felt some lifting of her heart when she saw the old woman, but Woman of the Sky did not speak to Kiin. Instead, turning her attention to the Raven, she said something in the Walrus tongue and then listened as the Raven spoke to her.

Finally Woman of the Sky turned and spoke to Kiin, and though the old woman did not smile, Kiin saw the light of a smile in her eyes.

"Raven wants you to know that you are his wife now," she began.

"Yes," Kiin said.

"This other woman is called Lemming Tail. She is now his first wife and you must do what she says. First of all, she will teach you to speak the Walrus tongue. Raven says you must learn quickly.

"Yellow-hair, the one your brother bought, she was once first wife. Now Lemming Tail gathers Yellow-hair's things to take to her. Do you have any questions?"

"The old man we saw when we came into the ulaq. Who is he?"

"Grass Ears," Woman of the Sky said. "He is Raven's uncle. He has two wives. His daughters are grown. Raven is more like a son than a nephew, at least in the honor Grass Ears gives him. But Raven gives little in return."

Again the quivering came into Kiin's spirit. A man who did not honor his uncle—how would he treat his wives?

And as though she read Kiin's thoughts, Woman of the Sky said, "You should have chosen Ice Hunter."

"Yes," echoed Kiin's spirit, "Woman of the Sky told you that Ice Hunter was strong enough to be your husband. You should have chosen him."

But then Kiin thought, What mother does not see her son as

being stronger, wiser, greater than he truly is? I have chosen. I will not fill my mind with thoughts of what could have been.

"I could not choose him," Kiin said, but did not look into Woman of the Sky's eyes as she spoke. "He is a good man. I could not take the chance I would curse him."

Woman of the Sky nodded. There was sadness in her eyes, but no anger. She turned and spoke for a time to Lemming Tail. Kiin saw a sullenness in Lemming Tail's face, the look that Qakan wore when he was forced to do something he did not want to do. Finally the Raven spoke, interrupting Woman of the Sky, but the old woman continued to speak to Lemming Tail, as though the Raven's words were nothing more than the wind. Even when she finished speaking to his wife, Woman of the Sky did not answer the Raven, but instead said to Kiin, "If you need me I will come, or my sister."

She left the ulaq and the Raven spoke to Lemming Tail, his words hard.

She said something to the Raven, anger in her voice, and the Raven slapped her. He took Yellow-hair's basket and left the ulaq, left Kiin alone with Lemming Tail.

Then some spirit seemed to whisper to Kiin: "So, you have two small fox furs, your suk, the necklace that Samiq made, the carving from Chagak and a whale tooth shell. No woman's knife, no needles or scraping tools, no pounding stone, no chunks of sinew or sealskins."

"But I have two babies," Kiin answered, speaking out loud. And her words were brave, her voice strong, without stuttering.

When Kiin spoke, Lemming Tail raised her eyebrows, then she began to laugh. Kiin did not like her laughter. It was too much like Qakan's laughter, like the laughter her father used when he ridiculed her. But then Kiin's spirit whispered, "You have traveled from one end of the earth to the other, a journey most hunters never make; you have danced with Walrus men, and are loved by a man who is now a Whale Hunter. What is a little laughter?"

Lemming Tail reached out and touched Kiin's suk, then she fingered Samiq's necklace, but Kiin pushed the woman's hands away. Again the woman laughed, and the laugh, high and screeching, made Kiin's skin pull up in tiny shivering bumps. But then Kiin, too, began to laugh. She laughed as she looked at the filth on the floor, at the tumbled pile of baskets heaped in a corner, the torn walrus hide curtain that hung over the food cache, and in rudeness, she pointed. In rudeness, she laughed.

Lemming Tail's lips curled, and she hissed angry words. Then she dug into a pile of half-finished baskets, threw one to Kiin.

Kiin took the basket to a place near the oil lamp; she waited, sure Lemming Tail would give her grass for weaving and a water skin, but Lemming Tail went over to the sleeping platform and lay down, curling herself under the furs with her back toward Kiin.

For a time Kiin watched and waited, but finally she put the basket down and began to straighten the room. Hides had not been kept dry, and floor mats had begun to mold. The whole ulaq carried their smell. She wished for Kayugh's clean, well-kept ulaq. Even her father's ulaq was clean, the floors padded with heather and new mats, bones collected and thrown out or saved for carving.

When Kiin had picked up the bones and food scraps on the floor and replaced the worst mats with several she found in a pile beside the food cache, she gathered the debris and carried it outside, far from the ulas to a place where the wind would carry the smell away from the village.

Fireweed, tall and glowing, grew at the edge of the village. Kiin twisted the tough stems until they broke and she had six pink flower heads in her hands. They were old, beginning to go to fluff, but the blossoms were still sweet, perhaps something that would help the stink of her husband's ulaq.

She returned to the ulaq, again politely refused the food Grass Ear's wives offered her, smiling at them this time. Their hair, though cut bluntly to shoulder length, was dark and shining, and they were so much alike in looks, with long narrow faces, slanted eyes and wide mouths that Kiin knew they must be sisters.

When she came back into the Raven's room, she noticed that Lemming Tail was breathing the long, quiet breaths of one who slept, so Kiin worked quickly to scatter the fireweed she had picked, then began to straighten the basket corner, sorting baskets according to size and shape, piling them so they could be used. Three were full of something that had once perhaps been food and were good for nothing now but to be thrown away. These she stacked beside the dividing curtain and continued to work until she had another pile of refuse: molded skins, old baskets, a water bladder full of holes. Again she gathered the load and took it outside, again she returned to the ulaq to find Lemming Tail asleep.

Kiin wished she could go through the food storage cache as well, but as second wife, she had no right, and so finally returned to the basket Lemming Tail had given her. Kiin had found a bundle of ryegrass laying against the ulaq wall. She took a clay-lined basket that she hoped would be water-tight and poured it full of water from a walrus bladder that hung on one wall. The water was tepid and had a brackish smell, but she dipped her hands into it and ran her wet fingers over several blades of grass.

A song began like a thin thread in her mind, words that spoke of the sea, of the ice and the blue men that lived in the ice. She sang as she split grass into fine strands with her thumbnail and twisted it into a coil.

But as she sang, worried thoughts, like wisps of smoke, curled into Kiin's words. The Raven was her husband now. He would expect her in his bed that night.

"You have had men you did not want in your sleeping place before," her spirit whispered. "At least the Raven is your husband. Do not forget that you are as strong as he is."

But Kiin knew her spirit spoke only to comfort her and was

not telling the truth. The Raven was strong, strong enough to own two wives, to trade for another. Strong enough to stand against the curse that Kiin carried.

She worked until some prodding of her spirit made her look at the sleeping platform. Lemming Tail was sitting up, her ears covered with her hands. But singing was one thing Kiin knew she did well, so she allowed herself to smile at Lemming Tail, allowed herself to smile in the way a woman smiles at a bothersome child.

There was a noise on the other side of the curtain and suddenly, so suddenly that even Lemming Tail looked startled, the curtain was drawn back, and Kiin saw that many women, perhaps all the women of the village stood in the Raven's ulaq.

Kiin stopped singing and put down her basket. She stood, and when she stood, Woman of the Sky came forward and said to her, "They come bringing gifts to Raven's new wife."

Then each woman came, first Woman of the Sky, then Woman of the Sun. They each brought a basket of herbs and laid them before her, then Woman of the Sun took a place beside Kiin and as each woman came, Woman of the Sun leaned forward to whisper in Kiin's ear, saying names and telling Kiin the Walrus People words for each object as the women brought everything a wife needs: needles, awls, rolls of babiche and chunks of sinew for sewing; sleeping mats and furs; grinding and cooking stones; baskets and containers for oil; storage containers for meat; fish gorges and a digging stick.

The women laughed and joked, and only Lemming Tail and Yellow-hair seemed sullen. Kiin was included in the laughter because Woman of the Sun or Woman of the Sky explained what the others said, so that soon Kiin learned many words in the Walrus language.

And once when one of Grass Ear's wives said how fortunate Kiin was to be wife to Raven, Woman of the Sun, after telling Kiin what the woman had said, eased Kiin's fears by whispering, "No one will dare treat you like a slave. And you will even have many months before Raven will take you to his bed. No Walrus man will enter a woman who is pregnant. She would curse his hunting."

So Kiin pulled these words close inside her chest and found herself smiling more easily, laughing more quickly.

Yellow-hair, on her turn to give a gift, held closed hands out to Kiin and when Kiin cupped her own hands under Yellow-hair's, Yellow-hair opened her fingers to show she would give nothing. Even then, Kiin laughed, laughed so hard that the other women, standing with faces red at Yellow-hair's rudeness, began to laugh as well until Yellow-hair, blushing, pushed her way through the women and sat down, knees drawn up to her chin, on the sleeping platform. Then Kiin saw Lemming Tail go quickly to a basket in the corner of the ulaq, and when she gave Kiin a gift, it was a crooked knife, something quite beautiful, the blade a thin slice of chert inserted in the side of a caribou rib, and Woman of the Sun told Kiin that the rib had been given in trade from the Caribou People, who lived far to the east where ice marked the edge of the world.

Kiin smoothed her hand over the rib and thanked Lemming Tail, Kiin hoping that perhaps this gift would mark the beginning of a friendship, but as Lemming Tail turned away, Kiin saw a look of mockery pass between Lemming Tail and Yellow-hair, and so Kiin knew the gift was not a gift of the heart.

When the women left, the Raven returned to the ulaq. Kiin was at the back of the large main room finishing the grass basket. The Raven sat down on a floor mat, leaned back against a pile of furs, and watched her through the narrow slits of his eyes. The man was so still that at times Kiin thought he was asleep, but if she reached to dip her hand into the water basket, she could see the gleam of his eyes following her, and his gaze seemed to weaken her fingers, making them shake as she worked. She tried to calm herself by repeating the new words she had learned that day, but the dread again seeped into her chest and grew so large that it pushed against her heart, making it skip and tremble.

"Remember what Woman of the Sky told you," her spirit whispered. "You are with child; no Walrus man will take you. The Raven will not touch you. You would curse his hunting." But though the words had comforted Kiin that afternoon, now she doubted what Woman of the Sky had told her. Who could say what powers the Raven possessed? He was not a man who would obey the rules of his people.

Lemming Tail watched Kiin also, but from the corners of lowered eyes and with quick glances.

When the Raven had come back into the ulaq, Lemming Tail gave him food then removed her suk and fur leggings and oiled her legs. Kiin had tried not to show her surprise when she saw that Lemming Tail's legs, from ankles to knees, were tattooed in a complex pattern of triangles and dots. Kiin thought the marks made Lemming Tail's legs look black and ugly, but she could tell by the way Lemming Tail smoothed the oil carefully over the designs that the woman though they were beautiful.

When the Raven finally rose, he pulled Lemming Tail to her feet, slid his hands over her back, then up around her neck. And Lemming Tail looked at Kiin with a taunting smile as she followed the Raven to the sleeping platform. But Kiin also smiled, trying to keep the relief from her eyes.

The Raven said something to Kiin and pointed to a place beside him on the sleeping platform. Again, Kiin's heart began its troubled beating, but the Raven turned his back to her and Kiin crowded herself into the farthest corner of the platform, also turning her back.

Soon the Raven and Lemming Tail filled the ulaq with the noise of their lovemaking, and Kiin could not sleep. But then Kiin pulled a song into her mind and held it there to cover the Raven's groanings, Lemming Tail's sighs and callings.

And for once Kiin was glad she did not yet understand the Walrus tongue.

40

"*There will be more changes,*" Fat Wife told Samiq as she handed him a shell filled with a broth of ugyuun and cod.

But Samiq would not look at the woman. He did not want to see her smile as she told him about another of his punishments. It had been enough to spend the remainder of the summer learning with the small boys, to miss the fall hunts. Many times Samiq had decided to go back to his mother's people, to return without the secret of the Whale Hunters' poison, but the thought of Kayugh's disappointment kept him with the Whale Hunters, made him decide to wait at least until the spring.

And perhaps Kayugh would not welcome him back if he came without the skills he had been sent to learn. Then where would he belong?

But that morning, Many Whales had given him another harpoonhead. It was not as fine as the one that had been lost with the whale, but Samiq knew the weapon was a sign that Many Whales still wanted him to hunt.

If I am allowed to hunt, Samiq had thought, I can bear to stay here until I am skilled enough to teach the First Men. Then I will return to my people and I will see what truth Kayugh hides in his heart, and I will know whether to stay or to find another beach. And if I must find another beach, I will come to the Whale Hunters and to the First Men only in trade.

But now Fat Wife's words made Samiq uneasy, and he turned away from her and began drinking his broth.

Fat Wife continued to talk, speaking of the women in the village and of the children. Then she said, "Children again in this ulaq will be a fine thing." She chuckled and said through her laughter, "Who knows, perhaps tonight the noises in this ulaq will make Many Whales come again to my sleeping place." She patted her thick middle and said, "There is still time for me to make another son."

Samiq listened with open mouth, trying to make sense of the old woman's words. Then Fat Wife held up the thick furred parka she was sewing, and Samiq saw it was nearly finished.

"It was supposed to be for Many Whales," Fat Wife said and chuckled, "but he has one as every husband should. So it is for you."

Samiq spilled his broth, and he gasped as the liquid splashed on his bare chest. Now he knew the reason for Fat Wife's smiles, and he was angry that he had not been told. Many Whales treated him like a woman, always making decisions for him.

He looked down at her round, fat head and asked, "Who is to be my wife?"

Fat Wife smirked. She was without her side teeth and the gaps made black holes in her smile.

"My husband tried to buy you Small Flower, but her father is afraid that you will take her away, back to the Seal Hunters. And Speckled Basket has been promised to Crooked Bird, so your wife will be Three Fish."

Three Fish, Samiq thought, and felt as though he had been hit, the blow knocking the wind from his lungs. Speckled Basket would have been bearable. How could he forget their time together in the grass? But Three Fish . . .

Fat Wife flipped her apron like a young girl and turned, then said, "My husband says that there is no man in this village with hands large enough to hold her." She slapped her buttocks and laughed.

It was a joke best told by a man, and Samiq pretended he did

not hear. He set his dish down. He had nothing to say to Fat
Wife. What good would it do to protest? What difference
would it make?

Fat Wife's chuckling stopped, and Samiq was surprised at her
next words for she said, "Whale Killer, all women are the same
in the dark."

Three Fish's parents brought her to Samiq that night. Samiq
made himself smile when they came. But each time he looked
at Three Fish's wide face, at her broken teeth, he felt an ache
begin in his chest, and in his mind he saw Kiin, her delicate
features, her gentle smile, and he remembered her hands firm
but soft against his skin.

I will please my grandfather, Samiq told himself. Then perhaps he will tell me the secrets of the whale poison and I will be
able to return to my people.

"But you will have a wife to take back with you," an inside
voice said, arguing within his chest like the Whale Hunter
women argued within their ulas.

No, she will want to stay with her people, Samiq told himself.
She will not come with me, and I will be free of the Whale
Hunters. But now I must do this to please my grandfather.

And he made himself smile, made himself say words of welcome to Three Fish's father and to smile at Many Whales, to
laugh at the jokes the two men told about the taking of women.
Fat Wife sat in the corner, her back to the men as was the
custom, her hands busy weaving a basket, but at each joke,
Samiq saw her shoulders shake, so he knew she was listening.

Three Fish stood behind her father. She was wearing an otter
fur suk, the bottom edge banded with dangling shells and curls
of colored seal esophagus. Her hair was smoothed back into the
tight bun married women wore, and her face was painted with
red ochre, something Samiq knew women painted on sealskins
to preserve them, and he wondered what custom among the
Whale Hunters said that new brides should have red faces.

Three Fish's father was as large as Three Fish, his shoulders and hips making a wide square within his parka, the man twice as big as Many Whales, his face round and smiling like Three Fish's. His chin tattoos ran in three vertical lines, and his eyes were full of light.

"You know he is a good man," Samiq's inside voice told him. "He will make a place for you in hunting trips and will welcome you into his ulaq." But still the ache remained in Samiq's chest, and he could feel no joy.

Finally, when the joking was done, Fat Wife left her corner and fed the men. As new husband, Samiq was not allowed to eat, but made to sit watching as Three Fish's father and Many Whales ate ugyuun broth and whale meat.

Then the men stood. Three Fish's father took her hand and placed it in Samiq's hand, then Fat Wife, now allowed to be part of the ceremony, pushed the couple into Samiq's sleeping place and pulled the curtain shut behind them.

"Make babies," she called after them and Samiq heard Many Whales and Three Fish's father join her laughter.

Samiq squatted down. He had released Three Fish's hand and, in the darkness of his sleeping place, was not sure where she was. Then she moved, pushing herself against his arm, slipping her hands inside his parka. She giggled and stroked Samiq's chest, but Samiq thought, Fat Wife listens and laughs, too.

"You do this for your father," his inner voice said. "For your people." But then he thought, How much does a man give to his father? How many years for the years given? How much shame in exchange for learning? A life forever with such a wife?

With Three Fish as wife how can I make a life for myself? I will be like a child in my own ulaq, her words louder than mine.

He suddenly pushed Three Fish from him and stood up, his head brushing the ceiling of his sleeping place.

"Lie on your back and be quiet," Samiq ordered and Three Fish's giggles turned into a small gasp. "I am your husband and you will do as I say. Do you understand?"

He waited, wondering if Three Fish knew he was afraid she would not obey. But her answer was small and quiet.

"Yes, husband."

"And tomorrow, begin a new curtain for my sleeping place. This curtain is old. And make the new curtain wider."

Three Fish did not answer, but she did not laugh, and Samiq closed his eyes and thought of Kiin, Kiin in his bed, Kiin soft under his hands. And when Samiq was sufficiently aroused, he dropped to his knees and spread Three Fish's legs, holding himself up with his arms so his chest did not touch her when he took her as his wife.

41

*A*mgigh *pushed his paddle* into the water, three strokes left, three strokes right. The North Sea was calm, and its calmness made Amgigh uneasy. It was not a usual thing to have the water this clear green-blue; it seemed clear enough to see far under the surface, to the depths where the spirits lived, to the depths where the whale had pulled him. . . .

No, he told himself. This is always the color of the North Sea. It is always this clear. The many days I had to spend in the ulaq made me forget what the sea was like. I have forgotten. I have only forgotten.

Gray Bird—Waxtal—had wanted to come with him this first time out since the whale. So had Kayugh. But Amgigh was not sure how he would react. What if he could not make himself paddle out? Would he want other men to see his shame?

When he had finally emerged from the ulaq, out of the safety of close, dark walls, just watching the sea had made his stomach tighten in fear.

It is better that I go alone, he told himself. There was that chance that the sea had stolen his courage. And so he went, ignoring the tears on Chagak's face, the fear in Kayugh's.

But now all things seemed different: the cold of the water; the windless silence; the heavy gray of the shore. Even the paddle did not seem to fit his hand. He wished there was someone with him, someone who would sing hunting songs, who would sing songs of men stronger than the sea.

Then he remembered something Chagak had told him when he was only a child—if he was alone or afraid to tell the sea of his strength.

So Amgigh raised his voice, called out toward the open water, "I am strong. I do not boast to you. I tell you only the truth. I am strong. Even the whale could not kill me."

"Yes," he whispered, and he lowered his head to speak in toward the center of his chest so his spirit would hear his words. "I am strong."

Even after the days lying in his sleeping place, his legs were powerful, not as thick as Samiq's legs, but well-muscled. Even now with each stroke of his paddle, his thighs pushed hard against the bottom of the ikyak.

He lifted his voice, began a song. It was an old song, a song that praised sea lions and called the otter brother. Even Kayugh did not know who had first thought of the words. A grandfather, Kayugh said. Someone who hunted well.

As Amgigh sang, he remembered other songs and then remembered the full richness of Kiin's voice singing, the songs she sang, sometimes with new words, old songs sung in a new way. Then, even as he paddled, in his mind Amgigh saw Kiin's small hands against his skin, felt the feather-touch of her fingers. He closed his eyes, shook his head. Her spirit should be gone now, should be at the Dancing Lights. But who could say? Perhaps it had been captured by the sea, perhaps each ripple of water held a small part of her soul, enough so that Amgigh would see her, feel her, each time he was in his ikyak.

Perhaps the water pulled his thoughts to her. Who could doubt that the sea was a living thing? Who could doubt the powers it carried? Surely the spirits of whale and sea lion were part of the foaming, breaking waves. Amgigh remembered his first time in an ikyak. His legs had been small, thin, his arms as weak as birdbones. The sea had clasped his paddle, tried to wrest it from his hands. And what hunter did not say the same? What hunter did not know that the sea tested, proved, until it was sure the boy would be a good hunter, worthy of taking seals, worthy of taking sea lions.

Amgigh could still remember the ache of his muscles after that first day in the ikyak. Arms, shoulders sore from lifting and pushing his paddle, sore from fighting the suck of the water if he plunged his paddle too deeply, the chop of waves when he did not plunge it deeply enough. He remembered the ache of his hips as he sat with legs outstretched and wide apart to help him balance the ikyak. And he remembered that he had been afraid.

Samiq had not been afraid. Even the first day, Samiq had purposely flipped his boat, emerged laughing as their father rolled the ikyak and brought Samiq back from the sea. Though Amgigh returned from that first day with his new chigadax still dry, while Samiq in his exuberance had flipped his ikyak twice —and each time been scolded by their father—Amgigh knew that Samiq was again the one with the gift. Samiq would learn to move like a seal, and Amgigh would be left behind.

And now Waxtal said Samiq would return from the Whale Hunters and expect to be leader of the First Men. Yes, Waxtal said, Samiq would teach them to hunt whales, but he would also proclaim himself chief hunter.

Amgigh and Waxtal had been sitting together at the top of Waxtal's ulaq. Amgigh was weak from the days he had spent in his sleeping place, and his eyes were still not right, seeing darkness at the edges of all things, sometimes seeing double.

For a long time, they had sat without speaking, but then Waxtal shook his head, made a choking noise in his throat. "Your father has made mistakes," he said. "I have seen his mistakes, though I kept my words to myself, but he is a good leader, and he is wiser than Samiq will ever be. Samiq will be a man who boasts of his own skills. He will come back from the Whale Hunters with nothing but boasts. But what else could we ex-

Sue Harrison

pect? Samiq's true father . . ." And then his words drifted off, but Amgigh had finished Waxtal's words in his head. Samiq's father was a Short One, a man who killed men.

Then Waxtal's words were low and murmuring, as if he had forgotten Amgigh was beside him: "Samiq will think that he has earned the power to be chief hunter. He will not think of Kayugh. He will think only of himself."

And Amgigh, pulled into his own thoughts, wondered if Waxtal was right. As a boy Samiq did not boast, did not push himself ahead of others. But Waxtal knew the Whale Hunters better than Amgigh did. Who could say how Samiq would change after living with them for a year?

"Even if Kayugh no longer wanted to lead our people," Waxtal leaned over and whispered to Amgigh, "you would be the better chief." And Amgigh had laughed, but Waxtal said the same thing the next day and again the day after that, until finally one night, in Amgigh's dreams, animals came to him: otters and lemmings and seals and sea lions. Each told him he should be chief, chief above Samiq.

But now, alone on the open sea, away from Waxtal's whisperings, Amgigh knew his own thoughts, and he realized that he did not want to be chief. He did not even like to hunt, though his aim was true and he was often the first to see the dark head of sea lion or seal above the waves. But he also knew he did not want Samiq to be chief.

Amgigh sighed, studied the shore. Aka's island seemed to have more birds than Tugix's island but he had not come here for birds. He had come to climb Okmok, the mountain on the far side of Aka's island. There, on the north side of Okmok, was the shining bed of obsidian, the sacred stone of their people.

Amgigh pushed his ikyak farther out on the sea. Yes, there, he was sure. He saw the glint of obsidian, the dark gash that seemed to grow down from the white and blue glacial ice above it.

It was a long and difficult climb, but he had done it before. Once with his father, another time with Samiq. There were several good beaches on this island, good places for villages . . . someday, perhaps, he and Kiin would . . . No, Amgigh thought, not Kiin. But he would find another wife, perhaps someone from the Whale Hunters, and when he gave Samiq obsidian knives in return for teaching him to hunt the whale, then Amgigh would find a wife, would trade for her with whale meat and his obsidian knives.

Then he would have sons and his sons would learn to make weapons, even finer blades than Amgigh could make, until every hunter wanted a blade made by Amgigh or one of his sons. It would be that way. Yes, and then Samiq would see who had the greater power.

The climb was long, and the wind was cold as it pulled against Amgigh's parka, against his fingers as he sought handholds in the dead grass. But in his concentration, Amgigh did not feel the cold, did not allow himself to wonder if the wind pulling against him was Kiin's spirit, calling him to follow her into the spirit world. He had too many knives to carve, too many blades to make. He needed to be a man, strong enough to carve rock, his hands hard with calluses where his fingers gripped the stone. What could a spirit do with stone? Stone and spirit—their worlds were separate.

Three nights he spent on Aka's island, three nights with Aka's spirits, with the grumblings from Okmok's great fires deep beneath the rock. But what did he have to fear? Okmok was a powerful mountain, but Aka was more powerful, and Okmok was known to have good spirits. Why else would the mountain pour forth the shining black obsidian, the spirit stone of the mountains? And who had more right to that stone than a man who made knives, the best knives. No, he was not afraid. No.

Each day of the three days Amgigh climbed. Each day he pried and chipped and picked up spalls of obsidian that had been torn loose by wind and rain and sun, all the powers of the sky, and by ice and rock, grinding slowly, the powers of the earth working patiently. Where else did a man gain the knowledge to knap stone, but from the sky? Where else did a man learn such patience, but from the earth?

Each day Amgigh gathered the stone he had won from the mountain, rolled it up in a thick piece of sea lion skin and bound it to his back. Often as he made his way down the mountain, holding fast and letting go, grass to rock to grass again, he checked the leather to be sure the obsidian did not cut through. And so in three days, he had three sea lion skins full of stone.

Then before beginning his journey back to his people, he threw out the ballast stones in the bottom of his ikyak and replaced them with the spirit stones. And as he began the journey back to his people, back to his own village, he sensed the difference in his ikyak. It was stronger, faster, and even when the calmness of the North Sea surrendered once again to high, white-foamed waves, Amgigh felt as though his paddle cut into the water with a new sureness, and the ikyak itself skimmed easily, wave to wave, like a bird, flying. And as he paddled, he thought of the new obsidian knife he would make for himself, to replace the one he was sure Qakan had taken. And he would make knives for Samiq, each blade itself worth the knowledge of whale hunting.

42

S amiq smoothed his harpoon shaft with a chip of lava rock and
looked across the ulaq at Many Whales. The old man's head
was bent, his eyes closed. Once Hard Rock had become chief of
the Whale Hunters, Many Whales had suddenly seemed to
grow old, as though he were no longer a man, but again a boy
dependent on others for his food, for the necessities of each
day's living.

Samiq thought that Many Whales had learned to trust him
again, that Many Whales saw him once more as a man, but
perhaps Many Whales saw him as a man only because Many
Whales himself was once again boy. And still the other men of
the tribe did not include him in their evening gatherings, did
not ask him to tell stories of his hunts.

"They will see you as a man when you put a son in Three
Fish's belly," Fat Wife told Samiq. "Then they will give you a
place as whale hunter." And leaning forward she would glance
over her shoulder and if Many Whales seemed to be sleeping,
she would whisper, "Then they will tell you the secrets of their
poison."

But again this morning Samiq had heard Fat Wife's comforting words to Three Fish, "It is a good time to rest. It is a good
time to rest." And he knew that once again he had been unable
to plant a child in his wife's womb. Three Fish would be spend-

ing several nights in the hut set aside for women who were in their time of bleeding.

The Whale Hunters were more strict than the First Men about a woman's bleeding. In all other things among the Whale Hunters women were nearly as important as men. Women were allowed to sit in counsel on all things but hunting plans. Men often prepared their own food and sometimes even repaired their own parkas, but during a woman's bleeding, she had to leave the ulaq for fear her blood would curse her husband or his weapons. It seemed strange, but who was Samiq to question the Whale Hunters' customs? They were the ones who knew how to take the whale. Who could say what a woman's blood could do to a whale harpoon? Even the First Men made women in their first bleeding live alone.

Samiq shared his wife's disappointment. What man did not want a son? But that night as he lay on his sleeping mats, he thought, It is a good time to rest—for both of us.

He was asleep when he felt a gentle prodding, and at first, still caught in dreams, he pulled away. Then, thinking that it was Three Fish, he sat up. Anger pushed back the remnants of his dreams. How dare Three Fish come into his sleeping place during her bleeding? Did she care nothing about his weapons?

But then the woman spoke, and Samiq realized it was Fat Wife, not Three Fish.

"Many Whales needs you," she said.

There was the choke of tears in her words, and suddenly, Samiq's heart was beating at his throat. His voice was dry and raspy when he asked, "What has happened?"

"He is very sick. He cannot see. He cannot move."

Samiq jumped past Fat Wife and ran to his grandfather's sleeping place. Many Whales lay on his sleeping robes. One side of his mouth was strangely crooked, and Fat Wife crouched beside him to wipe at the spittle that bubbled from his lips.

"He cannot see," Fat Wife said, her words broken by her tears, the fat under her chin trembling.

Samiq knelt beside the old man and touched his forehead. "I am here, Grandfather," Samiq said softly.

There was a gurgling in the old man's throat, and Samiq turned toward his grandmother.

"He cannot speak?"

"At first he could speak, and he told me he could not see. Then he called your name, and now . . ."

Many Whales groaned and then slowly lifted his left hand. Samiq reached for the trembling fingers, but Many Whales suddenly shuddered. His hand jerked toward Samiq's face, and the fingernails left scratches on Samiq's cheek as the hand fell.

Many Whales lay still and Fat Wife leaned over him. She licked her fingers then held them over his mouth; she pressed her head to his chest.

She sat up and straightened the robes that lay over him. "He is dead," she said softly.

A misty rain surrounded them as they stood beside the mound of rocks that was Many Whales' grave. When they covered Many Whales' body with rocks, Samiq was uneasy. He thought of the discomfort that the old man's spirit must feel, the weight of rocks against it, but no one made an objection and so Samiq did not speak. He remembered from his mother's stories that different people cared for their dead in different ways.

The women ended their mourning cries, and Hard Rock, his whale spear in one hand, spoke to Many Whales' spirit, to the spirits that always gather near the dead, then he used the spear to pierce the bottom of Many Whale's ikyak, and the boat was laid over the pile of rocks. Hard Rock began a death chant, but over the sound of the chant, Samiq heard the calls of geese on the beach. And Samiq wished he could be one of those geese, white and silver-gray, spreading wings in the wind, away from this burial, away from sorrow, from mourning.

There was a strange emptiness in Many Whales' death—a loneliness—and Samiq realized that Many Whales had been the cord that bound him to the Whale Hunters.

Now why should I stay? Samiq wondered. What keeps me here? If I did not have a wife, I would leave, he thought, and was suddenly, foolishly angry at Many Whales for dying.

But then, as though Many Whales spoke to him, Samiq thought, What good would it do to go back now, knowing only in part? I need to stay so I can teach my people.

Someday, Three Fish would give him a son. He had lost Many Whales' power, but with a son, there would be something gained. Perhaps enough to learn the secrets.

During the forty days after Many Whales' death, that time of mourning, Samiq avoided his wife, taking care not to look at her, not to be alone with her. Of what use was she? In mourning, a woman could not share her husband's sleeping place. What man wanted a son conceived in mourning, a daughter that reminded him of death?

Samiq spent much time away from the ulaq, fishing with the old men, digging clams with the children. But as the mourning time passed, Samiq noticed that Three Fish had grown thin, her face pale, her laughter hollow.

It is not her fault that she is my wife, Samiq finally told himself. It was chosen for her as it was for me. Besides, it was as Fat Wife had said: in the darkness all women were the same. Sometimes Three Fish was Speckled Basket, sometimes Small Flower, always Kiin.

That night, as they sat in the dimly lit ulaq, Samiq found he could not work on his weapons as he usually did. He wanted to walk, to be away from the Whale Hunter people. In his restlessness, he raised his eyes to study the women who sat sewing close to the oil lamps. They were quiet, Fat Wife's face gray and drawn, Three Fish looking smaller, less formidable.

Samiq stared at Three Fish. Did she know that yesterday was

the last day of mourning? Did she count the days with marks on the ulaq floor like Fat Wife? Did she watch the moon as he did? Three Fish looked at him, but glanced down quickly when Samiq met her eyes. There was a sadness in her look, a hurting that Samiq had thought Three Fish was too insensitive to feel.

"Wife," he said softly, and she looked up at him, and when he stood she stood also, and even Fat Wife looked up and smiled. But Samiq did not care. Let her think what she wants, he thought. Perhaps it will ease her sorrow.

In the darkness of his sleeping place, Samiq waited for Three Fish to lie down, but she remained beside him until he gently pushed her toward the sleeping mats. Three Fish's hand closed around his wrist and she leaned close to his ear, then whispered, "You are of the Seal Hunters and I know your spirit is with them."

Samiq was surprised at her words, but before he could answer, she said, "In my heart, I call you Samiq."

He could not see her, but he reached in the darkness to touch her face. I am to her as Kiin is to me, Samiq thought. And a sudden aching came to his chest, an understanding.

"Before you return to your people," she said. "Give me a son."

A sudden lightness filled Samiq's chest. She had given him his release, asking no more from him than what he wanted to give. And as he laid her back on the sleeping robes, in the darkness, Three Fish was Three Fish.

LATE WINTER, 7038 B.C.

Chagvan Bay, Alaska
and
Yunaska Island, The Aleutian Chain

43

Kiin awoke in pain. The muscles of her abdomen pulled
until the pressure that had begun in her back encircled
her hips and ground into her bones. She turned to her side and
took several deep breaths. The pain stopped and she relaxed.

She wished she could stay on the sleeping platform, but as
second wife, it was her morning duty to light the lamp and lay
out food.

She pushed herself to her hands and knees, her belly hanging
nearly to the sleeping mats. The pains had begun four, five days
before, and were infrequent, but they made it difficult for Kiin
to sleep nights or to finish her work during the day.

She crawled out into the ulaq, added oil to the lamp and
blew gently on the smoldering wick until it caught again and
burned brightly. But the effort brought another pain, this one
more intense than the pain that had awakened her.

It had been more than eight moons since Qakan had taken
her. For much of that time, she had lived as second wife to the
Raven, though not truly wife. Since she was pregnant, he had
not taken her to his bed, but she knew once the babies were
born, he would expect her to be wife in all ways.

Kiin went to the food cache and pulled out several storage
containers made of stiff dried walrus hide. One contained
smoked halibut, the other roots. The Raven ate much halibut,

and he also liked the tiny bulb roots that the women dug from mouse caches in the sod.

Kiin scooped out a bowlful of the bulbs and began to peel off the outer coating. They were so tiny that Kiin used her fingernails to skin them. Now in the spring, after storage through the winter, the roots were beginning to soften, but the Raven still liked to eat them raw.

Kiin tried to be a good wife to the Raven. She had learned what foods he liked most and how to prepare them, how to make the long furred leggings both men and women wore and, most important, to speak the language, though her frequent mistakes still brought muffled laughter from the women, smiles from the men.

Kiin heard Lemming Tail groan. Some mornings the Raven was awake before Lemming Tail, and then he would nod to Kiin and eat in silence, but if Lemming Tail woke first, she would order Kiin to bring something from outside, even when the snow was deep and the winds strong.

Lemming Tail crawled from her sleeping place, combing her fingers through her thick black hair. Each day, she oiled her hair and brushed it with a bundle of reed stalks, and Kiin also had gathered reed stalks and begun brushing her hair, hoping to make it shine as Lemming Tail's did.

Lemming Tail, in the custom of the Walrus People women, wore only her short aprons front and back. She stood beside Kiin, watching as Kiin peeled the last of the bulb roots then said, "There is nothing fresh here. My husband is tired of dried winter food. Go to the beach and find sea urchins."

Kiin laid aside the bulbs and rose without looking at the woman. There was no choice. Lemming Tail was first wife and so must be obeyed. She knew as well as Kiin did that there would be no sea urchins. Kiin pulled on her suk and leggings and the long thick fur boots that Woman of the Sky had made for her. The boots were soled in ridged walrus hide to make walking on the beach easier.

When she left the ulaq, the sun was still only a hint of brightness in the southeast, and once Kiin was away from the protection of the village, the wind hit her strong and cold, bringing on another pain. She bent forward to relieve the pressure in her back and protect her face from the wind, but continued to take small, slow steps until she reached the beach.

The pain ended, but when she straightened, she saw that someone was there before her—a man. She began to back slowly toward the village, afraid that he was someone from another tribe, someone who could not be trusted.

A gust of wind swirled up from the frozen bay. The man raised his hands over his face, turning slightly toward her, and Kiin realized it was Qakan.

Another argument with Yellow-hair, Kiin thought, for the two fought often, and Qakan, always the loser, was sent out to walk the beach or find warmth in another ulaq.

Qakan had stayed the winter in the Walrus People's village, and though he often said he would leave in spring, he had made no preparations to do so.

Usually, if Qakan saw Kiin, he would not acknowledge her, but this time, he grinned and ran over the icy beach to meet her.

"You are awake early," he said, speaking in the language of the First Men.

"N-no, I usually r-r-rise before my husband to prepare food," Kiin said, and she spoke in the Walrus tongue.

As soon as she said the words, Qakan's smile faded, and he curled his lips. "You think your husband will honor you because you have learned his language so quickly?" he asked.

He lowered his face to Kiin's and stared at her, but Kiin felt no power in his eyes, and she said to him, "What m-m-my husband d-does is not your concern. He has made you a rich man. That sh-should be enough." Then she turned her back and walked away. It was good to speak to him without fear that her angry words would bring retaliation. What man would dare hit the Raven's wife?

But then Qakan called to her, the high whine of his voice

bringing back memories of their earliest years together. She turned and waited for him, saying nothing as he began his complaints about Yellow-hair and Ice Hunter's ulaq where Qakan and Yellow-hair lived.

Finally Kiin interrupted him. "Will you r-r-return to our . . . people this summer?"

"Perhaps," he answered, "but Yellow-hair wants to stay here."

"The wife d-does n-not rule the husband," Kiin said.

Qakan snapped, "She does not rule me."

"Then g-go. But r-r-remember people from our village gave you things to trade for them. Make g-g-good trades."

"I cannot trade at this village," Qakan said. "They know what Raven paid for you. They will expect high trade prices from me. All I will be able to get is lemming meat."

For once Qakan spoke without whining, as a man stating a fact, and Kiin realized that he was right. And with the realization came the emptiness of knowing that she would have no chance to influence her brother's trades. Any trades would be made in villages many days' journey from the Walrus People's camp.

She turned away, but then felt the strength of her spirit, of the babies she carried. She took a long breath and looking back over her shoulder said loudly and without stammering, "After you trade, come back to this village. That way I will know whether you have traded well."

Qakan began to laugh. "Why should I?"

"If you trade well," Kiin said, "I will ask the Raven to give you an amulet of power."

Qakan shrugged and walked away, but Kiin had seen the interest in his eyes. Perhaps it would be enough to make him choose wisely.

Kiin turned to look out at the cove, and another pain twisted out from Kiin's spine. She squatted on her heels. After the pain peaked, Kiin's spirit whispered, "You are stronger than the pain."

Kiin stood slowly. She was alone on the beach. Qakan's tracks made a trail back to the village. Then remembering why she had come, Kiin grimaced at the thick rim of ice that had built up on the shore. How could Lemming Tail expect her to bring sea urchins?

"Do not worry about Lemming Tail," Kiin's spirit said. "Today you will give your husband something greater than fresh food."

Kiin started to walk the long curve of the beach, stopping only when a pain came. Woman of the Sun had told her to stay outside as long as possible once her labor began, to walk and speak to her sons, to tell them of all things created.

So Kiin walked, but for a time her thoughts went to Samiq. Perhaps even now, he had forgotten her. Perhaps he had a beautiful wife, one of the Whale Hunter women.

"Yes," Kiin said. "And when he returns to our people, they will tell him I am dead. And that is best. He is not strong enough to stand against my curse, or even against the Raven."

But Kiin's feet seemed to walk to the rhythm of Samiq's name, and the image of his face was so bright in her mind, he might have been beside her.

Then a pain pressed in on Kiin, pulling her into a tunnel of darkness, a place without thought or remembrance. And when the hurting ended, Samiq's face was gone, but in her mind she saw the faces of two infants, one asleep, one crying. She could not say who they looked like, Amgigh, Samiq or Qakan, but already she had made her choice, already she had decided. Of the two, if one looked like Qakan, he would be the cursed one, the one given to the wind spirits. And so she prayed that one would look like Samiq or Amgigh so her choice would be clear, then she stood and began to walk again, singing to her babies of the sun and the stars, the earth and the sea, of rivers and mountains, all things created, all things sacred to men.

44

W<i>oman of the Sky found her</i> on the beach. Kiin was crouched down, clasping her knees, grinding her teeth against the pain.

"Tugidaq?" Woman of the Sky said, and Kiin felt the woman's hand on her head. "How long have you had the pain?"

Kiin could not answer, could barely understand Woman of the Sky's words, but then the pain passed and Kiin looked up. "Several days. Hard since this morning."

Woman of the Sky glanced at the haze of light that showed the sun's place in the clouds. "Do you feel the need to push?"

"No," Kiin said. "Only the pain."

Another pain came. It drew Kiin back into the darkness at the center of her mind. Then her spirit said, "Samiq." And the name was like an amulet, something to hang on to, something to hold Kiin above the pain.

"The birthing shelter is ready?" Woman of the Sky asked.

And when the pain had ended, Kiin said, "Yes." She had spent the last few days building the framework, layering mats over the poles that the Raven had cut from a stand of willow, taller than a man, that grew in a sheltered place in the valley tundra between mountains. He had brought her five willows, dragged them out, three on his right shoulder, two on his left, and Kiin had set them back beyond the village, away from the wind, out of the path of smoke that rose from the roof holes of the ulas.

She bound the willows at the top as she had seen her mother bind the driftwood poles of the bleeding shelter, then Kiin layered mats over the poles and sewed grass over the mats in an overlapping thatch that would keep out rain or snow.

Inside, she put the things a mother would need: sealskins, softly napped, to wrap the babies; old mats to soak up the blood of the birth; full water skins; and a seal stomach of dried fish— the humpback fish that Kiin had not tasted until she had come to the Walrus People—a summer fish so that Kiin would not curse hunting by eating flesh of fish or animal that was caught during the time of the birth.

She had a woman's knife to cut the babies' birth cords and sinew thread to bind the cords so they would not bleed. Woman of the Sun had given her a basket full of soft moss, good to pad a baby's carrying strap and absorb a child's wastes. She had oil to clean and soften the babies' skin, and dried nettle leaves to steep for tea, the leaves something the Raven had bought from traders, the leaves more difficult to get than even nettle twine and good to help the afterpains of childbirth.

Woman of the Sky pulled Kiin to her feet, held her up during the walk to the birthing shelter, and when Kiin was inside, Woman of the Sky went to get Woman of the Sun.

When the two sisters returned, Kiin had her eyes squeezed shut against a pain. The pain ended, and Kiin saw that the sisters were tying the ends of a thick braided cord of sealskin strips to the shelter's willow poles. Woman of the Sun pulled the cord over to Kiin. "Hold on to it," she said, wrapping Kiin's fingers around the braid. "When a pain comes, pull. Your shelter is strong enough to stand, even against all your strength, and your pulling will help push the babies into the world."

The pains came again, harder, faster, until Kiin was so tired that it all seemed as though she were living in a world of half-sleep. Dimly she heard Woman of the Sky's chant: pull, breathe, pull, breathe, breathe, breathe, pull. And through the words, through the pain, Samiq's face, Samiq's name, Samiq's voice. In the pain Kiin forgot all else—forgot that she was Amgigh's wife, forgot the Raven, forgot Lemming Tail, forgot Qakan, forgot the Walrus People—remembered only Samiq, Samiq, Samiq.

The babies came in the night, under the rise of the full moon. Kiin felt the pressure of the first head in her birth canal; then a different kind of pain, this time worse, the tearing of skin, the wideness of the baby as it passed from her body. Then quiet, no pain, the murmurings of the old women.

At the baby's sudden cry, Kiin called out, "No!" For her first thought was that Woman of the Sun or Woman of the Sky had used their knives against her son. Then Woman of the Sun held the child up, and Kiin saw that the boy was whole and strong.

"Remember, Tugidaq," said Woman of the Sky, "one is cursed."

"Listen to the spirits. They will tell you which one," Woman of the Sun said as the baby wailed.

But Kiin saw no curse, only her son, only the long fingers and toes, the fine straight hair, the short wide nose of the baby's father: Amgigh. "No curse," she said. "No curse."

Then again the pain, this time so sudden that Kiin could not keep from crying out, and so her second son was delivered to his mother's screams, and when Woman of the Sky held the child for Kiin to see, she closed her eyes in sudden joy at the wide shoulders, the thick black hair, the slant of the gull-wing brows. Samiq's son. Samiq's son. No curse. No curse.

Kiin sat holding her babies. Already she had forgotten her pain. She had forgotten her fear of the curse that had been a part of each day's wait while she carried her sons. She had forgotten her dread when Woman of the Sky first held each of the babies for Kiin to see, her fear that she would see babies with features like the fish that sometimes washed up on the beach, huge and scaley with bellies as white as dead man's skin.

To calm her dread, Kiin had told herself it would be enough to be alone in the birthing hut, without the Raven's orders, without Lemming Tail slapping her or pinching her.

Also, since the Raven had seen her whale tooth shell, he demanded that Kiin carve. Each day, he brought in driftwood from the beach, and Kiin, using a small crooked knife, carved. And as she carved she saw that her knife brought forth the same misshapen animals her father had carved.

And though Kiin held the true image of the animal in her mind, her fingers could not make what she saw come to life. There was always some flaw, one eye larger than the other, one paw too small, flippers turned the wrong way, but the Raven was pleased with her work, grunted his approval, and each night he collected her carvings, wrapped them in soft pieces of furred sealskin and packed them in baskets. He had even brought her a piece of walrus tusk, and Kiin had carved it into an ornament for his hair.

Lemming Tail hated Kiin's carvings, and she often taunted Kiin about their ugliness. Kiin was ugly also, Lemming Tail said, too ugly to be in Raven's bed. Did Kiin think he would take her as true wife once the babies were born? No. He did not want her. He wanted only the two sons Woman of the Sun had said Kiin would bear. But Kiin only smiled and wondered why Lemming Tail should care. Yes, the carvings were ugly. It amazed her that only she and Lemming Tail should be able to see that.

But though the carvings were ugly, Kiin knew she was not ugly. Men do not give up so many furs for an ugly woman. And Lemming Tail herself should know that the Raven took only beautiful wives. Lemming Tail was beautiful, her eyes not dark, but a golden brown, her hair with flecks of red in its blackness. And what of Yellow-hair? Was she not beautiful, her body as graceful as water falling? So Kiin knew she was not ugly, though as the days passed she had grown clumsy and large-bellied with her two sons.

But now, in the birth hut, she did not have to carve. Now she was alone and could make up songs, could sing and nurse her sons. But most of her joy came from seeing that one of her sons looked like Samiq and the other like Amgigh, neither at all like Qakan. So in that way, she loved them both, seeing no curse in their perfect arms and hands, in the long fingers and toes of Amgigh's son, his thin straight hair and long legs; in the strong wide shoulders of Samiq's son, in his large hands, his thick hair.

No curse, she said. No curse. Why should she have worried? Qakan was not strong enough to curse sons given by Amgigh and Samiq. Qakan had given no curse, and if he had not cursed these sons then how could she believe he had cursed her? She would return to her own people, yes, in some way, she would return. When she was strong again, before she had to go back to the Raven's ulaq, she would leave the birth hut in the night, bind the babies under her suk and steal an ik. She would return to the First Men. Yes, it would take her all spring, all summer, but who had paddled most of the way last summer? Not Qakan.

She would take her babies back to the First Men. Amgigh would be proud to have a son, and when Samiq returned from the Whale Hunters, he, too, would see that Kiin had given him a son. And what greater gift can a woman give?

45

T *hree days after the birth,* Woman of the Sky came to Kiin's hut. The babies were asleep, each one in a cradle hung from the willow poles.

The Raven had made the cradles, each a rectangle of wood with a length of sealskin attached to the long sides to form a sling that held the baby in the center of the rectangle. Each wooden side was like one direction of the wind—east the direction of new life; south the direction of the sun; west, death; and north, the place of the Dancing Lights.

"They sleep?" Woman of the Sky asked while still standing in the door of the hut.

Kiin nodded, "Yes, Grandmother."

"Good," the old woman said, but for the first time since Kiin had known her, Woman of the Sky seemed nervous, unsure of what she should say, her hands twisting themselves together, her eyes blinking too rapidly.

"The spirits have spoken to you?" she asked.

With a trembling that made Kiin's heart work in short, hard beats, Kiin answered as though she did not know what Woman of the Sky meant. "N-no," she said and tried to smile, tried to act as any woman, mother of two sons, would act.

Woman of the Sky came into the birth hut and sat cross-legged on the grass mats of the floor. The oil lamp gave out a puff of smoke as the door flap settled into place.

"Kiin," Woman of the Sky said, her voice firm, her eyes so dark that even the flames of the lamp did not show in their depths, "one of your sons is evil. One has to die."

"No," Kiin said, her voice loud. "My s-s-sons are not evil. You c-can s-s-see that neither belongs to Qakan. If you knew my husband, you would s-see that the first born is his, in all ways he belongs to my husband. If you knew my husband's brother, S-S-Samiq, you would see that the s-second born belongs to him. In all ways he is Samiq, even in the st-strength of his cry, the thickness of his hair."

"And why should this second born belong to Samiq?" Woman of the Sky asked and bent close to Kiin, peering into her eyes.

"Samiq has n-no wife and was s-sent to the Whale Hunter tribe to learn to hunt . . . to hunt the whale. My husband Amgigh sh-shared me with Samiq for a n-night as a comfort before he left."

Woman of the Sky nodded.

"My s-s-sons are as all m-m-men, with good and evil m-mixed, the choice to be theirs, not s-something decided by s-some spirit before they were born," Kiin said, and the heat of her words rose and stirred the air near the cradles until Amgigh's son began to cry.

Kiin stood and pulled the baby from his cradle. The baby's carrying strap was still slung under Kiin's suk, the strap fitting over Kiin's shoulder, across her back and under her other arm. Kiin slipped the baby into the wide section of the strap so it supported the baby's back and head and ran between his legs. Kiin pushed her nipple into his mouth.

"My sister's dreams are never wrong," Woman of the Sky said. "And she saw this before you came to us. Did she not say you would have two babies? Did she not say they would be sons?"

But Kiin would not look at the woman, would not lift her eyes to the brown and wrinkled face.

For a long time Woman of the Sky sat without speaking, but finally, when Samiq's son began to cry and Kiin stood to take him from his cradle, Woman of the Sky stood also, and before Kiin could take the crying infant into her arms, Woman of the Sky picked him up from the cradle. For a time, she stood holding the child, rocking him until he no longer cried, then she looked at Kiin, and Kiin saw there were tears on the old woman's face.

"All my sons except Ice Hunter died when they were babies," she said, her voice a whisper. "Kiin, Woman of the Sun has had no dream on this, but my own spirit tells me that this baby is the evil son, this child with the dark hair is the one who will bring destruction."

Kiin said nothing, only reached for Samiq's son, held the baby close so the feathers of her suk lay soft against his bare skin.

"I will leave now," Woman of the Sky said, and she spoke in the Walrus tongue.

"G-g-go, then," Kiin said, speaking also in the Walrus tongue, but her throat closed so she could not say the rest of the words: Come again to visit.

Woman of the Sky left, closed the door flap behind her, but Kiin still felt the woman's presence and knew she was standing outside the hut. Finally she called in to Kiin, "Let your spirit speak to you. Let it tell you what is true. Would you curse us, the people who have let you become one of us?"

Kiin slipped Samiq's son into his carrying strap. No, I would not curse you, she thought. But do not ask me to kill one of my sons. Do not ask me.

"Wife," someone called.

Kiin, in her dreams, thought the voice was Amgigh's, and for a moment she was again in Kayugh's ulaq. Then she opened her eyes and when the voice came again, she knew it belonged to the Raven.

"Husband," she answered, keeping her voice low so she would not awaken the babies, "I am here."

"Come out," he said.

And Kiin, surprised that he would ask such a thing, answered, "Take care for your weapons. I st-still bleed."

She heard him shuffle back from the hut, then she crawled outside and was surprised to see that the night had nearly ended, the sun already red on the horizon.

"I have spoken to the old women, Grandmother and Aunt," he said, and his words brought dread to Kiin's spirit, a heaviness that made her want to hide in the dark shadows near the hut.

"Your p-power is st-stronger than theirs," Kiin said, spitting out the words in anger.

And the Raven surprised her by answering, "Yes, my power is stronger. You should not kill your sons. They are my sons also, do not forget. I traded a good woman for you. You must do as I say."

Kiin lowered her head, did not let herself see what was in her husband's eyes. So, if her husband told her she should not kill her sons, could she disobey? She was wife. She must do as her husband said.

"T-t-tell the Grandmother I m-must obey my husband. I am wife. Tell the Aunt I m-must d-do as my husband says."

Low and soft on the wind, Kiin heard the beginning of the Raven's laughter. Low and soft on the wind, she heard the sound as the Raven turned and walked away from the birth hut.

And though, as she went back into the hut, she heard nothing from her own spirit, heard no voice agreeing or disagreeing, a song came, whispering at her from the peak of the willow poles:

> *I will not choose for my children,*
> *Which son is evil and which is good.*

What mother could choose between two sons?
What mother could choose?

Each son will decide for himself.
Each must choose as every man chooses.
As Amgigh and Samiq chose.

Then she heard the murmur of her spirit. The voice, still and small, singing from within: "As the Raven chose."

46

The morning fogs were longer, thicker. The snow became rain; the rains thinned and became mists.

"Soon the whales," Hard Rock said.

The men had gathered on the beach. The fog seemed to isolate them from the village, but Samiq knew that it also carried their voices clearly to the ulas.

"We need a watcher," Dying Seal said, pushing a chunk of dried meat into his mouth. "The son of Puffin. . . ."

"He is too young," Hard Rock interrupted.

Samiq looked at the man in surprise. Puffin's son was Hard Rock's nephew. It was an honor for the boy to be mentioned, but Hard Rock's face was set in a scowl.

"Whale Killer will be our watcher."

Dying Seal laughed, but Samiq knew Hard Rock had not made a joke.

"You are more boy than man," Hard Rock continued, his eyes on Samiq's face. "You will be our watcher."

The men around him began to murmur, but Samiq said, "I have never learned the skills of a boy. Hard Rock chooses wisely. For a little while, I will be a watcher."

"There is no need," Dying Seal said to Samiq.

But Samiq replied, "This is not a dishonor. Do not think that it is." Then he turned to Hard Rock and said, "Let us go now. I will be watcher, but first I must speak to my wife."

Samiq saw the surprise and disappointment in Hard Rock's eyes, and he knew the man had wanted a fight. Samiq had often seen two of the Whale Hunters fight, thrusting with words instead of knives. To the Whale Hunters the wounds made by words were as deep as those of any weapon, and Samiq understood that he was not equal to Hard Rock's skill, the fighting with words still new to Samiq, his own replies too slow, too awkward.

"It is better this way," he quietly told Dying Seal. "But watch over Fat Wife and Three Fish for me."

"I will send you food," Fat Wife promised as she packed Samiq's chigadax and boots into a sealskin sack. "Puffin's boy will bring it to you."

"Puffin's boy should be watching," Three Fish said.

"It will not be long, wife," said Samiq laying a hand on her shoulder.

Hard Rock went with Samiq to the watching place. It was situated on a narrow ledge at the side of a ridge. It was freedom for a boy. A place where mothers did not come. A place where a boy could test his weapons. There was a hut on the widest section of the ledge, and the shelter was protected from the wind by a shallow cave.

As Samiq placed his food and clothing inside, he noticed that the shelter's walls were tightly woven and strong, but that the mats on the floor had begun to rot, filling the hut with the smell of something dead. In disgust, he pulled the mats from the floor and carried them to the edge of the ridge and tossed them into the rocks and grasses below.

He turned to Hard Rock expecting some protest and saw that Hard Rock was holding a fist-sized stone, gripping it tightly with the tips of his fingers. Samiq's stomach muscles tightened, and he reached slowly toward the handle of the obsidian knife

Amgigh had given him. In a fight with Hard Rock, there would be nothing but loss.

But Hard Rock held the stone toward Samiq and said, "This is the signal rock. Three times against the wall of the cave for a whale. Twice for seals."

Samiq dropped his arms to his sides and listened as Hard Rock tapped the stone once against the rim of the cave. It echoed loudly, throwing a clear tone down toward the beach. "Three times," Hard Rock said as he placed the stone in a niche at the edge of the cave. "Then light the fires." He said nothing more and did not turn to look back at Samiq as he descended the side of the ridge, dislodging dirt and stone as he went.

Samiq waited until Hard Rock was lost in the fog, then he turned and strained to see beyond the edge of the mist where the sea lay as black as the center of an eye.

For three days and nights, Samiq watched, sleeping only when the fog was too thick to see the water. On the fourth day, Puffin's boy came. He carried water and meat and a packet of bitterroot. He set down the water then squatted beside Samiq, handing him the package of roots.

The First Men ate the root cooked. Samiq did not like the sour taste it had when raw. He made a face and the boy smiled. The boy popped a handful of bitterroot bulbs into his mouth. Samiq felt his throat tighten as the boy chewed. But the boy only laughed and ate more.

Unlike most of the Whale Hunters, Puffin's boy was small and thin, but Samiq had heard him more than once best several of the older boys in word fighting.

"I can stay two, three days," the boy said.

"Good," Samiq answered, "perhaps you will finish all of these." And he tossed the packet of roots back on the boy's lap.

"I will if you cook them," the boy said laughing.

"You are the cook," Samiq said, running his hand over the top of the boy's head.

The boy nodded and began to unpack the supplies he had brought. He laughed and talked, his words sometimes so rapid they came from his mouth like a song.

But even as the boy talked, Samiq watched the sea. There was an ikyak far out on the water, and Samiq wondered if it might be Kayugh or Amgigh. But Puffin's boy gestured toward the thin, dark line and said, "Hard Rock. He hunts today."

Samiq grunted, feeling disappointed. "They have seen seals?"

"No," the boy said, then grinned. "Fat Wife misses you. She says it is shameful for Hard Rock to send you here. Now all the women of the village are angry. Even Hard Rock's wife. That is why he hunts today."

Samiq's laugh echoed down the ridge, and the boy laughed as well, then said, "Hard Rock will return before night. The ceremony must be made. The old men are all dead now and only Hard Rock and Dying Seal know how to make whale poison. This morning, Hard Rock made the poison."

Samiq turned toward the boy. "How do you know?"

"I followed."

Samiq drew in his breath, but he turned again toward the sea, noticing that Hard Rock's boat was now closer to the shore.

"You followed?" he finally asked.

The boy pulled a broken flake of stone from the ledge and cupped it in his palm. He took a piece of bone from inside his parka and used it to chip at the rock.

"You will cut your hand," Samiq said and leaned back toward the hut to pull his spearhead basket from the sleeping mats. He opened the basket and took out a strip of hide and tucked it in the boy's palm.

"It is also the wrong kind of rock," Samiq said, then seeing a flush stain the boy's face, realized that he was only working the stone to avoid Samiq's questions, but Samiq again asked, "You followed?"

"Yes," the boy said, his eyes still on the stone, now discarded at his feet.

Samiq handed him a piece of andesite from his basket and the boy turned it in his fingers.

"It is ready," Samiq said, pointing to the thinned base, the top that narrowed to a point. "Except for the edge." He put the stone in his own palm and steadied his hand against his thigh, pressing with a piece of bone to force flakes from the edge.

"Use this piece to practice," Samiq said, flipping the stone back to the boy. "My brother makes the best blades of any man I know. I tell you what he has told me. The bone goes here," Samiq said, placing the punch on the edge of the blade. "Now press in toward the center. Lean into the punch. Use your shoulders for the force you need." Samiq waited until the muscles in the boy's arms grew taut. "Now press down."

A flake came cleanly from the edge of the stone. The boy studied the blade, moved the punch.

Samiq shook his head, "No," he said, "put the punch here, nearly flat to your stone." He watched and grunted his approval when another flake broke from the edge, then he placed his hand on the boy's wrist.

The boy stopped, looked up at him.

"No one is to watch the alananasika make the poison," Samiq said. "Why did you watch?"

"I wanted to know," Puffin's boy said. "I heard my father say that only Hard Rock and Dying Seal know how to make it. What if something happened to them? Hunters die. Black Berry's father drowned last summer; Red Bird's father was killed by a whale. What if that happened to Hard Rock? What if that happened to Dying Seal? Then we could not be whale hunters. None of us. I watched so I would know. I think all the men should know."

Samiq heard the earnestness in the boy's voice and remembered what his grandfather Many Whales had once said to him. "I think I would have done the same thing," Samiq said softly.

The boy met Samiq's eyes and did not look away. "There is a small plant. The women call it the hunters' hood. . . ."

Samiq nodded. "Yes," he said. "I know the one."

The ceremony fires were lit. Samiq saw the flames from the ridge. "I will watch," he told Puffin's boy, ignoring the wide eyes that told of the boy's interest. No one but whale hunters were allowed to watch the ceremony. "You do not have to watch," Samiq said.

But the boy squatted down beside him saying, "I watched them make the poison."

Samiq smiled, and knowing that the boy did not see the smile in the darkness, he reached to pat the boy's knee.

The chanting began, and Samiq recognized the same words that were spoken when he became Whale Killer, a repetitious chant that he still remembered from the ceremony the summer before. The men wore the same masks, and Samiq watched the dancing, memorizing the pattern that Puffin's boy showed him, the boy explaining, "It is a dance taught to all boys."

Samiq felt a sudden elation. What more did he need before he returned to his own people, now in one short day having learned both dance and poison? He placed a twisted handful of crowberry heather on his own fire, watching the flickering of his shadow against the side of the cave. Echo of the ceremonial fires, Samiq thought. Whale Hunters and whale hunter.

He had reached again to throw more heather on the fire when his eye was caught by another glowing, this one beyond their island, perhaps on the First Men's island, a light where there should be no light, a redness in the night sky. He stood and the boy did, too.

Suddenly, Samiq felt the earth move under his feet, and he dropped quickly to all fours, pulling the boy down beside him.

"It is mountain spirits," Samiq whispered, but he did not think the boy heard him. The noise was too great, the tremors knocking rocks and gravel from the side of the ridge.

Samiq crawled into the hut, pushing the boy ahead of him. The boy did not speak, but once in the hut, he crowded close to

Samiq, and Samiq tucked the boy under him until the shaking and the noise stopped.

The glow in the sky lasted through the night. Samiq could not sleep, but the boy slept for a short time. When the gray haze of sunrise lighted the sky, Samiq crawled outside to the ledge. Morning fog blended with smoke, and Samiq could not see as far as the fingers of his own hand.

Suddenly there was a small voice beside him. "We should not have watched. The mountain spirits punish us."

"No," Samiq said, but could think of no reason for his disagreement and so again said, "No."

The boy said nothing and Samiq looked down at him, the boy's face only a darkness at Samiq's side. "You should go back," Samiq said. "You will be safe at the village."

"No," the boy said, turning to Samiq. "I will stay another day. I will watch. You must sleep. I have slept. Now you must sleep."

Samiq raised his hand to ruffle the boy's hair, but drew it quickly back and instead said, "What do they call you?"

"Puffin's boy."

"No," Samiq said. "Your true name."

"I am called Small Knife."

A good name, Samiq thought. A man's name. The knife, life itself. "I will sleep, Small Knife," he said.

47

When Samiq awoke, Three Fish was kneeling beside him. Her face was cut and dirty, her eyes red from crying. He looked over her shoulder to see if Small Knife was behind her, but Three Fish put her face close to his, blocking his view of everything except her wide mouth and broken teeth.

"Many have died," she said, her voice hoarse with sobs, "and Hard Rock blames you. Some of the hunters have gone out into the North Sea. They say it is Aka that spits fire. Hard Rock says that Aka does the will of the Seal Hunters and that you have cursed us by watching the Whale Dancing."

The ridge shook again, sending a small scattering of rocks to the ledge, and Three Fish screamed.

Small Knife rushed into the shelter, his eyes wide. "She is frightened by the rocks," Samiq said. "Can you see anything? Has the fog lifted?"

"No. There is smoke and fog. Ash falls from the sky and covers everything." He shook his head sending a puff of white from his hair.

Samiq grasped Three Fish's shoulders. "Three Fish," he said sternly, "stop crying." The woman closed her eyes. "Stop crying," Samiq said again. "Tell me what happened."

She took several short breaths and wiped her eyes. "We were

sleeping. Fat Wife and I. The ground began to shake and suddenly the timbers of the ulaq were falling."

Her eyes were wide as if she were seeing the ulaq fall once again, and Samiq was suddenly afraid. When she first woke him, had she said that many were killed?

"Fat Wife was screaming," Three Fish said, tears again on her cheeks. "Fat Wife was . . . there was blood in her mouth and her eyes were open. And then the roof fell on the oil lamps and I could not see, but I pulled her until I got her to the hole where the roof once was and then I could see. . . . The blood . . ." Three Fish wiped her nose on the back of her hand.

She took a long shuddering breath. "Fat Wife is dead," she said. "Hard Rock's ulaq stands and Dying Seal's also, but everyone in Puffin's ulaq was killed, even the baby. Puffin, my brother!" she wailed. "My father and mother. . . ." Again Three Fish began to cry but Samiq felt more anguish for Small Knife, and he looked up at the boy still standing at the entrance of the shelter, the boy's body rigid, his fists clenched.

"Small Knife," Samiq said softly, but there were no words to comfort the boy, and Samiq felt suddenly empty, thinking how Small Knife must feel losing father and mother, brothers and sisters. Then suddenly, Samiq thought of his own people, so much closer to Aka than the Whale Hunters. Perhaps even now, his mother and father, his sisters and Amgigh were dead, buried in the rubble of their ulaq. And what about Kiin?

"Kiin," he whispered, and he pushed Three Fish from him.

The woman looked up, her eyes swollen from her crying. "Hard Rock blames you," she said again. "He says that you called Aka, that you could see the Whale Dancing from this ridge and you watched to curse us."

"Hard Rock is a fool," Samiq said angrily. "What man could make fire come from a mountain?"

"He says that you called the whales and that you also have the power to call Aka."

Samiq stared at her, saw the questions in her eyes.

Could I have called the whales without knowing? Samiq won

dered. Could I have wished Aka to do this thing? But then remembering his own family, he said to Three Fish, "Would I hurt my own people also? They are closer to Aka than the Whale Hunters. Hard Rock is a fool."

Samiq crawled from the shelter, but stopped in surprise when he saw the depth of the gray flakes that covered the ledge. He scooped up a handful, and turned to find Small Knife at his side.

"I should not have watched the dancing," Small Knife said softly.

Samiq flung the handful of ash to the ground and said loudly, "What hunter does not watch? What watcher does not see?"

But the pain did not leave the boy's eyes, and he said again, "I should not have watched. I am not a hunter. I am not a watcher."

"You would have been a watcher."

"But I am not."

"I am a whale hunter," Samiq said. Then shouting into the fog, into the falling ash, he said, "I am a whale hunter. I have chosen Small Knife as watcher."

And when Small Knife said nothing, Samiq pushed past him to the hut. "Gather your things," Samiq said to him. "We will go back to the village."

But when he entered the hut, Three Fish grasped his parka. "You cannot go back. Hard Rock will kill you."

"I am not afraid of Hard Rock."

"It is not only Hard Rock. All the men of the village have sworn to kill you."

"Dying Seal?"

"Everyone. And Hard Rock will cut off your head to destroy your spirit. You cannot go back."

"I said I am not afraid."

"Then you are a fool," Three Fish said suddenly, speaking in a loud, strong voice not unlike Fat Wife's.

Her words made him angry, and Samiq said, "You have lived too long with my grandmother. You speak like a man."

Three Fish swallowed and her nostrils flared, but she said softly, "Who will teach your people to hunt the whale if you are killed? What can you do now to help the Whale Hunters?" She stopped, looked at Small Knife, then looked back again at Samiq. "If you called Aka, causing this, then call again and make it stop. Then go back to your own people and leave us alone. But if you did not call Aka, what can you do to help anyone if you are killed? Go to your own people and help them."

Samiq looked at Three Fish in amazement. Who would have thought there could be such wisdom behind the broken teeth, behind the rude laugh?

"You are my wife," Samiq said. "Dying Seal will care for you if you return to the Whale Hunters, but if you want, you may come with me."

She stood still for a moment, looking at him. "You have not yet given me a son," she said. "I will go with you."

They climbed down from the ridge while the smoke and fog still layered the beach. Ash made handholds treacherous, footing slippery. Small Knife fell once, cutting a knee, skinning an arm, but he did not call out, and Samiq said nothing as he supported the boy long enough for him to get his breath, then they began to descend again.

When they reached the beach, Samiq started toward the ikyak racks.

"No," Small Knife said. "I will go. No one will bother me. You stay here. Hide in the grass."

Samiq studied the boy's eyes. Did he speak the truth or would he bring Hard Rock?

The boy waited, not speaking. "I will go with him," Three Fish offered.

But Samiq drew her down beside him in the grass. "No," Samiq said. Who could trust Three Fish? Who could say what foolishness might come into her mouth the next time she remembered her sorrow? "Go quickly," Samiq said to Small Knife and pulled the long grass over Three Fish and himself.

It was a long time before Small Knife returned, and with the thickness of the fog, Samiq did not see the boy until he was nearly upon them. Small Knife carried an ik, the bulk of it like a huge awkward shell over the boy's head and back.

Samiq strained to see through the fog. Perhaps there were others behind the boy, hidden in the haze, hidden by the bulk of the ik. He drew his knife from its scabbard and waited. He pushed Three Fish behind him and then moved a short distance from her. If the Whale Hunters planned an attack, perhaps Three Fish would decide to fight with them.

Small Knife set the ik down, but Samiq remained in the grass.

If he comes close enough for me to touch, Samiq thought, I will know he intends no harm.

Small Knife crouched low, creeping through the grass to Samiq, then he sat cross-legged before him, close to Samiq's right arm. The boy said softly, "I went to my father's ulaq. It is as Three Fish said."

Samiq felt the boy tremble, but there was no sound of tears in his voice.

"Did anyone see you?" Samiq asked.

The boy hesitated, finally meeting Samiq's eyes. "Dying Seal."

"What did you say?"

"I said you were dead, lying at the bottom of the ridge, killed by Aka."

"What did he say?"

"He said nothing."

"Then we must go. When you return to your people, say nothing. Tell them you have not seen me. Tell them you have not seen Three Fish."

"I will go with you," Small Knife said.

"You cannot. You belong here with your people."

"You are my people," Small Knife said.

Samiq stood and pushed his knife back into its sheath.

What would be the best thing for the boy? For himself?

But suddenly, there was a man's voice. "Let him go with you."

Again Samiq gripped his knife.

Dying Seal moved from the gray of the fog, his hands extended before him. "I am a friend. I have no knife," he said softly.

Samiq looked into the man's eyes. Did he speak the truth or were there others behind him, waiting? Samiq glanced toward Small Knife. Did the boy know he had been followed?

Dying Seal waited, his eyes fixed on Samiq's hands. "Did you call Aka?" he asked.

"Aka obeys no man," Samiq answered.

"But are you man or spirit?"

"I am man."

For a time, Dying Seal did not speak, his eyes on Samiq's face. But then he said, "Does Three Fish want to go with you?"

"Yes," Samiq answered.

Dying Seal looked past Samiq toward the woman, but Samiq did not allow his eyes to be drawn away from the man.

"Yes," Three Fish said. "I will go with him."

Then Dying Seal said to Samiq, "Let the boy go, too. He needs a father now. It would be better for him. He may be blamed since he was with you, and then who can say what will happen to him?"

Samiq glanced at Small Knife. "If you want to come with us, you may come," he said.

"Yes, I will come."

Dying Seal nodded and said quietly to the boy, "Be strong. Be a good hunter." He turned to Samiq, holding Samiq's eyes with his eyes, then finally gave the blessing of the alananasika, "May you always be strong. May many whales give themselves to your spear. May you make many sons." Then he turned and walked away.

48

Samiq paddled the k around the edge of the cliff; a feeling of dread lay heavy in his stomach.

"Here?" Small Knife asked.

"Yes, this beach," Samiq answered, his voice sounding high and thin even in his own ears.

They had traveled two days and in the traveling, the fog had not lifted; the ash, fine as silt, continued to fall. The bottom of the ik was layered with it, and Three Fish sneezed often and loudly, moving in the boat, stirring the ash until Samiq's mouth and nose burned, his lungs ached.

"Your people will not be here," Three Fish said. "They will have left. Or perhaps they are already dead."

Samiq pulled his paddle from the water and looked at Three Fish sitting in the center of the boat.

"Do not say what you do not know," he said quietly, holding down the anger that rose against her.

Then Samiq guided the ik to the center of the beach where the finer gravel would cause less damage to the sea lion hide bottom.

As soon as they stepped from the ik, the ground moved beneath them.

Three Fish dropped to her hands and knees. When the shaking stopped, she looked up at Samiq. "We should go," she said. "There are bad spirits here."

Samiq did not stop to answer her but strode up the rise of the beach, not caring whether she or Small Knife came with him.

The grass was clotted with ash and caught at his legs as he walked. He blocked all thoughts from his mind, hoping to calm the rapid beating of his heart, but his stomach twisted when he saw his father's ulaq. Driftwood rafters stuck through the sod of the roof like the bones of a rotting carcass. Large wall stones leaned at odd angles, skewing the ulaq to one side.

Had some of his people escaped or had all been killed? He stood on one of the displaced boulders and looked over at Big Teeth's ulaq. Its roof was caved in, the ulaq merely a gaping hole in the side of the hill.

The island was quiet; Samiq heard no voices, no bird callings, nothing but the slap of waves, one rushing after another, their rhythm too quick, as though even the sea were afraid of the mountains.

The ground shook again, and Samiq heard Three Fish's voice carried by the wind from the beach, fear in the whine of her words.

It is sad that women are so necessary to a man, Samiq thought. But what man can hunt and sew also? And he realized with a sudden numbness that he had brought Three Fish with him to assure his survival, some part of him thinking that his people had been killed.

But then he felt a hand on his shoulder, heard the quiet words: "Perhaps they left before."

Samiq spun and saw that Small Knife had followed him.

"Perhaps," Samiq said.

"I will look," the boy offered.

Samiq saw the compassion in his eyes. "We will look together," Samiq said, then hesitating, he finally pointed to Kayugh's ulaq. "We will start here," he said. The most difficult first.

The fall of ash grew heavier, and the day darkened early, as though it were winter, but Samiq could see black clouds moving toward Tugix's peak, and he worked feverishly to move the sod and rock that lay in the ulaq.

"There is nothing," Small Knife finally said. "No one dead. No one living."

Samiq did not reply. Pulling a piece of curtain from the wreckage, he recognized the pattern that his mother made on all her weaving, dark squares on light background, and he felt a small flicker of hope. Perhaps as Small Knife had said, they had escaped.

They went then to Big Teeth's ulaq, again moving sod and stones to seek what Samiq hoped was not there.

"Nothing," Small Knife said after they had cleared away most of the fallen sod.

Samiq looked at the boy. A cold, hard rain had begun to fall, and Small Knife's hair was molded by the wetness into a tight black hood over his head. His parka shed the water in rivulets to his bare feet, and he looked like a small boy, too young to take the responsibilities and sorrows of a man.

I cannot ask him to help me now, Samiq thought, and said, "Go back to Three Fish. Pull the ik to the cliffs on the south side of the beach. You will find caves there and the water will not reach you. Go and wait. I will come soon."

Samiq watched the boy leave. What sorrow will I find that the boy does not already know? Samiq asked himself. Perhaps my people still live. My mother and father. Amgigh and Kiin. But Small Knife's parents . . .

Samiq went to the burial ulas, first to the one where his grandmother, Shuganan's wife was buried. The roof was not as badly damaged as the other ulas' roofs; only a portion of it had caved in. Samiq walked carefully over the top to the roof entrance, the hole sealed by a wooden door. When he removed the wood, some of the roof sod crumbled into the interior, but most remained, and he lowered himself into the ulaq. Gray light filtered in through the broken roof, and he saw the bundle that was his grandmother, still intact in the center of the ulaq. There were two bundles beside her, one old, the size of a baby. But the other, the size and shape of a child or small woman, made Samiq's heart thud heavily in his chest. The death mats were new, still the color of dried grass, not darkened by time. He knelt beside the bundle, wanting to tear the mats from the body.

What spirits will I anger? he wondered. What curse will come upon my hunting? But if it were Kiin . . .

He unsheathed his knife and cut the matting from the dead person's head. The mats pealed away in layers and Samiq saw the darkness of the hair. Some of the flesh pulled away from the bones of the face and at the stink of rotting flesh, Samiq's stomach heaved. Then a small piece of wood fell from the folds of the weaving, the wood carved in the shape of a seal. Samiq's head was suddenly light with relief, but then he thought, a boy of this age and size would be Little Duck's son. How would the woman survive the loss of her only child?

Samiq carefully rewrapped the boy and left the ulaq. He climbed through the roof hole, set the door back into the opening, trying not to dislodge more dirt on the dead.

He stood for a time looking at the other death ulaq. His father, Shuganan's son, was buried there. Samiq began digging through the broken sod roof.

When Samiq reached the floor of the ulaq, he found nothing resembling a dead one and no one recently dead from Aka's rage. Was it possible that all his people had escaped? But if no one were buried here, why was the place honored as a death ulaq? Where was his father?

Samiq turned and began to climb from the hole, but he slipped in the rain-soaked dirt, landing back on the floor, his hand jamming against something sharp. It was a bone, and Samiq jerked it from the sod, then studied the palm of his hand to see if the bone had left splinters to fester in his flesh. But then he realized that the bone he held was not from whale or sea lion, not something broken from a rafter, but the bone of a man, and he held it against his forearm, seeing the thickness of it, the indentations where muscles were once attached. The bone of a man, powerfully built.

He laid the bone in the dirt at his feet and began to dig in the sod where he had found it. He uncovered the long bones of the legs, and small bones, once parts of hands and feet. Finally the skull. None of the bones were wrapped. Why? What had happened to cause such a thing? Had his mother's silence about her first husband not been a silence of respect, but of hate?

Samiq looked at his own arms, his legs and hands. Truly, they were not the long thin limbs of the First Men. Not even the thicker bones of the Whale Hunters. Who was his father? Who were his people?

Samiq looked at the bones lying at his feet. What spirits would he offend if he reburied the bones? What spirits would he offend if he did not?

Samiq closed his eyes, wiped the rain from his face with the sleeve of his parka. He was too tired to worry about spirits. Laying out the mat that he had carried from Kayugh's ulaq, he wrapped the bones carefully, then pulled stones from what had once been the ulaq walls. He clustered the stones over the bundle, making a burial in the manner of the Whale Hunters.

amiq nodded his approval. The cave Small Knife had chosen
was high above the tide line and had a dry sand and gravel
floor.

Three Fish crouched at the entrance, her arms held just
above a cooking fire. Water dripped from her suk to sizzle on
the burning crowberry heather. "Did you find anything?" she
asked.

"One dead. A boy, son of the man called Big Teeth and of his
second wife, Little Duck. But the boy died some time ago. Not
from Aka."

The mountain shook then, and Three Fish jumped up, her
hands over her mouth.

"It is nothing," Samiq said. "Tugix often shakes the earth."

Three Fish sat again but Samiq saw the doubt in her eyes.
"You are safe," he said with some irritation, then thought, I
should be alone. Or perhaps only with Small Knife. I would not
wish Three Fish's complaining on Dying Seal, but I should have
left her with her own people.

They stayed the night, Samiq careful to make his bed beside
Small Knife, making sure they were together on one side of the
fire, Three Fish on the other. Several times in the night, he
heard Three Fish moving in the cave, but he did not look to-

ward her. He did not want her close to him. Tonight, no imagination would make her Kiin.

They awoke in darkness, the fire gone out, Samiq angry that Three Fish had not kept it fed. She who would sit in the ik without paddling should not expect the men to keep the fire. But he said nothing to her; he was too tired for arguing. He groped in the darkness for his belongings and wished they had brought more food. The amount they had taken from the watching place would last only a few days.

The gray circle of light from the cave entrance told of a heavy fog, and as he stood looking out, Samiq felt disoriented, unable to see the sun or even a brightness where it stood in the sky.

"It is morning," Small Knife said.

"There is no way to be certain," Samiq replied.

"The tides."

"Aka makes new tides. Who can tell if it is the morning or Aka that pulls the water?"

Small Knife lifted his shoulders, and by his smile, Samiq realized the boy had not meant to argue.

"My people have a cave for ikyan," Samiq said, trying to fill the silence that had come between them. "Perhaps they left some supplies there."

"And if we find some, we will leave?"

"I do not know. Perhaps we will go, perhaps not."

They made a torch with sodden matting from the ulas, winding the mats around a narrow length of driftwood. Three Fish, wading in the muck of Big Teeth's ruined ulaq, found a sealskin of oil, and Samiq used the oil to douse the wet mats. Three Fish trailed after them as they walked to the cave, the torch blazing in Samiq's hand, but Samiq turned at the cave entrance and told the woman to remain outside.

"It is forbidden for women to enter," he said, and went inside before Three Fish could argue with him.

The torch cast circles of light in the cave, showing the narrow bottom where sand and gravel had made a smooth floor and the widening sides that narrowed again at the top. Kayugh once said that long ago Samiq's grandfather Shuganan had wedged posts into the floor and into cracks in the cave walls. When Big Teeth, Gray Bird and Kayugh had come to Tugix's island, they built platforms on the posts and stored their ikyan in the cave each winter.

Samiq held the torch close to the racks. They were empty. He had hoped to find some ikyan and perhaps some sign showing where his people had gone. There was nothing.

"Look!" Small Knife exclaimed, pointing up.

Samiq lifted the torch, illuminating the top of the cave. A post had been driven into a high crack in the cave wall and hanging from the post was an ikyak, cords tied around each end, the ikyak suspended from the post like a child's cradle.

"They hung it so the sea would not reach it," Small Knife said.

Samiq handed the torch to Small Knife and pulled himself to the empty ikyak platforms. Reaching up, he wedged his toes and fingers into the small cracks that scored the cave walls. He stretched up toward the ikyak, meaning to tip it toward the floor, but the ikyak lurched away from him. Bracing his feet against the cave wall, he grabbed the post and swung himself up to straddle it.

"Push the torch into the wall," he called down to Small Knife. "Come and help me."

Small Knife was soon beside him, and Samiq explained, "There is something in the ikyak. We will have to empty it before we can pull it down."

Samiq clung to the post and reached into the ikyak. He pulled out a chigadax, new. The feathering at the sides showed the work was Chagak's. Samiq smiled and dropped the garment to the floor, then reached back into the ikyak. He brought out a basket with a drawstring sealskin top. He opened it. Sewing supplies: needles, awl, sinew. Handing it to Small Knife, Samiq said, "Carry it down."

Samiq waited until Small Knife was again beside him, then he reached once more into the ikyak.

"Boots, sealskins."

He dropped them to the floor. Two spear shafts and two paddles were lashed to the ikyak, and Samiq pulled these out and dropped them also.

"I cannot reach the rest," he said. "I will have to unlace the cover bindings."

"I can reach it," Small Knife said.

Samiq watched as the boy gripped the post with his legs and arms and allowed himself to swing upside down over the ikyak. Releasing the post with his hands, he hung by his knees, lowering himself through the hatch head first, his legs still tightly wrapped around the post. He pulled out a filled seal belly and handed it to Samiq.

"Fish," Samiq said.

"They knew you would be hungry," said Small Knife, grinning, then he lowered himself again into the ikyak.

Samiq balanced the seal belly behind him on the post and reached with one hand as Small Knife brought out a bladder of oil. "One more thing," the boy said, his voice muffled in the ikyak.

He brought out a bundle of mats, finely woven, bordered with a pattern of dark squares. Small Knife dropped the mats to the floor and pulled himself back to the top of the post. He took the bladder of oil from Samiq's hands and climbed down to the cave floor, cradling the bladder in one arm. Samiq dropped the seal belly down to the boy, then pushed the ropes to the end of the post, until one jerk would free the ikyak. He tilted the ikyak so Small Knife could grab the narrow bow, then climbed to the floor. He placed his hands above Small Knife's, bracing to receive the weight of the ikyak, and they pulled it from the post, swinging it gently down to their feet.

They set the ikyak at the cave entrance and loaded the fish and oil back into it. Samiq stuffed the chigadax, sealskin and boots into the ikyak hatch. Then sitting on his heels, he unwrapped the bundle that was bound in his mother's mats.

He set the things before Small Knife: a rope woven of kelp

fibers, a small stone lamp, braided wicks. A scraping stone —a woman's tool—but something he might need. "For Three Fish," he said, holding the stone. She was not what most men wanted in a wife, but she was a woman, able to sew, able to prepare skins.

He unwrapped patching fat and a long bailing tube, tapered at both ends. Then thinking the mats to be empty, Samiq began to rewrap the supplies, but Small Knife reached between the folds of two mats and pulled out a small white object. It was strung on a cord like the amulet Samiq already wore, and when he took it from Small Knife's hands, Samiq saw that it was ivory, carved in the shape of a whale.

Samiq turned the carving in his fingers. Where had this carving come from? It was too beautiful to be one of Gray Bird's.

Perhaps it was something his grandfather had made. His mother kept many of Shuganan's carvings wrapped in oiled sealskin in baskets in Kayugh's ulaq. Samiq slipped the cord over his head, pulling the carving to lie beside his amulet.

"You will wear it?" Small Knife asked.

"You have not heard of my grandfather Shuganan?" Samiq replied and smiled at Small Knife's wide eyes.

They carried the ikyak from the cave. Three Fish crowded close, peering inside, running her fingers over the ikyak seams. Samiq handed her the scraping stone.

"For you," Samiq said, then was embarrassed by the gratitude that shone in the woman's eyes. It was only a small blade. Why had he given her nothing before? But what had been his to give when he lived among the Whale Hunters?

50

Kiin *returned to the Raven's* ulaq fifteen days after the babies were born. She returned to find that Lemming Tail had kept the main room of the ulaq clean, had kept the lamp wick trimmed. There was no food rotting on the floor. Two seal stomach containers were full of newly dried fish and the Raven's chigadax was freshly mended and oiled and hanging from a peg in the wall.

Lemming Tail was not in the ulaq, but Kiin, seeing that all things were in order, closed her eyes and took a long breath. She had been afraid she would come back to days of work to make up for Lemming Tail's laziness.

A small raised platform was set on the other side of the room from the Raven's sleeping platform and Kiin noticed that four loops of willow had been tied securely to the rafters. Cradle hooks? she wondered. So perhaps the Raven had acted on his promise to her that both babies were to live, both babies would be safe in his ulaq.

Kiin set the babies' cradles on the platform. The platform was a pile of furs and grass mats over a willow and driftwood frame that had been lashed tightly with babiche. The furs were not the fine thick pelts that padded the Raven's bed, but what could Kiin, a second wife, expect? It was good enough that she had been given a bed.

The babies were strapped against her chest, and she wore her suk with the fur in, soft against her babies' skin. Her sons were sleeping now, though she felt Samiq's son occasionally suck lazily on her left breast.

She set the grass bag that held her sewing supplies on the floor and crouched on her heels beside the platform. She leaned her head back on the furs of her new bed. She had done little that day, but she was tired, and she already wished for the night so she could sleep.

It was good to come back to find the ulaq empty and clean, to find that the only work she had to do was to prepare food, care for the babies. She should take off her suk, hang the cradles and let the babies sleep.

For a moment Kiin let herself think what it would have been like if she had stayed in Kayugh's ulaq. Chagak would now be helping her. There would be food cooking, and she would have her own sleeping place where she could close the curtain, be alone if she wished. Yes, Kiin thought, Chagak was grandmother again and Kayugh grandfather, though they thought she was dead. And Amgigh and Samiq were fathers, though since she was Amgigh's wife, both babies would be raised as his sons. Still Samiq would know, know by looking; everyone would know.

Kiin could see little of herself in either of the babies. Perhaps, she thought, in the curve of the eyebrows, perhaps in the shape of ears. But what could she expect? She did not have a strong spirit. Her spirit could never stand against Samiq's or Amgigh's. But what did that matter? Once she had thought she would always be in her father's ulaq, never be wife, never be mother. Now she had two sons.

Kiin yawned and closed her eyes. The babies had been restless the night before, perhaps feeling her dread at returning to the Raven's ulaq. They were not yet named, so had no spirits of their own, nothing to separate them from her spirit, so of course they would feel her fear, her anxiety. As wife, she must ask her husband to name them, soon, though she did not like to think of the babies having Walrus People names.

But, she told herself, better to have a Walrus name than no name at all.

She did not mean to fall asleep, but the babies were warm against her chest and belly, the furs of the sleeping platform soft against her back. She did not dream and, later, did not know what woke her. Slowly, she opened her eyes. Her neck was stiff and she hunched her shoulders, then she caught her breath with a quick start of fear. Woman of the Sky and Woman of the Sun were in the ulaq, both sitting on the Raven's sleeping platform, sitting as Walrus People sat, legs stretched out straight before them, backs against the ulaq wall.

Kiin wrapped her arms around the babies, felt both squirm under her tightening grasp. She was suddenly glad she had fallen asleep with them still tucked inside her suk. Perhaps if they had been in their cradles, Woman of the Sky and Woman of the Sun might have been able to take them, even while Kiin slept.

"We brought food," Woman of the Sun said and reached up to hang a sealskin from the rafters over the oil lamp.

"We did not know if Lemming Tail would have any thing prepared for you or for Raven," said Woman of the Sky.

Kiin stared at the women. When she had first come to the Walrus People these women were her friends, the ones she trusted, but now that she knew her sons did not belong to Qakan, she did not want Woman of the Sun or Woman of the Sky near her.

"Thank you," Kiin said. "My sons and I thank you," she added.

"The babies are growing?" Woman of the Sky asked.

"Yes," Kiin answered. "Yes."

"We have talked to Raven," said Woman of the Sun. "He says his power is greater than your sons' curse."

Kiin lifted her chin. "He has spoken to me also," she said. "He wants both sons. I will kill neither."

"You have no sign—nothing from some spirit that tells you which son is evil?"

Kiin pushed herself from the floor and stood. She was afraid, but her spirit whispered: "What power do these old women have over you? The Raven is your husband. He will protect your children." She wanted to pull the babies from their carrying strap, to hold them out to the old women so they could see the babies' faces, their strong fat arms and legs, their smooth round bellies. But what did she know of power? What did she know of curses? Perhaps the women had come hoping she would show them the babies, hoping they could see them away from the protection of suk or cradle. Perhaps they controlled some spirit of death. Who could say?

"My sons are n-not evil," Kiin said. "They are as all m-men are, able to do evil, able to do good, the choice their own, something they will decide when they are older. It is n-not for m-me to decide for either of them, though I wish I could."

Kiin stood with legs splayed, feet flat and firm on the ulaq floor. It was the way Kayugh stood when he told stories of fighting the Short Ones, the evil ones who had destroyed so many of the First Men's villages many years before. That was the way a man stood to fight, Kayugh said. Legs apart for balance, feet pulling up strength from the earth.

She would not kill one of her sons, would not let Woman of the Sun or Woman of the Sky kill them.

"The Raven will n-not let you kill them," Kiin said, and for the first time since Qakan had sold her, she was glad that Ice Hunter had not won the bidding. Who could say what would have happened? Surely Ice Hunter would have listened to his own mother, would have chosen to give one of the babies to the wind spirits.

"Raven is wrong," Woman of the Sun said.

But then a voice came from beyond the dividing curtain, a man's voice. "Speak in the language of the Walrus People, old woman." It was the Raven. He came into the room, glanced at Kiin, then turned and faced the two sisters.

"My sister said that you are wrong," Woman of the Sky said.

"One of the babies is cursed and will bring terrible evil to his people."

"You think I fear evil?" the Raven asked, then laughed. "Kiin," he called without looking back at her, his eyes still on the old women. "Bring the babies here."

Kiin's heart jumped, throbbed until her blood pulsed hard against her temples. "N-no," she said softly.

The Raven spun as though he had been hit. "Who are you to tell me 'no'!" he bellowed.

Kiin took a step forward. "I am . . . I am Kiin, m-mother to these sons," she said. "These women want to kill them."

"Only the evil one," Woman of the Sky said, but her words were blotted out by the Raven's anger.

"You are wife before you are mother!" he shouted at Kiin. "I bought you and your sons. They are my sons now!"

"No," Kiin said again. Anger pushed away her fear, pulled the words smoothly from her mouth. "They are not your sons if you would let them be killed."

The Raven's face was red, his jaw so tense that Kiin saw the ridges of muscle moving against the skin of his cheeks. "No one will kill my sons," he said, the words hissing out between his teeth.

Slowly Kiin walked toward him. Slowly, she raised her suk. She brought out Amgigh's son first, then Samiq's, cradling both boys in her arms.

"Which was first born?" the Raven asked.

"This one," Kiin said, pointing to Amgigh's son with her chin.

The Raven took the baby from her arms and held him toward the old women. "This is Shuku," he said. "Shuku, a man who understands the power of stone, who holds that power in his heart. A strong hunter, good with weapons, a man who will take many walrus and have many sons."

He handed Shuku back to Kiin and took Samiq's son.

"This is Takha," he said. "Takha, a man who moves over

water without fear, who holds the power of water spirits in his heart. A wise man, good with speaking, with trading, a man who will also take walrus and have many sons."

The Raven handed Takha back to Kiin and said to Woman of the Sun and Woman of the Sky, "Leave my ulaq. Do not curse them or my woman. Any of my women."

"The curse has already been made," Woman of the Sun said. "It is not our curse, nor would we curse an infant who has no protection from us. But this I will tell you as a protection for yourself when you are old. These babies share one spirit. They must live as one man. When one hunts, the other must stay in his ulaq. They must share one wife and one ikyak. Do not give them too much power."

As Kiin heard the words, her anger grew. She waited for the Raven to reply, but then saw that both women held their eyes on the man, both stared without blinking, and the Raven, his eyes on them, did not move.

"He will beat them," Kiin's spirit whispered. "You beat them, and you are weaker than the Raven."

But then the Raven shook his head, looked away and closed his eyes, and with beating heart Kiin saw the look of triumph on Woman of the Sky's face, the slow smile that came to Woman of the Sun's lips.

"Perhaps my sons share one spirit," the Raven said. Then without looking at Kiin he said, "I am hungry, wife."

Kiin turned her back on all three and placed the babies on her sleeping platform. She pulled Qakan's fox pelts from the cradles and tucked the soft furs around her sons. When she turned back to the Raven, Woman of the Sky and Woman of the Sun were gone. The smell of meat simmering came from the sealskin hung over the oil lamp. For a moment Kiin hesitated, then she went to the skin, scooped out a serving into a wooden bowl with a ladle made from a caribou scapula. She handed the food to the Raven. He grunted his thanks and Kiin went back to the babies.

Shuku and Takha, she thought. Good names even if they

were Walrus People names. So now they had their own spirits, were separate from her, stronger, yet not as easily protected. But who was she to protect them, her own spirit scarcely older than their spirits?

She smoothed her hand down Shuku's cheek, brushed a wisp of hair from Takha's forehead. We will grow up together, she thought.

51

Kiin stood on her sleeping platform and hung each cradle from the rafters. The Raven finished his meat and held his bowl out toward her. She stepped down from the platform and took the bowl and filled it again.

"It would be good," her spirit whispered, "if men could sometimes fill their own bowls." Such a little thing when a woman was busy and a man only sitting, doing nothing. But Kiin chided herself for the thought. Had she not come back to a clean ulaq, lamp wick trimmed, night baskets washed, even new grass on the floor?

The Raven took the bowl and grunted at Kiin. Kiin waited, watching him eat. When he was finished, he tossed the bowl in a corner and crawled up on his sleeping platform, sitting there, his back against the wall. He watched as Kiin filled her own bowl and ate.

Kiin cupped the bowl in her hands and waited until the meat cooled. She sat with crossed legs, her head down. She was not hungry. To have Woman of the Sky and Woman of the Sun in her ulaq, telling her she must kill one of her sons, had twisted her stomach until it felt too small to hold any food. But she must eat or she would have no milk for her babies. She dipped her hands into the bowl and scooped a portion of meat into her mouth. It was good. The muscles in her arms and legs and at the back of her neck slowly relaxed.

The Raven pushed himself to the edge of the sleeping platform. Kiin expected him to interrupt her eating with requests for more food or for water. But he only looked at her and said, "I am not a good man."

Kiin swallowed. Did he expect her to answer him? To agree or disagree?

But then he continued, glancing away from Kiin and speaking as though he spoke, not to her, but perhaps to her sons, maybe to some spirit only he could see. "But I am not evil." He cleared his throat.

"There is one thing I want," he said. "I want to be shaman of this village. I want men to come to me to get power for their hunting. I want women to bring their children to me so I can give them powerful names."

Kiin lowered the bowl to her lap and nodded. This man was her husband, the one who protected her sons. If he honored her by speaking to her about his dreams, then she would listen. She would try to understand him.

The Raven stood and walked to her sleeping platform. For a long time he watched the babies as they slept. Then he turned to Kiin. "They do not look like you," he said.

"N-no," Kiin answered. "M-m-my spirit is weak, n-not even s-strong enough to touch a baby that I carry in my belly."

"But your carvings have power," the Raven said.

Kiin thought of the poor faint lines of her carvings, features only hinted, obscure, like something pictured in the clouds, and she remembered the carvings Shuganan had made, the carvings full of detail, each mark of the knife sure and true. Kiin's carvings were nothing more than a small way to please the Raven, a way to make him see her with favor, perhaps to make him want to protect her sons. But then her spirit pushed into her mouth, controlled her tongue, said what Kiin would not have said, "Yes, they are powerful. They have great power. All my power goes into my carvings, all except what I save for my songs."

Sue Harrison

The Raven nodded, turned away from the babies and walked over to where she sat. Kiin took another scoop of food from her bowl. "Your sons do not look like their father."

"Qakan?" Kiin asked, puzzled. "They are n-not his sons. They belong to my husband, Amgigh, a m-man of the First M-Men tribe."

"Amgigh," Raven said and again went over to look at the babies. "Which one is most like Amgigh?" he asked.

But there was some strangeness in the question, something that made Kiin wary. "They both look like . . . like Amgigh," she said, and seeing the Raven frown, said, "One looks like Amgigh's father and one like his mother."

The Raven slowly smiled. "So," he said, "will you miss Qakan when he leaves this village? He plans to go soon. He told me that he will return to his own people."

"I will n-not m-miss Qakan," Kiin said. "I will be happy when he g-goes."

As though he had not heard her, the Raven said, "If you want to go, to return with him to his people, I will let you go. You must leave your carvings and you must leave your sons. Someday, your sons will bring me power. By then, those old women, the Grandmother and the Aunt will be dead and this village will need a shaman."

Kiin took a long breath. Why did the Raven think he was strong enough to be shaman? Why did he think he was strong enough to stand against her sons' curse if he could not even hold his eyes open against two old women?

"Qakan does n-not want me to go with him and I do n-not want to go," Kiin answered. "Qakan has Yellow-hair. She can paddle and she will be a wife for his bed."

The Raven smiled. It was not a pleasant smile. It opened his mouth too wide, showed too many of his teeth, and Kiin had to hold her shoulders stiff to keep from shuddering.

"Yellow-hair will not go with him," the Raven said. He paced the length of the ulaq, turned and spoke to Kiin as if he were explaining something to a child. "You are my wife. You are a

322

good wife because you keep this ulaq clean and you have given me two sons. Lemming Tail is my wife. She is a good woman in a man's bed. Good to make the nights pleasant. Perhaps I will keep both of you; perhaps someday I will trade you to another man, but for now you are my wives. But Yellow-hair, whether she is wife to another or not and whether I have many other wives, Yellow-hair is my woman. She belongs to me and I belong to her.

"Yellow-hair is not a good wife. She is lazy and sometimes she is good in my bed, very good, better even than Lemming Tail. But only sometimes. She cannot sew and she cannot prepare meat. But I, too, am lazy. I do not hunt too often and I do not help when someone in the village puts up a lodge. I do not make my own weapons and I do not build my own ikyak. But there is some spirit that binds Yellow-hair to me. That is why she will not go with Qakan. And that is why I say to you, if you are willing to leave your sons, you, too, are free to go with Qakan, to see if he will take you back to Amgigh. Perhaps you and Amgigh are like Yellow-hair and me."

For a long time Kiin did not answer. Her thoughts were not on Amgigh, but on Samiq. Yes, perhaps it was as the Raven said. No matter who Kiin had as husband, no matter how many wives Samiq took, Kiin belonged to Samiq and Samiq belonged to her. But how could she return with Qakan? He could not risk taking her back, letting Kayugh and Amgigh know that he had taken Kiin against her will, had cursed Amgigh's sons by using her as wife.

So she turned her thoughts to the Raven. He was not a good husband, though he had never beaten her, and Lemming Tail said he had beaten her only once. But Kiin had seen Kayugh with Chagak, Big Teeth with Crooked Nose and Little Duck, so she knew what a good husband was. She knew the difference between a man who kept a woman only for his bed and his ulaq and a man who cared about his woman as he cared for himself. No, the Raven was not a good husband, but he was not a terrible husband.

If she left on her own and took her sons, he would come after them. As long as he would protect Shuku and Takha she would stay. Perhaps she would have to go to his bed, but she had had worse. She would wait for her chance, leave the Walrus People when the Raven was away on a trading trip, when her sons were stronger.

"N-no," she answered the Raven. "It is not like that with Amgigh and me. I will stay with you."

52

"**P**erhaps we should leave," Small Knife said. "Seven days is long enough to wait."

"Who is boy and who is man?" Samiq snapped, pacing the short length of the cave.

Three Fish sat huddled in the corner, but Samiq, afraid she would back Small Knife in the argument, did not look at her.

"They may return," Samiq said, speaking with his back toward Small Knife. He did not think the boy would answer.

"They will not return," Small Knife said, his voice sounding tired, flat, like a father speaking to a sullen child. And Samiq suddenly felt foolish. The boy was right. Why else would they take everything except his belongings? Had he not said so himself? What spirit bound him to this beach?

His thoughts were interrupted by a grinding roar, and the ground moved; dirt and dust sifted down from the top of the cave.

Three Fish screamed.

"Three Fish," Samiq said loudly, straining to be heard above the roar of the earth. The woman grabbed her suk and ran to the cave entrance.

"Three Fish!"

She stopped and looked back at him.

"Stay here. It is safer here."

"I cannot," she said. "I cannot." Her words were sobs. "You were not there. You do not know. The walls fell on Fat Wife. I could not get her out."

"This is not a ulaq," Samiq said, looking also at Small Knife, seeing that the boy had not panicked, but was waiting for Samiq to speak.

"Perhaps it would be best to leave," the boy said quietly, his voice clear, calm. "Your wife is too frightened to stay."

Three Fish's eyes were round, her lips open in a dark square like the mouth of a wailing child. Samiq's people would not return as long as Aka burned, so what would be the purpose in staying? To torment Three Fish?

"We will go," Samiq said, taking his spears from where they leaned against the cave wall. "Leave nothing."

They lashed the ikyak to the ik to form a more stable craft, weighting both boats with their supplies and stones from the beach. Samiq sat alone in the ikyak, while Three Fish and Small Knife sat in the ik. They paddled out until the land was only a thin line obscured by the haze and ash that grayed the sky.

Samiq's chigadax kept him dry, but he knew that Small Knife and Three Fish would soon be wet from the sea spray. "We will find land and stop," Samiq called to them. Small Knife did not answer, but seeing the boy's soaked hair, Samiq shivered. For the first time since they had left the Whale Hunters' village Samiq thought of his fine whaler's hat. Where was it now? Crushed beneath the walls of Many Whale's ulaq?

Lashed to the ik, Samiq's ikyak was clumsy and difficult to paddle. When he and Amgigh had hunted seal, they had often lashed their ikyan together to ride out a sudden storm. Then they had paddled only to stay afloat, but now Samiq must also keep the boats moving, even in the midst of waves that obeyed Aka and not the wind, waves that a hunter could not judge and know.

And this ikyak was not his own, not made to the measure of his arms, legs, hands. His other ikyan were with the Whale Hunters: the ikyak Samiq had made as a boy, the one from which he had taken his first seal, and then the ikyak he and Many Whales had made—light, narrow, a craft that went through the waves like an otter. What had Kayugh taught him? That his ikyak was a brother.

Yes, Samiq told himself, this ikyak was made for someone else, but it is a good ikyak. He stroked the craft's sides, rubbed his fingers over the tight sea lion skin. Yes, it is a good ikyak. Strong, well-made.

"Brother," he said, hoping the ikyak would hear, would feel the bond. Who could say what the ikyak would do if it knew Samiq longed for his other ikyan? "Brother."

The water was coming over the sides of the ik, and Samiq handed his bailing tube to Small Knife, the boy paddling with one hand while he sucked water into the tube and dumped it over the side.

Samiq knew of small islands not far to the east, a place where he had hunted seals, a good place for bird eggs. "There is an island," he called to Small Knife. "We will go to it." But the sounds of the sea drowned out his words, and finally he only gestured, pointing toward the east, wishing he would have given Small Knife the ikyak, Samiq stronger, more able to paddle and bail the ik.

The day was forever. The waves pushed them back toward land and they strained to make headway against the wind. Samiq's shoulders ached and his throat burned. The salt spray stung his lips and tongue. But I am a hunter, he thought. What about Small Knife, only a boy, and Three Fish, a woman? He closed his eyes and again pulled his paddle through the water. We should have stayed, he thought. I told them we should have stayed. Aka would have calmed. We could have made an easy trip on smooth seas.

"I cannot!" Three Fish's voice broke over the noise of the

waves and Samiq opened his eyes. The woman had slumped down in the ik, allowing her paddle to drag in the water at the side of the boat.

"Do not lose your paddle," he called to her, surprised that he felt no anger only despair, but Small Knife looked back at her and shouted, "Rest. I will paddle." And Samiq was ashamed of his own weariness.

"An island, soon!" he called to Small Knife, and he hoped that the boy heard.

Samiq had lost the faint light where the sun shone behind the gray of the fog, and he did not know how much time had passed. A dangerous thing. A foolish thing, he told himself. What hunter allows such a thing to happen? But the tides and the sun together had seemed to desert him, each behaving as though it, too, had forgotten its place.

Samiq continued to paddle, the movement so often repeated that his arms seemed to move by themselves. He noticed that since Three Fish no longer paddled, his stronger paddling was turning the boats, so he lifted his arms, dipping more shallowly into the water, matching his strokes with Small Knife's.

He watched the surface of the water for the change in color that would show they were near the island, but the floating ash altered all colors, and the first difference he noticed was the turning of the waves, the swells capping as they sped over shallow seas.

"The water changes," Small Knife called to him, and Samiq marveled that the boy had noticed.

"We near the island," Samiq called back. "Three Fish must paddle."

The woman put her paddle into the water, and Samiq was again able to work more quickly, pulling the ikyak with greater speed.

The south side of the island had a gravel beach and few rocks, so Samiq motioned for Small Knife to turn the craft south, Samiq resting for the few moments it took to make the turn.

The ikyak was near enough for Samiq to see the shape of the shore, and they paddled more slowly, Samiq using his paddle to skim the ash from the top of the water, his eyes scanning for rocks that might rip through the hide coverings of the boats. He saw some movement on the shore, but was too intent on maneuvering his ikyak to worry.

Seals, he thought. We will have meat.

The waves carried the boats, pressing them toward the rocky point that protected the beach. Samiq untied his knife from the top of the ikyak and, steadying the boat with his paddle, called to Small Knife, "I will cut the lashing now."

The ik lurched away from the ikyak, Small Knife and Three Fish now paddling at opposite sides of the boat. Samiq stayed slightly behind as the ik rounded the point of the cove. It was caught by the waves, and skimmed smoothly toward the beach. Samiq pushed his own craft around the point, easily avoiding the few boulders that stuck above the water. There was little surf, so Samiq used his paddle only to slow the ikyak and avoid the rocks. He looked toward the shore, his eyes again catching movement.

What if it were not seal, he thought. What if it were one of the Whale Hunters? What if they had come after him? They would kill him, he had no doubt. But would Small Knife and Three Fish be safe? Samiq saw Small Knife pull a spear from the bundle of supplies in the center of the ik, and Samiq pushed his paddle deep into the sea, driving his ikyak to a place beside the ik.

"Something behind that rock!" Small Knife called to him and Samiq fixed his eyes on the shore. Something too tall to be seal. A man! Whale Hunters?

The man carried a spear. Samiq untied his harpoon from its lashings on the right side of his ikyak. Small Knife raised his spear in his arms. Three Fish crouched low in the front of the ik. The man on the beach also raised his spear, then drawing back his arm to throw, made a quick sideways run.

The run was suddenly familiar, something Samiq had often seen.

"No! No-o-o-o!" Samiq screamed.

Small Knife hesitated and so did the man on the beach.

"Big Teeth. I am Samiq! I am Samiq!

"It is a friend," Samiq said to Small Knife. "Put down the spear."

Then there were others on the beach. First Snow and Gray Bird and Amgigh.

Samiq searched the dim shore beyond the men. Kiin? His mother? Were the women also here?

Then splashing out toward him through the cold water, his parka thrown aside, was Amgigh. Samiq plunged his paddle into the water, bringing the ikyak to his brother's side.

In the shallows, Samiq unlaced his hatch skirting and jumped from his ikyak. Samiq clasped Amgigh's shoulders and blinked to hide the tears that stung his eyelids.

"Our mother?" Samiq asked.

"She is well."

"Kiin?"

But when Samiq asked for Kiin, Amgigh turned away. Samiq's heart beat quickly, but before he could go after his brother, Big Teeth had grabbed him in a rough embrace and First Snow was ruffling his hair.

"My sister?" Samiq asked First Snow and First Snow grinned.

"She is good and so is our son."

"We did not know if you would find us," Big Teeth said. "And soon we must move again. Aka shakes us from this small beach."

Samiq nodded, seeing that Big Teeth knew what he himself had finally understood while paddling to the island. Aka would destroy anything near.

Then looking at the men, Samiq realized that his father was not among them. "Our father?" he asked Amgigh and was suddenly afraid. There was so much he needed to tell Kayugh about hunting the whale.

"With your mother. He will be glad to see you."

Then Big Teeth stepped forward. He cleared his throat, placed a hand on Samiq's shoulder. "We have lost two," he said quietly. "Neither to Aka. And Qakan is trading with the Walrus People."

"Two?" Samiq said, knowing one was Big Teeth's son, knowing and yet unable to tell Big Teeth he knew. How did a man tell another that he had desecrated his son's grave?

"My son," Big Teeth said, lowering his head. "To some spirit. We do not know what. He would not eat and there were lumps in his neck. His belly bloated, and finally he died."

"I am sorry, Big Teeth," Samiq said, but could not meet Big Teeth's eyes, afraid of seeing the sorrow there, afraid also of what Big Teeth would tell him next.

"Kiin is dead, Samiq," Big Teeth said.

"My beautiful daughter," said Gray Bird, the words high and wavering like the beginning of some woman's mourning cry.

Samiq could not breathe, could not speak. Kiin. Kiin. How could Kiin be dead? She still came so often into his dreams. Could the dead do that?

"No," Samiq said, and spoke quietly as if refusing some morsel of food, as if telling his baby sister Wren to stay away from his weapons. He looked at Amgigh. "No, Amgigh," he said.

Amgigh did not turn away, did not try to hide his eyes. Samiq saw the anguish there, the sorrow of a man for his woman and so knew that Big Teeth spoke the truth.

"Amgigh, I am sorry," Samiq said.

"It was when I was with you at the Whale Hunters," Amgigh said. "She went fishing. . . ." His voice broke and he looked down. "The sea took her."

For a moment, silence, then Samiq knew if he did not speak, he would cry, cry for another man's wife, cry like a child, and so he said the first words that came to him, nothing about Kiin, nothing about Aka: "I have learned to hunt the whale. I have come back to teach you. To teach all the First Men."

Amgigh looked up, smiled, but the sorrow was still in his

eyes, and then Samiq noticed something more, something he had seen before. The look Amgigh had had as a boy whenever Samiq beat him in a race, whenever Samiq had thrown rocks farther or harder. Anger.

Sorrow, yes, but why anger?

53

Then *Samiq had no words*, nothing to say. His need for Kiin was an emptiness in his chest that pressed his heart and lungs up into his throat. Each breath was pain. Each heartbeat.

The men had begun to ask questions, but their voices were only a babble of sounds, like the croaks and chatter of cliff murres.

What would his life be without Kiin? He would rather be dead himself. Then he could be with her at the Dancing Lights, but he did not have that choice. He was father and husband. His life belonged to those who depended on him. Besides, he had promised to teach Kayugh to hunt the whale. He had promised to teach Amgigh and Big Teeth.

He heard Small Knife's voice above the babble, clear and high above the men's voices. He stood with Three Fish beside the ik, the boy shifting from one foot to the other, Three Fish tugging at her suk.

"I have brought someone with me," Samiq said, interrupting the men.

"Come here!" he called to Small Knife and Three Fish.

They came quietly, skirting the group of men gathered around Samiq, but Samiq pulled Small Knife to his side and said loudly, "Small Knife, my son." Big Teeth grinned, and Samiq was glad that he had brought the boy. It was always good to give a son, and how much more a son who was nearly a man, ready to be a hunter.

"He will be a good man," Amgigh said quietly.

Samiq nodded. "He is already a man."

Samiq turned to Three Fish. She stood with her head lowered. He placed his hand on her shoulder, and she looked up at him. "She is called Three Fish," Samiq said to the men. "She is my wife."

He saw a look of dismay on Amgigh's face, a smirk on Gray Bird's lips. "She is a good worker," Samiq said defensively and hoped she would not smile and show her broken teeth.

For a time, no one spoke, and Samiq looked away, wished that Three Fish had stayed with Dying Seal. Then Three Fish giggled, and Samiq saw with horror that she purposely smoothed her hands over the front of her suk, molding the garment over her breasts, her eyes on Big Teeth's face.

"Go back to the ik!" Samiq said to her. Three Fish looked up at him and giggled again, then walked slowly to the ik, glancing back over her shoulder at the men as she walked.

"She is mother to Small Knife?" Amgigh asked.

"No," said Samiq. His anger made his words harsh. "She is mother to no one. I did not take her willingly."

"Perhaps she should go back."

Samiq looked at his brother in amazement. "She cannot go back. If Aka did not kill her, the sea would."

"She is a big woman," First Snow said. "She will help the other women carrying."

Yes, Samiq thought, she is big. There is at least that.

"I will show you where the women stay," Amgigh said to Samiq. "Our mother and father will want to see you."

"I will stay here with Three Fish," Big Teeth said. "Do not worry about her." Then he turned to First Snow and said, "Take Small Knife to the stream. Show him the ikyak you are building." And Big Teeth said to Samiq, "It is good you brought the boy."

The boy, not the woman, Samiq thought, but he said nothing.

"Our shelter is up in the rocks," Amgigh explained as they walked. "My father was afraid that a camp nearer the sea might be swept away."

Samiq nodded but did not reply, his mind still on Three Fish's behavior. At least our mother will not have to sew my chigadax, Samiq thought, and she will have another daughter to help her gather eggs and berries, to tend the cooking pits and trim the oil lamp wicks.

He shook his head, wanting to forget his embarrassment, to forget the pity he had seen in Amgigh's eyes. His brother had changed in many small ways. He was more certain of his words and seemed to plant his feet more firmly when he walked. Perhaps his time as husband to Kiin had given him the confidence he needed; perhaps his time away from Samiq had made him more sure of his own skills.

When they reached higher ground, Amgigh stopped and motioned toward an outcropping of rock. Sealskins hung from the rock and two women stood beside a cooking pit.

One of the women coughed, and even from a distance, Samiq knew it was Chagak, the one beside her, Blue Shell. Chagak seemed smaller than Samiq remembered her, and he saw that her hair now had several streaks of gray.

She looked up at them as they approached, her eyes suddenly wide. She pressed her hands to her chest and Samiq ran to her, not caring what the others thought, hugging her as Big Teeth had hugged him, stroking her hair, wiping the tears from her cheeks.

Laughing and crying, Chagak pointed toward a pile of skins and Samiq saw the small, round face of a little girl smiling up at him.

"Wren?" Samiq asked.

Chagak nodded.

The child looked at him, one finger in her mouth, and Samiq

lifted her from the mound of skins, seeing the features of his mother and of Kayugh blended on the tiny face.

"Sister!" he said and swung her up into the air, the girl laughing as she clutched at his hair.

He settled Wren on his shoulder and turned to face Blue Shell, but he could not bring himself to look into Blue Shell's eyes.

"I am sorry about your daughter," he said and had to stop, the words he wanted to say caught in his throat.

Blue Shell mumbled some reply Samiq could not hear.

Samiq nodded as though he understood then said, "Gray Bird says your son is on a trading trip."

"Yes," Blue Shell said. "Yes. He is a trader now."

"You found your ikyak?" Chagak asked.

Samiq set his sister back on the pile of skins and said, "Yes, we would not be here if we had not found the ikyak."

"Your father was the one who left it there for you," she said.

His father. No, not his father. Kayugh. And Samiq remembered the bones he had found in the death ulaq, the small bones of hands and feet scattered as if a trader had rattled them together, cast them out in a game of chance.

The sealskin curtains moved and Crooked Nose joined Chagak at the cooking pit. Her mouth dropped open when she saw Samiq, and in a whispered voice she asked Chagak, "He is not a ghost?"

Samiq laughed and strode over to her, placed a strong hand on each of her shoulders. "Not a ghost," he said.

Crooked Nose laughed, too, but through her laughter Samiq saw the shine of tears, and Crooked Nose had to turn away, wipe an arm across her eyes.

Then Chagak called, "Red Berry, I need you!"

Samiq looked toward the sealskin curtains and waited for his sister. When she came, Samiq smiled. She was again pregnant, the bulge of her belly beginning to curve over her apron, her faced lighted with the glow that was the beauty of pregnancy.

There would be jokes among the men, Samiq knew. Two babies so close together. When did First Snow have time to hunt?

Red Berry gave a small screech, and then, unlike Crooked Nose, did not try to hide her tears. And though, being sister, she could not reach out to him, could not hold him, she clasped her hands over her growing belly and rocked herself from one side to the other until her tears had stopped, and she could finally say, "I am glad you are home."

"I, too," Samiq said, and he looked at the rocks and the shelter beneath the rocks. Home, he thought. Yes, home.

Then Amgigh, stepping forward, watching as Chagak peeled back the layer of mats that covered the top of the cooking pit, asked, "Where is my father?"

Chagak looked up, surprise in her eyes. "He was not on the beach with you?" she asked Amgigh. "Does he know Samiq has returned?"

"No," Amgigh said. "I thought he was here with you."

Crooked Nose reached down into the pit with a long forked stick and drew out a piece of meat.

By the smell, Samiq knew it was harbor seal meat, the animals abundant near the island.

"Seal meat," Chagak said quietly. "Thank you for the whale meat you sent us. Your father has your spearhead."

"You did not eat the poison," Samiq said.

"Big Teeth knew. He cut it out," said Crooked Nose. "The oil was enough for much of the winter. Kayugh says you are a great hunter, providing for two villages."

Samiq's face reddened at the praise, and wanting to draw attention away from himself, he asked, "Where is Little Duck?"

There was a quick sadness in the eyes of those around him, and Chagak said, "Her son died, and since then Little Duck does not speak, seldom eats. For a time, she walked when she was told to walk, worked when she was told to work, but now she is so weak, she only waits to die."

Samiq closed his eyes.

"I will talk to her," he offered.

"It will do no good. She listens to no one. No one can help her," Crooked Nose said.

"She is in the shelter?" Samiq asked.

"Yes."

"Go to her now, Samiq," Amgigh said. "Maybe seeing you will help. Who can say? I will find my father."

Samiq looked at his mother and she nodded, saying to Red Berry, "Go with him."

Red Berry smiled sadly as they entered the shelter, then whispered, "She is very thin."

Grass mats covered the entire floor area of the overhang, and the ground sloped up to a small cavelike shelter. Sleeping skins were scattered over the mats and Samiq stepped around them as he followed Red Berry. A movement drew Samiq's eyes toward a pile of mats.

"Little Duck," Red Berry called softly. An oil lamp burned beside the mats, and as Samiq's eyes adjusted to the darkness, he saw Little Duck. He stepped closer and shivered in disbelief. Little Duck's skin stretched over her bones like the covering of an ikyak over its skeleton of wood.

"Little Duck," Red Berry called again.

This time the woman lifted her head, and in the shrunken face Samiq recognized Little Duck's eyes. Her skin fell in folds from her chin to her shoulders, and her hands shook as she raised them toward Samiq.

"Samiq?" the woman said. "You are not dead?"

Samiq knelt beside her. "No, Little Duck, I am not dead. I am here. I have come back to my own people."

"We thought you were dead," Little Duck said. "Aka . . . when Aka . . . We thought you were killed."

"I am alive," said Samiq.

"My son is dead," the woman said, her voice quivering.

"I am sorry."

"Soon I will be dead, too. Then I will be with my son."

"You must eat," Samiq said, bending closer as the woman lowered her head to the mat.

"There is no reason to eat."

"Big Teeth needs you."

"He has Crooked Nose."

"You could have another child."

"No. There are no more children in me."

"It is no use," Red Berry said quietly. "There is nothing that can be done."

"I will stay with her a little while," Samiq said.

"There is no need," Red Berry answered. "She only sleeps. She will not even know you are here."

"I will know I am here," Samiq replied.

Red Berry stood beside him as he squatted on his heels. He took Little Duck's hand in his own and watched in quietness.

It was not his place to cry. She was not his mother nor grandmother nor wife, but Little Duck's grief for her son seemed to settle deep into the center of Samiq's chest, drawn by the pain he carried for Kiin.

The curtains parted and Samiq looked up. Kayugh had entered the cave. Gladness mixed with the sorrow in Samiq's throat and he could say nothing. A glance at Little Duck told him she slept, and he carefully placed her hand at her side and rose to greet his father.

A year had not changed Kayugh, his hair was as black, his face the same. Chagak had once told Samiq that Kayugh never changed, that he looked the same as he did when she first became his wife.

"You are safe," Kayugh said.

"You should have known I would be," Samiq answered, then regretted his words, thinking he sounded too much like a boy pretending to be a man.

"Yes, I should have known," Kayugh said and smiled.

"When I came to our beach," Samiq said, "I thought that you . . . that Aka had . . ."

"You should have known we would be safe," Kayugh said, and he smiled when Samiq laughed.

Little Duck stirred on her mat, but did not open her eyes.

"She is dying," Kayugh said.

"It is her choice," Samiq replied.

Kayugh nodded and walked to the far wall of the shelter. He sat down and motioned Samiq to a place beside him. Kayugh was silent for a time, then asked, "You have seen your sister?"

"Red Berry?"

"Wren."

Samiq grinned. "She has grown."

"She is beautiful like her mother."

Samiq was surprised at Kayugh's words. He had never thought of his mother as beautiful.

"I have met the one you brought from the Whale Hunters," Kayugh said.

"Small Knife?"

"Yes, I have seen the boy," Kayugh said, "but I meant the woman."

"Three Fish. She is called Three Fish."

Kayugh nodded. "I did not know you would take a wife."

"It was not my choice," Samiq said. "Many Whales thought I needed a woman."

"Many Whales," Kayugh said. "He is a strange man." Kayugh rubbed his hand across his chin. "They marked you," he said.

Samiq touched his own chin. He had nearly forgotten the dark lines that Many Babies had sewn into his skin.

Kayugh frowned and looked away. "Did Aka shake their village also?" he asked.

"Yes," Samiq replied, his voice soft. He cleared his throat, a harsh sound against the quietness of the shelter, against the gentleness of Little Duck's breathing. "Fat Wife died. Also Three Fish's parents and her brother, Puffin, who was Small Knife's father."

"It is good you brought them then."

"I did not want to," Samiq said. "But I am glad I brought Small Knife. He is more man than boy."

Kayugh nodded then asked, "Many Whales?"

Samiq looked away. His father had been fond of Many Whales. "He is dead."

Kayugh closed his eyes and pressed his chin into the collar of his parka. When he raised his head he looked toward Little Duck and asked, "Aka?"

"No," Samiq said. "A sickness. It took him quickly and without pain. He could not move, and his mouth was . . . it was . . ."

"I have seen the sickness before," Kayugh said. "An old woman I knew when I was still a child. She lived for a long time. Be thankful that Many Whales died quickly."

They sat in silence until Samiq finally spoke, telling Kayugh the thing that had seldom left his mind since he fled from the Whale Hunters. "They thought that I called Aka. That I told Aka to destroy their village."

Kayugh snorted. "Why? Why would they think that?"

"Because so many whales came to the Whale Hunters' island last summer. More than they had ever seen. Many Whales said it was my power, and some of the hunters were angry that a man from the Seal Hunters should have such power."

"Was it your power?"

"How could it be? I am just a man. I learned what they taught. I did what they told me to do. That was all. I sought no great power. I called on no spirits."

"Then the Whale Hunters are fools," Kayugh said. "What man could call Aka? Who has such power?"

Samiq was relieved at Kayugh's answer. To have someone else believe as he did made the Whale Hunters' accusations seem less important.

"But you learned to hunt the whale," Kayugh said, and Samiq saw the hope in the man's eyes.

"You found my whale on your beach," Samiq answered.

Kayugh laughed. "When Aka quiets we will go back, and you will teach us to hunt the whale," he said. He reached to grip Samiq's shoulder. "You have been a fine son to me."

The words were more than Samiq ever hoped to hear, and he found he could not speak, the quietness of the cave broken only by Little Duck's shallow breathing.

"I am sorry about Kiin," Kayugh said suddenly.

"Yes," Samiq said, the sorrow of her death again full and hard in his chest until each breath brought pain. "Amgigh . . . it must be hard for Amgigh," Samiq said.

He turned and saw that Kayugh's eyes were on his own, holding him so he could not look away. "It is more difficult for you," Kayugh said. "I promised her for Amgigh because he was my child and you were not." He clasped and unclasped his hands. "I did not know then that your mother would become my wife and you would become my son. And I did not know how deeply you would care for Kiin."

Samiq's face colored. "Amgigh was a good husband to her," he said.

"He is a good man. A fine son. But in some ways . . . There is caring, but . . ." Kayugh shrugged then said, "I have never told you about Amgigh's mother."

Samiq was surprised. People seldom spoke about the dead, usually only to tell others that they had died. And even then a man had to choose his words carefully. Who could say what the spirit of a dead one might do?

"She was called White River. She was a good woman. Strong. She gave me Red Berry and Amgigh. Two good children. When she died, I did not want to live. I did not think a man could care for a woman more than I cared for White River. But then I found your mother. And when she took Amgigh and nursed him so he could live . . ." He shook his head. "There is no way to say how much I care for your mother."

Samiq looked at Kayugh in amazement. Who could truly know what was in the heart of another man?

"Kiin was to Amgigh as White River was to me. But to you, Kiin . . ." He stopped. "You see, I understand, because I have your mother."

Samiq nodded and Kayugh said, "I planned to go with you

this summer to help you find a wife, a woman of the First Men or perhaps of the Walrus People. I did not know you would bring a Whale Hunter wife."

Samiq bit at the inside of his cheek. A wife—Three Fish had always been an embarrassment, and here among his own people how much worse. A wife! Better to live alone. But he smiled at his father, a stiff smile, and said, "Yes, I have a wife. A strong, healthy wife."

54

Y ellow-hair smirked at Qakan and threw another chunk of dried fish. Qakan ducked and the fish thudded against the curtain that divided their part of the ulaq from Ice Hunter's.

Qakan looked at his wife in disgust. Her hair was matted and her skin streaked with soot. Except for the first time he had seen her, the time she was dancing, helping Raven cheat Qakan out of his trade goods, she had been dirty. Her hair was filthy, caked with rancid fat, her grass aprons frayed. Their portion of the ulaq was not much better. Ice Hunter's mother, the one the Walrus People called Grandmother, first berated Qakan for not making his wife take better care of the ulaq. Later, perhaps when she realized Qakan was powerless to control his wife, she talked to Yellow-hair, shamed the woman into throwing out the worst of the scraps that littered the floor.

Today, Grandmother had visited them, had shouted at Yellow-hair. "Your filth stinks up my son's half of this ulaq," she had said, her old woman's neck stretched long and thin, her voice rising to a screech as she spoke of Yellow-hair's laziness, of Ice Hunter who was kind enough to allow a trader to live in his ulaq for the winter.

She did not look at Qakan as she spoke, did not offer him the courtesy of acknowledging his presence, and Qakan was not sure which was the greater shame: that he could not make his wife keep the ulaq clean, or that Grandmother saw him as being worthless, as having no more power than a basket set in the corner.

When Grandmother left, Qakan had sneered at his wife, though he dared not utter a word to her, but the scorn in his smile had been enough. She took the few fish still in their storage cache and began throwing them at him. At first she threw silently, anger reddening her face. The only sound was the thud of fish striking curtains or walls, and once the low gurgle of Yellow-hair's laugh when Qakan was too slow and a fish hit him.

Finally Qakan left, stopping before he went through the curtains to pick up a few fish from the floor and take them with him. At least he would have something to eat.

It was spring; he had a good amount of trade goods—things he had hidden from Yellow-hair once he realized she was trading his furs, carvings and necklaces for seal stomachs of dried fish, for berries and roots so she would not have to spend her days finding food.

Yes, he would go, Qakan decided.

He walked the beach, watching as all men watch for signs of seal or fish. He had never liked the sea, but during the long winter, he had found himself looking forward to the calmer waters of summer, when a man could go out and fish, away from a lazy wife who never allowed him into her sleeping place, who teased with flipping apron and wide-spread knees, but demanded furs and necklaces for any night spent as wife.

Now after a winter of Yellow-hair's taunts, Qakan was not only angry with his wife, but also with all the Walrus People. Why did they allow their women to be so foolish? Did mothers not care how their daughters behaved? Did fathers have no pride?

And what about Kiin? She was honored now among the Walrus People. Had she forgotten her shame among the First Men? Had she forgotten that she had lived without a name and without a soul? Now she was mother of two sons, Qakan's sons. Sons he had given her. Instead of a curse he had given her life and honor—as wife of one of the most powerful men among the Walrus People. Had she forgotten that all this was hers because of him?

Well, he would not stay among the Walrus People. He was a trader. Yes, he had taken a wife for the winter. To warm his bed and prepare his meals, to sew his parka, but now he was ready to travel to other villages, to enjoy the hospitality of other women. He would leave Kiin. Why worry about her? He had found her a good husband. He would take Yellow-hair with him, give her in trade to another village, one of the First Men's villages scattered between the Walrus People and Tugix's island. He would stop in those villages closer to Tugix, the places he had not stopped last summer for fear Kiin would be seen and remembered.

Yellow-hair—clean and in a new suk—would bring much in trade. Too bad he could not take her back to his own village. Samiq needed a wife. What would Samiq give? How many furs for a woman who could dance like Yellow-hair?

The bay ice had melted, and the hunters said that even the sea ice was breaking up. A trader, if he was careful, could begin spring trading trips. Qakan picked up a stone and flung it out into the water. The wind was strong enough to force his stone into a curved path. Qakan laughed. He would like to see Samiq with Yellow-hair as wife, would rejoice in Samiq's dishonor: a filthy ulaq, torn clothing, poor food.

With Yellow-hair as wife, Samiq would have no sons. How could Yellow-hair, as contrary as she was, as few times as she came into her husband's bed, give sons? Even Raven with all his power had not gotten sons from her.

So, yes, Qakan would go back now, tell Yellow-hair his plans. He would speak sternly to her, let her know he was more powerful than she was. Who was she? A woman. Only a woman. Not even a First Men's woman, but a woman of the Walrus People. She had no power.

He returned to the ulaq. Ice Hunter was not there, nor his sons. Qakan straightened, stood tall as he entered his side of the ulaq. Yellow-hair had not trimmed the oil lamp's wick, and the light was dim. At first Qakan saw nothing but the heap of furs that made up their bed on the sleeping platform. Then he saw movement. He closed his eyes, waited for a moment as they adjusted to the dimness. Yes, he saw the light color of his wife's hair. So, in the middle of the day, she slept. No wonder he had no food. No wonder his parka was not mended, the fur matted with old grease.

He strode to the sleeping platform, reached down and clasped her by the hair. At the same moment a hand reached out of the furs, a man's hand, and grabbed his wrist. Qakan gasped, heard Yellow-hair's laughter, and a deeper laugh—a man's laugh. Then Yellow-hair was standing beside him, her grass aprons askew, and lying naked in the furs was Raven, the man's hand so hard on Qakan's wrist that Qakan began to whimper from the pain.

"You have a fine wife," Raven hissed. He released Qakan's wrist and stood up. He reached into the furs and brought out his leggings and parka, slipped them on. He cupped a hand around one of Yellow-hair's breasts.

"She is ready for you," he said, then pushed Qakan back so that he tipped slowly into the heap of furs, then Raven left the ulaq.

Yellow-hair stood over Qakan laughing. She reached down and stroked one of Qakan's legs, but Qakan sat up and slapped her hand away.

"You are not my wife," Qakan hissed. "Get out of my ulaq. You are no one's wife. You belong to no one. Get out. Get out. I do not need you. A trader has many women. Any woman he wants."

Yellow-hair's eyes widened. For a moment Qakan thought she was afraid, but then she laughed, laughed until she was doubled over, holding the laughter into her belly with both arms. But as quickly as she had begun laughing, she quit and began gathering her belongings, furs, baskets, food.

For a time Qakan watched, then suddenly his anger spilled

over from its place in his chest, slid down through his legs and into his feet, pushed its way also down his arms and into his hands. He ran to the corner where he kept his weapons, pulled out a spear.

Yellow-hair was kneeling with her back to Qakan, stacking baskets from the jumbled heap near the storage cache. Qakan took two steps, running steps. Yellow-hair turned, screamed. Qakan stopped, spear in one hand, ready to strike.

Yellow-hair's eyes narrowed. She threw back her head and laughed. "Kill me," she said. "You cannot throw. You are no hunter. Kill me."

She stood up, thrust out her arms. Qakan lowered the spear. Yellow-hair smiled, then turned away from him, back to the stack of baskets. For a time she worked, packing, but then with a short laugh, she faced him again and spat at him. The spittle landed in a glob in Qakan's left eye.

Qakan flinched, wiped his eye. Yellow-hair's laughter spun up and out, filling the ulaq. Qakan turned away, but then he turned back, and quickly, quickly, as quickly as Samiq moved, he raised the spear. He threw it—as hard as Big Teeth threw.

Yellow-hair's laughter ended, seemed to pull itself back into her throat.

When he threw the spear, Qakan had closed his eyes. Now he opened them. Yellow-hair was standing, but the spear protruded from between her breasts. Blood was already pooled at her feet. She fell.

Qakan watched as her eyes rolled back in her head until only the whites showed beneath the lids. She took one shuddering breath, then was still.

Qakan walked to his wife, pulled out his spear, then leaned over and moved the baskets so they would not be stained by Yellow-hair's blood. Her baskets were not as beautiful as Chagak's baskets or even the baskets that Kiin made, but they would be good for something in trade.

Qakan began to pack the bedding furs, mats, the small amount of food in the storage cache. When he had finished, he stood over Yellow-hair once more. He waited a long time to see if she still breathed. No, no. He leaned over, careful that his parka did not touch her dead flesh. He unclasped the necklaces from her neck. One was a shell necklace, another was of bear teeth, the third was a leather thong that held one of Kiin's walrus carvings.

They would bring a good price in trade, each of them.

Then he stood, and speaking to Yellow-hair, to her spirit, said, "Yellow-hair, you fool, now who is going to paddle my ik?"

55

Q *akan smiled at the men* gathered around him. It had been
a long winter, a hard winter, mainly because of Yellow-
hair. But he had learned. He would not be taken by a beautiful
face again.

And now that the Walrus men knew he would soon leave,
they eagerly offered him trade goods in exchange for furs, knives
and even for Kiin's carvings that Qakan had bought from
Raven. Raven had demanded two of Amgigh's knives and three
sealskins for a basket of those carvings.

Qakan had made the trade, rolling his eyes and forcing his
lips into a pout, had bowed his head under Raven's laughter,
but only to hide his own smile. Raven did not know about the
other knives he had, knives finer and with longer blades, knives
also made by Amgigh. He did not know that Kiin's carvings with
their fine smooth lines, the shape of head and flipper curving
into the whale tooth or walrus tusk would bring him much more
than the knives and sealskins he had given for them.

Yes, this evening he was making many good trades, but
Qakan was careful not to let any man see his eyes. Someone
might have power to read what was there, to find the truth in
the depths, to know that they could make much better trades.
They might also see the secret of Yellow-hair's death, see that
Qakan had left her in the ulaq, covered her in the sleeping

platform with the worst of the skins, the moldy mats, things he could not trade.

So when he had taken all he could take, what would fit in the ik and what was good enough to barter on his way back to his own village, he held up both hands and again with head bowed, eyes hidden, said, "No more. I have nothing left. You have taken it all. I must leave you. But someday I will return and will bring whale oil from the Whale Hunters' island at the far western edge of the world, and I will bring obsidian knives from the First Men and mats woven with the finest stitches, baskets for your women, sealskin boots and ivory needles and parkas made of otter fur.

"So now leave me. I must pack my ik. I will go in the morning."

Some of the men protested. Some made references to Yellow-hair, but Qakan turned his back on all of them and began filling the ik, bundling furs and sorting shells into baskets. But then he felt a hand on his shoulder.

He turned and saw that it was Raven. "A good trade," Raven said and held up his two knives.

"Yes," Qakan replied. "Amgigh's knives are always worth much."

"Amgigh?"

"A young man from my village. He is skilled in making weapons. He is also a great hunter. Two summers ago, when he was still a boy, Amgigh killed a whale."

"He alone took a whale?" Raven asked and tipped his head back, looking at Qakan through slitted eyes.

"He and his brother," Qakan said and was not afraid to return the man's slow smile. He did not care if Raven knew he was lying. Raven would repeat Qakan's claim. Did it not make the knives more valuable?

"So, do you plan to take Yellow-hair?"

Qakan drew in his cheeks, turned and spat. "You should know," he said.

Raven shrugged. "Why should I know?"

"She will not go with me. She wants to be your wife again."
Quickly Qakan lowered his eyes. He hoped the man's spirit did
not sense the truth.

Raven laughed. "I like Kiin," he said. "She keeps the ulaq
clean, makes good food and warm parkas, but Yellow-hair, she is
a woman who puts joy into a man's loins."

Qakan made himself smile. Made himself laugh. "Yes, it was
a good winter," he said and watched as Raven turned and left
him.

He leaned down over the ik, packed the last of the baskets,
tied them with double strands of kelp line so they would not
shift. Yes, he thought, It was a good winter. But I have traded
Yellow-hair. To the wind spirits. Now I will see what they will
give me for her. Perhaps another woman to paddle my ik. He
laughed and the wind took his laughter out over the sea. Perhaps they would give him Kiin.

56

K iin looked up from her weaving. Qakan pushed aside the
dividing curtain and stood, arms crossed over his chest,
eyes roving the ulaq walls. Kiin was weaving a mat in the manner of the Walrus People women, the weaving done on the lap,
two strands of grass twined across a long fringe of warp grass,
the cross strands twisting over each warp grass to make a tight,
strong mat.

Qakan had lost weight over the winter, and the bones of his
face were sharper, his eyes deeper in their sockets.

"I have g-given you everything I have to g-give," Kiin said.
"The other b-baskets and m-m-mats are for my husband's ulaq,
and I have m-made no carvings since the babies were born."

"I do not need your mats," Qakan said, spitting out the
words, disdain in his eyes. "What good thing can a trader expect to get from woman's work?"

"You d-do not need my carvings then," Kiin replied, her voice
even, her eyes on her weaving. "Bring them back. Perhaps m-m-
my husband needs them."

She did not look up at Qakan, but knew he would be scowl-
ing. "You are hungry?" she asked. Sometimes, when Yellow-hair
was angry for several days, Qakan came to her to get dried fish
or to stay for a night.

"No."

Kiin sighed. "Why are you here?"

"You should come with me to the beach," he said. "I need to talk to you."

Kiin looked at him, narrowed her eyes. "You are leaving s-soon. To t-trade," she said.

"Yes."

"Will Yellow-hair g-g-go with you?"

"No."

"You want m-me to p-paddle your ik."

"No," Qakan said.

"Do n-n-not take Yellow-hair back to our people."

"I told you she will not go with me."

Kiin felt the corner of her mouth twitch. Everyone in the village laughed about Qakan and Yellow-hair; everyone knew about their arguments; everyone knew Yellow-hair often kicked Qakan from her bed. Twice Kiin had found the Raven with Yellow-hair in their sleeping platform. Three times Lemming Tail had found them, and though it did not matter to Kiin what the Raven did with other women, each time Lemming Tail found them, she became sullen and angry.

It would be that way when the Raven finally took Kiin to his bed, Kiin knew. Each night Lemming Tail watched the Raven, and each time he looked at Kiin, Lemming Tail went to him, distracted him with the stroking of her hands, with teasing and giggling. And so the Raven had not yet taken Kiin.

"Come to the beach with me . . ." Qakan pleaded, his voice the whining little boy's voice Kiin remembered from their childhood.

She set aside her weaving and stood on tiptoe to look into her son's cradles. They both slept, Samiq's son sucking on his fist, Amgigh's son with eyes squeezed tight in sleep, mouth moving in a dream.

Kiin slipped on her suk and deliberately walked over to the weapons corner and picked up a long-bladed stone knife.

She looked up at Qakan, saw that his eyes had widened. "It is m-mine," she said. "M-m-my husband g-gave it to m-me to protect our s-sons."

She followed Qakan out the entrance tunnel and into the gray misty rain of the day.

"To the beach," he said.

"N-n-no here," she answered. "You d-do n-not remember that the Grandmother and the Aunt have s-said one of the babies should d-die?"

Qakan's eyes narrowed. "Why do you think I want to talk to you?" he said. "I have heard of their plans. Raven has spoken to all the men."

"The Raven?"

"You think he wants to protect the babies?"

Kiin held up the knife. "He g-gave me this," she said.

Qakan shifted his weight from one foot to the other, then answered, "I do not know, but something has made him change his mind. He has decided Grandmother is right. He thinks one of the babies should be killed. He has made a plan."

"So why d-do you tell me, Qakan? What d-do you gain?"

"You are my sister."

Kiin laughed.

Qakan flushed. "I am the babies' father," he finally stammered. "They are my sons."

Kiin saw the whiteness in his face, the truth that was in his eyes. Yes, Kiin had been careful not to let him see the babies. He did not know how much they looked like their true fathers. For a moment she closed her eyes. Of course Qakan would believe he was father. Perhaps that was enough to make him want to protect the babies. Perhaps. Or perhaps he only wanted Kiin to go with him so he could trade her again and trade the babies. Babies were not worth much. They could not hunt or fish, but these were sons, born at the same time. Even the Raven admitted their power.

So whether as father or as trader, Qakan would want to protect the babies. But Qakan was Qakan. Who could believe what he said?

"I d-d-do n-not . . . believe you," Kiin said. "The Raven will protect his s-sons."

"They are my sons," Qakan hissed, "and soon they will be dead if you do not go with me tonight."

"You l-leave tonight?"

"Yes. Come with me. Bring the babies."

Kiin turned away from Qakan. "No, Qakan," she said. "N-no."

"If you do not believe me, then believe this, Raven will tell one of the women to get you, to bring you to the beach. He will say that Lemming Tail is hurt. When you leave the ulaq, Grandmother will come in and kill one of the babies."

"Samiq's child," Kiin's spirit whispered. "She will kill Samiq's child."

But Kiin said to Qakan, "You lie," and crawled back into the ulaq.

Qakan waited. Nervously, he watched. Raven was fishing, and as long as he stayed away . . . It had taken two necklaces to coax Lemming Tail to spend the evening in another ulaq, but they were small necklaces. If this did not work, he would have to wait another day, and each day he waited gave more chance that Yellow-hair's body would be discovered. Yes, as husband he owned his wife. A man might beat his wife, but kill her? No. And who could say what Raven would do when he found out?

Then Shale Thrower came to the beach, and Qakan knew the spirits honored his plan. Shale Thrower was a young woman, easy to fool, quick to believe what others told her. Qakan flung back the hood of his parka and mussed his hair, then darting out from between the ulas, he grabbed her arm.

"Quickly, quickly," he gasped. "Raven says to bring Kiin. Tell Kiin Raven wants her. Lemming Tail has been hurt. They are there, behind the village. He is afraid Lemming Tail is dying. Raven needs Kiin."

For a moment Shale Thrower stood and stared at Qakan, her

mouth curling into a circle, her eyes wide. Qakan pushed her toward Raven's ulaq. "Go, now. Tell Kiin Raven needs her."

Qakan watched the woman run to Raven's ulaq, then he walked to the beach. The ik was ready.

Kiin clasped Shale Thrower's shoulders and shook her. "It is the Raven who wants m-me?" she asked. "The Raven?"

"Yes!"

For a moment Kiin stared at the girl. So, she thought, Qakan told the truth.

"G-g-go and tell him I am coming," she said. "Go n-now."

Shale Thrower left the ulaq, and Kiin took a long breath. She pulled the babies from their cradles and slipped them into their carrying straps. "Do not cry," she whispered. "Do not cry; do not cry," the words like a song, a lullaby. She pushed a breast close to each baby's face and waited until she felt each child begin to suck. Then she threw a few of her belongings into a basket—needles, chunks of sinew, coils of kelp twine, the long knife the Raven had given her, a short-bladed woman's knife. A walking stick, a bag of dried fish.

Her chest ached with the knowledge that Woman of the Sky and Woman of the Sun would do such a thing to trick her. But she heard the voice of her spirit whisper, "It is to protect their people. Their village. Even the Raven wants to protect his village."

Quickly, Kiin crawled out of the ulaq. Quickly she slipped down to the beach. Night was coming; the sun was dark beneath clouds, the sea black. Qakan had said he would not leave until morning. She knew where he kept his ik. He said he would sleep there for the night. But then she saw the ik, out already into the bay, Qakan alone, paddling.

Fear grew thick and hard in her chest, clogging her throat so she could not even call out. Once, twice, she waved her hands, then finally found her voice and called to her brother.

She heard her spirit speak: "He cannot hear you."

Once again she called, felt the wind cold on her cheeks, cold on the wetness from her tears. She squatted down. Let the Raven find her here; she had a knife. She would fight for her sons.

Then she heard a call, coming in from the water. Faint. She looked up. Qakan had turned the ik. He was coming for her.

57

"Three nights *I have waited* for you!" Three Fish yelled. "Three days I have lived here and you act as though I am no longer your wife. That you do not know me."

"You are my wife," Samiq said. "But that does not give you reason to decide where I sleep. You are my wife, and you will do what I say."

"I will return to my own people!" Three Fish said.

"Go. I will not stop you."

"Small Knife will go with me," Three Fish said.

"It is his choice. Ask him."

Her small eyes slid away from Samiq's face and she muttered, "He will not go unless you say so."

Samiq shrugged. Small Knife had already become one of the First Men. Even in the few short days they had been on the island, Small Knife was learning their ways. He was often with First Snow, each teaching the other different skills, both benefiting. Even Samiq's mother had mentioned that it seemed as though Small Knife had always belonged to them, had always been a part of their village.

"I will not make him go," Samiq said to Three Fish.

"If I go alone, I will die."

"It is your choice. You can try to return or you can belong to my people. The wives of the First Men do what their husbands say, and it is an honor to be a good wife."

Three Fish narrowed her eyes but Samiq continued to speak.

"The skills of a good wife are like the skills of a good hunter," he said. "Does the hunter say to the sea lion, 'Come to my beach this day or that? Come here and make my hunting easy'? Does a hunter get meat by telling the whale what to do? No. The hunter must go to the animal. And it is the same for the wife. Who brings skins for her clothing, oil for her fire?"

"Who sews a man's ikyak cover?" Three Fish retorted. "Who makes his chigadax? Who makes his parka?"

For a time Samiq did not answer, but instead stared at Three Fish, his anger first directed at Many Whales, the man who had forced him to take this loud and stupid woman as a wife. It would be a good thing to be rid of her, but Samiq would not ask Small Knife to take her back to the Whale Hunters. He would not sacrifice a son for a worthless wife. And so Samiq spat on the ground, near enough to Three Fish's feet so that she would know his disgust, and then he said, "Perhaps this year a different woman will make my chigadax." And he walked away.

Samiq was asleep and the rumbling woke him. He reached for his harpoon and went to his father's sleeping place. His mother was curled beside his father, the two with arms around each other, and for a moment Samiq hesitated, but then he knelt and grasped his father's shoulder, gently shaking him awake.

Kayugh sat up quickly, reached for his spear, but Samiq clasped his arm and said, "It is Samiq. Listen."

His mother awoke, sat up and pulled a sealskin around her shoulders. "It cannot be Aka," she said. "We are too far away."

"We are not far enough," Samiq said as another tremor shook the cave.

"But we are safe here," Kayugh said. "A small shaking will not hurt us. Go back to your sleeping place."

Samiq felt the burn of anger at the center of his chest. He was not a child to be ordered to his bed. He left his father's sleeping place and walked to the mouth of the cave. So now the rumbling had reached this small island. What if it grew worse? In the morning he would talk to his father. He must make him understand.

But in the morning, Kayugh felt the same way. "There is no need to leave," he said. "We can wait here. There are few whales, but there are seals. Surely before winter, we will be able to return to our own beach. Then you will teach us to hunt the whale, and we will trade again with the Whale Hunters."

"The Whale Hunters think I brought Aka's anger on them," Samiq said. "They will not trade with us. They will kill us."

Kayugh frowned. "Perhaps Aka will kill them and there will be no worry. If not, we will find another place, one nearer the paths of the whales."

"We must go now," Samiq said. "This island is too small. Aka could shake it into the sea. There would be no escape for any of us."

Kayugh sat quietly for a time. "You are a man," he finally said, but did not look at Samiq, "but you are my son. We will stay."

Samiq rose slowly to his feet and left the shelter. Yes, he was Kayugh's son. Kayugh's son and the son of that one who had been cut apart, buried without honor. Who could say what weakness was passed to Samiq through that one's blood? Perhaps there was some truth in what the Whale Hunters said. Perhaps Samiq carried evil he did not understand, could not control. If so, who was he to disagree with Kayugh? Instead Samiq should learn from him.

Who was a better father than Kayugh? Samiq claimed Small Knife as son, and already knew what it was to take pride in Small Knife's skills. But Samiq in learning to be father, should remember Kayugh's example.

Early the day before, Small Knife had taken a seal in the water just off their beach. "You have brought us luck!" Gray Bird had said to Samiq, and Samiq felt a father's joy when Small Knife took the hunter's share of flippers and fat.

Small Knife had begun work on his own ikyak. He was young, younger than Samiq had been when he had made his first kill, but many things had changed. They lived in a new place. They must accept new ways. There were fewer berry bushes here and the beach was no long stretch of sand and gravel sloping gently into the sea, but a sudden drop, giving few places to find clams or chitons, even at low tide. There was not as much food available for the women to gather and so boys must become hunters.

But that morning, the falling ash had been worse, and so Samiq and the others had brought in their ikyan soon after Small Knife took his seal.

Even this morning, as Samiq strained his eyes toward the water, he could see little but gray. And as the women worked, each wore a cap of ash. Samiq heard Crooked Nose exclaim, "In our eyes, in our hair, between our teeth!"

Samiq smiled. Crooked Nose. Who was more ugly? Who was more beautiful?

Samiq's eyes fell on Chagak, tending both the fire and Wren, the tiny girl running among the women, often straying too near the cooking pits.

Samiq stood up and stretched, then caught his mother's eye and motioned toward Wren. His mother picked up the child, and Samiq grinned at the small girl's scream of protest.

Chagak hugged Wren then brought her to Samiq. Wren held her arms out to her brother, babbling and giggling when he threw her up into the air and caught her.

"You do not hunt?" Chagak asked.

Samiq looked at his mother in surprise. She had seldom begun a conversation with him since he returned from the Whale Hunters. He was now fully a man, a hunter with a wife.

"Too much ash," he replied, but he knew that Chagak understood why the men were not hunting.

She nodded. "Yes, for us also," she said looking back at the cooking pits.

Samiq smiled. "I heard Crooked Nose."

Chagak laughed but said nothing.

She stayed with him as he walked to the beach. And Samiq realized that since his mother had spoken first, there was something she wanted to say to him, but when she did not speak, Samiq began to run toward the water, bouncing Wren in his arms. Perhaps his mother only needed him to watch Wren. "I will keep her here while you work," he called back to his mother.

But Chagak hurried to Samiq's side. "I will walk with you," she said.

Samiq hoisted Wren to his shoulders, the girl holding tightly to his hair, her legs wrapped around his neck.

"When I left, she was a baby," Samiq said. "Now look how tall she has become. Taller than her mother."

Chagak looked up at her daughter and laughed. "Yes, but she walks before she talks and that is not good. She gets into everything and understands nothing."

"Perhaps it is to her advantage to understand nothing," Samiq replied.

"Like Three Fish," Chagak said suddenly.

Samiq looked quickly at his mother. There was no laughter in her eyes now, and Samiq waited for her to continue.

She lowered her head and asked quietly, "If I speak to you about her, will you be angry?"

"No."

"She laughs at Crooked Nose's jokes, but she always leaves before we begin any hard work. She smiles and takes her gathering bag, pretending there is nothing more for her to do than walk on the beach.

"Blue Shell says she is forever bothering Waxtal, flipping her apron. . . ."

"I did not choose her," Samiq broke in. "I did not want her."

"You think Three Fish does not understand that? She cannot go back to her own people, yet she feels she does not belong here. Why should she work for us? Why should she do anything but please herself?"

Chagak smiled at Samiq and laid her hand on his arm. "In many ways, it is very difficult to be a wife," she said softly. "Nearly as difficult as being a hunter."

Near the end of the day, the trembling stopped. The waves rolled to the shore smoothly, without jerking and splashing. Kayugh was right, Samiq thought. I call myself a man, but in many ways I am still a boy. I let fear rule my thoughts. Kayugh said we are far enough from Aka. Kayugh is right.

Samiq took his place near the fire at the entrance of the cave. Big Teeth was telling a story, something Samiq had heard before, but Gray Bird—now Waxtal, Amgigh had told Samiq—interrupted him.

"They were eating mossberries," Gray Bird said.

"Mossberries, then," Big Teeth agreed. "Both hunters were eating mossberries when the blue men came to them."

"There were three hunters," Gray Bird said.

"Three, then," Big Teeth agreed, then said, "Gray Bird, you should tell the story. You have told it before. Besides, I am tired."

"Waxtal," Gray Bird said. "I am Waxtal." He nodded and said, "Yes, I will tell it."

So Gray Bird began, but soon Big Teeth, yawning, stood and left the story circle, then Kayugh and First Snow. Samiq tried to listen, to follow the story, but Gray Bird's story wandered, the man telling first one part of a story, then interrupting to tell another part and going back to the first until the whole story was lost, and Samiq felt like a child who had spent the day following the strange and twisting path of a puffin. So Samiq left and Small Knife. Then only Gray Bird and Amgigh sat near the fire, the two with heads together, Gray Bird murmuring, Amgigh nodding.

Samiq squared his shoulders and went to where Three Fish sat. The other women were working on parkas or baskets, but Three Fish sat doing nothing, her hands idle in her lap.

Samiq leaned toward her and whispered, "Come with me to my sleeping place."

Three Fish jumped up, her mouth open. She ran her fingers through her hair and straightened her apron. Like a First Men wife, she waited for him to enter the sleeping place first, and, closing the woven grass curtains, she dropped to her knees to smooth the sleeping robes.

Samiq sat down beside her and stroked her wide, strong shoulders. When he slipped one hand beneath her apron, she giggled and spread her legs, and then Samiq lay down beside her, thinking for a moment of Kiin, of Kiin's spirit watching as Three Fish grasped his buttocks and pulled herself close to him.

"Wait," Samiq whispered in the darkness. He pulled away and clasped her hands to control her. "First, I must speak to you."

Three Fish giggled and tried to break his hold.

"Three Fish, you are my wife. You are a good, strong woman and I wait with pride for the day you will give me a son. But I want you to be a part of my people, for then you will be my wife in all ways." Her hands were slippery with seal oil and sweat, and Samiq was afraid that she would pull away from him before he finished speaking. "Three Fish, listen," he said, hoping she could hear his whisper above her giggling. "I want you to become one of the First Men as I became one of the Whale Hunters. You must learn the ways of my people."

Three Fish laughed loudly. "I know the ways of your people," she said. "But Many Whales said our ways were better than your ways."

"Perhaps they are," Samiq answered. "But ways change slowly

and people will not listen to your ideas if you insult them with rudeness."

Three Fish slid her hands up over Samiq's chest. For a time she said nothing, but Samiq held her eyes with his own, would not let her look away.

"Yes," she said, lowering her voice to a whisper. "You are right. I have not been a good wife. I mourn my people and my mourning keeps my hands idle."

"Mourn in your heart as I mourn, for I was part of the Whale Hunters, too. But we cannot mourn with our hands. There is too much to do."

"You are right," Three Fish whispered. "You are right."

And clasping his wife to him, Samiq thought, Ah, Chagak, my mother, you are wise.

58

amiq squatted, hands between his knees, head bowed. Ash fell thick from gray skies. Though the trembling of the ground had stopped for one night, it had begun again the next day and had not stopped since. He did not want to dishonor his father, but Kayugh was wrong. They had to leave the island. If they did not they would all die.

"You are still a boy, not a man," Samiq's inside voice told him. "You are not ready to make a man's decisions. Your father is right; you are wrong."

But then once again Samiq remembered the horror in Small Knife's eyes after he returned from his parents' destroyed ulaq, and he saw the sorrow in Dying Seal's face. Should he let what had happened to the Whale Hunter village happen to his own people? And if his father did not agree with Samiq, then at least Samiq had a responsibility to Small Knife and Three Fish. If Kiin were alive, he would do anything to save her. Could he do less for the boy who was his son, the woman who was his wife?

It was early morning. Samiq had crept from his sleeping place, leaving Three Fish, her mouth open in deep snores. The night before, Samiq had asked Small Knife and Three Fish to meet him outside the shelter in early morning before the others had awakened.

But now he wondered at the wisdom of his request. "You

have no choice," he told himself, speaking the words into the morning fog. "You have no choice."

Samiq had spent the last two nights with Three Fish, and now she was taking her share of the work, and also was not so ready to dishonor him with apron flipping. He hoped she would be willing to help him when he explained his plan.

When Three Fish and Small Knife came from the cave, the boy squatted beside Samiq; Three Fish stood in front of them, her arms crossed over her breasts, a sleeping robe flung around her shoulders.

The ground shook and a rumbling seemed to come from the rocks. Three Fish covered her mouth with both hands. And Samiq, leaning one hand against the ground to hold his balance, said, "You both know that we must leave this island."

The rumbling stopped and Three Fish wrapped her sleeping robe more tightly around herself. "Yes," she said. "We must leave."

Small Knife said nothing, but he moved closer to Samiq, the two with arms almost touching.

"We cannot return to the First Men's island," Samiq continued, "and each day, Aka's anger grows. Perhaps Aka will send more waves, more fire. The last time, many died. Perhaps this will happen again."

Samiq turned to look at his son and saw that Small Knife's face had paled, his eyes grown large.

"Small Knife," Samiq said, "you and Three Fish have lost the most to Aka. My people have lost only their homes. And they think by waiting that they will be able to return."

"We will all die," Three Fish said.

"No, we will not die," said Small Knife. "Samiq will not let us die." Then he asked, "Have you spoken with your father?"

"I have tried," Samiq replied, surprised but pleased with the boy's confidence in him.

"We should leave. The three of us," Three Fish said. "We have Samiq's ikyak and the ik. And Small Knife now has an ikyak."

Her words angered Samiq. Did she care so little for his people that she would leave so easily? But then he thought. Why should she care? She does not know them. Finally he said, "Perhaps we can make the others understand."

"There is not much time," said Small Knife.

"You are right," Samiq replied. "But we must try. Three Fish, you must speak to the women. Do not speak urgently. Perhaps even the first time, speak with laughter about your fears. But speak often. Tell them again what happened to your village and your people. Then you must do the most difficult thing."

Three Fish straightened and gave a quick sideways glance at Small Knife.

"Tonight when the men sit by the fire, you must come to me. Pretend you are frightened and beg me to take you away."

Three Fish blinked her small eyes. "I can do that."

"For a little while, I will speak to my father and the others," Samiq said. "Do not come until I give you a sign."

"What sign?"

"I will stand and stretch, then sit again. Come soon after that. And during the evening, act as though you are sad. Keep your eyes lowered when you serve food. Cover your face when you sew. Pretend to cry."

Three Fish laughed.

"And what should I do?" Small Knife asked.

"You must speak to First Snow and Big Teeth," Samiq answered. "Tell them your fears about Aka. Then tonight, if you have the opportunity, and if you are strong enough, tell of the deaths in the ulas of the Whale Hunters."

"I am strong enough," Small Knife said.

Amgigh watched from the shadows of the cave as Small Knife and Three Fish left Samiq. For a time Samiq stood outside, his eyes on the sea. He had grown some in the year he had been with the Whale Hunters, but he was still not as tall as Amgigh, though his shoulders were wider.

Amgigh had heard Samiq speak to their father, two, three times about leaving the island, about following the land east, away from Aka.

Away from whales, Amgigh thought. Away from any chance my father and I will have to learn to hunt the whale.

Amgigh's anger was like a chunk of lava rock chafing inside his chest. Samiq comes back with a wife and grown son, Amgigh thought. He comes back knowing how to hunt the whale. I have nothing; no wife, no son. Now he wants to tell our father what to do.

Then Waxtal's words came back to him: Samiq did not care about Kayugh, did not respect Kayugh's power. Samiq would try to become chief.

Perhaps it was time to tell the other men about Samiq's true father. It seemed that what Waxtal feared was true. The evil that had been in Samiq's true father had come to Samiq, was forcing its way into Samiq's spirit, telling Samiq what to do. Why else would Samiq, more boy than man, seek to take his father's place as chief of the village?

Small Knife came to Samiq after the night fires had been lit. "There was no need to convince," Small Knife said. "Big Teeth and First Snow feel as we do.

"And Three Fish says, that of the women, only Chagak does not want to leave. Chagak says without Aka there is nothing. And Little Duck gives no answer. She is too near death to care."

That night, Samiq was one of the last to come to the fire. He sat facing the cave so he would know when Three Fish was ready. Small Knife sat beside him and on the other side were Gray Bird and Big Teeth.

Samiq had thought of many ways to bring up the subject of leaving, and finally decided to speak directly as soon as the customary time of silence had passed.

Samiq waited, squatting on his heels, his hands clamped tightly over his knees. He had a sudden fear that his voice would sound like the voice of a boy, high and cracking, and he clasped his amulet. There was, he reminded his spirit, the power of two tribes in the amulet.

Then to give himself courage, he whispered into the damp night air, "I am Samiq, father of Small Knife, caller of seals, hunter of whales, alananasika among my own people. What other man has as much?"

Samiq closed his eyes for a moment, concentrating on the powers that were his, and when he looked up, he was ready, the pulse of his strength deep and sure in his chest.

"I want to speak," he said.

He saw that his father's eyes were on him. Seldom did anyone other than Kayugh break the silence of the evening fires. But Samiq did not allow himself to think of Kayugh's power. Always in some small way, a man was a boy in his father's eyes. But now, to all, Samiq must be a man.

"Speak," Kayugh said.

But before Samiq could say anything, there was a loud roaring and the island shook, throwing rocks from the shelter walls. Over the roaring, Samiq heard Three Fish's low wail.

The shaking subsided and the dust settled. "Is anyone hurt?" Kayugh called. Samiq stood and looked into the darkness of the shelter.

"We are not hurt," Chagak said.

But then, Three Fish came hurtling out of the cave. Her face was streaked with tears and dirt. She ran up to Samiq and knelt at his feet. "Go back," he hissed, but Three Fish wrapped her arms around his legs, and her shoulders jerked with sobs.

"Take me back to my people," she cried. "Aka will kill us all. We must leave. Do not make me stay here! We will all die!"

Chagak came from the cave and knelt beside Three Fish. "Come with me, Three Fish," she said. "You are safe."

"No!" Three Fish screeched, clinging more tightly to Samiq.

"Be still," Samiq said. "Be still. Go with my mother."

But Three Fish would not release her grip. "You must go," Samiq said. Then raising his voice, he called Crooked Nose.

Crooked Nose came and helped pull Three Fish up. The three women walked together into the shelter. Samiq looked across the circle of men to see that Small Knife's eyes were on him, but Samiq did not say anything.

He turned back to the fire and closed his eyes, rubbing the dust from his face. The men spoke in whispers and suddenly Kayugh's voice was loud among them. "You wanted to speak, Samiq?"

Samiq looked at his father. "Yes," he finally said. "I want to say what should not have to be said." He paused, studying the faces around the fire. "We must leave or we will die."

In the murmur of voices, First Snow turned to Kayugh. "He speaks the truth. I and my wife and our son will leave, even if we have to go alone."

"You are a fool," Kayugh said. "Soon we will return to our own beach. We will hunt the whale. We will never be hungry. If you leave now, where will you go?"

First Snow looked toward Samiq and Samiq answered, "We must get away from the sea. Aka's shaking makes waves tall enough to cover all but the mountains."

"There is nothing away from the sea but ice," Kayugh said.

Then Amgigh stood, Samiq feeling a sudden relief, knowing his brother would support him against their father.

But Amgigh said, "Who are you to argue with my father?"

The words, cold and hard, settled into Samiq's chest and, though Samiq opened his mouth to speak, he could not.

"Your mother Chagak told us your father was one of the First Men," Amgigh continued, "that he had been killed by the Short Ones, but there are some of us who know the truth."

Samiq's eyes traveled over the faces of the men. Each man looked surprised. Big Teeth even shook his head to disagree with Amgigh, but then Samiq's eyes fell on Gray Bird. The man was smiling.

Samiq saw a quick movement at the entrance of the cave and realized that his mother was there, her face pale.

"Samiq's father was a Short One," Amgigh said, his lips

drawn back from his teeth. And Samiq looked at Kayugh, saw that the man's eyes were wide, his mouth open, and Samiq realized that if what Amgigh said was true, Kayugh had not known.

Then Samiq looked at his mother. Chagak held a bola in one hand, an obsidian knife in the other. He remembered the scattered bones in the death ulaq and knew that his mother was strong enough, fierce enough, to have killed the man who was his father.

Samiq stood and stared at Amgigh. Refusing to let the anger in Amgigh's eyes make him look away, Samiq said, "We have always been brothers."

"I am not your brother," Amgigh said.

"You lost no one to the Short Ones, Amgigh," Samiq said. "My mother lost her whole village and there were many lost in Small Knife's village. They are the ones who should take revenge. They are the ones who may seek my death." He looked back at Chagak, his mother now closer to the circle of men.

"You are my son," she said. "I am not a hunter or a warrior, but if anyone here seeks to take your life, I will kill him as I killed the Short One on the Whale Hunters' island. As I killed the Short One while Gray Bird cowered behind me."

Gray Bird sneered at her, then laughed, but said nothing.

Small Knife stood and walked around the circle to Samiq's side. "I am your son," he said quietly. "If any of these men want to fight you, they must fight me, also."

Samiq looked at Kayugh, hoped to see some caring on his father's face, but Kayugh's eyes were on Chagak.

"I leave tomorrow, then," Samiq said. "I and my son and my wife. Tonight we will take our things from your cave and stay outside."

He turned toward the cave, saw that his mother stood there, her hands still tight on the weapons. Samiq was man now, had no right to touch his mother, but he reached out to her, took her in his arms, felt the wetness of her tears against his neck. And he felt no shame.

59

Samiq built a fire from driftwood and seal bones, and closed his ears to Three Fish's complaining.

"I would have stayed in the cave one more night," she said. She tucked the tail of her hair into the collar of her suk and turned her back against the wind. "It is too cold here."

"You wanted to leave," Samiq said. "We will leave. Sleep now. Tomorrow you must paddle the ik, alone."

They had already packed their few belongings into bundles. Chagak had given them three seal stomachs of dried fish and a container of oil. Big Teeth had given them several seal hides.

They would leave after both Samiq and Small Knife had a chance to sleep. Now Samiq watched, his eyes on the paths that led to the cave, and Small Knife slept. But Samiq's thoughts were on Amgigh. Why had his brother come to hate him? They had had no choice in which one of them went to the Whale Hunters, which one stayed in the village and was husband to Kiin.

Kiin, Samiq thought. Kiin, dead. These days with his people had also been days of mourning, mourning that he could share with no one. He had not been Kiin's husband; he had not suffered the loss that Amgigh suffered. But how many times during his stay with the Whale Hunters had he imagined himself telling Kiin some story of his life there? The foolish ways of the

Whale Hunter women, always fighting, always angry. The lazy way they rendered seal oil: stuffing strips of fat into a sealskin turned hair side in, the women leaving the fat until it melted itself into oil. How a man, wanting a good meal of fish and seal oil, in eating would find his teeth full of seal hair from the oil. He wanted to tell her that the women who were so lazy with seals could flense a whale in only three, four days. He wanted to tell her the Whale Hunters' jokes, their stories. But now he would share none of these things.

He remembered how frightened he had been that he would find Kiin's body in the destroyed ulas, but then when Amgigh told him of Kiin's death, it was as though the words were only words in a dream, as though Amgigh did not speak the truth.

Now, he would lose not only Kiin, but all of his people. But then he told himself, You suffer no more than Small Knife or Three Fish. They have lost their people, too.

Samiq slept while Small Knife watched, and while Samiq slept he dreamed, dream piling on dream, the dreams pushing into one another like broken pieces of ice at the edge of a river. The dreams were so strong that when Small Knife shook him awake, the shaking became part of a dream, became the shaking of Aka, and Samiq woke angry at the spirits of the mountain, those spirits that had taken so much from a people who honored them.

"Your father, your father," Small Knife whispered.

Samiq's first reaction was gladness, but then he remembered the evening before and reached for his spear. He was a Short One. Any of the First Men might decide to kill him.

He stood and slowly his father approached him, hands outspread. "I am a friend. I have no knife," he said, and Samiq saw the sadness in the man's eyes.

Samiq set down his spear.

"Come with me. I need to talk to you," Kayugh said.

Warily Samiq's eyes swept the beach, the rocks and grasses

that bordered the paths from the beach, then he turned and said to Small Knife, "Help Three Fish load the ik." Then he followed his father to a place among the rocks that was sheltered from the wind.

For a time Kayugh said nothing and Samiq studied his father, seeing what he had not seen before—that there were changes in the man: strands of gray hair that blended with the black, lines around his eyes, a new scar across the top of his left hand.

"I spoke to your mother last night," Kayugh finally said. "What Amgigh said was true. Shuganan had no son. Your father was a Short One. He forced your mother to be wife to him. She was wife one night. Only one night. That night she and Shuganan killed him and left his body in the ulaq." Kayugh cleared his throat, ran both hands through his hair.

For a long time, Samiq said nothing. The wind whined as it buffeted them from between the rocks, and waves crashed against the beach. Samiq felt old, older than his father, older than any man had ever been. "So I am grandson only to Many Whales and son to a Short One," Samiq finally said, and he suddenly felt as though his spirit was something unclean.

"Samiq," Kayugh said and laid his hand on Samiq's arm. "Leave us if you think this island is not safe. Do not leave us because of what your brother said last night. His sorrow over Kiin's death twists his words and dims his spirit.

"A man is not what his father or grandfather was. A man is what he himself does, what he thinks, what he learns, his own skills. You are a hunter of whales. You are good to your mother. You are patient with your wife, good to your new son Small Knife." Kayugh picked up a handful of beach gravel, released it slowly from his fingers. "Samiq," he said, "you will always be my son."

Samiq felt Kayugh's voice wash through his spirit like something clean, something good, pushing away the ashes of his anger, the blackness of Amgigh's words.

"I am glad my mother chose you to be my father," Samiq

said, then looked away, afraid that Kayugh would see the tears that stung his eyes.

They walked back to the beach together, Kayugh's hand on Samiq's shoulder. Samiq heard the calling first. Big Teeth's voice. Then Kayugh turned, waited until the man was beside them.

"Little Duck," Big Teeth said. He lowered his head, closed his eyes. "She is dying. She asks for Samiq."

"Samiq?" Kayugh said, surprise in his voice. He looked at Samiq.

Small Knife came up to Samiq. He carried a knife in one hand, stood slapping it against his palm.

"I will go," Samiq said. "Gray Bird is not strong enough to kill me, and Amgigh . . ." He hesitated.

"Amgigh will not kill you," Big Teeth said.

"I go, too," Small Knife said, still slapping the blade of his knife against his palm.

They went together to the cave; Samiq and Small Knife walked between Big Teeth and Kayugh. When they came to Little Duck's bed, Samiq squatted beside the woman. She did not look like Little Duck. Her face was wrinkled, her hands gnarled and bent like eagle's claws. She opened her eyes, the eyes moving until they were upon Big Teeth, then she said in a thin voice, "I am sorry that I leave you no son."

She closed her eyes again and Big Teeth knelt beside her, drawing one of her hands to his chest. "You have been a good wife," he said.

They were silent then as Little Duck walked the thin line between two worlds. And Samiq thought, Perhaps there will be some small sign, one thing she will see and tell us before she becomes one of the spirits. There was always that hope with the dying.

Her eyes opened again and Samiq thought that perhaps she had died, the lids opening to free the soul, but she looked at him and he saw she was still alive, still seeing as a woman. "You

did not die, Samiq," she said. "We thought Aka killed you."
She coughed. A drop of spittle sprayed from her mouth and
settled on Samiq's cheek. "You are too strong. You are stronger
than Aka. . . ." Suddenly she gasped, and Samiq realized that
her eyes were now on Small Knife who stood beside him.

"My son," Little Duck said softly. Tears began to run down
her face. "My own son. Samiq brought you back to me." She
tried to sit up, her arms pulling against Big Teeth's hands.
"Samiq, Samiq," her voice was urgent, "you must take him
away from here. This is a place of death. Take him to a good
place. A safe place. You must leave. Please, Samiq, you are
stronger than Aka. You are stronger. . . ." Her words ended
with a soft sound of choking, and she fell back on her mats. She
closed her eyes, and when they opened again, they opened to
release her spirit.

Crooked Nose began to wail, and Chagak looked at Samiq.
"You are right," she said. "We must leave this island."

But Kayugh turned and walked away.

60

*C*hagak *did not try to follow* her husband. First she must help in the washing and preparing of Little Duck's body. Then, if Kayugh threw her away, said she was no longer his wife, then she would decide what to do. Then she would weep for what she had lost.

Chagak dug through her supplies until she found a seal bladder of the fine oil from Samiq's whale. This she had strained and set aside for special times of ceremony, for burials and namings. She found the piece of driftwood Kayugh had notched into a comb for her hair, and took it into the shelter.

Already Crooked Nose was smoothing a paste of oil and red ochre over Little Duck's face, and Red Berry and Blue Shell were washing the woman's legs and feet. Chagak sat down and raised Little Duck's head into her lap. She began combing the woman's hair, pulling out all the tangles before she kneaded in the oil. Little Duck's hair had grown dull and thin since the death of her son, since she had stopped eating. Chagak had to comb carefully so the strands would not snap under her fingers.

Crooked Nose had already cut her own hair short at both sides. Not all first wives would mourn their husband's second wife, but Chagak knew Little Duck had been like a sister to Crooked Nose, not a rival for Big Teeth's attention.

As her hands worked, Chagak's thoughts went to Kayugh.

She had always known Gray Bird would someday tell the truth about Samiq's father. Poor Shuganan, how careful he had been to tell the story of Samiq's birth so that Kayugh and his people would think the child was son of the First Men. Then in his dying, his visions of the spirit world, Shuganan had told all—to Gray Bird, the man who always used knowledge to his own benefit, who rejoiced in bringing sorrow to others. If she had not killed the Short One while Gray Bird cowered in fear, Gray Bird would have told what he knew long before now.

At least Samiq was old enough to defend himself. And he had proven himself equal to any, first sending his people a whale, then bringing them another hunter, a boy nearly grown. Except for Gray Bird and perhaps his son Qakan, there was no one who would want Samiq dead. And Gray Bird should know he did not have power enough to kill Samiq, and Qakan. . . . Who could say where Qakan was or whether he would ever return?

She finished Little Duck's hair, then stood. "I go to find Kayugh," she said. She stepped past the others but stopped when Red Berry caught her hand.

"Be wise, my mother," the girl said, and Chagak smiled, glad to know this one, Kayugh's oldest child, still considered her mother.

Kayugh was, as Chagak knew he would be, on the beach, pacing at the edge of the water, as though all his desire was to leave this place, to push himself out into the sea as a seal pushes from the beach and is soon a part of the waves.

Chagak stood until Kayugh saw her, moved toward her. She lowered her head, but kept her eyes up so she could see him.

"You should have told me," he said, and Chagak heard the hurt in his voice. "Did you think I would kill Samiq?"

"How did I know what you would do?" Chagak asked. "When you came to us, I did not know you. You were not my husband."

"Not then," Kayugh said and turned from her, his words carrying back to her as he paced. "After you became my wife, then did you think I would kill your son?"

"No, I knew you then. I knew you would not hurt Samiq."

"So why not tell me?" he asked.

"I was afraid you would not want me as wife."

Kayugh stopped, turned. Slowly he walked toward her, reached out for her. He tipped her head up so she was looking into his face, saw what was in his eyes. "Always, Chagak, always," he said, "you will be my wife."

"Little Duck is ready," Chagak said.

Samiq was nearly asleep, and he jumped when his mother spoke, then shook his head. "Kayugh has not returned."

"He will not return until the burial is finished," she replied.

"How do you know?"

She smiled at him, a smile that made him feel as though he were a child. "I spoke to him," Chagak said. "This is his way of giving you his place. He knows the one who leads the people must be first to give the death chant. There will be no question among us if he is not here.

"Samiq," she said, "it is very hard for a man to step away from what he has been, to give his place to another man, even if that man is his son. But he said to tell you that you are alananasika now and so are chief hunter and proper leader of our village, but remember, you are young, and wisdom is something that comes only with years. Remember then to rely on your father's wisdom, to use his judgment when you are not sure of your own."

An unexpected anger rose in Samiq's chest. Why suddenly am I leader? he thought. Must a man be leader for others to follow the wisdom of his words?

He bit at the insides of his cheeks and for a moment closed his eyes. "I do not want this," he finally said. "I do not want to be leader."

Chagak opened her mouth as if to speak, but then the earth shook again, stirring the ashes from the rocks around them, and Chagak dropped to her hands and knees to keep from falling.

The shaking stopped, and Chagak stood, brushed off her knees and the palms of her hands. "A man does not choose whether or not he is leader," she said. "The people choose. They follow a man's wisdom; they follow a strong hunter. They are ready to follow you."

"They want to leave this island, that is all," Samiq answered.

"That is the first thing," Chagak said.

"And you and my father?" Samiq asked. "Will you stay or go?"

"I do not want to leave Aka," Chagak said. "It is a mountain sacred to my village, to my people, but those people are at the Dancing Lights, and I must do what my husband wants me to do."

"Do you think Kayugh will go?" Samiq asked.

"I do not know," his mother said.

"Come with us," said Samiq.

But Chagak only shook her head, then turned from him and walked back toward the cave. Once she called back to him, "The burial ceremony, Kayugh says it is yours."

And again Samiq felt the anger and with it despair. "What do I know of burial?" he shouted, but his mother did not appear to hear.

Then the ground shook again, and Samiq thought, If it is the only way to bring my people to safety, I will lead. Among the First Men I am alananasika. I will prepare like the alananasika.

He stood and scanned the hillside, finally seeing a small darkness, a boulder in the grass, and he climbed there. He settled himself back against the stone and tried to find the words that would best guide Little Duck's spirit to its place in a new world.

Kayugh watched the burial ceremony from a distance. Yes, he thought, Samiq is right. We need to leave this island, find another place to make a village. Who knows if we will ever be able to go back to Tugix's beach? But the farther east we go, the fewer whales there are to hunt. How much power will we give up if Samiq cannot teach us to hunt the whale?

Kayugh sighed, rubbed his eyes. When Aka's fires first began, he had thought of moving to the Whale Hunter island, but he had been afraid that with the First Men there, Many Whales would decide Samiq could no longer be a whale hunter.

But even the Whale Hunters' island had not been safe. Nor was this island. And who knew how far they would have to go to get away from Aka's anger, the anger of the mountains east and west of Aka?

So Samiq was right. They must leave this little island. Even the center of the island was low, low enough that waves could come, could drown them all. How could Kayugh forget what had happened to his own family years before? How could Big Teeth or Gray Bird forget? Even Samiq and Amgigh had heard their father's stories about that time of giant waves.

And why should Kayugh think that Samiq was too young to lead? When Kayugh had led Big Teeth and Gray Bird and their wives to Tugix's beach, he had only eighteen, perhaps nineteen summers.

No, Kayugh could not forget what happened to his people, but neither could he forget what that leadership had cost him. Two wives: the old woman Red Leg, the young, beautiful White River. And he had nearly lost Amgigh as well.

The spirits always test the man who leads his people. Samiq was alananasika. A strong young man, wise even though he had few summers. Let him lead, Kayugh thought. He has already lost Kiin. That loss should be enough. The spirits will ask nothing more from him. But I . . . how could I chance the loss of Chagak?

The air was damp with a misty rain and the dampness brought the words of Little Duck's burial ceremony clearly to Kayugh's ears.

Samiq spoke of the need for people to work together, of the strength of many compared to the strength of one. Then he stooped and pulled a strand of grass from the earth, snapped it easily in his hands. Then pulling a handful of grass, he twisted it and tried to break the twisted strand.

The strand would not break, and Samiq held it up. He moved his eyes to each of the people, even Amgigh and Gray Bird.

"I do not want to leave alone," Samiq said. "I am weak when I am by myself. But together we are strong."

Then he led them in the death chant and explained that the women had decided to make the burial in the manner of the Whale Hunters since they had no death ulaq and no time to build one. Samiq picked up a stone, placed it on Little Duck's shallow grave.

Then Kayugh walked down to stand with his people. He picked up a stone then plucked three pieces of grass. He laid the stone against Little Duck's feet, turned to Samiq and handed him the blades of grass.

"I will go with you," he said. "I and my wife and my daughter, Wren."

Big Teeth did the same, for himself, for Crooked Nose. First Snow, and finally Gray Bird did the same. For a time Amgigh stood alone, away from the others. Then he, too, picked a blade of grass, piled his stone on the grave, then turned, not to Samiq, but to Kayugh, handed him the grass.

"I go where you go," he said.

61

For many days Qakan paddled almost as hard as Kiin. They rested on rocky shores, bypassing coves and good beaches to stay during low tide on dangerous narrow ledges of rock near the sea, places Qakan thought the Raven would not look for them.

But one afternoon, the sun still high in the sky, Kiin saw a wide beach protected by circling arms of land. At the center of the beach, a narrow stream cut down into the sea.

"We should s-stop here," she said to Qakan.

But Qakan shook his head. "It is a place Raven would look, the beach where men from many villages come to trade during the middle of each summer."

But Kiin, seeing the curve of the beach, remembered that she had heard some of the Walrus women speak of this place, of its good water and many birds.

"Our ik is s-slow," she said. "If the R-Raven was following us, he would have caught us b-by now. What . . . what d-does he care? He d-d-does not want m-me. He wants my s-sons, and if the Grandmother and the Aunt convinced him to k-kill one of the children, then perhaps he is glad that I am g-gone."

"He does not want you?" Qakan asked. "How do you know?"

"He t-told m-me," Kiin answered. "He wants power as a sh-shaman. He thinks my s-sons have p-p-power. But perhaps the Grandmother and the Aunt convinced him . . ."

"They are my sons," Qakan said. "I will not have them taken from me."

Kiin shrugged. She and Qakan had argued in such a way each day since they left the village. The first day, Kiin had explained that the babies belonged to Amgigh and Samiq. She had showed Qakan the children, Kiin sure that even Qakan would see that Takha had Samiq's nose and eyes, his thick dark hair, and that Shuku had Amgigh's mouth, his long fingers and toes. But Qakan had pointed to the babies' ears, flat to their heads like Qakan's ears, like Kiin's ears, and claimed them as his sons.

But now Kiin's spirit warned, "Why argue? Perhaps the children are safer when Qakan believes they are his."

So Kiin did not speak about the children, but instead said, "Qakan, we n-need water and perhaps I can dig clams at low t-tide. See the cliffs s-set back . . . back there? Perhaps I can find m-murre eggs."

Qakan lifted his paddle from the water, and sat for a moment looking toward the shore. "Yes," he finally said. "It is a good beach. We can spend one or two days gathering food."

He laid his paddle in the bottom of the ik and motioned for Kiin to guide them into shore.

Kiin, disgusted at his laziness, opened her mouth to speak, but then decided to say nothing. Who could know what Qakan would do if she made him angry? She had two babies to protect. It was enough that he had said they could stop here, could stay to gather food.

Together, they pulled the ik up on the beach, then Qakan took his trade goods from the boat and waited while Kiin hauled the ik up over the grassy hills at the back of the beach. Kiin had begun to stake mats and sealskins over the ik when Qakan came, hauling two of his packs with him.

"Make two shelters," he said. "I will sleep under the ik with the trade goods. You go far enough away so that I cannot hear the babies cry. If we are going to stay here a few days, I want to be able to sleep."

Kiin gritted her teeth. They did not have enough sealskins to make two good shelters. But then her spirit said, "This beach is a sand beach; even some of the hills are sand. Finish Qakan's shelter, then dig into the back of a hill, cross the paddles over the hole and stake mats over that. It will be enough for you and the babies. At least you will not have to sleep next to Qakan."

For a little while, Qakan watched Kiin work, but then he wandered away and did not return until she had finished his shelter and was digging the hole for her own.

"The ik is well-hidden," he said, and Kiin nodded.

Yes, it was well-hidden. Two hills away from the beach. If the Raven did stop at this place, he might not even realize that they were here, especially if they were careful to brush away any tracks they left in the sand. And Kiin's shelter was even farther from the beach. Well away from the ik. Harder to find than Qakan's shelter.

"The river is fresh water," Qakan said.

Kiin stopped digging and went to the small pack she had brought from the Raven's ulaq. She handed Qakan several walrus bladders, and when Qakan scowled, she said, "I want to set bird snares at the cliffs when I am done here. You can do something. It is not difficult to get water."

Qakan turned back toward the beach and Kiin called, "Be careful; watch for ikyan on the sea."

Qakan trudged away from her. "I am not a child," he said, his voice a whining in the wind.

Kiin sat back on her heels. The pit was deep enough, although it was only as wide as her arms stretched out and long enough for her to lay down in, full-length. She must cover it well with skins and mats. She did not want it to fill with water if it rained. She laid paddles across the hole, then layered sealskins in the bottom of the pit and curled them up the sides, sewing them with large, quick stitches to the mats and skins she laid over the crossed paddles. She left a hole at the bottom edge of the pit so she could crawl in and out. She went to Qakan's ik. He was lying inside the shelter, his eyes closed.

"I-I came for the w-water," she said, "and my sleeping mats."

Qakan did not open his eyes, merely pointed to the place where he had put the water bladders. He had filled only two and Kiin picked up both. The basket with her sleeping mats was beside them. Kiin took the basket and left.

At her own shelter, she hung the water skins from the crossed paddles, spread her sleeping mats over the sealskins, then the furs. She took the babies from her suk, tucked skins over them and sang softly until they both slept. Then she unpacked a roll of kelp twine from her pack and wound long strands of it around each of her wrists. When she was sure the babies were asleep, she left the shelter.

The climb to the base of the cliffs was difficult. The dark sand shifted under her feet and twice she cut her toes on sharp edges of beach grass. She brought a walking stick with her, not a good stick, carved to fit the hand, but only a stout piece of driftwood she had found on the beach. It helped her keep her balance as she climbed, and she did not stop until she found a place where she could see the entrances of murrelet burrows. She tied her twine into nettings that would cover a hole entrance, leaving a slipknot in the center so the twine strands would act like a noose when the bird flew out. Then she tied the netting into place over each entrance. She had enough twine for five traps. That evening when the birds left their burrows, her traps should catch two or three.

When she returned from the cliffs, she made her way past a long sloping ledge where black and white murres stood as stiff and straight as basket poles over their nests. Usually murres chose ledges that were difficult to reach, but this ledge, a dark gray outcropping of rock thrusting from the side of a grassy hill, was not.

Kiin knew that the murres' eggs—one egg per nest, sometimes two—would lie on the bare stone, perhaps with a scuffling of dirt or a few stems of grass around them. Kiin slapped her walking stick against the grass above the ledge until the murres, bleating and croaking, left their eggs. Then Kiin took six eggs.

It is good, Kiin thought. Tonight we have eggs, and in the

morning I will cook birds. Then perhaps Qakan will decide we can stay an extra day, can trap more birds, gather more eggs.

That night, Kiin woke often. Since they had left the Walrus People's village, she had not let herself sleep too deeply. Why take the chance that Qakan would sneak from his shelter to hers? Why take the chance that he would attack her again, use her like a wife? But so far he had made no move toward her, treated her almost as though she were another man, allowing her a fair share of the food and doing at least some of the work.

But still she was uneasy. Qakan was Qakan, lazy and selfish and often foolish, sometimes putting his wants above his safety, unable, it seemed, to look ahead and see that what he did this moment might hurt him later. He would try to trade her, probably before they reached any First Men's villages, and now that they were far from the Raven's village, perhaps the best thing would be to leave him. Kiin needed only a short time to launch the ik, to paddle far enough into the sea so that Qakan could not wade out and catch her.

Kiin's heart beat quickly at the thought of it: returning to her village with her sons and an ik full of trade goods. She smiled in the darkness. Her father would be furious and Qakan would hate her forever.

"He has always hated you," Kiin's spirit whispered. "Samiq and Amgigh would protect you. You are strong enough to escape. It would not be easy, but you could do it. There are ways, ways it could be done. You have a knife. You are not tied. . . ."

Yes, Kiin thought, Yes. There are ways. And she planned until the sky showed a thin line of white to mark the dawn.

Qakan slept hard. His dreams were good dreams, dreams of Yellow-hair, a good Yellow-hair, as fine a woman as her dancing had promised she would be. They had his sons and other sons in a ulaq so large that it took a row of lamps to light it. Qakan dreamt his hands were stroking Yellow-hair's soft round breasts, the long, firm muscles of her thighs. And Kiin was there, too, her belly again bulging with babies. She was weaving baskets and smiling, smiling while Qakan took Yellow-hair, Kiin smiling and singing, smiling and singing, while Yellow-hair groaned and writhed under Qakan's hands.

When the babies woke, Kiin nursed them and cleaned them, smoothed seal oil over their fine, soft skin. She nursed them again until they slept, then left them in the shelter while she went to check the bird snares.

When she reached the bird holes, she found that three of her five traps held murrelets, the birds dead, trap strings wound tightly around their necks. She dismantled the traps and used one of the trap strings to tie the birds together, then carried them back to the shelter.

When she reached the shelter, the babies were both crying. She laid the birds down then pulled the babies to her, removed the soiled grass that lined their sealskin wraps and put in fresh grass. She raised her suk and put each baby in his carrying strap, pressing her right nipple into Takha's mouth, the left into Shuku's. Then she went outside and cleaned the birds.

Qakan stretched out his arms and yawned. He was hungry. Kiin should have food ready by now. She better have after leaving the babies so early in the morning. They had begun to cry, first one then the other, making so much noise, Qakan, two hills away, had been pulled from his dreams. He had not gone to them. He had walked past Kiin's shelter, then went a short distance into the hills, relieved himself, stayed there until the crying stopped, then picked a few handfuls of crowberry heather, good for starting a fire.

When he returned to Kiin's shelter, she was cleaning birds outside. He threw down the heather. "I am hungry," he said.

"Build a fire." And he continued past her, down to his own shelter, a place to be out of the wind while he waited for her to fix the food. She was slow, always slow, and if he stayed at Kiin's shelter, prodding her to work more quickly, she would think of something for him to do. Bring water; hold the babies.

Yes, the babies were his sons, but what man took care of a baby? And also it made him uncomfortable to see the thick thatch of hair on the one called Takha. The hair was too much like Samiq's hair. But, of course, the child could not belong to Samiq. Samiq had never even had Kiin in his bed.

Qakan thought again of the babies' ears, the round shape of their faces. They were his sons. How could Kiin even question it? He had proven his manhood on Kiin, had proven that he was as much man as Amgigh, even if he had never taken a seal. And now he had two sons. He wished his father knew.

Never in all the stories Qakan had heard as a child, had there been one about a man who fathered two sons at the same time. And Qakan had taken other women, not just Kiin, but women from First Men's villages. Then he had Yellow-hair. But what man could beget a son on her? She never came to a man's bed without demanding some gift.

Sometimes a man had to make a choice. What was more valuable, a wife who could not keep a ulaq clean, who never cooked, never sewed, never came to his bed—or his trade goods? He was not a fool.

He had not meant to kill her, but what man would not have killed her seeing what she had done?

Qakan knelt beside his packs. The middle pack contained a seal belly of dried fish. He took several fish and hoped Kiin would not notice they were gone. She was always scolding him about how much he ate. What did she expect? He was a man, not some woman, small and weak, who needed little. He pushed the seal belly back into place and set the sealskin that held Amgigh's knives on top. Suddenly, he stopped.

He had tied each package of trade goods differently, a certain number of knots for knives, another for chopping stones, an-

other for ivory, different knots for each thing he traded. He had
tied the pack of knives with three knots, one after another. Now
it was tied with two knots. Qakan opened the pack, counted out
the knives. He had had five left, now there were four.

Kiin had taken a knife, not just one of the greenstone knives,
but the beautiful obsidian blade Qakan had taken from
Amgigh's weapons corner.

But why should he be surprised? Kiin had always been greedy.
Why think she would ever change?

Perhaps it was time to show her what a knife was for. He
unwrapped the largest of Amgigh's greenstone knives. The
blade was perfect, the edge so sharp that Qakan had accidently
sliced his fingers on it when he wrapped it. True, if he scarred
Kiin, he could not sell her as a wife, only as a slave, but even
slaves brought good prices, and he would trade the babies sepa-
rately, making sure his sons were given to strong hunters, raised
to honor their father. And each year in his trading he would
stop to see them, would bring gifts, would let others know that
they were his sons.

Qakan heard shuffling footsteps in the sand behind him.
Kiin, Qakan thought. Qakan gripped the knife in his hand and
stood up. Yes, he would show Kiin she could not steal from him.

He turned. It was not Kiin.

Qakan's heart pulsed so suddenly that it caught, with his
breath, tight in his throat. For a moment he could not think,
could not react, but finally he smiled and, holding the knife in
one hand, he laughed then said, "Raven, you frightened me. Do
you wish to make another trade before I reach the villages of the
First Men?"

Raven drew back his lips. His breath hissed through his teeth.
He held the missing knife in his right hand.

"You brought Yellow-hair?" Qakan asked, fear pushing the
words from his mouth before he could think about what he was
saying. "I did not bring her with me because she did not want
to come."

"Where are my sons?" Raven asked, his voice louder than the

roar of wind or waves, even louder than the beating of Qakan's heart.

"I do not have your sons," Qakan said and pointed at the heap of packs behind him. "Look, I have only the goods I need to make trades."

"You took Kiin, you took my sons, you traded them. Where are they? Which village? Which hunters?" For a moment Raven's eyes were on the packs, then he said, "You killed Yellow-hair."

A trembling began in Qakan's hands and it moved up his arms to make the walls of his chest quiver. "I killed no one," Qakan answered, his voice a high squeak, like the voice of a boy. "I killed no one. Perhaps your wife Kiin killed Yellow-hair. Perhaps she left on her own. Why blame me because you cannot control your own wife?"

Raven kicked at Qakan's packs, scattering Amgigh's knives.

Qakan did not turn his head, but watched Raven from the corners of his eyes. Raven, Qakan thought, the man was not a hunter. He said he was a shaman, but in all the months Qakan had lived with the Walrus People, he had not seen Raven speak to any spirits, heal any sicknesses.

Raven is nothing, Qakan thought. He has no power. And Qakan repeated the words in his mind until the trembling in his hands stopped, until he could once again hold his knees still.

Raven knelt, pulled more packs from the ik. Now, Qakan told himself. Now, before he can fight back. With a quickness Qakan knew even Samiq would envy, he spun and plunged his knife through Raven's parka, through the seam where the hood joined the shoulder and into Raven's neck.

But Raven turned as fast as Qakan had turned, and thrusting out with his arms, knocked Qakan to the ground.

Then with a sickness that spread from Qakan's stomach up into his mouth, Qakan saw that his knife was caught in the hood of Raven's parka and the cut on the man's neck was only deep enough to make a fine beading of blood.

Then Raven was kneeling on Qakan's chest, the blade of the

obsidian knife thrust under Qakan's chin. "You killed Yellow-hair," he said, then raised his voice to scream it on the wind. "You killed Yellow-hair. Where are my sons?"

"I killed no one," Qakan said, the knife so tight against his skin that he had to mumble his words so the blade did not bite into his flesh.

"You traded my sons," Raven said.

"Kiin . . . Kiin did it. She killed Yellow-hair. She took your sons. It was Kiin. . . ."

Kiin crouched at the top of the nearest hill, her arms clasped tightly around the babies under her suk. She had heard Qakan's pleas, his voice rising into shrieks, and hurried from the shelter to the top of the hill, but when she saw the Raven, she dropped to her hands and knees and hid herself in the tall ryegrass.

She watched the Raven thrust the knife into Qakan's throat, heard the gurgle of her brother's last words. She watched while the Raven went through Qakan's packs, while he took Amgigh's knives, took furs and a seal belly of dried fish, a lidded basket of hooks.

She waited while the Raven stood over Qakan's body, while he cut the head away, sliced all the joints so Qakan's spirit could not take revenge. She waited while he smashed Qakan's ik, as he cut the sea lion covering to shreds and scattered the shreds in the wind. Even after the Raven had tied Qakan's packs to his ikyak, after the Raven had paddled far enough away so that Kiin could not see the dark line of his ikyak on the water, she waited.

And finally, when the sun was setting, she took her babies back to her shelter then went down to Qakan. She did not let herself look at what was left of him, but using a flat piece of rock dug a shallow grave in the sand next to where he lay, and again using the rock, she pushed him in, trying to keep her hands from being marked by his blood.

She covered him with stones and then went to the edge of

the sea and washed her hands, rubbing them with sand and water.

Then she came back to the place, to the mound that was now Qakan. And knowing that his spirit was there with his body, unable to move to the Dancing Lights since the Raven had cut him apart, she said, "All your life, Qakan, always, you blamed me for your choices. So you killed Yellow-hair. For what reason? In anger? To show your power? You have no power, Qakan. You never had power. You used all the strength of your spirit to hate others instead of building yourself into what you should be."

She turned and walked back to the hills, back to the shelter where her babies were waiting for her. But at the base of the hills she turned and called, "I *will* go back to our village, Qakan. My sons belong to Amgigh and Samiq. They are not cursed. You were never strong enough to curse anyone."

And it was not until both babies were in her arms that she realized she had spoken without stuttering, that her words had come as easily as her songs, had flowed as smoothly as water over sand.

62

The voice came, *something that* was a part of her dreams, a whining voice. Qakan's voice. Kiin awoke, sat up, listened. No, there was no voice. Only the waves on the shore, only the sound of wind as it sped over the mats and skins of her shelter, as it pushed through the pile of broken wood and torn skins that had once been Qakan's ik.

Kiin had brought the pieces of the ik and the few trade goods the Raven had not taken, back to her shelter. Better to have them here, not visible from the beach. There was ivory, a few small pieces—broken whale teeth, a thin piece of whale jawbone. There was a skin of dried fish, though when she opened it, she noticed with disgust that the bag was stuffed with handfuls of grass and only half full of fish. Qakan. Always taking what he should not take.

Kiin had dug another hole beside her shelter, stored the fish and pieces of the ik cover still large enough to be usable, then she covered the hole with grass mats.

She had finished before dark, and so had rested, beginning a song to her babies, and while her mind was caught in the words of the song, her hands became restless, needing some kind of work to do. And so she unsheathed the hunting knife the Raven had given her and picked up a bit of broken wood from one of the ik's thwarts. At first she only whittled, cutting through the ochre that had been painted over the thwart and down to the pale yellow of the inside wood.

But then she saw that her hands were making an ikyak, pulling a boat out of the wood like a man pulls his feet from a pair of sealskin boots.

"An ikyak," she said, then let the carving become a part of her song.

"An ikyak you will have," she sang to Shuku, to Takha.

> *It will be another brother.*
> *Together you will build it;*
> *Together you will go into the sea;*
> *You will hunt; You will hunt;*
> *The three of you, brothers together.*

She had sung and carved until the only light was from the early rising moon. Then she had slept until Qakan's voice . . . Qakan's voice. . . .

"Qakan is dead and his spirit cannot move from the grave," Kiin's spirit told her. "It was a dream."

Kiin laid her hand on Shuku's back, then on Takha's. Both babies slept, their breathing soft, slow.

Kiin lay down, pulled her mind from thoughts of Qakan, instead planned what she would do the next day, the bird traps she would set. She had to catch as many birds as she could. Dry their meat. Save their fat for winter oil. If the First Men did not come to this island or if the Walrus People came and she had to hide during the days of trading, she might have to spend the winter here. How would she and the babies live without oil, without meat?

The Raven had splintered Qakan's ik into pieces so small that Kiin could not repair it, and though she could fish from the beach, she would not catch as many fish as she would if she had an ik.

"There will be crowberries to eat and crowberry heather to burn," her spirit whispered. "You can gather chitons without an ik. You will find sea urchins and clams. There is ugyuun and there is kelp. You have seen salmonberry blossoms.

"And who can say," her spirit continued, "a sea lion may come, as sea lions do." The words, a comfort, flowed like a song and carried Kiin's thoughts into dreams. Dreams of seals and sea lions, of food, enough food for her and for her sons. . . .

Then again the whining came; again Kiin awoke. Qakan's voice; Qakan's voice.

Kiin woke up her sons, silenced their whimperings with a quiet song. She put them into their carrying slings and let them nurse. Then she left her shelter, taking with her a bird egg, something left from her gathering the day before.

She walked to the mound where Qakan was buried, stood a small distance from the pile of rocks there. She listened, but heard nothing. Then the wind cut in sharply from the beach, and she heard Qakan's complaining again.

"Qakan!" Kiin said. "You have brought yourself to this place. You and your greediness. There is nothing I can do for you."

She threw the egg into the rocks of Qakan's burial place, saw in the moonlight that the egg landed and broke, draining itself into Qakan's grave. "There," she said. "Eat and be quiet."

63

amiq lost count of the days they had traveled, men in ikyan, women in iks. Enough days to see the moon from full to full again and beyond. Long enough to use much of their food. After four, perhaps five days, they could no longer feel any but the most violent of Aka's trembling, but even yet, the waves acted according to some force other than the wind or the tides.

The ash had thinned and was now only a slight haze, a dust that colored the sky in pinks and browns, and at night seemed to settle in a shimmering circle around the moon.

The land was now unfamiliar to everyone but Gray Bird. The grass was interspersed with willow, this willow sturdier and taller than the tufts that grew by the streams of Tugix's island. He still pointed out beaches where he had traded with people of one village or another. Twice they had stopped and stayed at First Men villages, but in both places Samiq had felt the uneasiness of the people. New hunters—would that mean new leaders for the village, women who expected to have a share in the food already cached for winter? So they had stayed long enough to catch fish, to tell the people why the sea acted strangely, to tell of the powerful spirits that ruled the mountain Aka. Then they went on.

One night, with their small skin shelters set behind hills above a rocky beach and the wind blowing first in from the sea and then with a cold fierceness over the center of the island from the mountains, they sat together, their bodies shielding the three small oil lamps burning in their midst. Red Berry with her son and Chagak with Wren sat in the most sheltered place at the center of the circle. Gray Bird, his face pinched and sullen, cheeks rough from many days of wind and sea spray, began to speak of a beach where Walrus People and sometimes even Caribou People came to trade with the First Men.

Samiq leaned forward to hear Gray Bird over the whistling wind. Samiq smiled, laughing at himself for his interest in Gray Bird's words, and the smile cracked the skin of his lips, bringing the sweet taste of his own blood into his mouth. How often had he ever wanted to hear what Gray Bird would say? How often did the man ever say anything that was more than a boast or a complaint? Yet now he spoke with a certainty in his words that drew Samiq's attention, and Samiq caught his father's eyes over the circle of people and gestered toward Gray Bird so that Kayugh, too, would listen.

"It is a good beach," Gray Bird said. "Open to anyone, a place where women come to gather bird eggs in the spring, but where no one is living."

"When were you there last?" Big Teeth asked, and Samiq noticed that First Snow and Crooked Nose were also leaning toward Gray Bird, also listening to the man.

A small shivering went through Samiq's body. Had the traveling worn their spirits down to the place where they would listen to anyone, even Gray Bird? But then Samiq thought, Who else but Gray Bird has been in this place? Who else can we listen to? Kayugh had lived nearly this far east, but that had been many years ago, and Kayugh's people had lived on the South Sea and this was the North, the two with different fish, different animals, even different colors, the South Sea blue, the North Sea green.

Samiq looked slowly around the circle of his people. His sister Red Berry, big with a second child in her belly, was holding her son Little Flat Stone on her lap, rocking gently to comfort the child. Wren was asleep on Chagak's lap and Chagak was watching Gray Bird, her eyes occasionally going to Samiq and then to Amgigh. Amgigh was sitting beside Small Knife, and though he spoke occasionally to the boy, Amgigh would not look at Samiq, had scarcely spoken to Samiq since they began their journey, but his eyes were now on Gray Bird's face.

He feels the same hope I do, Samiq thought. Perhaps this one time, Gray Bird knows what he is talking about. Maybe there is a beach not far from here where we can stay, a place where we can build a new village. It should be facing the North Sea for it seemed that most waves in the North Sea that rose from Aka's trembling, from other mountains whose spirits had joined Aka's spirits in anger against all men, were smaller than waves coming from the South Sea. What had his father told him? That they had found Tugix's island when Samiq was still a baby because they were forced from their own beaches by the waves of the South Sea.

Samiq turned his thoughts back to Gray Bird's words. Gray Bird had seemed to notice that everyone was listening to him and he sat straighter, his mouth tight with pride, and the thin string of whiskers on his chin danced with each of his words. "The Walrus People say that near this beach I speak about, the North Sea turns to ice each winter. If we choose to stay on this beach, our women will have to prepare warm clothing for us."

"If you take enough seals," Crooked Nose said, "we will make enough clothing."

But Gray Bird continued as though she had not spoken. "So we must stop soon. There is still a good part of the summer left, time to hunt and fish and build ulas before winter."

Yes, Samiq thought, we must stop, soon. Even though the women dangled fishing lines as they traveled, catching cod that they split and hung on the edges of their boats, they were able to prepare only what was needed for each day's food. And fish was not enough. Who could live through winter without oil, without the thick fat of seal or whale?

Their clothing, too, was wearing out. Samiq's chigadax

needed to be replaced, although Three Fish repaired it each night.

"Some of the Caribou People make their chigadax from bear gut," Gray Bird had told them, but Samiq was not sure that such a garment would be acceptable to the sea animals. Instead he had continued to encourage Three Fish in her repairs, noticing that he was not the only one who suffered. Cold salt water burned faces and hands. Even Wren's face had blistered although she was often tucked inside Chagak's suk.

The women, without waterproof chigadax, suffered the most. The constant moisture made their garments rot, and Three Fish had only one suk. The other women had two and wore them both, so one suk covered the holes of the other.

Samiq, caught in his own thoughts, did not realize that Gray Bird had finished speaking, that everyone was looking at him to see his reaction. Finally Amgigh, his mouth fixed in a sly smile, said, "Brother, you have nothing to say about what Waxtal has told us?"

And Samiq, startled back to the circle of his people, smiled at Amgigh, an open smile, without anger, without embarrassment. What man at times did not find his own thoughts louder than another's words?

"My father," Samiq said, "you are older and wiser than I am. What do you think?"

Kayugh, his head lowered, his eyes on the driftwood stick he was using to mark the bare gravel of the ground, said, "Gray Bird speaks wisely. We need to stop. We must build ulas, we must hunt before the winter."

He lifted his head. "Gray Bird, how much farther to this beach?" he asked.

Gray Bird shrugged. "Two days, three at most."

Kayugh looked at Samiq, but said nothing.

From the corner of his eye, Samiq saw the smirk on Amgigh's face. "If the beach is as you say, Gray Bird," Samiq said, "we will build our village there. And since it is a place where traders come each summer, perhaps Qakan will find us there and help us trade for things we need for winter."

Big Teeth smiled and First Snow laughed. Soon everyone was speaking and even Blue Shell seemed happy, all the women smiling and talking, Gray Bird's laughter as loud as anyone's. Only Amgigh sat without speaking, without laughing, and his eyes, meeting Samiq's across the light of the oil lamps, still held the glow of anger.

The third day, as the sun neared its high point in the sky, Samiq noticed a change in the sea, a subtle difference in color.

He guided his ikyak around the sloping mound of a green hill that ran itself down into the sea without beach or cliff to divide grass from water, and beyond the hill he saw a circling gray sand beach in a wide cove. He looked back. The other men were following him, the women's ik close behind.

Three Fish was standing up in the woman's ik, and in his astonishment at her stupidity, Samiq could not speak. Finally he bellowed, "Sit!" The heat of his anger cooled when Three Fish quickly dropped, but the babbling continued and he turned his ikyak back to face his wife, Three Fish coyly covering her face with her hands, only her eyes showing between her thick brown fingers.

"Wife!" he said sternly. "Are you a child that you stand in a boat?"

He waited, not expecting an answer, surprised when he heard Three Fish say, "Gray Bird says it is the beach."

Gray Bird pulled his ikyak in line with Samiq's. He pointed, saying, "Yes. There. See where the willows grow taller? We camped only a small way upstream."

Samiq turned his ikyak and paddled to Kayugh's side.

"I heard," Kayugh said, a smile at the corners of his mouth. "So, do we stop here?"

"It is a good beach," Samiq said.

Amgigh pulled his ikyak between Samiq's and his father's. "When has Waxtal ever been right? You trust what he tells you?"

Samiq, suddenly angry at his brother, at the days of silence, the scowls, the angry replies each time Samiq tried to include Amgigh in decisions or conversations, said, "You believed him when he told you about the man who was my father."

Amgigh, his mouth set in a narrow line, his nostrils wide, hissed, "Do what you wish. If Aka or any mountain wants to kill us, we will be dead no matter what you decide."

He paddled away from them toward the shore and Samiq watched him go, watched as Amgigh's long hard strokes soon pushed the ikyak up onto the sand of the beach. Then Samiq and Kayugh followed.

Samiq was pulling his ikyak from the water when he heard Kayugh gasp, Amgigh cry out. Samiq spun, ripping his harpoon from its ties on his ikyak as he turned. But then he, too, cried out.

Standing at the top of the beach was Kiin.

64

A spirit. *She must be a spirit,* Samiq thought.

"Do not go too close," some voice within seemed to whisper, but he could not stop himself. He left his ikyak, forgot about the others with him, walked up the rise of the beach toward Kiin.

Then he saw that she was crying; though she stood straight and held a lance in one hand, she was crying. Did spirits cry? She brushed one hand across her face and he saw that her wrist was ridged with scars. Did spirits have scars?

"Tell me you are real," Kiin said, and Samiq noticed that her voice was whole, without breaks, without stuttering. Kiin never spoke so clearly. Perhaps then she was a spirit.

"I am real," Samiq said. "We are real. But your father said he found your ik, that you had drowned."

"I am alive. I am not a spirit. Qakan took me, traded me to Walrus People. I was trying to get back to you . . . to Amgigh."

Samiq was close then, close enough to see that she wore a new suk, something made of otter and fur seal skins. He saw that she had a thin, pale scar on her forehead, the scar nearly hidden under the edge of her dark hair.

"We are all here," Samiq said and held out a hand to her.

"Amgigh, your mother and father, Kayugh and Chagak, Crooked Nose . . . all of us."

She reached out her hand, and it was warm and hard in his own. She was real, not a spirit. Then Amgigh was beside them, and Kayugh came and the women. Samiq dropped the hand that he had no right to claim, turned away.

"It is a dream," some spirit whispered.

Then I will not wake up, Samiq thought.

65

Waxtal *pushed his ikyak back* away from the beach, away from the pull of the surf. Kiin. How was it possible? Had Qakan no more sense than to sell her to some tribe that visited this beach? But then how could Qakan know that Aka would turn to fire, that the mountain spirits would send ash and tremors to drive the First Men from their village?

Besides, he could pretend that he did not know of Qakan's plan. It was a foolish plan. He had told Qakan that it was a foolish plan.

He turned his ikyak and let the waves take him into shore, used his hands to walk the ikyak up the sand, then unlaced his hatch skirting and stepped out. The women were on the beach, all of them clustered around Kiin. The men stood back; Amgigh and Samiq stood beside each other, the two speaking together —the first time Waxtal had seen them speak since they had begun this journey.

Blue Shell had sunk to the ground, like a small heap of tattered furs, and Kiin was now bending over her. Blue Shell was a foolish woman. Kiin was only a daughter. Better Blue Shell react like this for Qakan. Who could say where he was, whether he was safe? Why were Blue Shell's thoughts not for her son?

Waxtal went to his wife, stood behind her. "Wife, get up," he said, careful not to look at any of the women except Blue Shell, careful that his eyes did not meet Kiin's. "We must make a camp. There is driftwood on this beach. We can build a fire." He reached down and pulled Blue Shell roughly to her feet, but then Kiin was beside him, pushing him away.

"Leave her alone," Kiin said. "You are fortunate I let you stay on my beach. If you touch my mother, I will kill you."

Waxtal opened his mouth to reply, but found he could say nothing. And for the first time he noticed that she held a spear, point up, in one hand, holding it like a man holds a walking stick, and that her suk bulged in the front, the way a suk bulges when a woman carries a baby.

He glanced at the men behind him, saw that Amgigh's eyes were fixed on him, that Samiq stood beside his brother, the two watching, and Amgigh's face was dark with anger.

So Kiin thought she had more power than he did, more power than Waxtal, her father, a carver of wood and ivory, a hunter who had taken many seals, a warrior who had fought the Short Ones. She was a fool.

"You speak to me, your father, in such a way?" Waxtal shouted, his voice as loud as he could make it, his words trembling with his anger. "What then do you say to your husband?" Waxtal turned and pointed at Amgigh. "You left your husband and now carry a child. Whose child?" Waxtal thundered. "You have been more than a year away from us. You betray your own husband and carry another man's child."

He looked at Kiin, expected her to draw away from him, to lower her head, perhaps drop to her knees before him as she had when she lived in his ulaq. But Kiin stepped forward, walked past him so she was standing between Samiq and Amgigh. Then she lifted her suk and Waxtal saw with a start that she carried two babies.

"My husband is Amgigh," Kiin said. "My sons are Amgigh's sons."

Kiin took the babies from their carrying straps. There could be no doubt, Waxtal thought, when he saw the first child. It was Amgigh's son. The baby had Amgigh's eyes, his chin, the straight flat nose. She held the child out to Amgigh and Amgigh wrapped his arms around the baby so the wind could not catch the child's breath. Then Kiin took out the second baby.

"Second born," she said, "two or three breaths after his brother."

She held the child out, this time to Samiq, and Waxtal saw the joy on Samiq's face, the disbelief. It was Samiq's child. Did Kiin have no shame? Even Amgigh would be able to see that the second son belonged to Samiq.

"It is Samiq's," Waxtal said. He turned toward Kayugh and Big Teeth, even back toward his wife. "Samiq's son," he repeated.

But then Amgigh stepped forward. "Good," he said, looking into Waxtal's eyes. "Samiq is my brother. I shared my wife with him as brothers should."

Kiin took the babies back. She tucked her suk over them, and neither baby cried, neither baby fought against the cold or the wind.

"They are strong," Kayugh said. "I am proud of my grandsons."

Kiin smiled at him, but turned back to Waxtal. "You are not going to ask me how I came to this beach?" she asked.

Her insolence angered him. It was not her place as daughter to ask questions, not her place to speak to him without politeness.

He looked away from her, did not answer. What hunter would?

"Qakan brought me," she said, and Waxtal saw that the others, even Samiq's ugly wife Three Fish, his new son Small Knife, gathered close to hear her voice above the wind.

"Qakan took me the day that Samiq left with Amgigh and Kayugh to go to the Whale Hunter village. Qakan punched a hole in my ik so you would think I had drowned. We traveled many days to a Walrus People village."

"You did not try to get away?" Waxtal asked, interrupting.

"Yes," Kiin answered, again her eyes on her father, the

strength of her spirit showing in their dark centers. "Many times. But Qakan tied me so I could not get away."

She held her hands up, pulled back the sleeves of her suk so they could see the scars that circled her wrists. "He traded me to a hunter named Raven. Traded me for a wife for himself and many furs."

"Who would give that much for you?" Waxtal asked and spit into the sand.

For a moment there was silence, then Samiq said, "I would give that much for her."

"And I," Amgigh said.

"So you are wife to this man Raven," said Waxtal, ignoring Samiq and Amgigh.

"Never taken as a man takes a wife," Kiin answered. "The Raven hopes to become a shaman. He did not want my pregnancy to curse his powers, and I escaped from him soon after the babies were born."

"You escaped alone?" Kayugh asked.

"With Qakan."

"With Qakan?" Big Teeth asked.

"He had killed a Walrus People woman and needed to get away. I went with him to protect Amgigh's sons."

"They would harm your sons?" Chagak asked, her voice soft.

"The Walrus People believed they were cursed."

"All babies born together, two instead of one, have some difference," Crooked Nose said. "Something that draws special attention from the spirits. They should be raised as one man, sharing a wife and an ikyak."

Kiin nodded. "That is the way of the Walrus People, too," she said. "But there is another curse," and looking at Amgigh, she said, "Qakan took me by force, as a man uses a wife. Only once, after he knocked me out with his paddle and I could not fight him."

Amgigh's face blanched and his fists clenched. "I will kill him," he said.

"No," Kiin said, "but you must decide whether to take me

back as your wife and whether I can be part of your village. I do not want to curse you."

"Send her away," Waxtal said.

But Amgigh pushed past Kiin and clasped Waxtal by the front of his parka. Amgigh twisted his hand until the collar of the parka was tight around Waxtal's neck. "You knew Qakan had taken her and you did not tell me. I could have gone after them and brought her back. I should kill you, but first I will kill Qakan." He released Waxtal suddenly so that the man fell backwards to the ground.

Amgigh turned to Kiin. "You are my wife and they are my sons," he said. "If Kayugh or Samiq says you cannot be part of this village, then we will go ourselves and start a new village."

"Three Fish and I and our son will go with you," Samiq said.

And Waxtal saw that Samiq's eyes were on Kiin's suk, on the bulge that was his son. And Kiin's eyes went for the first time to the woman Three Fish, to the large round face, the small eyes, the thick lips and broken teeth. Waxtal saw her surprise and a shadow of something that might have been sadness. So now she knew that Samiq had taken a wife.

Waxtal pushed himself up from the ground. They could do what they liked. Let them curse themselves. Then they would know that he was right about Kiin, had always been right.

"You can stay in our village," Kayugh said to Kiin.

Blue Shell hurried to her daughter's side, stroked the sleeve of her suk, and Kiin reached out to clasp her mother's hand.

"Where is Qakan?" Amgigh suddenly asked, anger in his words.

"Dead," Kiin answered.

Amgigh's eyes widened. "You killed him?" he asked.

"No, I did not kill him. The Raven followed us. The woman Qakan killed had once been the Raven's wife. He followed us to this beach and killed Qakan."

"Why did Raven leave you here?" Amgigh asked, his voice now quiet.

"I hid so he would not know I was with Qakan. He does not

want me. He already has a wife, but I am afraid he would take our sons."

"No," Amgigh said. "He will not have the babies. He will not have you."

Waxtal had heard Kiin's words, had heard her say that Qakan was dead, but it all seemed like something done in a dream. Amgigh had made no sign of sorrow, no sound of mourning. He continued to ask questions as though Kiin had said nothing about Qakan at all.

Dead! Qakan was dead! Something inside Waxtal's head began to pound. His only son was dead. And even if Kiin spoke the truth, if she had not been the one to kill him, it was her fault.

"Qakan is dead?" he asked, the words rasping from his throat. His son. His son. Qakan, his son. Qakan the trader. Who could say what he might have become? Perhaps a great trader. Perhaps the chief of some village. Even a shaman.

Waxtal heard the women begin the mourning song, the wavering sound like something brought on the wind, like the voice of some spirit.

He looked at his wife. She stood beside Kiin, and though there were tears on her cheeks, Blue Shell's mouth was closed.

66

Kiin led the women to the place she had made her camp. She had found a good site, some distance from the beach but not in the marshy tundra. It was near a freshwater spring and only a short walk from a fissure in the earth that let out hot steam.

"See," she said and pointed to the cooking stone she had laid over the fissure. An easy way to cook without oil or wood."

But she did not look at the women's faces when they saw her crude shelter of skins and woven mats. They could think what they liked; she had been left here without supplies, and less driftwood floated ashore here than did on Tugix's island.

She watched as Crooked Nose, Chagak, Red Berry and her mother began opening baskets of goose fat and sea lion stomachs full of dried fish.

They said little, but worked quickly, and Kiin, many questions battering in her chest, asked nothing, for some reason afraid of the answers they would give her. Wren came to them, running from the beach. She stopped beside her mother and for a long time stared at Kiin. Finally Kiin said to her, "Do you want to see the babies?"

Kiin lifted her suk and took her sons from their carrying straps, and suddenly the women were around her, passing the babies from hand to hand, each woman gazing into the infants' eyes, stroking hair and counting fingers and toes.

"Your sons are beautiful," Chagak finally said and smiled at Kiin, then added, "We are so glad you are with us again."

And Kiin, her throat filling with tears, could not answer, but only nodded.

Then Wren said, "Kiin? Kiin?"

Kiin scooped the girl into her arms, pressed her face against Wren's thick dark hair and murmured to the girl, "I am your sister Kiin."

Then all the women were talking at once, Crooked Nose asking questions about the Walrus People, Chagak asking where Kiin had found food, her mother asking if she was strong, if she was well, and Kiin, after answering all their questions, asked them about Little Duck and about Little Duck's son.

"They are dead," Crooked Nose said. "The boy died of some sickness, and Little Duck, after he died, did not want to live. She stopped eating, and now they are both at the Dancing Lights."

Kiin looked at her own sons, Amgigh's son in Crooked Nose's arms, Samiq's son cradled by the woman Three Fish. Yes, she could understand how Little Duck felt. She would not want to live if her sons were dead. But there was some part of her that whispered, "No, Kiin, you would live. You would choose to live."

Kiin looked at Chagak, asked, "Why did you come here? This is a traders' beach. I thought there might be some small chance that in the next few years my father would come here to trade. But not all of you."

"It is Aka," Chagak said slowly, a sadness in her words.

And Kiin remembered that Aka was the sacred mountain of Chagak's village, the village that the Short Ones had destroyed. Chagak, when she prayed, usually prayed to Aka.

"Aka's spirits are angry; they send fire into the sky and shake the ground. They send ash that covers everything. Even the grass cannot grow and waves come sweeping everything from beaches." Chagak laid a hand on Three Fish's arm. "Three Fish is Samiq's wife from the Whale Hunters," Chagak said, her eyes steady, holding Kiin's eyes. "Her village was destroyed by Aka's tremors. Many people died. The boy Small Knife lost his family, so Samiq and Three Fish took him as son."

"Small Knife's father was my brother," Three Fish said in a quiet voice. "My mother and father also died."

"I am sorry," said Kiin and felt a pulling of her heart to this woman who had lost her people. But still, looking at her, Kiin wondered why Samiq had chosen the woman as wife. She was not beautiful, and several of her teeth were broken. Even her actions were rough, so that in some ways she seemed more like man than woman. But now that Three Fish held Samiq's son, Kiin could see a gentleness in her, perhaps the thing that had drawn Samiq to her.

Then the women were busy again, and Kiin felt as though she had never left them. She remembered how Chagak held her woman's knife in a different way than Blue Shell or Crooked Nose did, remembered how Crooked Nose cut with quick, hard strokes and Blue Shell cut slowly and carefully. And she saw that Three Fish had not yet found a place with them. Though Three Fish cut the fish and stacked it on skins to be taken to the men, her work was slow and slowed the other women, so Kiin took a place beside Three Fish, helping her, letting laughter show in her eyes if their hands accidentally touched, if they both reached for the same fish.

Then Chagak said, "Your father told us this is the beach where the Walrus People come to trade."

"Yes," Kiin answered. "I have heard that said."

"Waxtal says they will come here soon."

"Waxtal?" Kiin asked, and Blue Shell answered, "Your father took a new name when he thought you were dead. He said he was stronger in his sorrow."

"He knew Qakan had taken me," Kiin said but did not look at her mother.

"He is Waxtal now," her mother answered, and so Kiin dipped her wide, flat woman's knife into the goose grease, mixed grease with the chopped fish and said, "The Walrus People come sometimes in spring to gather eggs, but this year they did not come. So perhaps the traders will not come either."

Amgigh listened as Waxtal spoke. He thought back through the months that Waxtal had spent with him, the many times Waxtal had told him of the evil blood Samiq carried, the Short Ones' blood. Waxtal said that Kayugh had cheated Amgigh, favored Samiq, and Amgigh's grief for Kiin had fed his anger, until, slowly, over the days, his anger had grown into something that was near hatred. But now as he sat near Samiq, the hatred seeped from his body, leaving a great hollow within his chest that suddenly seemed to fill with shame.

Samiq had done no differently than he had; Samiq had done only what their father had told him. Samiq was Many Whales' grandson. Amgigh was not. Amgigh, as son to Kayugh, had been promised to Kiin, Samiq had not. There was no reason for hate. Now Amgigh watched Waxtal, sure that Waxtal had known Qakan took Kiin. He watched now as Kayugh questioned Waxtal about the Walrus People. When would they come here to trade? Would they be angry if Kayugh's people chose this place to stay, chose it for their village?

Waxtal sighed, shrugged, "Who can say?" he said. "You expect me to answer all your questions. My son is dead; I mourn."

He lowered his head, and Kayugh began an apology, but Waxtal interrupted. "Perhaps it would be good to have a village where the traders could stay. Perhaps if we made a special ulaq, one for the traders, they would consider it a good thing."

"And also if we allowed their women to come here to gather eggs each spring."

The voice—a woman's voice—came as a surprise to Amgigh, and he turned to see Kiin standing behind him, the other women standing behind her.

"This is my beach," she said, and Amgigh felt his face grow hot at her words. What woman could claim a beach?

"You are all welcome," she continued, "even Gray Bird. I would not want my mother to be without a hunter in her ulaq."

Waxtal lifted his head and narrowed his eyes. He pointed at Amgigh with his chin and said, "You will allow your wife to speak like this?"

Amgigh's embarrassment was suddenly replaced with a fierce and roaring anger. He stood then and strode across the circle to look down at Waxtal. "You, you who would give your own daughter to be traded, would speak to me in this way? My wife is right. She was on this beach first; she has claimed it as her home. Already she has two strong sons. Your son was weak. No one will sing songs in remembrance of what he has done, of his great hunts. Who are you to condemn my wife!"

Then Samiq was beside Amgigh, his hand on Amgigh's shoulder. "Amgigh speaks for me. He and I and our wives, we are one."

Then Amgigh turned to see that Three Fish had moved to stand beside Kiin, the two together like sisters.

Gray Bird stood. He walked away, but then stopped, turned and called back, "We do not know Kiin's husband, Raven. You think he will not fight for Kiin and her sons when he comes here to trade, when he finds her here with us? You, Amgigh, you think you are strong enough to stand against a shaman?"

But Amgigh turned to his wife and said, "Thank you, for allowing us to stay on your beach."

Then Crooked Nose said, "Food is ready."

And Amgigh noticed that Gray Bird, even in mourning, was the first to follow the women, the first to take food.

Kiin helped the other women build four shelters. Big Teeth and Crooked Nose took one; Chagak, Kayugh, Wren, Samiq, Small Knife and Three Fish were in the largest; Red Berry and First Snow in another; and Gray Bird with Blue Shell in another. Kiin invited Amgigh into her shelter, the place so small that Amgigh's feet and head touched wall to wall when he lay down.

Kiin fed the babies and Amgigh talked to her about their journey, of the beaches where they stopped and of the ash and fire of Aka. But even though Amgigh spoke, Kiin's thoughts were of Samiq. When the men had sat eating, she could not stop staring at him, and it seemed that her eyes were trying to pull all of him, the lines of his face, the shape of his hands, the way he smiled, into her soul.

The days alone on this beach had been hard days, and during those days, she had longed for Samiq, for his wisdom, his strength. Sometimes she thought she heard the whine of Qakan's voice, asking for something, pleading with her, but what could she do for him? She had no special powers. Finally, after she had taken him the egg, it seemed his whining stopped, but only for a few days.

So then each time Kiin took eggs, snared birds, dug clams or gathered sea urchins, she left something for Qakan. She had been on her way to his grave, bringing a piece of dried fish, when she first saw Kayugh's ikyan in the cove. She had hidden in the grass, her lance clasped close to her side. She had made the lance from a long piece of driftwood, smoothed it with lava rock and whittled one end into a point, hardened the point with fire. It was only a boy's lance, not much better than a child's toy, but she had speared fish with it. Perhaps it would be some protection if those who came were enemies.

She had waited, glad she had her sons with her in her suk, that way, if she had to, she could run into the hills, run to the sponge of the tundra behind the hills and up into the rocks of the mountains.

But then she had recognized Samiq and Kayugh and Amgigh, had come out to meet them. Then she was again with Samiq, able to see him, to hear his voice, watch his face. But Samiq had Three Fish, and Kiin had Amgigh. So each time Kiin's thoughts drifted to Samiq, she forced her mind to thoughts of Amgigh, to the good things about him. And when the other men finished eating and went to their shelters, Kiin invited Amgigh to her shelter.

When she had finished nursing their sons, she placed them in their cradles. She was wife; she must make herself ready for Amgigh.

She oiled her face and smoothed her hair with a comb she had made from a clam shell. Amgigh watched her, and she found pleasure in his watching, found it easier to put Samiq out of her thoughts. Then Kiin took off her suk, rubbed oil on her legs, moving as she remembered Lemming Tail moving, to make Amgigh want her. Then Kiin lay down on her side on the sleeping mats, and waited until Amgigh lay down beside her, but though he cupped his body around hers, he did not remove his apron, did not remove Kiin's.

Kiin lay, her eyes staring into the darkness, and wondered if during the year she had been away from her people she had turned ugly, or if her boldness with the men had angered Amgigh. Perhaps he had noticed that she spoke easily now, without the words stumbling and catching in her throat. Perhaps, now that she could speak, she spoke too much. But then hearing Amgigh's breathing ease into the rhythm of his sleep, a thought came that made Kiin tremble.

Perhaps Amgigh saw what she could not: the marks of Qakan's hands upon her body, the curse of his taking like scars on the smooth skin of her breasts and thighs and belly.

67

During the next nine days the women fished and gathered sea urchins. They walked into the hills to pull ryegrass for baskets and to check the crowberry and salmonberry plants. The men hunted the harbor seals swimming near the shore, and when they were not hunting, they helped the women build ulas.

The first ulaq was for Gray Bird and Blue Shell. Gray Bird asked that his ulaq be finished quickly so that Qakan, his body cut apart, his spirit without power and bound to the beach, would have a place to come, a place to live. And when Gray Bird's ulaq was finished, they built another larger ulaq where everyone else could stay as the men began work on a third.

Then the traders came. Men and women, babies, young hunters, their goods piled in iks or tied to ikyan. There were First Men and Walrus People and there were others with bear-skins for blankets, with chigadax made out of bear gut. They did not seem disturbed that Kayugh's people were already there. They greeted the two new ulas with smiles, with nods. "A good place to stay," Kiin heard one woman say in the Walrus tongue.

Driftwood and seal bone fires lined the great circle of the beach, and hunters' lamps were kept burning all night.

Chagak and Crooked Nose, Red Berry and Kiin hung skins of fish and broth over outside fires. Traders came, giving small things—a bear's tooth, a chunk of chert, a few shell beads—for a bowl of broth.

With each new ik or ikyak that came to the beach, Three Fish hurried away, asked the traders if they had heard anything about the Whale Hunter people. And each time Three Fish returned to the First Men's ulas, there was sadness in her eyes, and she told Kiin that the traders knew nothing, that they spoke of ash and fire and waves that kept them away from the Whale Hunter island. And watching Three Fish, Kiin again felt the ache that had been in her chest when she had been with the Walrus People, when she thought she would never be able to return to the First Men.

During the second day of the trading, Kiin slipped away from the cooking fires to watch. Most of the traders displayed their goods on grass mats or on sealskins dyed red with ochre. Even after being with Qakan, it was hard for Kiin to believe there could be so many things in the world. One trader had wooden dishes filled with bear claws and another had a basket of whale teeth that were as long and nearly as thick as Kiin's hand. One man had twists of rope made from coarse reddish-brown hair. Another had baskets, some finely woven of ryegrass fibers, some coarse, made of grass stalks and roots, of willow or of seal gut. Two traders had large pieces of chert, red jasper and greenstone, and another had harpoonheads made of whale jawbone with obsidian points. There were piles of bitterroot, hammerstones, bolas made with walrus tusk weights instead of stones, sea lion stomachs filled with dried halibut, rolls of dried seal intestine for chigadax, bundles of furs and skins. Others had grass mats, fur parkas and sealskin boots. Another had baskets full of rosy finch feathers, curls of orange and yellow puffin feathers and fragile disk beads cut from shells.

And everything Kiin saw, she wanted. Her eyes filled with the wanting, and when the wanting grew too large for her eyes, it slipped into her chest and pushed her spirit into a small corner of her body, leaving an ache that would not go away until she pulled her thoughts from the things she saw and instead walked up into the hills, instead thought of heather and sea birds and of the wide grayness of the sky.

Gray Bird was the first of Kayugh's people to trade. He took a few furs, a few of his carvings to the traders and came back to the ulas with bear claws and a whale's tooth.

"To carve," he said to Blue Shell and Blue Shell nodded, then quickly lowered her head.

But Crooked Nose spoke, loud enough for Gray Bird to hear, "So, he will carve this winter even if we do not have enough furs for parkas, enough food to eat. It is good to know that Gray Bird will carve!"

But Kiin stared in amazement. She had a basket full of the carvings she had made since Qakan's death. She had carved murres and cormorants, eagles and terns, harbor seals with great round eyes. She had made things that were important to her: carvings of her people's ulas on Tugix's island, things to help her remember what had been lost to her, to show Shuku and Takha what they should know about their fathers and about their true people.

Kiin opened her mouth to speak, to say something to Crooked Nose and Chagak, to tell them about the carvings she might be able to trade, but then her spirit said: "Will they think you are boasting? You think your carvings are better than your father's, but perhaps they are not. You know they are not as good as Shuganan's, cannot compare to his. Perhaps you will take them to trade and the traders will laugh at you, a woman, trying to trade small misshapen animals for food, for oil, for furs. Wait, wait, think about it, wait."

So Kiin continued to chop fish and stir the soup, to ladle out food to traders who brought beads or small bits of chert in exchange for what the women prepared. And she made herself stay near the ulas until she had grown used to the idea of trading, until it settled more deeply into her spirit and she knew the gleam of it would no longer show in her eyes. Then, she stood and stretched and left the cooking skins. She passed by her father, chortling over his treasures as he sat at the top of his ulaq. Kiin stood for a moment to watch Big Teeth and Kayugh working on a third ulaq, a place for Big Teeth and First Snow and their families. Then she went into the large ulaq where she and Amgigh lived.

She shook out the furs and straightened the mats in Amgigh's sleeping place. He still had not come to her sleeping place, and Kiin had begun to feel herself again drawn to Samiq, so that she knew she must keep her eyes and her thoughts away from him for fear everyone would see how she felt, for fear she would bring shame to Amgigh. But she also held her thoughts away from Amgigh, from worrying about why he shunned her, why he would not claim her again as true wife. Her sons were safe. That was enough. She would ask nothing more.

She went into her own sleeping place, then taking Shuku and Takha from their carrying straps, she set them into their cradles. "I will be back soon," she whispered, laying a hand on each baby's head. "Sleep, sleep."

Then she picked up a basket of her carvings, tucked it under her suk and left the ulaq.

The traders were noisy with stories and small arguments. For a time, Kiin only watched, listened. A man coming to trade talked first of the sky, perhaps the sea or sun, then small politenesses about rain and fog, perhaps a few jokes about other traders. The women did not trade, but sat silently beside their men, some laying out furs, stroking a hand against the nap of the fur as her man spoke of many days spent hunting for the animal, of the fur's unusual color, unusual thickness. And Kiin saw that if Chagak had furs to spare, she could have traded easily for many things. Chagak's skins were finer than any Kiin saw here. Amgigh's spearheads were better than most here, and whale oil was very precious since the traders lived so far from the beaches of the Whale Hunters.

At first Kiin wanted to go back to the ulaq, to hide her carvings. "Who will want them?" some spirit seemed to whisper. "The men will laugh at a woman who tries to trade." And it seemed that the bulge of the basket under her suk would tell everyone of her foolishness. But then she thought of the long winter ahead of them, of Shuku and Takha without food, of her milk drying up because she had nothing to eat, of Wren lying still and white, Kayugh and Chagak having nothing to feed her. And so she made herself stay to watch the traders, to decide what her people needed, and to see which trader had oil, who had fish, who had skins.

Then pulling a deep breath of air into her lungs, Kiin went to a man and woman who had baskets of kelp twine and seal stomachs of dried halibut. Kiin spoke first to the woman.

"Will you trade with me?" Kiin asked, forgetting in her nervousness to talk about the weather, about the sea and sky.

The woman's eyes widened and she pulled at her husband's sleeve, spoke to him in the Walrus tongue, quiet words, and she pointed all the while at Kiin.

The man stared at her, and Kiin, speaking in the Walrus language, said to him, "I want to trade for fish."

Almost, he laughed. Kiin could see the laughter. Though he kept it tucked behind his teeth, hidden in his cheeks, it came out in the crinkles beside his eyes, in the quivering of his chin. But Kiin, knowing how she must look, a woman, only a woman, with nothing in her hands, understood the reason for the laughter and smiled at him, for she could see herself through his eyes as something funny, something a trader did not often see, a woman with nothing to trade, asking to trade.

"What do you offer me?" he finally said. "I have a good woman. I do not need your hospitality for the night."

Kiin felt the sudden burning of her face, and knew the trader would see the redness there so she quickly reached into her suk for the basket of carvings.

She reached in, brought out a small gray walrus. The animal, carved in smooth lines from a piece of driftwood, was nearly as long as her hand. Its tusks were small white points carved from birdbone.

Kiin held the carving on the flat of her hand, and as she looked, she saw flaws in the work. The lines were not quite what she had wanted, not quite what she had seen before she started carving. But then she looked at the trader, at his woman; both were staring, eyes wide, at the walrus.

"Where did you get it?" the man asked.

"I made it," Kiin answered, and the trader shook his head and this time laughed out loud. "Women do not carve," he said.

But Kiin held in her anger and shrugged. Let him believe what he wanted. She knew the truth. "It is mine to trade," she said.

He looked into her eyes and for a long time said nothing, but then he whispered to his wife. She stood up, went to their ik and pulled out two seal stomachs of fish.

"Two," the trader said.

Kiin's heart beat hard in her chest. Two seal bellies of fish for a carving she thought had no value. But then something from within made her shake her head no, made her put the walrus back in her basket. Perhaps because the trader did not believe she had carved it. There were others who had fish.

"Three," the man said.

Kiin stepped around the man, her basket tucked tightly under her arm, and opened one of the containers. She pulled out a piece of fish, bit into it. It was firm and dry, the flavor good, no taste of mold.

"Three," Kiin said. She handed the walrus to the trader and she and the wife pulled the seal stomachs from the ik.

"You will keep them here for me?" Kiin asked. "I can carry only one at a time."

"They will be safe," the trader said.

But then Samiq was beside her, his hands over her hands, hoisting two of the seal stomachs, one to each of his shoulders. "I watched," he said.

Kiin looked up at him, saw the approval in his eyes.

"Leave the other. I will come back for it."

Kiin walked with him to the ulas, lowered her head as they passed the women, as Samiq called out to Blue Shell, "Your daughter is a good trader."

Gray Bird, his face drawn, eyes squinting, answered, "So she will bring traders into her husband's ulaq tonight. How much room does she have in her sleeping place?"

Then Samiq, speaking quietly, said to Kiin, "Do you have more carvings?"

"Many," Kiin said. "But they are not good."

"You do not see what others see," he answered. "There is a spirit in each carving, something more than what is carved. Go back. Trade again. We have not been able to hunt much this summer. You must be our hunter."

68

The man was tall, with dark skin; his hair, clipped back with an ivory ornament, was like woman's hair—black, straight, hanging to his waist. A black blanket of feathered puffin skins was slung around his shoulders, and as he walked, the blanket swung, making each of his steps seem larger than they were, making others move from his path to give him room. The man stopped at a trader's ik and Amgigh moved closer. Yes, Amgigh was sure now. This was Raven.

His skin was not as dark as it appeared. Bands of tattoo across his cheeks blackened his face, and it looked like he had rubbed soot over his eyelids.

A quivering began in Amgigh's stomach, something that numbed his hands and made his feet and legs seem slow and clumsy.

Raven stopped suddenly, and Amgigh heard the man's words, the full clicking sounds of the Walrus tongue. Raven reached out and grabbed something from a trader's ochre sealskin. The trader lunged toward Raven, hands clasping Raven's hands, and Amgigh saw that Raven held the driftwood walrus that Kiin had traded for three seal stomachs of fish. Raven released the walrus, backed away smiling, hands out toward the trader. He spoke, a question, again in the Walrus language, and the trader, the walrus held close to his chest, answered.

Sue Harrison

Amgigh had been amazed at what Kiin was given for the carving. After that first trade, Samiq had come to him, then they both went with Kiin, to help her as she traded other carvings for oil, fish, for furs and sealskins.

He had been proud that his wife's carvings were worth so much to others, and puzzled that the traders would see something more than the smooth lines of knife on wood, that they would see some power in what she had made. Everyone knew the power of Shuganan's carvings, but Shuganan was shaman, more spirit than man, even Gray Bird admitted that. And what was Kiin but a woman, a wife? What power could she give?

She was a good wife, yes, and at that thought Amgigh lifted his eyes again to Raven, saw for the first time that the ivory ornament in his hair was carved, a walrus at the top. Kiin's work, he was sure. Kiin's work. So even a shaman such as Raven would wear Kiin's carvings. Even a shaman saw power in her work.

Amgigh passed his hands up over his face, pressed his fingertips against his eyelids. Why did he not see what others saw? Her carvings were good, yes, but . . . Perhaps his eyes were blinded by his own hurts, by his own doubt. The first night they had come to this beach, he went to her shelter. He had watched her smooth oil over her legs, had lain beside her. He had meant to take her, but when he looked at her, he saw not only Kiin, but the face of Qakan floating like a ghost above her, and even an image of Samiq, strong and alive.

And overhead, sleeping in their cradles, were the babies. One his son, yes, but the other Samiq's son. The two would grow up together as he and Samiq had—rivals in all things. And would his son Shuku always be the loser, always catch less fish, the smaller seal, never run as fast, never be the best at anything?

If so, he, Amgigh, had done that to Shuku, had allowed Samiq to take Kiin, to put Takha in her.

And even with Kiin beside him, with her hair smelling of seal oil and wind, her breath soft like the seed puffs of a fireweed plant, Amgigh had felt little desire for her body. But now, seeing

428

Raven, Amgigh felt a sudden longing for Kiin. He needed to feel her pressed against him in the night, to know when he woke in the morning, she would be laying out food, and in the evening she would be sewing or weaving in his ulaq.

He turned, walked quickly away from the beach, back to the ulas. His mother and Crooked Nose were outside, scraping a sealskin. "Where's Kiin?" he asked.

Crooked Nose turned, pointed with her chin. Amgigh walked past the two finished ulas to the place that would be Big Teeth's ulaq. Red Berry, Three Fish and Kiin were dumping gravel and crushed shells on the floor. Driftwood rafters rose from chest-high rock walls. Amgigh watched as Kiin smoothed the gravel into the clay floor with a flat shale blade.

Her hair was mussed, falling over her eyes and into her face. She and Three Fish squatted with heads bent together, Three Fish speaking, Kiin laughing.

Amgigh had to call twice before Kiin heard him, but then she came, hurrying over the rock wall, squeezing between rafters.

She brushed the hair from her eyes and looked up at him. Amgigh reached toward her, and his fingers seemed to move by themselves to touch her face. But then he remembered his place as husband and dropped his hand, and would not allow himself to wonder at the sudden pain he felt, as though by drawing away he had somehow torn a small part of his spirit from his body.

"Kiin, come with me," he said, and she followed without asking questions.

When they were a short distance from the ulas, beyond Crooked Nose's sight and far enough so the wind would cover their voices, he stopped, turned and, this time with no one watching, allowed himself to reach out, to touch Kiin's face. To push the wisps of hair from her cheeks.

She did not speak, but Amgigh could see that her eyes were round with worry. "Amgigh?" she finally said, the name a question, and Amgigh squatted, pulling her down beside him.

"Raven," Amgigh said. "Tell me about him."

Kiin looked at Amgigh, her eyes still wide. "He is here?" she asked.

"No," Amgigh said and spoke so suddenly, that he was afraid Kiin would know he did not speak the truth. He took a breath, made his words come slowly. "No. He is not here. I just need to know about him. You were my wife, Kiin. I need you to be my wife again."

He thought he saw the beginning of a smile on Kiin's face, but she looked away from him and when she did not speak, Amgigh was afraid the spirits had taken her words, that she would once again stammer and hesitate as she had when she lived on Tugix's island.

But finally she said, "He is not evil, not good. He is something like . . ." She stopped, pushed her hands through her hair and then said, "He is himself, doing what he wants to do, and he does not think of others, how they feel or if what he does might hurt someone." She turned and looked into Amgigh's eyes. "I cannot explain it," she said. "He is . . . he is like the wind. The wind blows and brings in waves that destroy a village or the wind blows and brings in the body of a whale so everyone has oil. Good and bad, both, you see, and not caring either way."

"You were wife to him," Amgigh said, his words flat, hard.

"Not in his bed," Kiin said softly. "But I kept his ulaq clean and made clothes for him and carved if he told me to carve. I made a blanket of black puffin feathers for him. It was beautiful. I wish I could have brought it back for you."

Her words reached into Amgigh's chest and squeezed his heart so that its beat seemed small and faint. "You made a blanket for him?"

"I was his wife. He asked me to make it and I did."

"No," Amgigh said, and the word seemed to pry the fear away from his heart so it could beat again, so again he was a man, a man ready to fight for his wife, not a boy afraid of something he did not understand. "You are my wife. You have always been my wife."

"Yes," Kiin answered, but she turned her face away from him, and he could not see what was in her eyes. "I am your wife, but the Raven gave me food and a place to live. I took care of his ulaq and made his clothes."

"And warmed his bed," Amgigh said.

"No," Kiin said. "You know I did not."

Amgigh pulled up a stalk of grass and twisted it between his hands. "If Raven finds you, he will want you back."

Kiin turned toward him. Her face was white, and the black centers of her eyes suddenly pulled in, as though her spirit were shutting itself away.

"Kiin, he will want you back," Amgigh said. "He will want you and my sons."

"Yes," Kiin said, the word hardly louder than a breath. "At least Shuku."

Amgigh stood and pulled Kiin up beside him. Without looking to see if others saw, whether there was someone who might be offended, man, woman or spirit, sea animal or bird, he pulled her into his arms, laid his head against her hair. "He will not have you. You are my wife," Amgigh said, and knew he should have claimed her that first night in his bed. How else did a man drive away the memories and spirits of others?

"For the rest of the trading, I want you to stay away from the beach," Amgigh said. "I will have Three Fish bring you the babies. Take them into the hills and do not come out. Then if Raven comes, he will not know you are here. And when the traders have left, I will come for you."

Amgigh left her then, left without looking back. He did not want her to see what was in his eyes. What he knew he would have to do.

Kiin looked into Three Fish's eyes, tried to see if the woman knew what was happening, but Three Fish's large round face was flat, without trace of sorrow, anger or fear. She sat holding Samiq's son, the baby asleep, his fingers wrapped around one of hers, bubbles of milk from Kiin's nursing at the corners of his mouth.

Amgigh had come with Three Fish, had walked with the two women farther from the beach, around the boggy edges of a lake, over sedges to a high mound ringed with stunted willow. There, in the lee of the mound, Amgigh helped Kiin make a shelter of hides, driftwood and mats while Three Fish held the babies.

When they were finished, he left, again without looking back, stopping only to stroke each baby's face and to press his own cheek against Shuku's.

Now she and Three Fish were alone, each holding a baby, and Kiin wished Three Fish had gone back with Amgigh, so Kiin could be alone, could raise her songs to any spirit that might keep the Raven from coming to their beach. What if he came and saw the carvings she had traded? He would know she had been here. She should have thought of that before the trading, but what was worse—going back with the Raven to the Walrus People or seeing the First Men starve over the next winter?

Kiin tucked Amgigh's son under her suk, then to calm her spirit, she pulled out her crooked knife and a chunk of walrus tusk she was carving. She had traded a few of her carvings for more ivory—whale and bear teeth, walrus tusk and a strange chunk of yellow ivory, rounder than walrus tusk and without the brittle marbeling of the center; there was a faint pattern of checks at the rim of the cut edge, dark and light like the pattern Chagak put on the ends of her grass mats.

Kiin turned the partially carved walrus tusk in her fingers, let it warm with the heat of her hands, smoothed her fingers over the crevices. The chunk of tusk was as long as her hand, and at the broken end was as large around as her wrist. When she had first seen the tusk, she had seen also what was within it: an ikyak, sleek, one end pointed up with the curve of the tusk, the other end blunt. Already under her knife, the ikyak had begun to emerge.

She looked up at Three Fish, but Three Fish was murmuring to Takha. So Kiin began to carve, using her knife to shave away long curls of ivory. And as she carved a song came, something she could not hold within. So keeping her eyes on her work, she sang, the carving and the singing joining into one song, voice and hands.

Amgigh went to the beach. Most of the traders had packed away their goods for the night. Only four of the Walrus People ikyan were left—Raven's and the ikyan that belonged to a man called Ice Hunter and Ice Hunter's two sons. Ice Hunter spoke the First Men's tongue, and he spent most of that evening speaking to Amgigh.

"Kiin is a good woman, yes," Ice Hunter said, "but she is not worth a fight that will kill you, and Raven has killed others. He is not afraid to fight. Let him have the woman."

"And my sons?" Amgigh asked.

"No, do not let him take your sons," Ice Hunter said. "The women in our village think there is a curse. They think one of your sons must die. If you let him take your sons, one will be killed."

"Raven will kill him?"

"No, Raven wants both alive, but think how easy it is for a child to die. Think how easy it is for a baby to fall from an ik or for a young boy's harness to give way when he is gathering eggs."

Amgigh nodded. Yes, it would be easy to kill one son or another, and though he cared more for Shuku, he would also grieve if Takha were killed. And what of Kiin? How could he bear to lose her again?

"I will fight for her," Amgigh told Ice Hunter, and Ice Hunter, shaking his head said, "Then I will see you again when I come to the Dancing Lights."

Together they went to Raven, and Amgigh waited until Ice

Hunter spoke to the man, Amgigh watching as Raven's eyes narrowed, as his brows wove themselves into one line across his face.

"He wants her and both sons," Ice Hunter told Amgigh, and Amgigh listened, but did not take his eyes from Raven's face. Perhaps the man was without honor; perhaps he would kill Amgigh if Amgigh looked away, even for a moment.

Amgigh's hand lingered over his long-bladed knife. Raven might be a better fighter. What did Amgigh know of fighting men? But Raven would not have a better weapon. How many men knew the secrets of knapping obsidian? How many men knew the secret place on Okmok where the sacred rock was found?

"She is my wife and they are my sons," Amgigh said and he tried to catch Raven's eyes, to hold them with his eyes. How else does a man reason with other men? But Raven stared straight ahead, as though he did not see Amgigh, as though Amgigh were not even on the beach. So Amgigh spoke to Ice Hunter: "Qakan had no right to sell Kiin," Amgigh said, "but whatever Raven paid for her, I will return to him."

Amgigh waited while Ice Hunter, using his hands and many words, again spoke to Raven, but Raven flung his black feather blanket to the ground and with more angry words went back into his shelter.

Then Ice Hunter turned slowly to face Amgigh. "He will not trade for her, but he will fight you for her and for the sons," Ice Hunter said. "Spear or knife, he does not care."

"Knife," Amgigh said, his hand pressed against the sheath that covered his obsidian blade. Okmok was stronger than Raven.

The beach was empty, the traders still sleeping, some in the First Men's large ulaq, others in the shelters they had made under their iks. Amgigh had not told Samiq what was happening. When his brother sat down beside him the night before, asking about Kiin and Three Fish, Amgigh had explained that they were in the hills, away from traders, away from the noise that kept the babies crying. They would be back the next day, at least Chagak had said so, and Samiq had shrugged. But Amgigh knew Samiq was worried, and he understood without anger that his worry was as much for Kiin as for Three Fish.

But Amgigh could not tell Samiq the truth. Samiq had always been the one to help Amgigh, to wait for him, to teach him. Now it was Amgigh's place to fight, to be the man.

Amgigh walked the beach, the sand marred with footprints above the tide line, smooth below, his prints something new on the unmarked sand. He waited until he saw some movement in the shelter where Ice Hunter and Raven stayed. Then he walked over, stood outside the door flap until Raven came out.

Raven wore only his aprons, front and back. He was a tall man, taller than Kayugh and as wide as Samiq. For a moment he stood without speaking, then he called to someone in the shelter. Ice Hunter emerged.

"Amgigh," Ice Hunter called. "He asks if you still want to fight."

"Ask him if he will leave this beach, will leave my wife and my sons."

Ice Hunter spoke to Raven in the Walrus tongue and Raven laughed, said something and turned to Amgigh, one brow raised.

"He asks if you want to fight here or somewhere else," Ice Hunter said.

"On the beach, where it is flat," Amgigh answered, and without turning from Raven, gestured back toward the beach where the water had left the sand smooth.

Raven nodded and both men walked slowly to the place, then Amgigh, his left hand on his amulet, pulled his knife slowly from its sheath, let the blade move to catch light from its translucent facets.

Raven should know what he fought against. He should know that there was more here than the spirit of one man.

Amgigh saw the surprise in Raven's face, then a slow smile, and Amgigh watched as Raven drew out his knife, the blade longer than the blade of Amgigh's knife. Then Amgigh once more felt the fingers of some spirit clasp his heart. And the squeezing slowed Amgigh's heartbeat, pulled Amgigh's own spirit from his hands and feet, so his arms and legs were suddenly slow and weak.

It was Amgigh's obsidian knife, the mate to Samiq's knife. Qakan must have stolen it when he stole Kiin, stolen it and traded it to Raven.

Raven held the knife and laughed, but Amgigh thought, Perhaps the spirit of the knife will remember me, will remember its true owner.

Slowly Amgigh lifted his knife, slowly he began to circle.

A light mist had begun to fall, soaking the skins and mats of their shelter. Kiin was cold and hungry. In the night, Three Fish had eaten all the food Amgigh had brought them, and now the woman would not stop talking. Words flowed from her mouth like water from a spring, bubbling, pushing, frothing, until finally the shelter was so full of noise that Kiin wondered how there was room for the rivulets of water that squeezed between skins and mats to drip into her hair and run down her neck.

She pulled Takha from her suk. Maybe if Three Fish were holding him, she would be quiet. Kiin wrapped him in one of the few dry furs from her bed and handed him to Three Fish. The baby opened his eyes, looked solemnly at Kiin, then turned his head toward Three Fish and smiled. Three Fish laughed and again began to babble, this time to the baby.

Kiin sighed and looked down inside her suk at Shuku. Then suddenly she heard what Three Fish was saying, heard her say, "Your father will fight and you will be safe. Safe. Do not worry. He is strong."

Kiin clasped Three Fish by both arms. "What did you say?" Kiin asked.

"Only what Amgigh told me, that we must stay here because there are men on the beach who want to trade for women."

"And Amgigh will fight them?"

Three Fish pulled away from Kiin's hands and scooted herself back against the damp wall of their shelter. "He said he might," she answered.

"All I know is that I saw one of them," Three Fish said. "One with a black blanket over his shoulders. Even his face was black. I think Samiq and Amgigh were afraid he would want us."

"The Raven," Kiin whispered. And when she spoke the name, she felt as if her spirit shattered, as if its sharp edges were cutting into the outside walls of her heart.

Three Fish was talking again, her face close to Takha's face, but Kiin crawled over to the woman and waited until Three Fish looked up. Three Fish's smile faded and Kiin took one of Three Fish's hands into her own.

"Our husbands are brothers," Kiin said, and forced her words to be slow, to be gentle, so Three Fish would understand. "Our husbands are brothers so we are sisters."

"Yes," Three Fish said.

"I have to go to the beach now, Three Fish," Kiin said, "but you should stay here with Takha. Keep him from crying as long as you can. If he sleeps, that is good. But finally when he is crying too hard for you to stop him, then take him to Red Berry. She has milk. She will feed him."

Then Kiin untied the string of babiche that held the carving Chagak had given her and handed it to Three Fish.

"A gift for you," Kiin said. Three Fish cupped the carving of man, woman and child in her hand.

"Samiq told me about this," Three Fish said. "Shuganan made it. I cannot take it."

But Kiin closed her hands over Three Fish's hand and said, "You must. We are sisters. You cannot refuse my gift." Then she unwrapped what she had finished the night before, during the long night when sleep would not come. It was the walrus tusk ikyak. After she finished carving the ivory ikyak, Kiin had cut it crosswise into two pieces. To protect her sons, Kiin had done what Woman of the Sky had said. Her sons would share one ikyak. She took two braided sinew cords and knotted one around the front half of the ikyak, knotted the other around the back half of the ikyak, hung one cord around Takha's neck, the other around Shuku's.

"When I am not here, you are mother to Takha," Kiin said to Three Fish. "He is son to Amgigh, but also to Samiq. See, he has Samiq's wide hands, his thick hair. You are mother. Be sure Red Berry feeds him."

Kiin packed her carving tools and sleeping furs and strapped them to her back. Three Fish looked up when Kiin pushed open the shelter's door flap.

"Where are you going?" she asked.

"To help Amgigh," Kiin answered. Then, though she had not meant to turn back, Kiin held her hands out toward Takha.

Three Fish handed Kiin the baby and Kiin lifted him from his fur wrappings. She stroked her hands over his fat legs and arms, over his soft belly. She pressed him against her face, smelled the good oil smell of his skin. Then she handed him back to Three Fish and slipped out of the shelter into the rain.

"I will see him again tonight," Kiin said to the wind and waited for an answer, but there was nothing. No answer, no whisper to pull away her doubts.

Kiin tucked her arms around Shuku, alone in his carrying strap under her suk, and began to walk toward the beach.

69

Samiq was not sure why he awoke. He could remember no dreams, no whisperings from spirits, no sounds from the large room of the ulaq. Of course, Three Fish and Kiin were away, spending the night in the hills. Who could blame them? The noise and bother of the traders was not an easy thing to live with, especially for the women. Even Three Fish had traders following her, asking for a night of hospitality in her sleeping place. And what of Kiin, a beautiful woman known for her skills as a carver? Whoever heard of a woman who carved? Every man wanted her, wanted the chance to increase his own power by taking her to his bed.

Samiq slipped from his sleeping robes and went out into the main room of the ulaq. All but one oil lamp was out, but gray light filtered down from the roof hole. Samiq went to Amgigh's sleeping curtain and called to his brother.

"Lazy one, I go to fish. Come with me."

When Amgigh did not answer, Samiq pulled aside the curtain. His brother was not there. Samiq shrugged and went to the food cache, but as he was pulling out a skin of dried walrus meat that Kiin's carvings had bought them, he stopped.

Suddenly his heart was pounding, his chest full with a rush of blood. His hands trembled and when he clenched his fists, he felt the trembling move up into his arms. What foolishness was this? Samiq wondered. He was here in his own ulaq. There was no problem. Amgigh would have called him if there was. But again the trembling came, and again the pounding of his heart. Perhaps something had happened to Kiin, to one of her sons. Perhaps something had happened to Three Fish.

He pulled on his parka and climbed out of the ulaq. A cold wind blew in from the sea and the sky was gray with a misty rain. Samiq looked up toward the hills, where Kiin and Three Fish had spent the night, but he could see no one, then he turned and looked toward the sea. The ulaq was high, giving good view of the sea and the beach. There were no ikyan on the water.

It is early, Samiq thought. The traders have become lazy. But then he turned again, this time toward the flat sand near the line of high tide. And as he turned, his breath caught and he knew the reason his heart had raced while he was still in the ulaq. Amgigh's own spirit had called to his spirit, had called in pain, in fear.

Samiq ran toward the beach, toward his brother, toward the circle of traders who had gathered to watch. Samiq pushed through to the inside edge of the circle. One of the Walrus People was fighting Amgigh. The man's chest was bare and glistened with sweat. Amgigh stood before him, one hand clasping his amulet. The other hand, bleeding, held no knife, and Samiq saw that the Walrus man had cut through one of Amgigh's fingers and that the knife and finger lay together in the sand.

The Walrus man held up one hand, palm out.

He spoke, said something in the Walrus tongue, and by the tightness of his breathing, Samiq knew the two had been fighting a long time. He pointed at Samiq.

One of the men watching the fight held his hands out toward Samiq and said, "I am Ice Hunter. The one who fights is Raven. He asks if you are Samiq, Amgigh's brother."

"Yes," Samiq answered. "But how does he know who I am?"

"His wife, Kiin, she told him about you."

"Raven," Samiq said and Ice Hunter nodded. The one who had bought Kiin from Qakan. So he was here to claim Kiin, perhaps to claim her sons.

"You should have spoken to Kiin," Samiq's spirit whispered. "You could have helped her; kept a watch for this man; prevented the fight." But it had seemed enough that Kiin had been alive, that she had given Samiq a son. If he would have let himself speak to her, could he have kept from taking her into his arms, could he have kept from claiming her again as wife? She belonged to him. The belonging was in her eyes each time he looked at her. If he had taken time to ask the questions he wanted to ask, to speak to her, man to woman, how could he have kept from betraying Amgigh, from betraying Three Fish?

The man beside Samiq still held his hands out, still waited for Samiq's answer. "Tell your friend that if he kills my brother Amgigh, he should be ready to fight me also, for I will kill him."

Samiq glanced at Amgigh and saw his brother's arms drop, saw his eyes leave Raven to glance at Samiq. "Do not fight him," Amgigh called. "He has killed many men. What do you know of fighting?"

Almost Samiq said the same to Amgigh, but then stopped himself. Why pull away Amgigh's confidence?

Then Samiq had his own knife out, the one Amgigh had made him. He tossed the knife to Amgigh and Amgigh caught it with his uninjured left hand. He smiled at Samiq, but the smile was grim, edged in bitterness.

Then suddenly Raven thrust forward, catching Amgigh before Amgigh could bring Samiq's knife forward. Raven's knife cut deep along Amgigh's left arm. Samiq groaned, and his sleeve knife was in his hand before he knew what he did. But then Ice Hunter was beside Samiq, his hand tight around Samiq's wrist. "What is fair is fair," Ice Hunter said. "Who are you to say which man is right? Let the spirits decide."

Amgigh clamped his teeth tight, and Samiq knew he did so to keep the spirits that bring pain from entering in through his mouth. Then Amgigh lunged forward and drew his knife across Raven's bare chest. A line of blood beaded from the cut and dripped into the sand.

Then again, the knives were thrust, and again. Raven's knife drew blood, then Amgigh's. Both men backed away, stood for a moment, hands on knees, breaths drawn long and hard. Then Raven lunged again, and this time his knife hit Amgigh's knife. Amgigh's knife blade snapped, and the point of the blade flew in a wide arc, first up like a bird casting toward the sky, then down, to bury itself in the sand.

Then Samiq saw the fear in Amgigh's face, and with a sickness that pulled at his stomach, Samiq realized what Amgigh had known when Samiq threw him the knife, what Amgigh had known when he first gave Samiq the knife. But Samiq let his eyes hold his brother's eyes, let his brother see that Amgigh's fear was his own fear, that spirit to spirit they were still brothers.

Then also for the first time, Samiq saw the line of Kiin's carvings that stood on Raven's side of the circle. The carvings were the ones that Samiq and Amgigh had helped her trade for food and skins, life for their people this winter.

Raven stepped back, rested his hands on his bent knees and breathed deeply. Amgigh, too, stood, blood running in hard rivers from the stump of his finger into the sand.

"The animals," Samiq whispered to the Walrus man beside him, "they belong to Raven?"

"He traded for them. For all of them."

Ten and another ten, Samiq counted. Kiin's animals. Now they were giving power to the man who would kill her husband. Then Samiq felt a hand on his arm, turned and saw that Kiin was beside him.

"What have I done?" Kiin whispered. "What have I done to my husband?" And Samiq saw that her eyes, too, were fixed on the animals, on the ring of carvings that watched: soft gray of wood, hard yellow of ivory, the shine of many eyes, many spirits on the ground giving power to Raven.

Then suddenly Amgigh looked at Kiin, and Samiq felt the

pull of their spirits, one to the other, and the sorrow in Kiin's eyes was so strong that Samiq felt it crash against him like the power of the sea, wave after wave.

Again Samiq drew out his sleeve knife. He held it up for the Walrus men to see. It was a small knife, but sharp with a hard andesite blade. He tossed it to Amgigh, but as Amgigh reached to catch it, Raven sprang forward and thrust his knife into Amgigh's belly. Amgigh staggered back and the sleeve knife fell to the ground. Amgigh dropped to his hands and knees, his blood staining the sand. He grabbed the sleeve knife, but Raven aimed a kick into Amgigh's side, kicked twice, and then again. Amgigh drove the short blade of the sleeve knife into Raven's leg, but Raven kicked again, this time into Amgigh's face.

Amgigh's head jerked back and Samiq heard the snap of bone. Amgigh collapsed, and Raven was suddenly on top of him. He turned Amgigh over then drove his knife into Amgigh's chest. Samiq ran to his brother's side. Raven stood, moved back, let Samiq kneel beside Amgigh.

Samiq pushed his hands against the wounds, but his fingers would not hold the blood, could not stop the flow.

Then Kiin, too, was beside them, her arms over Amgigh's chest, her hair turning red with Amgigh's blood. She clasped her amulet, rubbed it over Amgigh's forehead, over his cheeks.

Amgigh took one long breath, tried to speak, but his words were lost in the blood that bubbled from his mouth. He took another breath, choked. Then his eyes rolled back, widened to release his spirit.

Kiin moved to cradle Amgigh's head in her arms, and softly, softly, Samiq heard the words of a song, not a mourning song, but one of Kiin's own songs—words asking spirits to act, words that begged Amgigh's forgiveness, that cursed the animals Kiin had carved.

Finally Kiin stood, wiped one hand over her eyes. "He is gone," Kiin said. "I should have come sooner. I should have known he would fight the Raven. It is my fault; I . . ."

But Samiq pressed his fingers against her lips, shook his head.

"You could not have stopped him," he said. He laid his hand on Kiin's head. "You are my wife, now," he said. "I will not let Raven take you."

"No, Samiq," said Kiin. "You are not strong enough to kill him."

But anger burned in Samiq's chest, in his throat, in the spaces behind his eyes. "A knife," he said and turned to the men gathered around him.

Someone handed him a knife, poorly made, the edge blunt, but Samiq grabbed it, his anger making him see the knife as something stronger than it was.

Raven clenched his teeth, screamed at him in the Walrus tongue.

"He does not want to fight you," Kiin said, her breath coming in sobs. "Samiq, please. You are not strong enough. He will kill you."

But Samiq lunged forward, wrist cocked so the longest edge of the blade was toward Raven. Raven crouched, and Samiq heard him mumbling—words spoken in anger, words coming from between clenched teeth. Samiq drew close, slashed his knife in an arc toward Raven, close enough to catch the back of Raven's hand, to rip the skin open, draw blood, but still Raven did not move.

The man called out to Kiin, something in Walrus words that Samiq did not understand, and he heard Kiin answering also in the Walrus tongue, Kiin's voice coming from the circle of her carved animals. For a moment Samiq looked toward her, for a moment he turned his head. Kiin was pushing her animals into the ground, heaping sand over them.

But in that moment of looking, Samiq felt Raven's knife. It slashed across the top of his right wrist, the obsidian blade biting through his skin into tendons and muscle. Samiq felt the strength leave his hand, as though Raven's knife pulled the power out through the wound. Samiq tried to open his fingers, to release his own small knife into his left hand, but he could not.

Then Kiin was beside him, standing between him and Raven. "No," she said. "Please, no." And then Small Knife was there also, his hands gripping Samiq's.

"You cannot win," Small Knife said. "Look at your hand."

Samiq glanced down at the blood, at his fingers that would not straighten when he willed them to.

"I have to fight," he hissed. "I cannot let him take Kiin."

But Small Knife looked away, not meeting Samiq's eyes.

"Do not fight," Kiin said again. "You have Small Knife. He is your son now. You have Three Fish. She is a good wife. Someday you will be strong enough to fight the Raven and win. Until then I will stay with him. I am not strong enough to stand against him, but I am strong enough to wait for you."

Then Ice Hunter was beside Kiin, reaching for Samiq's arm, wrapping a strip of seal hide around the bleeding wrist, pulling it tight to stop the blood. "You have no reason to fight," Ice Hunter said, "The first fight was fair. The spirits decided. Why else would your brother's knife break?"

Then it seemed to Samiq that not only the strength of his hand but the power he had left in his body flowed out with the blood from his wrist, and he had no words to argue with Small Knife or Ice Hunter, no promises to give to Kiin.

Kiin pulled off the necklace Samiq had given her the night of her naming. Slowly she placed it over Samiq's head. "Someday you will fight him," she said. "You will fight him and then you will give this necklace back to me."

She turned to Raven. "If I am to go with you, I must go now," she said, and she spoke in the First Men's language, then repeated the words in the Walrus tongue.

Raven asked a question, and again Kiin answered, first in her people's language, then in Raven's.

"I gave Takha to the spirit of the wind as the Grandmother said I must."

Samiq's spirit, heavy with Amgigh's death, was shattered by her words. She had given Takha to the wind? His son, without telling him, without . . .

Then Kiin lifted her suk, took Shuku from his carrying sling. She spoke to Raven in the Walrus tongue, then as though she still spoke only to him, said in the language of the First Men, "This is your son, but he is no longer Shuku. He is Amgigh."

And Samiq saw the anger on Raven's face, the clouding of Raven's eyes until they were as black as the darkest obsidian. But Kiin did not look away, did not flinch, even when the man raised one hand as though to strike her.

"Hit me," Kiin said to Raven. "Show these people that a shaman has only the power of anger against his wife, the power of his hands, the power of his knife." Then she dropped her voice to a whisper, "A man does not need a strong spirit when he has a large knife, a knife stolen from someone else."

Then Raven threw the obsidian knife to the ground. Kiin picked it up, walked back to Samiq, placed it in his left hand. Her eyes locked with Samiq's eyes, and he saw her pain. "Always," she said, "I am your wife."

Raven gestured toward the men who had come with him. One picked up Kiin's carvings; another brought Raven's ik to the water.

"We will not return to this beach," Raven said, but Kiin bent down and picked up a handful of pebbles from the sand. Once more she looked at Samiq, then she turned and followed Raven to the ik, stepped in as he pushed the ik into the sea.

Samiq raised his wounded hand to the necklace Kiin had given him. The shell beads were still warm from the heat of Kiin's neck. He watched as Raven's ik grew smaller on the water, watched hoping Kiin would look back once more, but some part of his spirit knew she would not.

He lowered his wounded hand. Blood escaped from the seal-skin wrap, and his fingers were still locked around the dull-bladed Walrus hunter's knife. In his left hand was Amgigh's obsidian knife, marked with Amgigh's blood.

His mother and Crooked Nose were on the beach, his mother kneeling beside Amgigh, cradling Amgigh's head in her lap, her voice raised in mourning, and Three Fish, too, was there, her face marked with tears.

"He took Kiin?" she asked. She wiped her eyes against her sleeve and also began a mourning song, a Whale Hunters' song, something different from Chagak's song.

Samiq moved away from her. He needed to be alone, away from the noise of mourning, from the sight of his brother, the sorrow of his mother, but Three Fish followed him, still singing, her voice harsh.

Then she thrust something toward him and Samiq looked down, saw his son, his and Kiin's, in Three Fish's arms. The baby looked into his eyes and Samiq felt a sudden power like the power of waves, spirit to spirit.

He dropped Amgigh's knife and reached out to his son. The baby's hand closed around Samiq's fingers, gripped tight. The mourning songs rose around them, but were not strong enough to cover the sound of the sea.

Acknowledgments

My Sister the Moon is founded on extensive research, but as a work of fiction is based on my interpretation of the facts and does not necessarily reflect the opinions of those experts who have so generously given their time and knowledge to this project.

My special gratitude to those who read *My Sister the Moon* in its various manuscript forms: my husband Neil; my parents Pat and Bob McHaney; my grandfather Bob McHaney, Sr.; and my friend Linda Hudson. Also my thanks to Neil for his computer work on the novel's maps and genealogy.

A sincere thank you to my agent Rhoda Weyr, who is not only an astute businesswoman, but also a careful and wise reader; and to my editors Shaye Areheart and Maggie Lichota for their meticulous work on this novel.

I will never be able to adequately express my gratitude to Dr. William Laughlin, who continues to support my work with resource materials and his encouragement.

A special thanks to Mike Livingston who lent me his extensive library about his people, the Aleuts. Many of these books, long out of print, would have been impossible for me to obtain otherwise. I also appreciate his willingness to share his knowledge about his people, his islands and kayaking.

My appreciation to those who provided resource materials,

both oral and written: Mark McDonald, The American Speech-Language-Hearing Association, Gary Kiracofe, Dr. Greg Van Dussen, Ann Fox Chandonnet, Rayna Livingston, Linda Little, Dr. Ragan Callaway, Dorthea Callaway and Laura Rowland. Thank you, also, to Sherry Ledy for her patience and good humor in teaching me basket weaving, and to Russell Bawks for his long hours of typing my research notes.

Neil and I both extend our thanks to Dorthea, Ragan and Karen Callaway, and Rayna and Mike Livingston for opening their home to us in our recent research trip to Alaska and the Aleutian Islands.

Thank you also to Dr. Richard Ganzhorn and his staff members Sharon Bennett and David Strickland, C.S.T., for answering my medical questions concerning knife wounds; and to Cathie Greenough for her willingness to share the expertise she has gained in her years counseling battered women and children.

My deepest admiration and respect to those four special women, abused as children, who opened their hearts and told me their stories of pain and fear, endurance and victory.

July, 1991
Pickford, Michigan

ABOUT THE AUTHOR

Sue Harrison lives in Pickford, Michigan, with her husband
and two children. She is currently at work on her third novel,
a sequel to MOTHER EARTH FATHER SKY and MY SIS-
TER THE MOON.

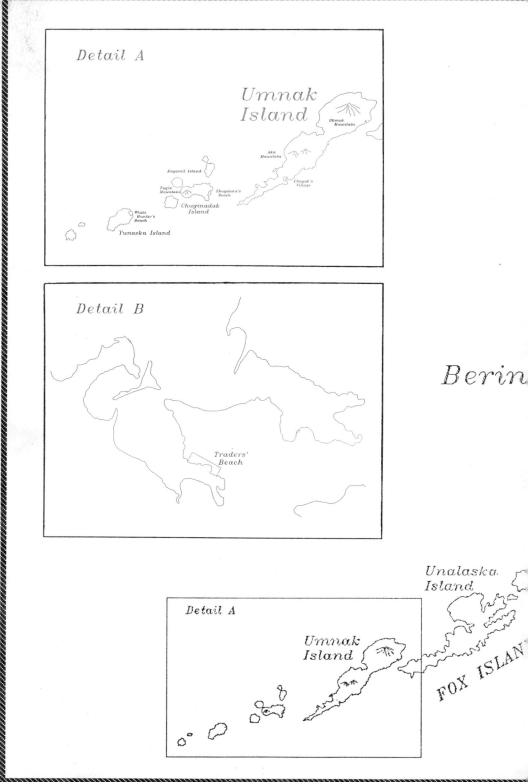